D1570672

# SYNTHESIS & OTHER VIRTUAL REALITIES

## MARY ROSENBLUM

### WITH ILLUSTRATIONS BY
### ELIZABETH LAWHEAD BOURNE

ARKHAM HOUSE PUBLISHERS, INC.

FOR SARAH
AND FOR NATE AND JAKE
WHO SHARE ALL THIS WITH ME

# CONTENTS

# YNTHESIS & OTHER VIRTUAL REALITIES

# ATER BRINGER

Sitting with his back against the sun-scorched rimrock, Jeremy made the dragonfly appear in front of him. It hovered in the hot, still air, wings shimmering with blue-green glints. Pretty. He looked automatically over his shoulder, as if Dad might be standing there, face hard and angry. But Dad was down in the dusty fields. So were Jonathan, Mother, Rupert, even the twins—everyone but him.

It was safe.

Jeremy hunched farther into his sliver of shade, frowning at his creation. It was a little too blue—that was it—and the eyes were too small. He frowned, trying to remember the picture in the insect book. The dragonfly's bright body darkened as its eyes swelled.

Bingo. Jeremy smiled and sat up straight. The dragonfly hovered above a withered bush, wings glittering in the sunlight. He sent it darting out over the canyon, leaned over the ledge to watch it.

Far below, a man was leading a packhorse up the main road from the old riverbed. A stranger! Jeremy let the dragonfly vanish as he squinted against the glare. Man and horse walked with their heads down, like they were both tired. Their feet raised brown puffs of dust that hung in the air like smoke.

Jeremy held his breath as the stranger stopped at their road. "Come on," Jeremy breathed. "There's nowhere else for two miles."

As if they'd heard him, the pair turned up the rutted track. The man didn't pull on the horse's lead rope. They moved together, like they'd decided together to stop at the farm.

Jeremy scrambled up over the rimrock and lurched into a shambling run. You didn't see strangers out here very often. Mostly, they stopped at La Grande. The convoys stuck to the interstate and nobody else went anywhere. Dead grass stems left from the brief spring crackled and snapped under Jeremy's feet and the hard ground jolted him, stabbing his twisted knees with bright slivers of pain.

At the top of the steep trail that led to the farm, he had to rest. He limped down the slope, licking dust from his lips, breathing quick and hard. They'd hear it all first—all the news—before he even got there. The sparse needles on the dying pines held the heat close to the ground. Dry branches clawed at him, trying to slow him down even more. They wouldn't wait for him. They never did. Suddenly furious, Jeremy swung at the branches with his thickened hands, but they only slapped back at him, scratching his face and arms.

Sure enough, by the time he reached the barnyard the brown-and-white horse was tethered in the dim heat of the sagging barn, unsaddled and drowsing. Everyone would be in the kitchen with the stranger. Jeremy licked his lips. At least there'd be a pitcher of fresh water out. He crossed the sunburned yard and limped up the warped porch steps.

". . . desertification's finally reached its limit, so the government's putting all its resources into reclamation."

*Desertification?* Jeremy paused at the door. The word didn't have a clear meaning in his head, but it felt dusty and dry as the fields. He peeked inside. The stranger sat in Dad's place at the big table, surrounded by the whole family. He wore a stained tan shirt with a picture of a castle tower embroidered on the pocket. He had dark curly hair and a long face with a jutting nose. Jeremy pushed the screen door slowly open. The stranger's face reminded him of the canyon wall, all crags and peaks and sharp shadows.

The door slipped through his fingers and banged closed behind him.

"Jeremy?" His mother threw a quick glance at Dad as she turned around. "Where have you been? I was worried."

"He snuck up to the rimrock again," Rupert muttered, just loud enough.

Jeremy flinched, but Dad wasn't looking at him at all. He'd heard, though. His jaw had gotten tight, but he didn't even turn his head. Jeremy felt his face getting hot and edged toward the door.

"Hi." The stranger's smile pinned Jeremy in place, crinkling the sunbrowned skin around his eyes. "I'm Dan Greely," he said.

"From the Army Engineers," ten-year-old David announced.

"To bring water," Paulie interrupted his twin.

"You're not supposed to go up there, Jeremy." Mother gave Dad an uneasy sideways glance. "You could fall."

"So how does the Corps of Engineers plan to irrigate the valley when the river's dry as a bone?" Jeremy's father spoke as if no one else had said a word. "God knows, you can't find water when it ain't there."

"Don't be so hard on him, Everett." Mother turned back to Dad.

"I ain't even heard any solid reasons for why the damn country's drying up," Dad growled. "Desertification!" He snorted. "Fancy word for no water. Tell me *why*, surveyor."

"At least someone's trying to do something about it." Mother was using her soothing tone.

They weren't paying any attention to him anymore, not even tattletale Rupert. Jeremy slipped into his favorite place, the crevice between the woodbox and the cold kitchen cookstove.

"We'll be glad to put you up while you're about your business," Mother went on. "It's like a dream come true for us, if you folks can give us water again. We've all wondered sometimes if we did right to stay here and try to hang on."

"What else could we do?" Dad said harshly. "Quit and go work in the Project fields like a bunch of Mex laborers?"

"I can't promise you water," the stranger said gravely. "I'm just the surveyor. I hear that some of these deep-aquifer projects have been pretty successful."

"It's enough to know that there's hope." Mother's voice had gone rough, like she wanted to cry.

Jeremy started to peek around the stove, but froze as Dad's hand smacked the tabletop.

"He ain't dug any wells yet. You kids get back to work.

Those beans gotta be weeded by supper, 'cause we're not wasting water on weeds. Jonathan, I know you and Rupert ain't finished your pumping yet.''

"Aw, come on," Rupert whined. "We want to hear about stuff. Are people really eating each other in the cities?''

"You heard your father," Mother said sharply. "The wash bucket's too dirty for supper dishes. Rupert, you take it out to the squash—the last two hills in the end row—and bring me a fresh bucket.''

"Aw, Mom," Rupert said, but he pushed back his chair.

Jeremy scrunched down, listening to the scuffle of his brothers' bare feet as they filed out of the kitchen.

"We don't have much in the way of hay for your pony," Jeremy's father grumbled. "How long are you planning on staying, anyway?''

"Not long. I can give you a voucher for food and shelter. When they set up the construction camp, you just take it to the comptroller for payment.''

"Lot of good money'll do me. There wasn't enough rain to make hay worth shit this season. Where'm I going to buy any?''

The screen door banged. Dad was angry. Jeremy frowned and wiggled into a more comfortable position. Why should Dad be angry? The stranger talked about water. Everyone needed water.

"Never mind him." From the clatter, Mother was dishing up bean-and-squash stew left from lunch. "You have to understand, it's hard for him to hope after all these years." A plate clunked on the table. "You keep pumping water, trying to grow enough to live on, praying the well holds out and watching your kids go to bed hungry. You don't have much energy left for hoping. When you're done, I'll show you your room. The twins can sleep with Jeremy and Rupert.''

She sounded like she was going to cry again. Jeremy looked down at his loosely curled fists. The thick joints made his fingers look like knobby tree roots. The stranger said something, but Jeremy didn't catch it. He'd only heard Mother cry once before —when the doctor over in La Grande had told her that there wasn't anything that could be done about his hands or his knees.

This stranger made Dad angry and Mother sad. Jeremy thought about that while he waited, but he couldn't make any sense out of it at all. As soon as the stranger and Mother left the kitchen, Jeremy slipped out of his hiding place. Sure enough,

the big plastic pitcher stood on the table, surrounded by empty glasses. You didn't ask for water between meals. Jeremy listened to the quiet. He lifted the pitcher, clutching it tightly in his thick awkward grip.

The water was almost as warm as the air by now, but it tasted sweet on his dusty throat. He never got enough water. No one did—not when the crops needed it, too. Jeremy swirled the pitcher, watching the last bit of water climb the sides in a miniature whirlpool.

Absently, he made it fill clear to the brim. What would it be like to live in the old days, when it rained all the time and the riverbed was full of water and fish? He imagined a fish, made it appear in the water. He'd seen it in another book, all speckled green with a soft shading of pink on its belly. He made the fish leap out of the pitcher and dive back in, splashing tiny droplets of water that vanished as they fell. Jeremy tilted his head, pleased with himself. Trout—he remembered the name, now.

"Jeremy!"

Jeremy started at his mother's cry and dropped the pitcher. Water and fish vanished as the plastic clattered on the linoleum. Throat tight, he stared at the small puddle of real water. The stranger stood behind Mother in the doorway.

"Go see if there are any eggs." His mother's voice quivered. "Do it right now."

Jeremy limped out the door without looking at either of them.

"Don't mind him," he heard his mother say breathlessly. "He's clumsy, is all."

She was afraid the stranger had seen the fish. Jeremy hurried across the oven glare of the barnyard. What if he had? What if he said something in front of Dad? His skin twitched with the memory of the last beating, when he'd gotten to daydreaming and made the dragonfly appear in church. Jeremy shivered.

The stranger's horse snorted at him, pulling back against its halter with a muffled thudding of hooves. "Easy, boy, easy." Jeremy stumbled to a halt, extended his hand. The pinto shook its thick mane and stretched its neck to sniff. Jeremy smiled as the velvety lips brushed his palm. "You're pretty," he said, but it wasn't true. It wasn't even a horse—just a scruffy pony with a thick neck and feet big as dinner plates.

He was ugly. Jeremy sat down stiffly, leaning his back against the old smooth boards of the barn. "Hey." He wiggled his toes as the pony sniffed at his bare feet. "It's not your fault you're ugly.'' He stroked the pony's nose. ''I bet you can run like the wind,'' he murmured.

The pony's raspy breathing sounded friendly, comforting. Eyes half-closed, Jeremy imagined himself galloping over the sun-scorched meadows. His knees wouldn't matter at all. . . . He drifted off into a dream of wind and galloping hooves.

''JEREMY! It's suppertime. Where the hell are you?'' Rupert's voice. Jeremy blinked awake, swallowing a yawn. It was almost dark. Straw tickled his cheek and he remembered. He was in the barn and a stranger had seen him make something.

''I know you're in here.'' Rupert's footsteps crunched closer.

By now, Dad probably knew about the trout. Jeremy rolled onto his stomach and wriggled under the main beam beneath the wall. There was just enough space for his skinny body.

''I hear you, you brat.'' Rupert's silhouette loomed against the gray rectangle of the doorway. ''You think I want to play hide-and-seek after I work all day? If I get in trouble, I'll get you.''

The pony laid back its ears and whinnied shrilly.

''Jesus!'' Rupert jumped back. ''I hope you get your head kicked off!'' he yelled.

Jeremy listened to Rupert stomp out of the barn. ''Thanks, pony,'' he whispered as he scrambled out of his hiding place. He shook powdery dust from his clothes, listening for the slam of the screen door.

Better to face Rupert later than Dad right now.

The pony nudged him, and Jeremy scratched absently at its ear. A bat twittered in the darkness over his head. Jeremy looked up, barely able to make out the flittering shadows coming and going through the gray arch of the doorway. He'd sneak in later. Jeremy's stomach growled as he curled up against the wall of the barn. The pony snuffled softly and moved closer, as if it was glad he was there.

The barn was full of dry creaks and whispers. Something rustled loudly in the loft above Jeremy's head, and he started. Funny how darkness changed the friendly barn, stretched it out so big. Too big and too dark. ''Want to see a firefly?'' Jeremy asked the pony. The darkness seemed to swallow his words. It pressed in around him, as if he had made it angry by talking.

He hadn't been able to find a picture. . . . The firefly appeared, bright as a candle flame in the darkness. It looked sort of like a glowing moth. That didn't seem right, but its warm glow drove back the darkness. Jeremy examined it thoughtfully. Maybe he should make the wings bigger.

"So I wasn't seeing things," a voice said.

The pony whinnied and Jeremy snuffed out the firefly. Before he could hide, a dazzling beam of light flashed in his eyes. He raised a hand against the hurting glare.

"Sorry." The light dipped, illuminating a circular patch of dust and Jeremy's dirty legs. "So this is where you've been. Your brother said he couldn't find you." The beam hesitated on Jeremy's lumpy knees.

The surveyor patted the pony and bent to prop the solar flashlight on the floor. Its powerful beam splashed back from the wall, streaking the straw with shadows. "Can you do it again?" he asked. "Make that insect appear, I mean."

Jeremy licked his dry lips. He *had* seen the trout. "I'm not supposed to . . . make things."

"I sort of got that impression." The man gave him a slow thoughtful smile. "I pretended I didn't notice. I didn't want to get you in trouble."

Jeremy blinked. This stranger—a grown-up—had worried about getting him in trouble? The bright comforting light and the surveyor's amazing claim shut the two of them into a kind of private magic circle.

Why not let him see? He'd already seen the trout, and he hadn't told Dad. The firefly glowed to life in the air between them. "What does a firefly look like?" Jeremy asked.

"I don't know." The surveyor reached out to touch the mak-ing, snatched his hand away as his finger passed through the delicate wings.

"It isn't real. It doesn't even look right." Disappointed, Jeremy let it fade and vanish.

"Wow." The surveyor whistled softly. "I've never seen any-thing like that."

He sounded like Jeremy was doing something wonderful. "Don't tell I showed you, okay?" Jeremy picked at a thread in his ragged cutoffs.

"I won't." The man answered him seriously, as if he was talking to another grown-up. "How old are you?" he asked after a minute.

"Twelve. I'm small for my age." Jeremy watched him pick up his marvelous light and swing its bright beam over the old pony.

"You look pretty settled, Ezra. I'll get you some more water in the morning." The surveyor slapped the pony on the neck. "Come on," he said to Jeremy. "Let's go in. I think your mom left a plate out for you." He gave Jeremy a sideways look. "Your dad went to bed," he said.

"Oh." Jeremy scrambled to his feet, wondering how the stranger knew to say that. If Dad was asleep, it was safe to go back in. Besides, this ungrownup-like man hadn't told. "Are you going to bring us water?" he asked.

"No," the man said slowly. "I just make maps. I don't dig wells."

"I bet you're good," Jeremy said. He wanted to say something nice to this man, and that was all he could think of.

"Thanks," the surveyor said, but he sounded more sad than pleased. "I'm pretty good at what I do."

No, he didn't act like a grown-up. He didn't act like anyone Jeremy had ever met. Thoughtfully, he followed the bright beam of the surveyor's flashlight into the house.

NEXT MORNING was church-Sunday, but the family got up at dawn as usual because it was such a long walk into town. Jeremy put on his good pair of shorts and went down to take on Mother in the kitchen.

"You can't go." She shoved a full water-jug into the lunch pack. "It's too far."

She was remembering the dragonfly. "I won't forget. I'll be good," Jeremy said. "Please?"

"Forget it." Rupert glared at him from the doorway. "The freak'll forget and do something again."

"That's enough." Mother closed the pack with a jerk. "I'll bring you a new book." She wouldn't meet Jeremy's eyes. "What do you want?"

"I don't know." Jeremy set his jaw. He didn't usually care, didn't like church-Sundays with all the careful eyes that sneaked like Rupert when they looked at his hands and knees. This time, the surveyor was going. "I want to come," he said.

"Mom . . ."

"I said that's enough." Mother looked past Rupert. "Did you get enough breakfast, Mr. Greely?" she asked too cheerfully.

"More than enough, thanks." The surveyor walked into the kitchen and the conversation ended.

When Jeremy started down the gravel road with them,

Mother's lips got tight and Rupert threw him a look that promised trouble, but Dad acted like he wasn't even there and no one else dared say anything. Jeremy limped along as fast as he could, trying not to fall behind. He had won. He wasn't sure why, but he had.

It was a long, hot walk into town.

Rupert and Jonathan stuck to the surveyor like burrs, asking about the iceberg tugs, the Drylands, Portland, and LA. The surveyor answered their questions gravely and politely. He wore a fresh tan shirt tucked into his faded jeans. It was clean, and the tower on the pocket made it look like it meant something special.

It meant water.

Everyone was there by the time they reached the church— except the Menendez family, who lived way down the dry creekbed and sometimes didn't come anyway. The Pearson kids were screaming as they took turns jumping off the porch, and Bev LaMont was watching for Jonathan, like she always did.

As soon as they got close enough for people to count the extra person, everyone abandoned their picnic spreads and made for the porch.

"This is Mr. Greely, a surveyor with the Army Corps of Engineers," Mother announced as they climbed the wide steps.

"Pleased to meet you." The surveyor's warm smile swept the sun-dried faces. "I've been sent to make a preliminary survey for a federal irrigation project." He perched on the porch railing, like he'd done it a hundred times before. "The new Singhe solar cells are going to power a deep-well pumping operation. They've identified a major aquifer in this region."

"How come we ain't heard of this before?" Bearded Ted Brewster, who ran the Exxon station when he could get gas, spoke up from the back of the crowd.

"Come on, Ted." Fists on her bony hips, gray-haired Sally Brandt raised her voice. "By the time news makes it here from Boise, it's gone through six drunken truckers. They're lucky they can remember their names."

"No. That's a good question." The surveyor looked around at the small knot of dusty faces. "You don't get any radio or TV?"

"No power, out here." Sally shook her head. "Anyway, we couldn't get TV after Spokane quit. There's too many mountains to pick up Boise, and I don't think there's anything big broadcasting this side of Portland."

The surveyor nodded and reached inside his shirt. "I have a letter from the regional supervisor." He pulled out a white rectangle. "I'm supposed to deliver it to the mayor, city supervisor, or whoever's in charge." He raised his eyebrows expectantly.

A gust of wind whispered across the crowded porch, and no one spoke.

"Most people just left." Jeremy's father finally stepped forward, fists in the pockets of his patched jeans. "This was wheat and alfalfa land, from the time the Oregon Territory became a state. You can't farm wheat without water." His voice sounded loud in the silence. "The National Guard come around and told us to go get work on the Columbia River project. That's all the help the *government* was gonna give us. If we stayed, they said, we'd dry up and starve. They didn't really give a shit. We don't have a mayor," he said. "There's just us."

The surveyor looked at the dusty faces, one by one. "Like I told Mr. Barlow last night," he said quietly, "I can't promise that we'll find water, or that you'll grow wheat again. I'm only the surveyor."

For a long moment Jeremy's father stared at the envelope. With a jerky awkward gesture, he reached out and took it. He pried up the white flap with a blunt thumb and squinted at the print, forehead wrinkling with effort.

Without a word, he handed the paper to Ted Brewster. Jeremy watched the white paper pass from hand to hand. People held it like it was precious—like it was water. He listened to the dry rustle of the paper. When it came around to Dad again, he stuck it into the glass case beside the door of the church. "I hope to God you find water," he said softly.

"Amen," someone said.

"Amen." The ragged mutter ran through the crowd.

After that, everyone broke up. After the Reverend had died in the big dust storm, they'd moved out the pews. Families spread cloths on the long rickety tables inside. There weren't any more sermons, but people still came to eat together on church-Sundays. The surveyor wandered from group to group in the colored shadows of the church, eating the food people pressed on him. They crowded him, talking, brushing up against him, as if his touch would bring good luck and water to the dead fields.

Jeremy hung back, under the blue-and-green diamonds of the stained-glass window. Finally, he went down the narrow stairs to the sparse shelves of the basement library. He found a little paperback book on insects, but it didn't have a picture of a firefly. He tossed it back onto the shelf. When it fell onto the dusty concrete floor, he kicked it, feeling guilty and pleased when it skittered out of sight under a shelf. Upstairs, the surveyor was giving everyone the same warm grin that he'd given Jeremy in the barn last night.

It made Jeremy's stomach ball up into an angry knot.

He wandered outside and found little Rita Menendez poking at ants on the front walk. Mrs. Menendez was yelling at the older kids as she started to unpack the lunch, so Jeremy carried Rita off into the dappled shade under the scraggly shrubs. She was too young to mind his hands. Belly still tight, Jeremy made a bright green frog appear on Rita's knee.

Her gurgly laugh eased some of the tightness. *She* liked his makings. He turned the frog into the dragonfly, and she grabbed at it. This time, Jeremy heard the surveyor coming, and when the man pushed the brittle branches aside, the dragonfly was gone.

"Do you always hide?" He reached down to tickle Rita's plump chin.

"I'm not hiding." Jeremy peeked up through his sun-bleached hair.

"I need someone to help me." The surveyor squatted so that Jeremy had to meet his eyes. "I talked to your father, and he said I could hire you. If you agree. The Corps's only paying crisis-minimum," he said apologetically.

Jeremy pushed Rita gently off his lap. This man wanted to hire *him*—with his bad knees and his lumpy, useless hands? Hiring was something from the old days, like the flashlight and this man's clean, creased shirt.

Jeremy wiped his hands on his pants, pressing hard, as if he might straighten his bent fingers. "I'd like that, Mr. Greely," he said breathlessly.

"Good." The man smiled like he meant it. "We'll get started first thing tomorrow." He stood, giving Rita a final pat that made her chuckle. "Call me Dan," he said. "Okay?"

"Okay, Dan," Jeremy said softly. He watched the man walk away, feeling warm inside.

JEREMY DIDN'T SEE much of Dan Greely before the next morning. It seemed like everyone had to talk to him about water tables, aquifers, deep wells, and the Army Corps of Engineers.

They said the words like the Reverend used to say prayers. *Army Corps of Engineers.*

Dan, Dad, and Jonathan stayed in town. Mother shepherded the rest of them home. The twins were tired, but Rupert was annoyed because he couldn't stay, too. He shoved Jeremy whenever Mother wasn't looking.

"I hope you work hard for Mr. Greely," Mother said when she came up to say good-night. The twins were already snoring in the hot darkness of the attic room.

"Waste of time to hire *him,*" Rupert growled from his bed. "The pony'd be more use."

"That's enough." Mother's voice sounded sharp as a new nail. "We can't spare either you or Jonathan from the pumping, so don't get yourself worked up. You don't have to go with him," she said to Jeremy. Her hand trembled just a little as she brushed the hair back from his forehead.

She was worried. "It'll be okay," Jeremy murmured. He wondered why. He almost told her that Dan already knew about the makings and wouldn't tell, but Rupert was listening. "I'll do good," he said, and wished he believed it.

It took Jeremy a long time to fall asleep, but when he did, it seemed like only moments passed before he woke up. At first, he thought Mother was calling him for breakfast. It was still dark, but the east window showed faint gray.

There it was again—Mother's voice. Too wide awake to fall back asleep, Jeremy slipped out of bed and tiptoed into the dark hall.

"Stop worrying." Dad's low growl drifted through the half-open door. "What do you think he's gonna do? Eat the kid?"

"I don't know. He said he needed a helper, but what. . . ."

"What can Jeremy do? He can't do shit, but Greely's gonna pay wages and we can use anything we can get." Dad's voice sounded like the dry scouring winds. "How do you think I felt when I had to go crawling to the Brewsters and the Pearsons for food last winter?"

"It wasn't Jeremy's fault, Everett. The well's giving out."

"No one else has an extra mouth to feed. No one but me, and I've gotta go begging."

"I lost three babies after Rupert." Mother's voice sounded high and tight. "I couldn't of stood losing another."

Jeremy fumbled his way down the hall, teeth clenched so hard they felt like they were going to break. *No one else has an extra mouth to feed.* His father's cold words chased him down the stairs. *No one but me.*

A light glowed in the barn's darkness. "Hi." Dan pulled a strap tight on the pony's packsaddle. "I was just going to come wake you. Ezra and I are used to starting at dawn." He tugged on the pack, nodded to himself. "Have you eaten yet?" he asked Jeremy.

"Yeah," Jeremy lied.

Dan gave him a searching look, then shrugged. "Okay. Let's go."

It was just light enough to see as they started down the track. The pony stepped over the thin white pipe that carried water from the well to the field. Above them, the old bicycle frame of the pump looked like a skeleton sticking up out of the gray dirt. In an hour, Jonathan would be pedaling hard to get his gallons pumped. Then, Rupert would take over. The twins carried the yoked pails and dipped out precious water to each thirsty plant.

"Did your dad make that?" Dan nodded at the metal frame.

"Uh-huh." Jeremy walked a little faster, trying not to limp. He had had a thousand questions about the outside world to ask, but the sharp whispers in the upstairs hall had dried them up like the wind dried up a puddle. He watched Ezra's big feet kick up the brown dust, feeling dry and empty inside.

"We'll start here." The surveyor pulled Ezra to a halt. They were looking down on the dry riverbed and the narrow rusty bridge. The road went across the riverbed now. It was easier.

The pony waited patiently, head drooping, while Dan unloaded it. "This machine measures distance by bouncing a beam of light off a mirror." Dan set the cracked plastic case down on the ground. "It sits on this tripod, and the reflector goes on the other one." He unloaded a water jug, lunch, an ax, a steel tape measure, and other odds and ends. "Now, we get to work," he said when he was done.

Sweat stuck Jeremy's hair to his face as he struggled across the sunbaked clay after Dan. They set up the machine and reflector, took them down and set them up somewhere else. Sometimes Dan hacked a path through the dry brush. It was hard going. In spite of all he could do, Jeremy was limping badly by midmorning.

"I'm sorry." Dan stopped abruptly. "You keep up so well, it's easy to forget that you hurt."

His tone was matter-of-fact, without a trace of pity. There was a knot in Jeremy's throat as Dan boosted him onto Ezra's back. He sat up straight on the hard packsaddle, arms tight around the precious machine. It felt heavy, dense with the magic that would call water out of the ground. Jeremy tried to imagine the gullied dun hills all green, with blue water tumbling down the old riverbed.

If there was plenty of water, it wouldn't matter so much that he couldn't pump or carry buckets.

Jeremy thought about water while he held what Dan gave him to hold and, once or twice, pushed buttons on the distance machine. He could manage that much. It hummed under his touch, and bright red numbers winked in a tiny window. He had to remember them, because his fingers were too clumsy to write them down in Dan's brown notebook.

Dan didn't really need any help with the measuring. Jeremy stood beside the magic machine, watching a single hawk circle in the hard blue sky. Mother had been right. Dan wanted something else from him.

Well, that was okay. Jeremy shrugged as the hawk drifted off southward. No one else thought he had anything to offer.

THE SUN STOOD high overhead when they stopped for lunch. It poured searing light down on the land, sucking up their sweat. Dan and Jeremy huddled in a narrow strip of shade beneath the canyon wall. Ezra stood in front of them, head down, tail whisking.

They shared warm plastic-tasting water with the pony, and Dan produced dried apple slices from the lunch pack. He had stripped off his shirt, and sweat gleamed like oil on his brown shoulders. His eyes were gray, Jeremy noticed. They looked bright in his dark face.

"Why do you have to do all this stuff?" Awkwardly, Jeremy scooped up a leathery disk of dried apple. The tart sweetness filled his mouth with a rush of saliva.

"I'm making a map of the ground." Dan shaded his eyes, squinting into the shimmering heat-haze. "They have to know all the humps, hollows, and slopes before they can decide how to build a road or plan buildings."

"I was trying to imagine lots of water." Jeremy reached for more apples. "It's hard."

"Yeah," Dan said harshly. "Well, don't count the days yet." He shook himself, and his expression softened. "Tell me about your fireflies and fish that jump out of pitchers."

"Not much to tell." Jeremy looked away from Dan's intent gray eyes. Was that what he wanted? "If I think of something hard enough, you can see it. It's not real. It's not any good for anything." Jeremy drew a zigzag pattern in the dust with his fingers. "It . . . bothers people," he said.

"Like your mom and dad."

"Dad doesn't like it." Jeremy smoothed the lines away.

"What about your mother? What about the other folk?" Dan prodded.

"Dad doesn't let us talk about it. I don't make things where people can see." Mostly. Jeremy shifted uneasily, remembering the dragonfly.

"Is that why you hide?" Dan was looking at him.

"The Pearsons had a baby with joints like mine. So did Sally Brandt—from the dust or the water, or something." Jeremy spread his thick clumsy hands. "They . . . died," he said. "There isn't enough water for extra mouths."

"Who said that?" Dan asked in a hard, quiet voice.

*I lost three babies,* Mother had cried in that scary voice. *I couldn't stand to lose another.*

Their old nanny goat had had a kid with an extra leg last spring. Dad had taken the biggest knife from the kitchen and cut its throat by a bean hill, so the blood would water the seedlings. The apple slice in Jeremy's mouth tasted like dust. Feeling stony hard inside, he made the dragonfly appear, sent it darting through the air to land on Dan's knee with a glitter of wings.

"Holy shit." Dried apples scattered in the dust as Dan flinched. "I can almost believe that I feel it," he breathed.

He wasn't scared. Jeremy sighed as the shimmering wings blurred and vanished.

"I don't believe it." Dan stared at the space where the making had been. "Yes, I do believe it, but it's fantastic." He slapped Jeremy lightly on the shoulder, a slow smile spreading across his face. "We could be the hottest thing in this whole damn dry country, kid. Think of it. The hicks would fall all over themselves to come see a show like that. *Hoo . . . ey.*" His grin faded suddenly.

"You're afraid of it, aren't you?" he asked softly. "Because it scares your dad?"

Scared? Not Dad. Jeremy shook his head. Rupert was scared of the brown lizards that lived under the rocks out back. He killed them all the time. Dad wasn't scared of the makings. He hated them.

"Look at this." Dan yanked a grubby red bandanna out of his pocket and dangled it in front of Jeremy's eyes. He stuffed the cloth into his closed fist. "Abracadabra . . ." He waved his hand around. "Watch closely, and . . . ta da." He snapped open his hand.

Jeremy stared at his empty palm.

"Your handkerchief, sir." With a flourish, Dan reached behind Jeremy's head and twitched the bandanna into view.

"Wow." Jeremy touched the handkerchief. "How did you do that?"

"It's pretty easy." Dan looked sad as he stuffed the bandanna back into his pocket. "The card tricks, juggling—it's not enough to keep you in water out here in the Dry. The sun's baked all the belief out of people. It would take a miracle to get some attention. You're that kind of a miracle," he said.

Dan acted like the making was a wonderful thing—not something shameful—not something that made Dad have to ask the Brewsters for food. Suddenly unsure, Jeremy bent to scoop up the apples that Dan had dropped. "You don't want to waste these."

"I'd give a lot for your talent." Dan's eyes gleamed like water.

Talent? Jeremy dumped the withered rings of apple into the pack, struggling to understand Dan's tone. "You're a surveyor," he said. "You don't need to do tricks."

"I guess I am." Dan's laugh sounded bitter. "So I guess we'd better get back to surveying," he said as he got to his feet.

Strange feelings fluttered in Jeremy's chest. Could Dan be right? Would people really look at him like Dan had looked at him, all excited and envious? What if Dan was wrong? What if everyone looked at him like Dad did, instead?

He could find out. If he went with Dan.

Jeremy thought about that—going with Dan—for the rest of the day, while he steadied the machine and pushed buttons. It excited him and scared him at the same time, but he didn't say anything to Dan.

Dan might not want him to come along.

IT SEEMED like everyone within walking distance was waiting at the house when they plodded back to the farm that evening. People had brought food and water, because you didn't ask for hospitality. Covered dishes and water jugs cluttered the kitchen table, and Dan was swept into the crowd and out of Jeremy's reach.

Dan didn't belong to him here, in the dusty house. Here, Dan belonged to the grown-ups and the Army Corps of Engineers. It was only when they were out in the dry hills with Ezra that Dan would be his. Jeremy slipped away to his barn sanctuary to pet Ezra and think.

What would happen if he walked away from the peeling old house? Dad wouldn't have to ask the Brewsters for food, Jeremy thought, and he pulled at the pony's tangled mane until the coarse horsehair cut his fingers.

AFTER THE first three days, the crowd waiting at the farm had thinned out. They'd heard what news Dan had to tell. They'd sold him the food and supplies that he'd asked for, taking his pale green voucher slips as payment. Now they were waiting for the construction crews to arrive. Even Dad was waiting. He whistled while he carried water to the potato plants, and he smiled at Dan.

Dan was the water bringer. Everyone smiled at Dan.

It made Jeremy jealous when they were at home, but they weren't home very often. He and Dan trudged all over the scorched hills along the river. Dan talked about cities and the Dryland beyond the fields, with its ghosts and the bones of dead towns. He told Jeremy unbelievable stories about the shrinking sea and the ice getting thicker up north, maybe getting ready to slide southward and cover the Dry. He taught Jeremy how to describe the land in numbers. He asked Jeremy to make things every day, and he laughed when Jeremy made a frog appear on Ezra's head.

Jeremy tried hard to make Dan laugh. His face and hands got scratched by the brittle scrub and his knees hurt all the time, but it was worth it. Dan never asked him outright, but he talked like Jeremy was going to come with him to the cities and the sea. Both of them understood it, and the understanding was a comfortable thing between them.

"Where did you come from?" Jeremy asked on Saturday afternoon. They were eating lunch under the same overhang where they'd stopped the first day out.

"The Corps's regional office at Bonneville."

"No, I don't mean that." Jeremy swallowed cold beans. "I mean before that—before the surveying. Where were you born?"

"South." Dan glanced out toward the dead river. His gray eyes were vague, like he was looking at something far away or inside his head.

"Everyone thought it would be a war," he said after a while. "No one really believed that the weather could do us in." He gave a jerky shrug. "We came north from LA, running from the Mex wars and the gangs." His eyes flickered. "California was dying and if anyone had water in the Valley, they weren't sharing, so we kept on going. You leave everything behind you when you're dying of thirst—one piece at a time. Everything.'' He was silent for a moment. The wind blew grit across the rocks with a soft hiss, and Jeremy didn't make a sound.

"I ended up with the Corps," Dan said abruptly.

The transition from *we* to *I* cut off Jeremy's questions like a knife. He watched Dan toss a pebble down the slope. It bounced off an elk skull half buried in drifted dust.

"I won't kid you about things." Dan tossed another pebble at the bleached skull. "If you come with me, you're going to find out that things aren't always what they should be. When you're on the road, you don't have any options. You do what it takes to stay alive. Sometimes you don't like it much, but you do it."

The sad bitterness in Dan's tone scared Jeremy a little, but it didn't matter. Dan had said, *If you come with me.*

*If you come with me.*

"Can you make a face?" Dan asked suddenly.

"I don't know." Jeremy looked into Dan's bleak, hungry eyes. "I'll try," he said uncertainly.

"She was about sixteen, with brown eyes and black hair. It was straight, like rain falling." His eyes focused on that invisible something again. "She looked a little like me, but prettier," he said. "Her nose was thin—I used to kid her about it—and she smiled a lot."

Straight black hair; thin nose . . . Jeremy formulated a face in his mind, watched it take shape in the air. No. That was wrong. He didn't need Dan's look of disappointment to tell him so.

"Stupid to play that kind of game." Dan laid his hand on Jeremy's shoulder. "Thanks for trying."

Jeremy shook his head, wanting to do this more than he'd ever wanted to do anything in his life. The face was wrong, but barely wrong. He could feel it. If he just changed it a little, maybe smoothed the forehead like *so*, widened the nose, it might be. . . .

*Right.*

She smiled, face brimming with warmth and sadness. Jeremy stared at her, sweat stinging his eyes. She was right in a way that no bird or fish or animal had ever been right.

"Amy!" Dan cried brokenly. "Oh God, Amy."

The sound of Dan's voice scared Jeremy. He felt the making slip and tried to hang on, but the face wavered, blurred, and vanished. "I'm sorry," he whispered.

Dan buried his face in his hands. That was scarier than if he'd cried or yelled. Hesitantly, Jeremy reached out and touched him.

"It's all right." Dan raised his head, drew a long breath. "You did what I asked, didn't you?" His eyes were dry as the riverbed. "I didn't know. . . ." He got up suddenly. "Let's go back." He looked down the dead valley. "I'm through here."

"You mean all through? Like you're leaving?" Jeremy forced the words through the sudden tightness in his throat.

"Yeah." Dan looked down at him. "The job's finished. I didn't expect to be here this long." His shoulders lifted as he took a long slow breath. "Are you coming?"

"Yes." Jeremy stood up as straight as he could. There was nothing for him here. Nothing at all. "I'm coming," he said.

"Good." Dan boosted him onto Ezra's back. "I'm leaving early," he said. "You better not tell your folks."

"I won't," Jeremy said.

NO ONE was pumping on the bicycle frame as they plodded past. Jeremy looked up at the brown hillside, imagining it all green with grass, like in pictures. Water would come, Dad would be happy, and he would be with Dan. Mother would cry, but she wouldn't have to protect him from Dad anymore.

The green landscape wouldn't take shape in his mind. Ezra broke into a jouncing trot, and Jeremy had to grab the saddle as the pony headed for the barnyard and the water tub there.

"Mr. Greely," Dad called from the porch.

Jeremy stiffened. Dad sounded cold and mad, like when he caught Jeremy making.

"We want to talk to you."

Mr. Brewster stepped onto the porch behind him. Rupert and Jonathan followed, with Mr. Mendoza, Sally Brandt, and the Deardorf boys.

Mr. Mendoza had his old deer rifle. They all looked angry.

"My brother got into town last night." Sally's voice was shrill. "He told me about this scam he heard of back in Pendleton. Seems this guy goes around to little towns pretending to be a surveyor. He buys things with vouchers from the Army Corps of Engineers."

"We searched your stuff." Ted Brewster held up a fistful of white. "You carry a few spare letters, don't you?" He opened his hand. "You're a fake," he said harshly.

The white envelopes fluttered to the dusty ground like dead leaves. Stunned by their anger, Jeremy turned to Dan, waiting

for him to explain, waiting for Dan to tell them how they were
wrong and remind them about the water.

"Dan?" he whispered.

Dan looked at him finally, his head moving slowly on his
neck, and Jeremy felt his insides going numb and dead.
"Mother gave you dried apples." Jeremy swallowed, remembering the tears and hope in her voice. "Dried apples are for
birthdays."

For one instant, Dan's gray eyes filled with hurt. Then he
looked away, turning a bland smile on the approaching adults.
"I heard about some bastard doing that." He spread his hands.
"But I'm legit." He plucked at the black insignia on his sweaty
shirt.

Dad took one long step forward and smashed his fist into
Dan's face. "He described you." He looked down as Dan
sprawled in the dirt. "He described you real well."

Dan got up very slowly, wiping dust from his face. Blood
smeared his chin. He shrugged.

They took him into town, walking around him in a loose
ring. Jeremy stood in the road, watching the dust settle behind
them. Even if Mr. Mendoza didn't have the gun, Dan couldn't
run. The dry hills brooded on every side. Where would he run
to? Jeremy climbed up onto the rimrock and didn't come down
until it got dark.

"I wondered about that guy," Rupert sneered as they got
ready for bed that night. "Federal survey, huh? The feds
couldn't even hang on to the Columbia Project. I don't know
how anyone could believe him."

"Hope is a tempting thing." Jeremy's mother leaned against
the doorway. She hadn't scolded Jeremy for running off. "If
there was any water around here, someone would have drilled
for it a long time ago," she said in a tired voice. "I guess we all
wanted to hope."

Jeremy climbed onto his cot without looking at her.

"I'm sorry," she murmured. "I'm sorry for us, and I'm sorry
for him, too."

"They'll hang him—like they did to that trucker over in La
Grande."

"Shame on you, Rupert." Her voice caught a little.

Jeremy buried his face in his pillow. She was feeling sorry for
him and he didn't want anyone to feel sorry for him. I hate him,
too, he thought fiercely. Why couldn't Dan have been what he
said? He could have gone with Dan, made things for him. Now,

they'd always have to pump and he would always be an extra mouth to Dad.

"They're gonna hang him," Rupert whispered to Jeremy after Mother had left. He sounded smug. "No wonder the jerk wanted you to help him. You're too dumb to figure out he was a fake."

Jeremy pressed his face into the pillow until he could barely breathe. If he made a sound, if he moved, he'd kill Rupert. Rupert might be almost sixteen and Jeremy's hands might not work very well, but he'd kill Rupert, somehow.

Rupert was right. They were going to hang Dan. He'd seen it in their eyes when they walked up to him. It wasn't just because he'd tricked them. They hated Dan because the government, the Army Corps of Engineers, didn't really care about them.

No one cared. Dan had made them see it.

He lied to me, too. Jeremy burrowed deeper into the pillow, but he kept hearing Dan's sad-bitter voice. *You do what it takes to stay alive. Sometimes you don't like it much, but you do it.*

Dan hadn't lied to him.

Jeremy must have fallen asleep, because he woke up from a dream of the woman with the black hair. Like rain, Dan had said. Jeremy opened his eyes. His throat hurt, as if he had been crying in his sleep. Amy, Dan had cried. She was dead, whoever she had been. Dan's *we* had turned into *I*.

Rupert snored, arm hanging over the side of his mattress. The sloping roof pressed down on Jeremy, threatening to crush him, trying to smear him into the dry darkness, dissolve him. Where was Dan now? In the church? Jeremy sat up, pushing against the heavy darkness, heart pounding with the knowledge of what he had to do. The house creaked softly to itself as he tiptoed down the steep stairs.

"Who's there?" his father said from the bottom of the stairway.

"Me." Jeremy froze, clutching the railing with both hands. "I . . . had to pee," he stammered. It was a feeble lie—the pot in the bedroom was never full.

"Jeremy?" His father bulked over him, a tower of shadow. "It's late. I just got back from town." He ran a thick hand across his face. "You liked Greely."

It was an accusation. "I still like him." Jeremy forced himself to stand straight. "He's not a bad man."

His father grunted, moved down a step. "He's a parasite,"

he said harshly. "His kind live on other people's sweat. You got to understand that. You got to understand that there's no worse crime than that."

"Isn't there?" Jeremy's voice trembled. "Who's going to share with him? Who's going to let him have a piece of their orchard or a field? He was just trying to live, and he didn't hurt anybody, not really. . . ."

"He lied and stole from us." His tone dismissed Dan, judged and sentenced him. "You get back to bed. Now!"

"No." Jeremy's knees were shaking, and he clung to the railing. "If it doesn't help the crops it's bad, isn't it? Nothing else matters to you but the land. Nothing."

His father's hand swung up and Jeremy turned to flee. His knee banged the riser and he fell, crying out with the hot pain, sprawling on the steps at his father's feet.

All by itself, the firefly popped into the air between them, glowing like a hot coal.

With a hoarse cry, Dad flinched backward, his hand clenching into a fist, ready to smash him like he'd smashed Dan. He *was* scared. Dan was right. Jeremy stared up at his father through a blur of pained tears. "It's not bad," he screamed. "It's just me. *Me!* I make things because they're pretty. Doesn't that count?" He cringed away from his father's fist.

His father hesitated, lowered his hand slowly. "No," he said in a choked voice. "It doesn't count. It doesn't count, either, that a man's just trying to stay alive. I . . . I wish it did." He stepped past Jeremy and went on up the stairs.

Jeremy listened to his slow heavy tread on the floorboards over his head. His pulse pounded in his ears and he felt dizzy. *It doesn't count,* his father had said. *I wish it did.* Jeremy put his forehead down on his clenched fists, and his tears scalded his knuckles.

JEREMY was right. Dan was in the church basement. Yellow light glowed dimly from one of the window wells along the concrete foundation, the only light in this dark, dead town. Jeremy lay down on his stomach and peered through the glassless window. Yep. Mr. Brewster was sitting on an old pew beside a wooden door, flipping through a tattered hunting magazine by the light of a hissing gasoline lantern.

He looked wide awake.

Jeremy glanced at the sky. Was it getting light? How long until dawn? Desperate, he leaned over the cracked lip of the well. Mr. Brewster wasn't going to fall asleep. Not in time.

The firefly had scared Dad. Jeremy lay flat in the dust, face pressed against his clenched fists. Mr. Brewster didn't know about the makings, not very much, anyway. Cold balled in Jeremy's belly, so bad that he almost threw up. Bigger would be scarier, but bigger was harder. What if he couldn't do it? The firefly popped into the air two feet from Mr. Brewster's magazine, big as a chicken.

"Holy shit." His chair banged over as he scrambled to his feet. "Mother of God, what's that?" His voice sounded strange and squeaky.

Nails biting his palms, Jeremy made the firefly dart at Mr. Brewster's face. It moved sluggishly, dimming to a dull orange. Oh God, don't let it fade. Sweat stung Jeremy's eyes.

Mr. Brewster yelled and threw his magazine at it. His footsteps pounded on the wooden stairs, and a moment later, the church door thudded open. Jeremy lay flat in the dust as Mr. Brewster ran past him. The ground felt warm, as if the earth had a fever. Sweat turned the dust on Jeremy's face to mud, and he was shaking all over. He couldn't hear Mr. Brewster's footsteps anymore.

Now!

He scrambled down through the window. A fragment of glass still embedded in the frame grazed his arm, and he landed on the broken chair. It collapsed with a terrible crash. Panting, Jeremy stumbled to his feet. Oh God, please don't let Mr. Brewster come back. He struggled with the bolt on the storeroom door, bruising his palm. It slid back, and he pushed the heavy door open.

Dan was sitting on the floor between shelves of musty hymnals and folded choir robes. The yellow light made his skin look tawny brown, like the dust. His face was swollen and streaked with dried blood.

"Jeremy?" Hope flared in Dan's eyes.

"Hurry." Jeremy grabbed his arm.

Dan staggered to his feet and followed Jeremy up the steps, treading on his heels. Someone shouted behind them, and Jeremy's heart lurched.

"That way." He pointed.

Dan threw an arm around him and ran, half-carrying Jeremy as they ducked behind the dark Exxon station. They scrambled under the board fence in the back, lay flat while someone ran and panted past. Mr. Brewster? This was like a scary game of hide-and-seek. Gray banded the eastern horizon as Jeremy led Dan across the dusty main street, listening for footsteps, stumbling on the rough pavement. They turned left by the boarded-up restaurant, cut through a yard full of drifted dust, dead weeds, and a gasless car.

Jeremy had left Ezra tethered behind the last house on the street. The pony gave a low growling whinny as they hurried up. Dan stroked his nose to quiet him, his eyes running over the lumpy bulges of the pack.

"It's all there, food, water, and everything," Jeremy panted. "It's not a very good job—I didn't know how to fix a pack. The ground's pretty hard along the river, so you won't leave many tracks. Willow Creekbed'll take you way south. It's the first creekbed past the old feed mill. You can't miss it."

"I thought you were coming with me." Dan looked down at Jeremy.

"I was." Jeremy stared at the old nylon daypack he'd left on the ground beside Ezra. It wasn't very heavy because he didn't have much. "I changed my mind."

"You can't." Dan's fingers dug into his shoulders. "They'll know you let me out. What'll happen then?"

"I don't know." Jeremy swallowed a lump of fear. His father was part of the land, linked to it. If the land dried up and died, Dad would die. "I got to stay," he whispered.

"Why? You think you'll make peace with your father?" Dan shook him—one short, sharp jerk that made Jeremy's teeth snap together. "You've got magic in your hands. Real magic. You think that's ever going to matter to him?"

"I don't know." Tears clogged Jeremy's nose, burned his eyes.

"Hell, my choices haven't turned out so hot." Dan wiped the tears away, his fingers rough and dry on Jeremy's face. "Just don't let him kill your magic." He shook Jeremy again, gently this time. "He needs it. They all need it." He sighed. "And I'd better get going. Keep making things, kid." He squeezed Jeremy's shoulder hard, grabbed Ezra's lead rope, and walked away into the waning night.

Jeremy stood still, the last of his tears drying on his face, listening to Ezra's muffled hoofbeats fade in the distance. He listened until he could hear nothing but the dry whisper of the morning breeze, then he started back. He thought about cutting across the dun hills and down through the riverbed to get home. Instead, his feet carried him back into town and he let them.

They might have been waiting for him in front of the church—Mr. Brewster, Sally Brandt, Mr. Mendoza, and . . .

Dad. Jeremy faltered as they all turned to stare at him, wishing in one terrible, frightened instant that he had gone with Dan after all. They looked at him like they had looked at Dan yesterday, hard and cold. Mr. Brewster walked to meet him, slow and stiff-legged, and Jeremy wondered suddenly if they'd hang him instead of Dan.

Maybe. It was there, in their faces, back behind their cold eyes.

"You little snot." Mr. Brewster's hand closed on Jeremy's shirt, balling up the fabric, lifting him off his feet. "You let Greely out. I saw you. Where's he headed?"

"I don't know," Jeremy faltered.

"Like hell." Brewster slapped him.

Red-and-black light exploded behind Jeremy's eyelids, and his mouth filled with a harsh metallic taste. He fell hard and hurting onto his knees, dizzy, eyes blurred with tears, belly full of sickness.

"Knock it off, Ted."

Dad, amazingly Dad, was lifting him to his feet, hands under his arms, gentle, almost.

"I lay hands on my kids," he said harshly. "No one else."

"He knows where that bastard's headed." Mr. Brewster was breathing heavy and fast. "You beat it out of him or I do."

"He said he doesn't know. That's the end of it, you hear me?"

Jeremy breathed slow, trying not to throw up. Silence hung between the two men, heavy and hot. It made the air feel thick and hard to breathe. Dad was angry, but not at him. He was angry at Mr. Brewster. For hitting him? Jeremy held his breath, tasting blood on his swelling lip, afraid to look up.

"You talk pretty high and mighty," Mr. Brewster said softly. "Considering you had to come crawling for help last winter. Seems like you ought to shut up."

Jeremy felt his father jerk, as if Mr. Brewster had kicked him. He felt his arms tremble and held his breath, wondering if Dad was going to let go, turn his back, and walk away.

"Seems like we all pitched in, when mice got into your seed stock a few years back," Dad said quietly.

Mr. Brewster made a small harsh sound.

"Come on, Ted." Sally's shrill exasperation shattered the moment. "While you're arguing, Greely's making tracks for Boardman."

"We got to split up," Mr. Mendoza chimed in.

Legs spread, shoulders hunched, Mr. Brewster glowered at Jeremy. Abruptly, he spun on his heel. "Shit." He jerked his head at Mr. Mendoza. "I bet the bastard headed west," he snarled. "We'll go down the riverbed, cut his tracks." He stalked off down the street with Mr. Mendoza.

Sally Brandt pushed tousled hair out of her face, sighed. "I'll go wake up the Deardorfs," she said. "We'll spread north and east. You can take the south."

Jeremy felt his father's body move a little, as if he had nodded at her. He stared down at the dust between his feet, heart pounding so hard that it felt like it was going to burst through his ribs. He felt Dad's hands lift from his shoulders, cringed a little as his father moved around in front of him, blocking the sun, but all he did was lift Jeremy's chin until he had to meet his father's eyes.

"I thought you'd gone with him," he said.

Jeremy peered into his father's weathered face. It looked like the hills, all folded into dun gullies—not angry, not sad, just old and dry.

"If we find Greely, we have to hang him," Dad said heavily. "Right or wrong, we voted—you got to know that, son."

"I was going to go." Jeremy swallowed, tasted dust. "You had to ask for food," he whispered. "Because of me."

His father's face twitched, as if something hurt him inside.

Without warning, the firefly popped into the air between them again, pale this time, a flickering shadow in the harsh morning light. Jeremy sucked in his breath, snuffed it out as his father flinched away from it.

"I'm sorry," he cried. "I didn't mean to make it, it just . . . happened. It makes Rita Menendez laugh." He took a deep hurting breath. "I won't do it anymore," he whispered, struggling to get the words past the tightness in his throat. "Not ever."

"Do it again." His father's hand clamped down on Jeremy's shoulder. "Right now."

Trembling, afraid to look at his father's face, Jeremy made the firefly appear again.

His father stared at it, breathing hard. With a shudder, he thrust his fingers into the firefly, yanked his hand back as if it had burned him. "It scares me," he whispered. "I don't understand it." He stared at his hand, closed his fingers slowly into a fist. "It's like this crazy drought." His voice shook. "I don't understand that, neither." He looked at Jeremy suddenly. "Not everyone's going to laugh. You scared the shit out of Ted. He ain't going to forgive you for that.''

Dad talked like he could keep on making things. Jeremy sneaked a look at him, heart beating fast again, throat hurting. "Hell," his father said softly. "I don't have any answers. Maybe there aren't any answers anymore—no good ones, anyway." He met Jeremy's eyes. "I've got to look south for Greely," he said. "Which way do you think he headed? Down Willow Creekbed or by the main road to La Grande?"

Jeremy hesitated for a moment, then straightened his shoulders with a jerk. "I think he went down the main road," he said, and held his breath.

His father shaded his eyes, stared at the dun fold of Willow Creekbed in the distance. "There aren't any good answers." He sighed and put his hand on his son's shoulder. "We'll look for Greely on the main road," he said.

# NTRADA

The rail was half empty, this early in the morning. Head aching, Mila Aguilar stared through the smeared window. Tract houses slid past below the concrete span—*los burbios,* acres of dust and junk, blotched with green wherever people could afford the water for crops. No gang on the rail today, thank God. Just techs on their way in to shifts at the Fed-Med clinics, child-care workers and service personnel. Asians. Latinos. A few blacks. No one looked at her. You didn't look—not unless you were asking for trouble.

The air smelled like sweat and urine and old plastic, as if it had been shut up in this car for weeks, breathed over and over again. It choked her suddenly, filled her with a squeezing claustrophobia that made the headache worse. Trapped. Every day of her working life she had taken this ride. She would do so until the end of her days, unless she found a way out. She clutched the grimy seat-back as they roller-coastered through the east hills. Little Cambodia slid by beneath the concrete track; a green patchwork of expensively watered vegetable plots. A flash of bright color caught her eye. Painted onto a crumbling highway overpass, Asian men and women fought strangling vines beneath tranquil blossoms.

Samuel Lujan had painted that mural. She had leaned over the crumbling wall in the middle of a hot night, watching those painted faces come to life beneath his hissing brush. They had made love afterward—right there on the overpass, cushioned by their tangled clothes. His long hair had showered down around her, and on that night, in that time and place, it had seemed that they would be together forever. There could be no other way for them to live.

But Sam had wanted out, too; out of the barrio. He had chosen his door and had walked through it. She had not followed. Mila's stomach clenched as the mural slid backward out of sight. The rail arched up and over the river, and the city towers rose to swallow them; so clean and bright after *los burbios*, surrounded by their well-watered park-blocks. Their shadows swallowed the rail, and hunger stirred in Mila's belly. It was not food that she craved. Those towers meant freedom. They meant escape. There were doors in those towers—for her, for Mila Aguilar. All you needed was an *entrada*; a way inside.

And she had found one. Mila slung her uniform bag over her shoulder and pushed her way down the aisle as the rail whispered to a stop. Orange plastic seats, grimy graffiti-covered walls, a crumpled condom wrapper on the gray composite floor; these were the images of morning, of hurry, of another precious step away from the barrio and *los burbios*. Put your card in the slot, touch in your number and run, because you're going to be late. A transit cop stared at her. Cops always stared if you were running and you weren't white. Lots of cops *here*, public and private. No gangs. No blades. Amelia Connor-Vanek's tower rose like a snowy mountain from its garden. She lived at the top, the old *bruja*. At the very top, where no one could look down on her except God.

Invisible security opened the door for Mila and closed it after her. It let her cross the carpeted lobby and opened the door of the lift. Mila combed her fingers through her short hair as the lift rose upward, shifting her bag to her other shoulder. By the time she got into her uniform, she would be late after all. But you didn't wear any kind of medical uniform on the street.

Ginger was waiting in the apartment anteroom, already dressed in her street clothes. "Rail running late again? The old girl's still asleep." She tossed her blonde head. "Bloodchem and biostats are normal. She was a case, last night. I had to call in a massage therapist at two AM. How do you *stand* her on days?" Ginger rolled her eyes. "If she puts her hand on my ass one more time, I'm quitting." She scooped up her uniform bag and a palmtop reader. "See you tonight."

"See you, Ginger." Mila went on into the apartment and peeked into the old *bruja's* bedroom.

Still asleep, and the monitor displays were okay. Mila stripped in the enormous living room, slowly and without haste. The handwoven carpet tickled her bare feet as she pulled on her uniform coverall. These were the symbols of escape; silk upholstery, wool carpet, the breathtaking view from this tower room. The headache had faded at last, but the hunger was always there. Always.

*Are you there?* Amelia's voice came over the comm on Mila's belt, shrill and querulous. *I've called you twice, damn it. I don't pay you to be late.*

"I'm sorry, Señora," Mila called out. Bullshit, on that *twice*. She quickly sealed the front of her coverall. "The rail was late. I'm coming right away."

"How many times do I have to tell you that if you want to say more than 'Yes, Señora' to me, you do it in person?" Leaning back in her reclining bed, Amelia Connor-Vanek glared as Mila came through the door. "I pay you for your physical presence, my dear. I already have a monitor."

The old *bruja* was in one of those moods. "Yes, Señora," Mila murmured. "I'm sorry, Señora." She looked like something dead, all wrinkled and ugly, no cosmetic work at all, and she could afford plenty. "I forgot." Mila kept her eyes on the white fold of sheet across Amelia's lap. The old *bruja* wore sexy see-through nightgowns, as if she was a fourteen-year-old *puta.* "I didn't sleep well last night, and I guess I'm tired."

"A new lover?" Amelia leered up at her as Mila came around the bed to read the monitor. "I hope you picked a pretty one, this time."

"I don't have a lover." Mila bit off the words as she uncapped the sampler. "I need to do your morning bloodwork."

"Touchy, dear?" Amelia chuckled deep in her throat. "You still miss him? The boy who went into the Army?"

"He was not a boy, Señora." Mila pressed her lips together as she slipped the sampling catheter into the port in Amelia's arm. "It was over long ago."

Sam had thought that the Army would be a door for him. Maybe it was, but it was not one she had wanted to take. They

had parted in anger, and there had been no word from him
since. What was there to say? The old *bruja* liked to mention
Sam, to play her little hurting games. She knew everything.
That was her trade—information. They made the big money, the
information brokers. She was a *bruja* with the spell to turn
rumor into gold. It scared Mila, how much she knew. And it excited her.

The monitor hummed, sipping its microliters of blood, test-
ing for signs of death, so that it could be expensively postponed
for another day or week or year. Death came to everyone, but
it came to the rich later and with greater difficulty.

Mila snapped the tubing out of the port and dropped it back
into the machine. "What would you like for breakfast, Señora?"

"Coffee."

"If you don't eat, Ginger will have to run IVs again tonight."

"So let her. I don't care what she does to my body when I'm
asleep."

Mila flinched as Amelia's withered hand closed around her
wrist. Head averted, she stood very still as Amelia Connor-
Vanek began to stroke her face. The old woman's fingers felt
like rat feet on her skin, dry and furtive. Mila closed her eyes
as the rat-feet fingers wandered lower; touching, caressing, lifting the weight of Mila's breasts with unhurried sensuality. It
had made her sick at first, the dry scaly touch of this woman's
hands. She bit her lip. Think of how many licensed medical
aides are on the agency waiting list. Think of the three years she
had waited for this job, any job. It could be worse, somewhere
else.

Even if it wasn't, she would stay.

Amelia laughed softly, possessively, as if she had been
reading Mila's thoughts. "Such lovely skin—it's your Spanish
heritage. You keep me alive, child," she said. "You're honest,
or perhaps honestly dishonest is more accurate, since no one
can afford to be completely honest in this world of ours." She
laughed again, a brittle sound, like breaking glass. "I've come
to appreciate the value of honesty, in all its guises. One of these
days, I'll give you a bonus, my child. A little gift."

"Yes, Señora." Mila shivered beneath those fingers—
couldn't help herself. The old *bruja* had felt her shudder and
was smiling. You don't own me, Mila thought fiercely. This is
a trade, *bruja*. Nothing more. Her head had started to hurt
again, throbbing with the beat of her pulse. It always got worse
when the old *bruja* touched her. Mila lifted her chin, fighting

sudden dizziness. "I need to do my log," she said, too brightly. "After, I will take you down to the fountain court. There are otters in the pool. Señora Anderson's aide told me."

"Don't patronize me." Amelia pushed Mila's hand roughly away. "I'm not impressed by holographic otters. Real ones might be interesting, but they'd never use real animals. They'd shit in the fountain. I see no reason to parade my decaying flesh in front of all those plastic parodies of youth."

There was a shadow in Amelia's eyes that Mila had never seen before—pain, perhaps? But the bloodwork had been normal. "What does it matter?" Mila asked with a sweet twinge of malice. "Do you care what they think, downstairs?"

"Cabin fever, child? Has the novelty of all this luxury worn off?" Amelia's withered lips twisted. "I don't need a mirror. I look at your face and I see my reflection. Why should I torture myself with the fountain court?"

"Oh, you're mistaken, Señora. You are a handsome lady. . . ."

"Stop the flustered Mex servant routine." Amelia seized Mila by the arms, pulling her close so that Mila had to look into her pale eyes. "I'm not going to fire you just because you see an old hag when you look at me, and by now you know it. Don't pretend that you don't, or I'll think that you *are* stupid and I *will* fire you."

The old *bruja*'s nails hurt, and her breath was sour in Mila's face. "I am Guatemalan, not Mexican," she said softly. "If you don't like the way people look at your body, why don't you get it fixed?"

For a long moment, Amelia stared into her face. Then she laughed, a deep booming laugh that seemed impossible for such a shriveled, wasted woman. As abruptly as she had started, she fell silent. "I am afraid." Her pale eyes pinned Mila. "Now you are the only person in this shitty world who knows that I am afraid of anything." She released Mila and reached for the raw-silk robe beside the bed. "I own you, child, and you hate me for it."

"You do not own me." Mila met Amelia's shadowed eyes. "No one owns me."

"You have ambitions, don't you?" Amelia's voice was a dry whisper. "Ambitions as large as my own once were. I respect that. I have decided that I want breakfast after all. Call Antonio's and have them send me smoked turkey and provolone

cheese on a sourdough roll. With fresh dirt-grown asparagus.
And then I want you to set up my dreams."
    Mila opened her mouth to protest, closed it without speak-
ing. "Yes, Señora." She looked away from those cold, shadowed eyes. "Right away."

MILA SAT beside the monitor, eyes on the bright numbers that
tracked Amelia Connor-Vanek's cheating of death. On the clean
white bed, Amelia fell into dreams beneath her VR mask. The
breakfast dishes lay piled on a tray beside the bed. That meal—
real meat, real cheese, and vegetables grown in irrigated soil instead of a tank—had probably cost more than Mila made in a
week. The old *bruja* had barely touched anything. Mila caught
a rich whiff of turkey and her stomach growled. She could eat
the leftovers if she wanted, but the thought of eating food that
Amelia's fingers had touched made her ill.
    She checked the monitor once more and got to her feet, too
restless to sit still. The blinds were open on the inside wall. In
this tower, the rooms ringed a central court that was roofed with
a clear composite, so that you could sit under real trees and look
up at real sky. All climate-controlled, of course. The recycled air
and water were tested hourly. You didn't have to worry about
what might be seeping into the river this week or which factory
had "accidentally" released what into the atmosphere yesterday. Far below, the fountain leaped into the air, shimmering
with light. The holoed otters would be sliding down a holoed
mud bank, playing and splashing. Were otters extinct? Mila
tried to remember.
    On the bed, Amelia made a soft noise. A sob. She did that
sometimes—cried. Crazy to pay all that money to a VR designer
for something that made you cry. Amelia's hands twitched, and
she sobbed again. It was an innocent sound, somehow. Like a
child crying for a lost treasure. It sounded strange, coming from
those pale withered lips. Mila checked the monitor. All normal
—as normal as it could be. Some drugs were illegal—even for the
Amelias of this world. Rev was one of them. But without Rev,
VR was just VR, no matter how good a designer you hired.
Shoot Rev into your veins and you *lived* it.
    *Get some,* Amelia had ordered when Mila had first started
working for her. She had assumed that Mila would have connections. Because she was Latina, from the barrio. Mila's lip
curled. She had done it—for the same reason that she stood still

beneath Amelia's hands. "Not because you own me," she whispered. The words hung in the cool, clean air.

Mila prowled to the far wall. At her touch, the tissue-thin strips of the blinds contracted into fine threads, letting in a flood of noontime sun. The river was a dirty brown trickle in the bottom of its bed. The green smear was Little Cambodia. Out there, in *los burbios*, your soul was up for sale. The government owned you for its subsidy dollars, or an employer who could claim your flesh as a bonus, because the only alternative was unemployment and the brand of full-subsidy on your personal file. Or the Army owned you. Sam had called it a contract. A way out, for a price. A choice between owners was no choice at all. Only up here, in the towers, could you truly choose.

Mila slapped the blinds closed. The monitor said that Amelia was dreaming, that she was healthy, in spite of the drug in her veins. *La Señora* had set the timer for three hours. It was time. Mila sat down at the main terminal in the living room. "Log on," she said. "Password *entrada.*"

*Harvard Equivalency Curriculum*, the terminal intoned softly. *Marketing Theory, 202. Do you wish to continue from your place of exit?*

"Yes." Text blinked onto the screen; assigned reading for the quarter. International Marketing Theory. How to figure out what needed to be sold, how to find the people to make it and the people to sell it to. Mila listened to the soft hum of the apartment's silence and began to read, struggling a little, because her mother had only been able to afford a public high school-equivalency and a decent vocational training program for her daughter. Words and comprehension came slowly at times—but HarvardNet had accepted her and that was something.

This was why she put up with Amelia's hands, why she risked supplying her with her drugs; this was the trade. HarvardNet was the best university-equivalency on-line, and she would never be able to afford it on her salary. A HarvardNet degree was her admission to the city. She could land a job with one of the smaller firms, maybe go freelance someday. This was her *entrada*; this was her escape.

If Amelia didn't find out about it. If she didn't look over her Net expenses and discover the tuition charges. It was a risk. So far, the accounting program hadn't flagged it, and the old *bruja* never bothered to look. God, the woman had money.

The global enterprise webs eliminate middle-level managers and push authority for product development and sales down to

independent engineers and marketers whose compensation is directly linked to the unit's profits. Brokers at the web's center provide financial and logistical aid, but give the unit discretion over spending, up to a point. Sony-Matohito, for example, is comprised of 287 autonomous companies. Line by line, Mila read, breathless with the sense of future that the words gave her. The headache was back again. She clenched her teeth and fought it.

In the most decentralized webs, brokers identify marketing potential and contract with independent businesses to fill production needs. Thus production moves to the cheapest labor market and does so at the wink of the stock market. Nationalism has become nothing more than an emotionally loaded mythology with no real connection to the international nature of commerce.

Adrenaline rushed through Mila's veins as fingers seemed to touch her neck. Blurred memory broke in her head; fright, the dry touch of fingers on her throat and Amelia's soft voice, whispering, whispering . . . then it was gone. A dream? Mila looked over her shoulder, but the room was quiet. Empty. She shivered. Nerves, she told herself, and turned her attention back to the screen.

A BEEPER went off, shrill enough to make her ears hurt. Mila jerked upright, groggy, vaguely aware that she must have fallen asleep in front of the screen. Her belt alarm! Amelia! She bolted to her feet and ran for the bedroom, adrenaline crashing through her system, the shrill electronic pulse trumpeting *death* throughout the apartment.

MILA HAD the Justice Center cell to herself. She sat on the narrow bed, staring vaguely at the dull-green wall beyond the expanded mesh of the cell. Overcrowding wasn't a problem anymore. You got the death penalty for so many things. Without appeals, cells emptied fast. You could get the death penalty for negligence if you were a licensed aide. The juries were always city people, and so many city people were old. They could afford to be old. Too many of those jurors would have aides at home. They would see themselves in Amelia Connor-Vanek.

But I didn't kill her, Mila told herself one more time. I gave her the usual dose. It was the same stuff, and there was no reason for her to die. The words carried no comfort. It *was* her fault. Rev was illegal, and she had administered it. Never mind that the old *bruja* would have fired her if she had refused.

If she had remained sitting beside Amelia's bed, Amelia

would not have died. She had died from an overdose of Rev.

Which meant that she had to have done it to herself, but there had been no note. The cops on the scene hadn't even bothered to record Mila's hysterical claim of suicide. The bored court-appointed lawyer had fed her case into LegalNet and had advised her to plead guilty. *Without a suicide note, you're dead, sweetheart. If you didn't do it, you'd better agree to full questioning,* he had told her. *Psychotropes, the whole nine yards. If you help them nail your connection, we can probably cut a deal with the DA.*

Her connection had been Sam. He'd gotten the stuff for her through his friend Salgado, because Amelia had offered twice street price and Sam had needed the money. So she'd told the lawyer to go to hell.

*Have it your way, sweetheart,* he had said. She hadn't seen him in the two weeks since her arrest.

Mila stared down at her hands, limp in her lap. How many days had she been here, waiting for her trial? Three? Ten? She had lost count. Mesh walls, concrete floor and ceiling, one bed, one toilet/sink combination, a table and a chair. No privacy. If you wanted to piss, the guards got to watch. And they did. Everything was painted the same dull green as the walls and bolted to the floor.

When she was nine, some of the boys on the street had snared a coyote in the scrubby field beyond the development. They had kept it in an old plastic airline kennel. She remembered how it had crouched in the tiny cage, yellow eyes empty of hope or fear, skinny and crawling with lice. It didn't snarl or bite at the sticks that the boys poked through the bars. It just crouched there. It had finally died.

A guard marched down the corridor. "You, Aguilar. On your feet."

Mila stood slowly, heart contracting in her chest. Her trial? Would her lawyer even *be* there? Would it matter if he was?

"You got a visitor. Turn around." The guard—a man—opened the cell and cuffed her hands behind her. He also put his hand between her legs.

Mila pressed her lips together, remembering Amelia's rat-feet fingers on her breasts. A visitor? Who was going to visit her here? Prison was contagious. Especially when the cops were looking for a drug connection. She stumbled as the guard shoved her forward. The visiting cubicles were just this side of the thick door at the end of the corridor. The guard pushed her inside, and the lock clicked. A video screen was set into the green wall. A battered plastic stool stood in front of it. The air smelled like mildew and fear.

"Sam?" Mila's eyes widened as the screen shimmered to life. No. It could not be. "What are *you* doing here?"

"I had some leave. I heard, when I got home." His face was anguished. "Mila, what *happened?*"

How many times had they asked her that question, over and over until her head pounded with the rhythm of the words? "I don't know," she whispered, and struggled with the tears that were trying to come. She hadn't shed a tear, not since they'd taken her from Amelia's apartment. If she started crying now, she'd never stop. She'd cry until there was nothing left of her but a shriveled husk on the floor, until her soul and her mind were empty. "Never mind," she said. "I don't want to talk about it, Sam, do you hear me? There's nothing you can do." Tell me how you are, she wanted to say. Tell me that you're fine, that your choice was a good one for you, at least. Please, *querido.*

She didn't say it. She could read the answer in his face, in spite of the grainy video. His hair was Army-short and his face looked skeletal, as if he'd lost weight. He had new muscles; stringy, lean muscles. He seemed harder, older. Changed.

"They sent us to Indonesia," he said. "For the UN—to stop this revolution, I guess. It was so damned easy. We only lost a few people—they might as well have been using sticks against what we had. We didn't even make the US NewsNet."

Mila had to look away. His eyes were the coyote's eyes. If she looked into the mirror, she would see the same eyes in her own face. We were human once, she thought bitterly. At least I think we were.

"*Cariña?* I love you." He stretched out his arms, as if he could reach through the video, through the concrete wall, could put his arms around her and hold her tight.

His face was full of grief. He was afraid for her, and his fear ate at the hard wall that she'd built around herself these past days. She could see her death reflected in his face. In a moment, that wall would crack apart and the terror would rush in to drown her. "Go away," she whispered. "Don't come here again, Sam. Not ever, do you hear me? I don't want to see you. I don't want to hear from you." She threw herself against the locked door, tugging at the cuffs, wanting to pound on it with her fists. "Turn it off!" she yelled to the invisible eavesdroppers. "I want to go back to my cell."

No one answered, but when she looked over her shoulder, the screen was blank again; a flat gray square of nothingness in the green wall. Trembling, she limped back to the stool and sat down. Her shoulder ached where she had slammed it into the door. I love you, *querido*. She held the words inside herself, like a charm, clenched in a fist. I love you. But it was too late. In her mind, she opened the fist and her palm was empty.

The door lock clicked behind her. Mila waited without turning for the guard to yank her off the stool and hustle her back to her cell.

"Ms. Aguilar?"

A woman's voice, much too polite to be a guard's. Reluctantly, Mila looked. The stranger stood just outside the door, flanked by a guard. She had dark red hair, cut short and stylish, and a strong bony face. She was dressed in a sleek tunic suit. The suit looked too expensive for a court-appointed lawyer. Mila waited.

"Ms. Aguilar, I'm Rebecca Connor. You've been released into my custody."

She stepped aside, obviously expecting Mila to hop to her feet and trot along at her heels. Mila sat coyote-still, waiting for the stick. "Why am I released?"

The guard started forward, but the woman put out a hand. "Ms. Aguilar, I am Amelia Connor-Vanek's daughter. I had my lawyer post bail for you." She was tapping her foot impatiently. "Could we discuss this in private, please?"

That made Mila blink. The bail figure had been astronomical. It always was, if you weren't an Anglo. Making bail was a pretty dream, like finding a pot of gold under a rainbow or winning the national lottery. Not applicable personally to Mila Aguilar. "Yes," Mila said with a cold glance at the guard. "I would prefer to discuss this in private."

THE GUARD took her back to her cell and gave her the clothes she'd been wearing on the day they arrested her. The day Amelia died. He cuffed her again and wouldn't take the cuffs off until they reached the front door of the Justice Center. He had given the rest of the things they had seized—her uniform bag and its contents—to the woman. As if Mila was a stray dog being claimed by its owner. Mila stalked through the door and out into the sunshine, half-blinded by the harsh, welcome light, resisting the urge to shake herself all over like a dog. Or a coyote.

"My car is over here." The woman put a hand on her elbow.

"You don't have to hold on to me." Mila touched the thin band of the parole collar around her neck. "It would be foolish to run away."

"I'm sorry." The woman took her hand away abruptly. "Were they all as bad as that jerk?"

Mostly they had been worse. Mila shrugged and watched the woman's lips tighten. She didn't like having her friendly overture rejected. You want something from me, Mila thought. You paid a lot for it, and I don't know what it is, yet. I do not think you are my friend. She climbed into the woman's car. It was a private vehicle, licensed for alcofuel. She revised the cost of the woman's suit upward. The old *bruja* had never spoken of a daughter. Not once. I should worry, Mila thought. I should be afraid. She merely felt numb. She kept seeing Sam's face in her mind; the new hard line of his jaw and the coyote-shadows in his eyes.

The woman drove silently, threading the manicured parkblocks that surrounded the big residential towers and their retail clusters. She was going to Amelia's tower. Mila recognized the neighborhood. The woman parked in the subsurface garage. Security's invisible eyes stared down from ceiling and walls. Mila felt the first stir of apprehension as the lift carried them upward. Some kind of trap? The lift door opened to Amelia's private anteroom. "Why did you pay my bail?" Mila asked.

"I need your help." The woman stepped out.

Sure. Mila followed her reluctantly through the anteroom and into the carpeted living room. In prison, her pre-arrest past had become brittle and unreal, fragile as old-fashioned movie film that could crumble at the touch. The familiar scent of Amelia's rooms brought it back to her in a staggering rush; Sam and the barrio and Amelia's dead, gray face.

"You look as if you're going to faint." The woman started to reach for her, caught herself and pushed a silk-upholstered chair toward her. "I think you'd better sit down."

"I'm fine, Señora Connor." Mila held on tightly to the chair back. "I told the police everything I know. There's nothing else to tell. I can't help you." Mila had escaped the kennel, now. She could be afraid again. "Who are you, and what is it that you want?"

"I told you who I am. I want a file." Rebecca Connor paced across the enormous carpeted space that Amelia had rarely used. "My mother bought and sold . . . information. I suspect you know that." She paused by the transparent inner wall, staring down into the upper branches of the fountain-court trees. "She had retired, but she would have kept some special information. As . . . insurance. I can't find it."

"I didn't steal it."

"I didn't say you did. Do I see otters down there?" Connor's shoulders moved, as if she had sighed. "What I did find was obsolete. Useless. And it was easy to find. That makes me think that there is more and that it isn't obsolete. I'm hoping that you can find it for me."

"Why me?" Mila lifted her chin. "I'm just an aide, Señora. A dumb Latina from the barrio. What would I know about a file? *La Señora* didn't tell me anything."

Connor turned away from the wall at last. Her eyes were cold. "Are you a dumb Latina? My mother is . . . *was* . . . very creative at hiding things in plain sight. What I want is your intuition. I want you to find her hiding place. The information has to be in hard-data form. It's not in her Netspace." Connor laughed coldly. "I'm better at that than she ever was, and she knew it."

"I can't help you." Mila crossed her arms, aware of the thin parole collar, heavy as a stone around her neck.

"You're going to try." Rebecca's eyes were a brilliant augmented green, cold as sea ice. "I bought you for the price of your bail and the leverage it took to get you off the DA's weekly conviction list. My mother kept a record of your course hours, you know. We could add theft to your negligence charge. We'll make a trade." She smiled thinly. "You cooperate, and I'll edit Amelia's financial records to hide your theft. If you find the file for me, I'll lean on the DA to drop the negligence charge."

So the old *bruja* had known about the courses all along. *Honestly dishonest*, she had called Mila, with her hands on her breasts. It had truly been a trade; the hands for the credit hours. "I have to help you." Mila didn't try to keep the bitterness out of her voice. "I have no choice, do I?"

"You have a choice," Connor said gently. "You know, you did quite well in your course work, for someone with a public education from the Net."

Mila turned away, hating this woman, hating her more than she had ever hated anyone in her life. Because she had all the power and Mila had none and had never really had any. Her *entrada* had been an illusion only, and this woman had flung it in her face. "Tell me what you want me to do," she said.

THIS WOMAN'S METHOD of looking for something was a strange one, Mila decided. She wanted Mila to touch, taste, smell, examine, and listen to every single item in the entire apartment. They started in the bedroom because that was where Amelia had spent most of her time. By evening, Mila decided that she would grow old before they finished.

"Nothing happens." She scowled at the holocube she was holding. "What do you expect? Trumpets? A sign from God?"

"You're not done with that yet. Taste it. Lick it. Just *do* it." Sitting cross-legged on the floor, Connor ran a hand through her rumpled hair. "Something will happen. I don't know what."

"I told you . . ."

". . . *La Señora* never told me anything," Connor finished for her. "I think she was playing a game with you and me. She knew that I'd come looking. I think you're the key."

"Why should you come looking? Why not just give it to you?" Mila touched the tip of her tongue to the black base of the holocube and grimaced. A man smiled at her from the center of the cube. He had a long face and warm green eyes, and his hair hung down in a dozen red-gold braids. "And why should I have some kind of key?" she asked.

"Amelia knew I'd come looking because she taught me this business and I knew her . . . methods. She didn't give anything away to *anyone*, honey, and certainly not to me. We are— were—competitors." Connor took the cube from Mila's hand. "It would be her little joke, to make you the key. She knew how I felt about her Mex girls."

"I am Guatemalan."

Connor shrugged and put the cube back on its shelf, straightening it carefully.

"Who is that?" Mila asked.

"He was Aaron Connor. My father—the only man she ever bothered to marry. I don't know why she did that. Maybe because he actually loved her. More the fool, he." She picked up a laptop reader. "Try this," she said coldly.

*Was.* So he was dead? Such bitterness in this woman. Mila took the reader. It was an old one—not the slick holomodel that Amelia had used, when she bothered to use a reader. Mila nearly dropped it as the screen brightened. You're getting warmer, Mila. The words glowed briefly and vanished.

Connor hissed softly through her teeth and snatched the reader from Mila's hands. "See this?" She pried a tiny silver disk from the reader's edge. "It was matched to your skin chemistry. It would only activate the message if you picked it up. I knew she was playing games." She threw the reader across the room.

Mila flinched as it hit the wall and cracked. "So she *did* this." Like a child's game—warmer, colder, you're getting hot. Hope and anger burned like twin flames in her heart. She had thought that the old *bruja* might have left a suicide message in her Netspace, that some Latino-hating cop had erased it. "She hid it," Mila whispered. "The note."

"What note?"

"The suicide note." Mila bent to pick up the broken reader. "She *hid* it. For me to find." A game, and the stakes were Mila's life. A *bruja* for real.

"Forget it, dear." Connor's voice was cold. "Amelia Connor-Vanek didn't suicide. Your connection sold you some bad drugs, and you didn't watch the monitor long enough to catch it. Who are you trying to protect, anyway?" Connor picked up a musicube and held it up to the light. "Negligence is no big feather for a DA's cap. I checked on your case. They'd pull your license and let you walk, for your connection." She tossed the cube to Mila.

Not that trade. Not now, not ever. "I don't remember who it was." Mila cupped her palms around the cube, touched it with her tongue, held it to her ear.

"It was your boyfriend, wasn't it? Yes, he's in my mother's file on you." Connor shrugged. "Poor judgment, honey. No full-sub Army bait is worth your life—no matter how good he is in bed."

"He was an artist." *Was.* She had put it in the past tense, as if he was dead—as if that part of him was dead.

"An artist?" The woman's lip curled. "I suppose you can call yourself anything you want, on a full subsidy."

"Do you think it is a pleasant life?" Mila hissed. "Living in the suburbs with enough to eat and drink—almost—and nothing ahead of you but another empty day? It was not his choice, Señora Connor. His mother was a hooker, okay? Her implant failed, and there he was." She touched the red-and-blue licensed-aide patch on her shoulder. "I could get this, only because my mother was never on full subsidy. Sam grew up on full subsidy. For him, there was only the Army."

This was what he had told *her*, so angry on that last day. And she had argued with him, yelled at him, wept. Mila laid her clenched fists gently on her thighs. "He saw what was all around him on the streets," she said. "He saw rage, fear, despair, and hope. He saw the things that we have stopped seeing because they are always there and it hurts too much. He took that hurt, and he painted it on the walls and the overpasses and the rail. He gave it life, all that hurt, but no one gave him a choice. Do you understand?"

"Are you telling me that you love him?" Connor's face was still, without emotion. "Love is a luxury of your class, Mila—a charming myth, like winning the lottery. In my game, you know better. Love is nothing more than a pretty type of loyalty, and loyalty is something that you sell for a very good price. My mother could have told you that. She never let loyalty get in her way—not to a lover, not to her daughter."

"Sam is not part of this, and he was not my connection." Mila threw the musicube back into its bin. "It was suicide."

"It was not suicide." Connor stood up, glaring down at her, fists clenched at her sides as if she wanted to hit Mila. "Tell me about your mother. Did she want you to have a better life than she? That's a part of your suburban culture too, isn't it? The kids have a chance at the future that didn't quite work out for Mom and Dad? Did you make your mother proud of you when you got your license? Or wasn't it enough for her? Is that why you stole course time from Amelia?"

"My mother died when I was twelve." Mila picked up the next cube. "She got cancer." The grief was so old that she barely felt it anymore. Her mother had worked nights at the Bon, playing dress-up with the wealthy. She had slept during the day while Mila did her lessons on the Net. Maybe it had been the leukemia that had made her sleep so much. Or maybe, when you finally realized that your life wasn't going to go anywhere else, that you had everything you were ever going to get, there was nothing else to do but sleep. Mila wanted to touch her forehead, to probe for the echo of the so-frequent headache. With an effort, she kept her hand still. "At forty-two, at her skill level, she didn't qualify for viral therapy under Fed-Med."

"I'm sorry."

"You're not. Why should you be?" Mila tossed the last of the musicubes back into the bin.

"Yes, you're Amelia's type. You'd react to her little cruelties, and she'd like that. But she'd break you, in the end." Conner got to her feet and yanked her tunic straight. "She taught me the business, but not enough to be better than she. Oh no. She was the queen. The one who could sell you anything, for the right price. Who was going where, with what product line, and why. The Cartel's top-secret plans for a better mousetrap. Who was in bed with whom and when. And how they did it, if you really wanted to know. That's the coin of the realm, these days. Information. And I'm better than she ever was." Connor stared down at Mila. "Much better, do you understand? She'll never forgive me for that."

"She is dead," Mila said softly. "It's late. Can I go home, please?" *Home.* An empty word for four walls and an empty bed.

"No." Connor looked around the room as if she expected something to leap at her out of the shadows. "You stay here until we're finished."

Mila shrugged. A cell was a cell. This one didn't smell as bad as the one at the Justice Center.

MILA WOKE to darkness and silence, head aching, hands clutching reflexively at the blanket tangled around her waist as she tried to remember where she was. Amelia's apartment. Memory returned, borne on the feel of the cushions beneath her shoulders. She was asleep on the floor, on the silk-covered cushions that no one ever used. Mila sat up, pushing hair back from her sweaty face. A sibilant whisper of breathing was Señora Connor, asleep on the sofa. Neither of them had wanted to sleep in Amelia's bed.

The darkness pressed in around her, thick and heavy, as if the air-conditioning had failed. She could feel the blood pounding in her brain, as if her skull might burst any second. Unwinding the blanket from her legs, Mila got silently to her feet. She had never been here in the dark. Faint light seeped in through the fountain-court wall. It stretched the room into vast unexplored dimensions. Mila longed suddenly for her small, neat bedroom. It was crowded, the crummy tract house where she lived. But in the darkness, it was always familiar. Angelina's baby would cry and wake Roberto up. Guillermo would get home from his shift at the clinic, making the pipes bang as he ran water in the kitchen. He would leave it on too long, and Angelina would come out to scold him for using up their water ration. They were landmarks, those baby cries and hissing whispers. Landmarks of safety.

*Safety* was a chain. It could tether you to the barrio forever. Here, it could bind her to this red-haired woman. You had to take risks, or be the coyote trapped in its kennel. Mila took a deep breath and tiptoed into Amelia's bedroom. In the doorway, she hesitated. The bed was in shadow, and for a terrible moment she thought Amelia was there, that she would reach out and seize Mila's arm with her rat-feet fingers. But it was empty, the bed; sheeted and white. Mila sat down on the edge and reached for the VR mask on the table. There *was* a suicide note. Mila was sure of it, never mind what Señora Connor said. It was here, for her to find. And somewhere, the old *bruja* was laughing at her.

The mask covered her face like thick pliable skin, made her breathless with claustrophobia, even though it stopped at her lips. Amelia had worn this. It had soaked up the feel of her ancient skin. Mila shuddered violently as she smoothed it down around her neck. The lenses in the mask made the room appear distorted and strange, like looking through the bottom of a glass. In a reality parlor, you paid to put on skinthins that covered your whole body, jumped up and down in some little room, while you pretended to be Spiderman or a ninja or an eagle. For all her money and custom-designed VR fantasies, the old *bruja* had only bothered with a mask. No gloves, even.

Mila hesitated. I am afraid, she thought. I am afraid she is here, waiting for me in the darkness; waiting to swallow me up. A small noise from the other room made her jump. Señora Connor, who held all the cards and would take whatever Mila found. Mila froze, hearing nothing but a hum of silence. "Log on," Mila said. Her voice sounded high and breathy, and nothing happened. Coded for Amelia's voice only? Relieved in spite of herself, Mila reached for the mask. Then she caught her breath as the lenses in the mask blurred with sudden light and color.

The Net must have recognized the VR connect and started to run a file automatically. Mila clutched the edge of the bed as the light brightened. A beach. She was on a beach of black sand with an endless blue horizon in front of her. Waves curled and broke into white foam with a low roar, and seagulls shrieked overhead. Mila caught her breath. It looked so *real,* but she felt the sheets beneath her palms. When she glanced down, she had no body, saw nothing but the black sand beneath her and a tuft of tough-looking grass that whipped in a wind she didn't feel—as if she was invisible, or a ghost.

Very strange.

A man and a child were running through the surf, laughing.

His damp hair trailed over his shoulders in red-gold tangles. The girl's hair was even redder than his. She squealed with delight as the man caught her and tossed her into the air. A woman had joined them. She was young too, like the man. Mila's age. They held hands, as in one of those slick ads for the vacation packages that you couldn't really afford, but paid for anyway, because it looked so damn good in VR.

Now they were walking across the black sand, walking toward Mila and laughing. The man and the woman were looking at each other over the little girl's head. Sam had looked at her like that. Before the anger and the Army. Mila swallowed, her throat tight. They walked past her. Invisible observer, Mila watched them climb the low dune beyond the beach. They were picking up clothes and a cooler that would be full of food, laughing and talking to each other about little things—about how the girl needed a nap and maybe they would take a nap, too, only you could tell that it wasn't sleep they were thinking about from the look in their eyes and the way they touched each other.

Mila raised a hand to her mouth, felt the soft thickness of the mask beneath her fingers. She recognized him now—the man in the holocube. Rebecca's father, the one man Amelia had married. So the red-haired child was Rebecca Connor? Mila looked again at the woman, at the line of cheek and jaw beneath the smooth young flesh. "Amelia," she whispered. As the trio disappeared over the crest of the dune, a gusty unfelt wind whipped up a plume of sand. The sand twisted into a whirling column. Mila recoiled as it solidified and took on human shape.

"I've been waiting for you." Amelia leered at her, shriveled and pale in a blue bikini. "You are ambitious, child. I knew that you would come looking for your bonus. You're not one to wait politely to be handed a bone, are you?" Her grin widened. "Well, it's yours. Almost. Just tell me my name."

"Amelia," Mila said. She was moving. Mila stared down and discovered that she had a body now. It looked like her own body, brown skin marred by the birthmark on her hip. Sam would kiss that small spot when they made love—would bite it gently. She was walking toward Amelia. In a rush of panic, Mila tried to stop, but she was only wearing a mask and she had no control over her VR body. "Amelia," she cried. "Your name is Amelia Connor-Vanek."

Still grinning, Amelia reached for her.

"Exit!" Mila tore the mask from her face, blinking in the sudden darkness.

"What's going on? Light!" Connor stood in the doorway, eyes puffy with sleep. "I heard you yell," she said as the room lights brightened. "What were you doing?" Her eyes narrowed as she noticed the VR mask clutched in Mila's hand.

"I thought that the file might be here." Mila dropped the mask back onto the bedside table. "I don't like VR. It scares me."

"I told you that the file isn't in her Netspace." Connor's tone was cold. "I checked. My mother never liked the Net." Her lip curled. "But she needed a good Net operator, so she made me into one. To serve her needs. I didn't hire you to check her VR files."

"You didn't hire me." Mila stood up. "You bought me, remember?" The file *was* in the virtual. The old *bruja* had said so. She must have fixed it, like she had fixed the reader—so that only Mila would summon her shriveled ghost. Mila shivered. "That was you," she said. "On the beach."

"You figured that out, did you?" Connor turned to stare down into the fountain court. "It was a vacation, on some island she rented. I'd forgotten about it," she said softly. "Lovers are a liability in this business. If they care about you, they make you too vulnerable. So you buy yourself ones who don't care, and if they're stupid enough to fall in love with you, you dump them. Your father died before you were born, but your DNA record makes you his. Is that why your mother named you Milagra? It means *miracle* in Spanish, doesn't it?"

"He had a heart attack. He smoked when he was younger, and it was on his medical record. So the ambulance wouldn't take him to the hospital. My mother didn't know she was pregnant when he died. She had to pay for the DNA match to prove I was his, or they would have cut our subsidy. Don't tell me that you're sorry, Anglo."

"No federal funds for illegitimate pregnancies. No federally funded treatment for self-induced illness." Connor turned slowly to face her. "Amelia divorced Aaron about a month after that vacation. She kept me, because she could turn me into something useful. Oh, she was generous. She gave him a lot of money. He used it to kill himself. Jet skiing. Hang gliding off Everest. High-altitude sky diving. It took him a couple of years. She didn't care. He didn't matter to her, and I only mattered because I was useful. What do you want from life, Milagra Aguilar? Tell me."

The soft light cast shadows beneath her cheeks, made her look old in spite of her smooth skin and bright hair. It had to have been a long time ago, that beach. If she ever gave up the cosmetic work and the fetal-cell implants, she'd look like Amelia.

"I do not want to be a coyote," Mila said softly. "I paid for the courses I took. I paid for them in full. I am going home now, because I do not want to sleep in this place. I will come back tomorrow to help you look for your treasure."

"That's the only VR file she had." Connor looked past Mila, as if she had forgotten that she was there. "What a crazy thing to keep."

Mila walked past her and out to the lift, heart beating fast enough to make her breathless. She knew where the file was, never mind what Señora Connor said about the VR. The treasure would be information. It would be valuable, and it would be hers. All she needed was the old *bruja*'s name. A riddle. More of her little games. The lift doors whispered open. Mila thought that Señora Connor might try to stop her, but the apartment was silent. As if it was empty.

It wasn't empty. It was full of ghosts. Mila shivered and stepped quickly into the lift.

SHE WENT to Salgado.

He didn't live in the barrio, but out on the fringe of the suburbs in a large house that must have belonged to someone very rich, once. He was what Amelia had been, but on a smaller scale; a local *brujo*. In the old times, he would have sold charms against the evil eye, love potions, and cures for warts. Now he sold fake kids for the subsidy role, news of a job that was going to open up, and the name of the person to bribe for the interview. Salgado was small, but he would know the right connections. She needed Salgado. It didn't matter that it was the middle of the night. Salgado worked at night.

His guards let her in; young punks with braided hair who undressed her with their eyes—and would do it with their hands if Salgado threw her out. Head high, Mila shouldered past them. The house took her breath away. Outside, it was shabby, a sagging ruin in a landscape of dead shrubbery. Inside, walls and ceiling glowed with real wood. Soft yellow light made the grain shine like satin. White carpet covered the floor, and tall porcelain vases held fresh-cut flowers.

"I am very impressed, Señorita." Salgado bowed her formally onto a coral-colored sofa, dark eyes glittering with laughter. "You are out of jail. That is quite an achievement."

"I am." Mila smiled back coldly, unwilling to be charmed.

He was like Señora Connor; sexy on the surface, but old underneath. His eyes calculated, always. "I have come to talk to you about a deal."

"What kind of deal?" The calculating eyes pinned her, shrewd and without warmth above his smile. "Your employer is dead. What do you have to offer me? Beyond your body, that is?"

Mila ignored his leer. "I am employed by her daughter. She believes that there is a file of very valuable information to be found. She has hired me to find it." Mila allowed herself a faint smile. "I have found it and she has not."

Salgado steepled his fingers and stared at the ceiling.

A waiting game. He knew who she worked for. It was his business to know. He wanted her to tell him, and then he would score points. Points mattered. Mila waited.

Salgado sighed at last, a concessionary sigh. "It is possible that information from that quarter might have value. If it is any good, I will give you something for it."

"If it is as good as I believe, I will want a lot," Mila said softly. They stared at each other silently for a long moment. "I will need to download it from a VR without anyone knowing."

Salgado smiled, but this time his smile was thoughtful, and he played gently with his perfect black hair. "I'll give you what you need," he said. "Come back to me if you get something, and we will discuss it."

ALL SHE NEEDED was the name, the answer to the riddle. Her *entrada*. It was almost dawn. In the gray light the neighborhood looked pale and colorless, as if all life had drained away during the night. The dead trees and rusting cars had always been there, but in this cold light they made the streets look like a ghost town, as if everyone had died overnight. This street was mostly Bangladeshi, the last refugees admitted before the borders closed to everyone except rich Anglos. The flea market on the corner was as drab and lifeless as the rest of the street, all color gone from the woven rag mats that divided the empty lot into stalls.

A bent sexless figure was sweeping dust with a frayed broom. A bundle of cloth beside the cracked sidewalk was a woman. Dead or just sleeping? Mila hesitated, saw the gentle rise of the woman's chest. Sleeping, with her arm tucked around a knotted-string bag of onions. Waiting for the market to open.

Almost to the barrrio, almost home. Think of a name, think

of the answer, the ticket inside, the *entrada*. Her headache was back, worse than ever. Mila sat down on the front steps of a tall house with arched windows and a circular driveway. The windows had been broken and mended with plastic. Black strands of electrified wire fenced in rows of carrots in the front yard. The adrenaline-rush of her find had faded, and fatigue made the muscles in her legs quiver.

Why did the old *bruja* do Rev and watch herself run on a long-ago beach? Mila blinked, eyes full of sand, too tired, almost, to think. She had spent hours dreaming. Every day. Mila had always assumed that she had a library of custom-designed diversions to play in.

But the beach had been the only VR. So her daughter had said. Crazy *bruja*. Crazy *vieja*. Movement caught Mila's eye—a shadow creeping along the house wall behind her. Danger? Awake in an instant, skin tingling with adrenaline, Mila stood. It wasn't stalking *her*. Mila almost slipped away—always the safe thing to do—but a thin hissing halted her. She knew the sound. An airbrush. She'd heard it too many times not to know it. Cautiously, Mila tiptoed closer to the house. No sign of life behind the sheeted windows. She edged around the corner, screened by the leafless skeletons of dead shrubbery.

It was a kid, thirteen maybe. He crouched in front of a bare stretch of wall, working on a picture. The hissing brush shaded in a human figure with sweeps of brown and gold.

Goose bumps rose on Mila's arms. He reminded her of Sam —the same hunched concentration, the same braid hanging forward over his shoulder. She must have made a sound because the kid looked up, eyes wide and darkly startled. ''Wait,'' Mila said, but he was already running, back bent, scurrying across the dusty yard. He vaulted one-handed over a battered chain-link fence at the back of the property and vanished.

He didn't look at all like Sam. The picture would be good, though, when he finished it. Mila touched a painted straggle of black hair, stared at the smear of wet color on her fingertip. I do not think of Sam anymore, she thought, and felt a quick pain in her chest. A deal with Salgado—a *deal*, and not just a sale— would include his bed. They both knew it. There would be no place for Sam in her life, even if he wanted to be there, even if the Army didn't own him.

*Love is a pretty type of loyalty*, Señora Connor had said. *And loyalty is something that you sell for a very good price.* It was the truth, Mila thought bitterly. She was already thinking of how to use Salgado, how to learn the way into that invisible labyrinth that hid wealth and power at its center. Someone tweaked the striped sheet that curtained the house's front window, and Mila hurried on down the street.

A lover who cared about you was a liability. The *bruja*'s daughter had said that too, in her bright, bitter voice. She had been right, and suddenly Mila knew why the old *bruja* watched her young self run down the beach over and over again with the man whose name she had kept, and their child.

Because she had loved him once, no matter what Señora Connor said. Because that time had been *hers*, not an item to be sold or traded, but a random moment that had no value to anyone except Amelia Connor-Vanek. Mila shook her head. The old *bruja* could have had her VR designer make that family see her, welcome her, forgive her—whatever she wanted. Rev would have made it *real*. But she had chosen to remain a ghost. An outsider forever, unseen and untouchable. To punish herself? To remind herself of what she had traded away? Or to remind herself of what she must be? *"Siempre solo,"* Mila whispered. "Alone."

*I had faith in you, child.*

Mila froze in the middle of the buckled sidewalk, skin going hot and cold in waves. The old *bruja*'s voice. Inside her head! The street faded to a blur, overlaid by an image of the terminal screen in front of her, of meaningless words frozen still. Now, she remembered her terror as Amelia touched her. *Caught!* Then the rat-feet fingers had stroked her throat, and she had felt the soft roughness of a drug patch before fear and surprise faded away to a dream of voices whispering, whispering in her ears. . . .

"What have you done to me?" Mila whispered, struggling with terror.

*There are some very specialized hypnotropes available on the drug market. Back in my early years, when I still operated in the flesh, I became quite skilled at implanting and blocking information. You can bury all kinds of things in the human brain—there is a lot of useful storage space there. When I am finished, you won't remember a thing, child. Until it's time.*

Rebecca Connor had been right. Mila smothered hysterical laughter. The file wasn't in the VR. It had been in Mila's head all this time.

*I told you I admired your honest dishonesty. I had a daughter once. Perhaps you find that hard to believe, but I did. I taught her everything that I knew, and I taught her too well. When she had learned everything I could give her, she walked away from me. She disdained me. I had entertained a dream that we would work together, that we would be the best. A youthful dream. In this business, you work best alone.*

*She is better than me.*

*It's funny. I thought about calling her the other day—just to speak to her again. It's too late for that. Never have children, Milagra Aguilar. You cannot afford to look behind you in this business, and children tether you to the past. They tempt you to look over your shoulder, to remember who you were and compare that person to yourself. Never look back. Keep your eyes on tomorrow, or you will turn into a pillar of salt. You will slow down, and the competition will take the world away from you. Remember that, child. So here is your bonus. Your gift. You will figure out how to use it. You know where you want to go, and you are willing to pay what it costs to get there. I predict that you will go far. Nothing is certain in this world, but I have made you my heir. Because you are like me.*

*And now, I'm going to go lie down. I have quit this game, and there is salt in my veins. I don't plan to spend the rest of my life hiding from boredom, and I am tired of bribing Death. By the time you wake up, it will be too late for you to intervene.*

Mila staggered as the street solidified around her, bright with morning sun. The old *bruja* had killed herself and left her suicide note in Mila's brain. Mila moaned with the pain in her head. A man shuffled past her, brown-skinned, with a wispy black beard, dressed all in white. He watched her nervously from the corner of his eyes, crowding the curb. Mila stared at him blankly.

Names, numbers, words without meaning, filled her brain. They pressed against the walls of her skull until she thought her head would explode. She had to record them, right now. She had to release them.

She ran all the way back to the house, burst through the door and past a startled Angelina. Not on a terminal, not when Salgado knew about the file—she was still thinking clearly enough to know better than that. Guillermo had paper, because he wrote poetry after his shift some nights and he said that the Net killed poetry. Mila hammered on his door until he woke. Angelina was babbling questions at her, clutching at her arm, but the words had no meaning, were lost in the jumble of syllables/numbers/names that filled her pounding head. Mila shook her off, snatched the dog-eared pad from the surprised and bleary Guillermo, and fled to her room, slamming the door in Angelina's face.

She wrote all morning. Sitting cross-legged on the bed, hunched over the pad, she filled page after page with her clumsy script. The words, dates, numbers, came to her one after another, without meaning, without control. As she wrote each one down, it vanished from her mind, popping like a soap bubble. She, Mila, watched from a small corner of her mind as her fingers scurried across the page. She had no control over them. She was merely a vehicle for the old *bruja*'s ghost, the skin of her hands a glove for those rat-feet fingers. How many times had the old *bruja* crept up behind her as she studied, with her drugs and her whispers?

Sometime in the afternoon, the words ran out. Mila dropped the pen onto the bed and straightened her fingers. An angry red groove marked the side of her finger where she had clutched the pen, and she smothered a cry as her hand cramped viciously. Her body ached, as if it had taken the effort of every muscle to get those words down onto the paper. One by one, she picked up the sheets, numbering them carefully. She recognized some of the names. They were on the NewsNet; politicians, and corporate names that *everyone* knew. Vilchek-Wasabe. EuroSynco. Sony-Matohito. The connections would be in the dates and account codes. In time, she would understand them. Mila folded the pages neatly. This was a ball of platinum string that she and Salgado could unravel for a long time. Each new thread would lead to others, would lead her deeper into the labyrinth of the old *bruja*'s world. This was, indeed, a treasure. This was her *entrada*.

She sat on the bed in the afternoon heat, pages in her hand, remembering black sand and a young woman laughing. In her mind, she heard the echo of Amelia's whispering. It made her feel unclean, as if those rat-feet fingers had groped across her soul. *You are like me*, the old *bruja* had said. Mila shuddered, folded the sheets of paper, and shoved them into her pocket.

REBECCA was asleep on the sofa when Mila let herself into the apartment. Her eyelids fluttered and she made a small sound in her sleep, like a sob. Like Amelia, dreaming of her lost beach. For a moment, Mila stood silent, looking down at her, then she bent and touched her shoulder lightly. Rebecca's eyes flew open, and she stood up in one swift motion.

"You came back." She thrust her fingers through her hair. "I didn't expect you to come back. You had the file when you left, didn't you?"

Mila nodded.

"I am not as good as my mother," Rebecca said with quiet bitterness. She looked out at the treetops beyond the interior wall. "She despised me for that—for being less than she was. That's why I finally split."

"She said you were better than she ever was."

"Ha." Rebecca's lip twitched. "So what do you want for it?"

"Everything in this life is a trade, is it not?" Mila pulled the folded sheets of paper from beneath her shirt and handed them to Rebecca. "This is the only copy," she said.

Rebecca took them without a word, her eyes on Mila's face.

"I will not trade," Mila said softly. "But I will ask you for two favors. I do not want to go back to jail. You said you can do that. And I want Samuel Lujan discharged from the Army. I will give you his ID number."

Still silent, Rebecca turned the crumpled pages one by one. Finally, she looked up. Her face was a mask of stillness. The green eyes were ice, but there were shadows in their depths. "You know what you have in this file." Her voice was cold. "You are too bright not to know, too bright not to guess how much you could get for it, from me or elsewhere. Why did you give this to me, Mila?" She waited one heartbeat. Two. "There are people I can hire to dig the truth out of you."

Mila felt goose bumps rise at the cold promise in this woman's tone. She could not trade, she could not sell this file. If she did, part of her soul would go with it, tangled in that ball of platinum string. It would consume her, as it had consumed this woman and her mother. It would own her in a way that Amelia Connor-Vanek never had. She would spend her life following that string, until she became a shriveled gray husk in a golden kennel. It still tempted her; that *entrada*, that ticket *out* and *up*, her entrance into the world of the towers. *You are like me,* Amelia Connor-Vanek had said, and it was true. Part of her longed to snatch those crumpled pages back from Rebecca, to run headlong into that labyrinth and find the center.

"It is not mine." With an effort, she met Rebecca's sea-ice stare. "Your mother meant this file for you, not for me. I do not want it. What matters to you?" she asked softly. "What is important to *you*, Señora Connor?"

"To be the best." Rebecca's eyes flickered. "But Amelia will never know, will she? I believe you." Her shoulders lifted slightly, as if she had sighed. "My mother would laugh, but I do. Keeping you out of jail is no problem, but it will take a little finesse to get your license reinstated."

"And Sam?"

"Your boyfriend." Rebecca stuffed the folded paper into the pocket of her tunic. "He can reenlist, you know. Unless you want me to stick him with a dishonorable?"

The city had painted out the Little Cambodia mural. She had seen the gray blotch of new paint from the rail. If she had opened that kennel, so many years ago, would the coyote have bolted? Perhaps. Perhaps not—if there was nowhere else to go. She had not opened it. "If he wants to reenlist, it is his choice," Mila whispered. "I will not come back here again."

"I was right about one thing." Rebecca's voice halted Mila in the doorway. "There was no suicide note."

Mila turned slowly. Was there a shadow of the coyote's stare in those ice-green eyes, too? What did Amelia's death mean to this woman? Would she blame herself, or would she see her own future in that empty bed? "There was no note," Mila said softly. "*La Señora* would never kill herself. It was an accident—a bad batch of the drug."

She went into the anteroom to wait for the lift. Some things you could not trade. Some things you had to give away. The lift whispered open to take her down and out of this tower world. Not forever. She would find her *entrada*. She would come back. Someday.

"Milagra?" Rebecca stood in the anteroom doorway. "I have this place in Antarctica. Near McMurdo, in the US reservation. The very big fish in this little global pond of ours live there. They pay their employees exorbitantly well. You should be able to pay for the rest of your degree with what you make." She pulled a small card from her pocket. "You have enough money to get there. I paid you for your time." She tossed the card to Mila.

Mila caught it. A key-card, with an address on it. She turned it over in her palm, mouth open to say no, wanting no obligations, no ties to this woman and her world.

"I wish," Rebecca said quietly, "that I had tried to forgive my mother."

She knew. Mila curled her fingers around the hard edges of the card, suddenly and intensely sorry for this woman. *Siempre solo.* Some things, perhaps, you had to accept as gifts.

"*Gracias,*" she said softly.

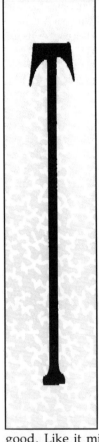

# THE CENTAUR GARDEN

Lonzo took the mag-lev out of the city. It was crowded at first, jammed with men and women going from apartment to job, or from job to play. They were dressed as brightly as tropical birds in city colors, their faces private and unreadable. Virtual faces, he thought, never mind that they were flesh. The real person was safely out of reach behind that mask. The music of it began to form in his head— rich, complex strings, hidden beneath a bright melodic surface. He leaned back in his seat as the mag-lev slid across the bridge, fingering the notes on his thigh, hearing it. It sounded good. Like it might work this time, really work.

The train slowed for the Perimeter but didn't stop on its way out of the city. It only stopped at the checkpoint on the way in—you were free to leave anytime. Lonzo stared out at the silvery thicket of tangled razor-wire that fenced the city towers. The fiberboard and scrap dwellings of shacktown crowded right up to the wire, huddled and hopeful in grimy tones of gray and brown. Figures scurried from doorway to doorway, furtive as night animals caught out in the light. In Lonzo's head, the bright city music segued to a soft melody of hoping in a minor key, punctuated with harsh notes of violence and despair, and graced with laughter, because laughter could happen even there.

It didn't quite work. He felt it, even in his head—the hole—that *absence* in his music. His fingers stilled as the train picked up speed. Lonzo reached down to touch his pack, to reassure himself with the hard outline of his muse-flute. Instead, he touched the roundness of his orb. He had almost left it in the apartment, cut off his access to the Net, to the city. To Roberto and Caryl, Jess, Sondra . . . all of them. But he'd told himself it was valuable, that he could sell it if he needed money.

His touching the orb instead of his flute felt like an omen.

He would come back to the city.

"Never," he said out loud. But the word—so strong this morning—was nothing more than air now, shaped by tongue and lips and teeth. The orb had sucked away its power.

Lonzo sighed and drowsed, the music in his head now muted, too soft to hear. He had been afraid to look at the other passengers before, afraid that he might recognize a face or, worse yet, watch a face recognize him. But now the car was almost empty. The bird-bright city folk had gotten off, and the thin scatter of men and women who were left wore the conservative and functional earth-toned clothes of ag-plex workers.

He had never gone much with 'plexers. They usually didn't come into the city, and it cost too much to travel very often beyond the Perimeter. In fact, he had never crossed it.

Until today.

Beyond the window, biomass bushes carpeted the land, a blur of dark green up close, their thriving branches and the black snakes of the irrigation hoses distinct and clear only at a distance. Life was like that, Lonzo thought sleepily. You only saw it clearly at a distance, when it was behind you or ahead of you. Up close, it was nothing but a blur.

Two or three at a time, the 'plexers got off, and finally, the car was empty. Lonzo sat up now, nudging his pack from beneath his seat, a tremolo of excitement in his head. The next stop, he told himself. The next stop should be his. The train was slowing, the rhythm of its speed altering, vibrating through the car, shaping the music to fit it. He didn't really know if Dyke had been straight about how to get into the Preserve. She liked to lie, even to her friends. Maybe this whole trip was all for nothing, maybe it was a good thing he hadn't thrown away his orb.

Going back to the city would be suicide. Truth, and it pierced him. Not death of the flesh, maybe, but something would die, some part of him. Lonzo reached for his pack, suddenly terrified that he'd miss the stop. He slung it awkwardly over his shoulder, wondering why it seemed so much heavier now than when he'd boarded. Maybe because it held Roberto, and Caryl, Sondra, and Jess, and Than, his current string. They were all there inside his orb, and maybe it wasn't *weight* he felt, it was them pulling on him, trying to drag him back.

He almost dropped it, left it there on the seat for anybody to steal. You can have them, he thought bitterly, I don't want them. He never had, for all they wanted him. But his flute was in there, too, and the mag-lev had stopped and there wasn't time to get it out. In a fever of panic Lonzo ran down the aisle, pack banging his hip. Heart pounding, he leaped off the step and onto the platform.

Behind him, the doors whispered shut and the mag-lev drifted on to other destinations, other cities. The sun clubbed him, hotter and brighter than in the city, where the tower-mounted solar arrays seemed to suck away the sun's power. Shading his eyes, dazzled in spite of his UV-protective contacts, he looked around. Not much—just a concrete pad at ground level cracked by heat and frost, a tile roof supported on two pillars. A few derelict houses, a couple of boarded-up stores, and a gas station lined a short section of street. A CLOSED sign creaked from the gas station. At either end of town, the road terminated in a wall of dusty green biomass bushes. Nobody had lived here for a long time.

It was an ag-plex stop; private access masquerading as a public stop and built with public funds. He didn't care, because the Preserve was . . . there. It fenced off the horizon beyond the bushes—a taller wall of green, random, not orderly like the city or the fields. The mag-lev rail arched gracefully up onto concrete pylons and ran into that forest wall, straight as a thrown spear.

So far Dyke was right. No gate, no guards, no wire. Looked like you could walk along the mag-lev track right into the Preserve. He shouldered his pack and started off. At first, he stayed close to the pylons. The ground was bare brown dirt, and he felt unaccountably hesitant, even if the sun made him sweat. On either side, the trees fenced the right-of-way with a solid wall of green, their branches thick and disappointingly regular. He wanted chaos—not the defeated ruins of former order like shacktown, but something truly random. Uncontrolled and uncontrollable. It was there beyond the wall of trees. He breathed, tasting it; pungent, spicy, dank, with a hint of mold and a musky whiff of living things. Forest. Wildness. He wanted to *play* it, but that hesitancy extended even to his music. So he left the flute in his pack.

Ahead, a small stream crossed the right-of-way, tumbling over gray stones. That sudden urgency squeezed him again, like it had at the Perimeter. He left the pylons, shoved head-down into the thicket of branches, following the stream. He closed his eyes as needled twigs whipped his face. Scratches—it was an automatic wince. That kind of damage would cost him an afternoon on bioenhanced healing because in the world of perfect virtual bodies, you couldn't afford any physical damage in the flesh unless it was aesthetic. Not in his trade.

But that didn't matter anymore, and he lifted his head, reveling in the rake of twigs across the cheeks, the sting of sweat in the scratches as he burst through into twilight.

Yes. He wandered slowly between huge tree trunks that were without pattern or order, leaning sometimes, healthy, dying, and in between. Twigs and fallen branches littered the needled ground and the air hung heavy beneath the trees, redolent with forest smell, almost too thick to breathe. Overhead, the treetops swayed as an unfelt wind struck them, filling the air with a susurration that was frighteningly loud. Storm coming? Lonzo tilted his head up to the sky, trying to read it, exhilarated by the sudden gray. In the city, you ignored the sky. Sometimes it provided a little variety or an annoyance in the form of rain when you wanted sun. Out here, it had tangible power.

The forest was empty, filled only by wind noise and the smell of rotting needles. Lonzo set his pack down slowly, gooseflesh bumping up on his skin as he fumbled open the flap. Took out his flute. His gloves felt clammy as he put them on, and he lifted the featureless tube of the flute tenderly. Gray sky full of threat and energy, trailing wisps of gray-green moss stirring in the heavy air—he began to play it. Human breath provided the core sound—a living thing, breath. His gloved hands caressed the flute, each tiny movement of the flesh a new sound or instrument, all overlaid on that moist, warm stream of life.

Low voices of oboe and bassoon sang the thick air, the dark patient age of the big firs. The stream tumbled through in strings and percussion, and the storm tension built in strident woodwinds and in the high clear voice of the flute itself. Lonzo let himself go, swaying to the twining rhythms, dissolving into the music. The flute was his refuge after he had been with one of *them*. He could play the sky, so clean and blue above the city. Playing, he too would be clean for a while, safe and remote from the hungry yearning people around him.

The music still wasn't right. Not even out here. Something bounced off his shoulder, and Lonzo's start crashed dissonance through the storm song. A fir cone. Lonzo stared at it, lowering the flute. Disappointment and silence flowed in around him like cold water. He had thought it would work out here, had thought the city—so structured, so created—had been the wound. Suddenly, Lonzo felt *alone*.

He hadn't been alone out beneath the mag-lev track. It retained the echoes of a thousand thousand people whispering along its rail, radiated those echoes like stored heat after the sun went down. If anyone had walked beneath these ancient trees, the trees had forgotten. Or didn't care. No human hand had planted them or shaped them. Why should they care? He wrapped the flute in its velvet cloth, his fingers trembling suddenly. The pack tipped as he stowed it and his orb rolled out. It bumped gently against his toe, heavy, shimmering with *their* invisible presence.

Lonzo reached, his hands moving without volition, and the holofield shimmered to life as he touched the velvet-purple orb. Bright images glowed in the twilight-colored field: a blood-colored rose. A tiny eagle. A golden scorpion. The rose was Mei Li's icon. Than was the eagle. The scorpion was Roberto's bit of posturing. There were others—Caryl's butterfly, Sondra's jade dragon—a constellation of need and pleading. Lonzo stared at them, tugged by temptation. *Lonzo, don't go. Who will come to the park with me?*

*I need you to read to me, how can I live without hearing your voice?*

*I love you. How can you just walk away?*

*I love you.*

*I love you.*

*I love you.*

He could hear their voices, even though he hadn't accessed their messages. Lonzo covered his ears, trying to block out Than's soft lisp that he thought was so sexy, Sondra's clipped Aussie accent, Roberto's sweet baritone. *I love you.* Their cries drowned the music in his head, and he should have left it behind, the orb, but he hadn't and it didn't matter; they'd follow him always, as close as any Net terminal, as close as weakness. If he reached out, if he touched any one of those message icons. . . .

He would no longer be alone.

The light was failing and the wind-noise filled the forest with emptiness. His fingers twitched, reached. He balled both hands into fists, shoved them between his knees. If he listened to their cries and pleading in his E-mail, he would go back.

Lightning sizzled across the sky, bright and blue, too fast to really see. And then thunder, a splitting *crack* that made him jump. Electricity pulsed through his flesh, as if the lightning was building inside him, making his short hair prickle on his head, as if *he* was full of the lightning. Any second now, it would leap from his skin, arc to the tree, and blow it apart. Caryl talked about lightning when she talked about being in love with him. And Than—he called it electrical. The orb had blanked and vanished in the gathering darkness, but they were still there, he could *hear* them, louder than the storm's music.

With a cry, Lonzo leaped against the trunk of the big tree. The bark shredded his palms, and the pain was like sex; pleasure and hurt together. His boots slipped and he kicked them off, climbing as though he was made for this, toes gripping the bark like it was flesh, like he was a kid climbing into his mother's arms, only if he'd had a mother—and everyone had one, right?—she was lost in a sea of whispering faces; Than, and Caryl, and Jeff, and Ziporah, all whispering I love you, I love you. . . . They drowned the music in his head, and it didn't work anyway, not even out here. All that remained was the sound of their pleading—and the storm.

He was into the branches now, hands sticky with sap or blood, needles pricking his face, twigs clawing at his shoulders. The tree swayed with the wind and his weight, and suddenly he was at the top. Some errant gust had broken it, left jagged splinters and a few thin branches jutting into the air. He wrapped his legs around the spindly trunk, let go and reached up to the storm's belly.

It didn't love him, that storm, didn't hate him, didn't care any more than the forest did. It didn't *need* him. Lightning forked the sky, blue-white and clean, so clean. Thunder crashed almost at the same instant. That meant it was close—old knowledge swimming up out of the past that had disappeared beyond the sea of faces. "Come on," he cried, reaching. "Come get me!" Electric orgasm without love or need. Nothing would matter—not the hole in his music, not the whispers on the Net—*I love you, I love you. . . .* ''Come *on!''* He reached, fingers spread, the tree's flesh bending and swaying between his thighs.

Bright blindness sizzled around him, exploded with a sound like the sky splitting. I'm dead, he thought. But pain stung his face and chest—splinters from the blasted crown of a taller tree—and he felt an instant of terrible disappointment. Then he was sliding, tumbling down, dropping through the tree's crown, nails tearing as he clutched automatically for a grip, twigs slashing his face, branches battering his ribs, arms, legs. And suddenly there were no branches and he was falling in blackness, and rain, and a shower of needles and twigs.

He landed hard and soft at the same time, fell into pillowing darkness, into a dream of their smiles, a hundred different faces, sucking the life from him, fingers gently shredding the flesh from his bones. . . . He tried to pull away, but his lips returned their smile, and his hands clasped theirs, fleshless and without power, the music silent in his head.

HE WOKE chilled and stiff to green light and birdsong. Sun shone, not hot yet, spangling the needled branches far above his head with droplets of glittering crystal. He moved, sucking in a ragged breath at soreness and bruising. Fabric rustled. Blinking he sat up, pushing aside a covering of pale green. It was tucked beneath him and half over him, and he shivered as it fell away. It had kept him more dry than not.

Stiffly, gracelessly, he got to his feet. His covering was some kind of rain poncho, sleeved and oddly proportioned. It was too long in the back, long enough to drag on the ground like a train if he put it on. Lonzo folded it, adding this puzzle to the puzzle of who had wrapped him in it. His pack had been tucked between the roots of the big fir from which he'd fallen. It was soaked, and he dropped to his knees on the sodden needles, cold water soaking through his leggings, afraid for his flute. The velvet wrap was damp, and so were his gloves. He pulled them on and picked up the flute.

The first notes were sharp and sweet with his relief. No damage. Squatting beneath the dripping tree, he caught the tone of the strengthening light, brought in strings, a percussive whisper of leaves as the morning breeze sprang up, then embroidered it with bright birdsong and the sparkle of sun on falling drops. He was trying too hard to close the hole. His shoulders drooped, bruised muscles aching from his squat. Sparrows fluttered at his feet and he kicked at them, the music dissonant with his anger as they scattered.

And felt . . . eyes on him.

He let the flawed notes trail away like mist, searching the shadows between the gray trunks, seeing nothing at first but a chaos of undergrowth and bark, clumps of dark sword fern. And then, as if someone had turned on a spotlight, he saw her. She stood on the bank of the stream watching him. Her hair was black, and her torso was lithe beneath the sleeveless shirt she wore. But where her hips should be, her waist flared into the shoulders of a black horse. She swished her long tail against her flanks and stamped one equine hoof.

Centaur, he thought numbly. And then: there are no such things. "What the hell *are* you?" he asked.

She grimaced, and in a single smooth motion she pulled her shirt off over her head. "Try *who*, not *what*. Why don't you get the staring over with? And ask anything you need to ask, okay?" She raised her chin, dark eyes steady in spite of her blush. "Then we won't keep bumping into all those questions."

The flicker deep in her eyes betrayed her hurt. And so he stared—because she wanted him to stare. "I apologize," he said. "About the *what*. I thought genens were illegal."

"You didn't get the death sentence for human gene manipulation when I was made. And Uncle paid the fine. He could afford it." She shrugged and turned, so that he could see everything.

Her black hair hung down her back, mixing with an equine mane that began like down between her shoulder blades, grew steadily thicker and longer as it descended her spine to her equine shoulders. Plumbing was a horse thing, he decided. Sex, too. Sixteen? Did she age like a horse or a girl? he wondered. She had stopped blushing as she turned, her hooves lifting daintily. But not quite gracefully. There was a hitch in her movements, like a sour note in an otherwise perfect piece of music.

He spotted the faint outline beneath the satiny black hide of her withers. Buried hardware. And also there in front of what would be her hips if she was human, and probably elsewhere, because how else could you coordinate all that muscle? He recoiled, repelled in spite of himself.

And she saw. Turned her head, her profile stark against the tree shadow, sparrows fluttering around her. "It didn't work." She pulled her shirt back on. "They thought it would, all the people who worked on me. But I couldn't walk. They did the surgery when I was four and implanted the hardware." She looked at him, her face harsh with truth. "I'm a failure. Ugly. But Uncle loves me anyway. You know, I thought you were a girl at first. Or a kid. But you're not."

His reaction had hurt her, so he forgave her quick, scathing words. "I should let my beard grow," he said, although he'd tried and it never did. Lonzo crossed the space between them and put a hand on her equine shoulder. Her head was nearly a meter above his and her skin shuddered beneath his palm, but she didn't move away. Up close he realized how big her human torso was. She looked right—in proportion to her horse self— but if she was fully human, she'd be a giant. She kept her face averted as he traced the outline of the hardware, feeling sleek horsehair, solid flesh, and buried plastic. Her strong animal scent—not unpleasant at all—tickled his nose, overlaid by a hint of musky woman-smell. "It's all right," he said, letting his hand linger. "It doesn't really bother me, you know."

And realized he was *doing* it, just like he'd done with Than, and Jess, and Mei Li, and all the others. Not trying to do it, just *doing* it—the lingering touch, that sense of awareness, his skin warming as he breathed her scent. In a few minutes, he'd start to perspire, never mind the morning chill. He would sense what she wanted him to say, then say it for her. It would happen like it always did. He jerked his hand away as if she had burned him, and she shied a little, hooves scattering rotted needles, startled.

"Did you cover me up?" He made his voice harsh, accusatory. It took a lot of effort to be harsh, because she didn't want that and it was so much easier to give her what she wanted. "Did you do that much and then just walk away, leave me to live or die there in the rain?"

"You didn't seem to be dying." She stamped one rear hoof. "Do you know what the penalty is for trespass on a Preserve? You were sort of conscious for a little bit. Don't you remember? You said you were okay, told me to go away." She shook her hair impatiently back over her shoulder. "Nothing seemed to be broken, so I gave you my poncho. *You* wrapped yourself up. Or would you rather I'd called somebody? You'd be in jail, or on your way to a community-service camp by now."

"I'm sorry. I . . . don't remember." He retreated, embarrassed. "Thank you."

"I listened to you play, yesterday. And this morning." She lay down, awkward and animal, folding her legs beneath her. Now she was shorter than he, looking up at him. "Can I see your flute?"

He unwrapped it, suddenly shy, and handed it over. She put on the gloves and raised it to her lips, eyes dreamy, hair and mane mixing and floating in the fitful breeze. Her notes were clear as rain, graced with rich woodwinds like tree shade and the bright chirp of birds. The sparrows answered her, fluttering down to peck among the needles in front of her. Maybe sparrows were the only birds who lived in this place, Lonzo thought.

She broke off suddenly. "Here." She handed the flute back reverently. "I only play for myself."

"Why?" Which was a silly thing to say, since he only played for himself. "You're good."

"Good, yes. Not great. Not like you." Serious expression, serious tone. "Will you play something?"

Great, she had said. He raised the flute, played the stream for a while, all bright with sun and white cascading water. And he ended abruptly, thirsty.

"Why did you come here?" Her eyes seemed to be all pupil, black as night in the shadows of the trees. "You're lucky, you know." She tossed her head again, like a horse might. "If I hadn't been surfing through Uncle's security, I wouldn't have seen you in time to delete you from the record. You'd be on your way to a camp right now."

Security? He looked up, startled, into the wild canopy above them, but if video eyes watched, he couldn't spot them. "Thank you," he said stiffly, a little irritated by her supercilious manner, a little angry because he hadn't wanted to know that city technology compromised this wild place. "I came here because I felt like it." He shrugged. "I was sick of the city."

"How were you going to live?"

"I don't know." He polished a speck of mud from the flute, not looking at her. Somebody always took care of him. It surprised him that she would even ask. "I'll figure something out."

"What?" She wouldn't leave it alone. "Are you going to live here like some kind of crazy hermit? Are you going to eat nuts and berries? Catch rabbits?"

"I don't know. You own this forest or what?" His anger burst out, startling her.

Her equine shoulders tensed as if she was about to lunge to her feet. "I don't own the forest." She sank down again, but her eyes were serious in spite of her smile. "I call it my garden, but that's only because nobody owns it. Nobody *made* it this way, so I love it."

That's what had drawn him—that this place hadn't been built or planted, hadn't been made. Lonzo's anger evaporated and he blew a soft apology on the flute.

She nodded in understanding. "What did you do in the city? Play music?"

She didn't guess, but why would she? She was no city child. *I play music.* He almost gave her that lie, spun her a story of live entertainment and noble poverty. He was already responding to her, reading the tiny clues of body language—at least of her human part—and sweating lightly.

But the forest mattered to her for the same reason it mattered to him. And she heard what he played in his music, and suddenly he didn't want to lie to her. "I'm a whore." The words came out harsh and ugly.

For the space of a single heartbeat, she stared at him. Then she laughed, but her laugh was uncertain. "A whore? How can you make a living at that, when people can do virtual sex with anyone or anything?"

He shrugged, and began to wrap the flute. A small part of him was pleased that he'd shocked her, that he'd jarred the familiar progression out of step. "Anyone can do sex, you're right." He smiled at her. "Love is something different. It's a living thing." Like his breath in the flute, never mind the electronics that augmented it. "I can make anyone fall in love with me. Even you." For a price. Always a price. "Nobody's been able to put that into a virtual yet—love." A lot of times sex wasn't even part of it. Sex was easy. Cheap. He lifted one shoulder in a lopsided shrug, shaped a leer that felt ugly. "It's a living."

"That's why you tried to die last night?" she asked softly.

*Tried to die,* not *tried to kill yourself.* He looked away from the dark intensity of her stare. "They always pay," he said softly. "Sometimes I don't even have to ask. And they never want me to go, but I always do after a while. They beg me to stay. Sometimes, they threaten suicide." Who had done that last? Jeff, or Mei Lin? He couldn't remember. "I don't think they ever do it," he said. Who would die for him? "I don't want to know."

"Why?" She touched his arm, eyes wide, her fingers light as the brush of the tender needles at the top of the tree last night. "Why can't you love them back?"

Her words startled him again. "I do," he said. "I give them what they want." He turned deliberately to meet her eyes, searching for the disgust that had to be there. "You'll love me and you'll get me a job with your uncle, feed me, dress me, just to keep me. And I'll be everything you want me to be."

"Is that what love is?" She tilted her head, frowning softly. "I don't know. I don't know at all." She got to her feet in a lunging surge of mass and muscle, hooves thumping hollowly on the ground. "I don't think Uncle will give you a job." She tilted her head in a measuring stare. "But he'll let me feed you breakfast. And you need to put something on those scratches."

"I'm fine." But her words brought stinging pain, as if she'd reminded his flesh of its injuries. He looked at his arms, noticing the red welts and the stripes of crusted brown blood for the first time. "Sort of fine, anyway."

"You should see your face." She turned, swinging her hind-quarters carefully so that she didn't bump him. "Come on."

He could see it clearly now—a roughness as she moved, a physical dissonance. It was part of her, not ugly, not alien. Just . . . her. "You're so beautiful," he blurted.

"Except for my limp." She rolled an eye at him. "You blush so prettily. Is it on purpose?"

"I'm not blushing." He glowered at her, then laughed. "And it's not really a limp, you know. More like . . . syncopation. I don't even know your name." He grinned up at her. "I'm Lonzo."

"Ailene." She looked down at him, ducking beneath a branch, her expression a mixture of wariness and curiosity. "What's so funny?"

"You're not falling in love with me. I can feel it. And part of me is disappointed." He laughed again, but it tasted bitter this time. "Maybe I don't really know what I want after all."

"Maybe we never do." She swished her long tail and broke into a trot.

But when he didn't run to keep up, she slowed down to wait for him. When he caught up with her, she offered to carry his pack. He handed it to her.

Apology offered and accepted. He wasn't at all sure who owed whom the apology, or why.

THE HOUSE was closer than he'd thought. Built against a line of gray cliffs, it hung above a small tumbling stream that cascaded down through a crack in the cliff face. It was built of weathered concrete the color of stone, shaped all in curves that harmonized subtly with the contours of the hillside. For a few moments he could only stand and stare, stunned by the unity of that architecture. It belonged here, jutting out of the rimrock in multiple levels as though it was part of the cliff.

At the same time it stopped him, as if an invisible fence blocked his path. He hadn't thought about who would live in a Preserve. Of course it would be the most wealthy, the topmost layer of the economic strata. A sparrow fluttered onto the path at his feet, chirped a bright note. Uncle could afford the fine for illegal genen work. He looked sideways at Ailene. "I don't know . . .," he began.

"Are you scared of him?" She cocked one rear leg, challenge in her eyes.

"No." He took his pack from her, slung it over his shoulder. "I'm not scared of him. I just. . . ." He shrugged, because it was too late to retreat anyway. This man would have security out to the rim of the Preserve. Although he'd been looking in every treetop for hidden video eyes and hadn't seen a single one. No wonder his music hadn't worked. This place wasn't so different from the city after all. He hiked the pack higher. "Let's go," he said, and sighed.

She led him toward the south end of the sprawling cliffhouse. Up close the place was huge, with vast windows and wide doors. Big enough for a centaur. "This is where I live," she said as she clomped up a ramp onto a stone-flagged terrace.

Plants cascaded from glazed pots, spilling clusters of tiny blue-and-white flowers over the rail. The stream tumbled below, full of foam and music. French doors opened into a huge suite. There were a couple of chairs and a table that was too high for him. And a wide couch at floor level, with a low table beside it. A laptop reader lay on the table. Ailene threw open the doors. "Bathroom is there." She pointed to an archway. "If you can handle the proportions."

This was another challenge, this invitation into her rooms. Challenges were playful things, masks for deeper questions. *I love you. Do you love me, Lonzito?* That was the usual question, but this time it didn't fit and it left him uneasy, treading warily on unfamiliar ground. "Thanks." He tossed his pack onto the couch as casually as if he lived here—answering her challenge—and went into the bathroom.

It was as big as an ordinary room with a walk-in shower closet large enough for her to stand in, a sink built to her height. The toilet had been designed for equine plumbing. Lonzo eyed the narrow rectangular pool and was glad he only had to urinate. The mirror above the sink showed him his scratches and he winced. Some of them looked bad enough to scar. But it didn't matter anymore.

It was hard to remember that. He stripped off his tunic, ran water and washed his face, bringing bright new blood to the worst of his injuries.

"This'll help." She stood in the doorway, a small plastic container in her hand.

Out among the trees she had fit. In here, in this house, she looked out of place, never mind the centaur-sized features that had been proportioned for her. "He built this whole place for you, didn't he?" The effect, instead of normalizing her, made her into a freak. Bare-chested, Lonzo walked past her into the main room and boosted himself up onto the tabletop. Now they were on a level. He took the container from her, sniffed at the white cream it contained.

"Yes, he built this house for me." She sounded sad. "Because he'd funded this project to do mer-type genens for the fisheries trade. And the engineer who was doing the designs was kind of a crazy genius, and he . . . did me. Just to see if he could do it, I guess." She looked away, her mouth twitching. "And then the Backlash happened, and people were rioting, killing genens, and the project was disbanded. The company that had contracted for the mers took care of them. But . . . I didn't belong to anyone. So Uncle kept me."

Kept me, she said, like you'd keep a dog. He'd built a house for her, spent a fortune to isolate her in her own uniqueness. *Just to see if he could do it,* she'd said about her creation. "That's how most of us get conceived, isn't it?" he asked softly. "On a shitty bed, or in an alley? Just to see if we can do it . . . make a life?"

"I think about it a lot." She looked away. "Are they the same thing—being born and being made? Or are they different? The World Court never decided. They just passed laws to stop human genengineering. They didn't decide if we were human . . . or not. I think they're waiting for all of us genens to die of old age. Give me that." She took the container from him, dipped a finger into it, and began to smooth the cream into his face. "Tell me about your mother. What was she like?"

Another question to surprise him. "I don't remember." Lonzo closed his eyes, the antiseptic tingling on his cuts. "I dream about her sometimes—she was dark like me. Smiling. In my dreams she's always dressed in white. She says, 'Come on,

Lonny, let's go see the doctor.' Maybe she was sick. I don't know what happened to her." Even back then there had always been someone to take care of him—in return for love. The faces layered like fall leaves in his memory, a lot of them nameless now, covering up whatever had been before. "I guess she died when I was little."

"Uncle loves me." Ailene's murmur sounded in his ear and her breath was warm against his face. "He built this house for me. He takes care of me. But I don't know. . . ." She shuddered, horse and human. "Sometimes I dream that the walls all crumble and trap me. And then the cliff falls in and crushes me."

"Maybe you should leave?"

"And go where?" Her words were a breath, barely audible. "And do what, Lonzo?"

"I don't know." Truth forced the words from him.

She nodded, her expression serene and resigned. "I think I'm unfinished," she said slowly. "I don't know what's missing."

"So is my music," he whispered. "Unfinished." It was his turn to look away.

"I heard it when you played." Her turn to be truthful. "But you're so close."

Somehow her truthfulness made the hole seem smaller. Lonzo fumbled the flute from his pack. It was cool in his hand, eager as he slipped on his gloves. *You're so close. . . .* He raised it to his lips and played . . . her. He played the sweet arch of her back in a soft minor key, graced it with the wind-lifted sweep of mane and hair. Added power and muscle with kettledrums and viols, played her the syncopation of her walk and let her hear how it was beautiful. And the hole was . . . smaller.

Eyes half closed, a soft smile on her face, she leaned close. She smelled of animal and woman, of the breeze beneath the forest canopy. Lonzo let the final notes trail away and laid the flute down. He took off his gloves, raised a hand to touch her face. Her skin stretched smooth and firm over her jutting cheekbones. She pressed her palm against his cheek as his hand traveled down the smooth muscles of her shoulder and back. Her waist was firm, blending into the sculptured muscle of her equine shoulders. So much power. So much grace. He followed the curve of her back, fingers tracing the muscled groove of her spine. "You're like the forest," he said softly. "You *are*."

Behind them, someone cleared his throat.

She shied like any horse, yanking him from the table. Her

shoulder slammed him in the hip, nearly knocking him off his feet, and the edge of the table banged his ribs. He caught himself and straightened, holding his side.

"Uncle." She faced the door, breathing fast, her cheeks flaming. "I wondered if you were home."

"I'm home." The figure in the doorway had the face and body of a man in his thirties, in his prime. Ash-blond hair, fair skin, eyes the azure color of the city sky. He was dressed in soft expensive trousers and sweater, and he nodded at Lonzo, then smiled. "I'm Sebelius Renfrew."

"Lonzo." If he had a surname, he'd never learned it. Or he'd lost it among the faces. "I met Ailene in the woods," he said, because a chasm of silence had opened at his feet and it needed to be filled.

"He plays the muse-flute." Ailene broke in, still breathless. "He's incredibly good."

"I've always liked the flute. I was just going to have a late breakfast. Brunch, I suppose." Renfrew smiled. "Care to join me on my terrace?"

The charm was a mask, like the city faces on the train were masks. And when Ailene said, "That would be nice," she was obeying a command, for all her smile. It made him angry—that she would smile and obey. Lonzo put a hand on her shoulder, took it away when her equine muscles bunched beneath his palm. Tense, her horse-muscles confessed. Nervous.

Her discomfiture banished his own, and he smiled at Sebelius Renfrew. "Breakfast would be very nice," he said. "Or brunch. You'll have to excuse my appearance." He tucked his flute into his pack, shouldered it. "I spent the night out in the forest."

"So I gather." Renfrew gave Lonzo a thoughtful look as he stepped back to usher them out onto the terrace again, past the potted plants, and up another ramp. "You popped up rather suddenly on my security system. Must be a glitch somewhere. I've got some technicians working on it." He draped a casual arm across Ailene's satiny back. "I don't want you to worry when you're out in the woods, dear."

"I don't worry, Uncle. I'd scare any intruders away." Her tone was light, but her tail whisked her flanks. "They'd think I was a monster and run."

"Lonzo didn't run." Renfrew smiled brightly. "Don't talk like that, child. You're *lovely.*"

His tone was passionate, full of truth. But somehow, like the perfectly proportioned house, his words made her seem ugly, a monster after all.

"And you're so sweet, Uncle," Ailene murmured. They had come to a small arched bridge of polished wood and she broke into a trot, her hooves shaking the planks as she crossed it. Lonzo and Renfrew followed behind her, side by side. Close together, because the bridge was narrow.

He had Renfrew's attention, for all the man wasn't looking at him. He was *old*. You could see the age in his movements, never mind the body-shop muscles and expensively purchased look of youth. And Lonzo was truly young. Beautiful, in spite of the scratches. He drew a shallow breath *tasting* the man, his skin prickling, warming. Perspiration dewed his forehead and he smiled. Refrew returned it. Sebelius Renfrew reacted to him, even if Ailene didn't. It was always like that. Always. Except with Ailene, and he wasn't quite sure why that was.

The bridge ended on another larger terrace. Orange trees bloomed in huge glazed pots, perfuming the air. A table of polished wood stood among cushioned chairs. It held a tray of food and various beverages. Ailene stood beside it, pouring coffee into cups. Her hair had fallen forward around her face, hiding her expression. There was no furniture designed for centaurs on this terrace, Lonzo noticed.

"Please, sit." Renfrew took the cup she offered, waved Lonzo toward another of the chairs. "So you play the museflute?" He seated himself and crossed his legs, leaning back with a sexuality that tugged at Lonzo's biochemistry. "Would you consider giving a private . . . er . . . recital later?" His eyes gleamed above his pleasant smile. "Ailene's quite fond of the flute."

"I just play for myself." And maybe always would, his music forever flawed. Lonzo moved his shoulders uneasily, not sure what was bothering him. Renfrew was reacting, attracted, but there was a hint of darkness to it, like a tingle of distant lightning. If he was a prospective client, Lonzo would make his excuses. Duck and run. "I'd disappoint you," he said.

"Let me be the judge of that." Renfrew turned his smile on Ailene. "I don't demand perfection."

She averted her head—just a twitch, but there was shame in it. You are perfect, Lonzo wanted to say to her. That uneven walk, the satiny horse-muscle, they're part of you, not a lack. He accepted the cup she handed him, silent, aware of Renfrew's intent scrutiny. Lonzo sipped at the coffee—real, not synthetic. "I really do play only for myself," he said.

"Well, that's the only valid motivation for anything." Renfrew leaned forward, picked up a rosy apple from the tray. "Although it's nice if you can do it and make a living, too. Have some food. The smoked fish is wonderful and the strawberries are from the greenhouse here. Very ripe. 'Lene?" He cocked one immaculate eyebrow. "Have you done your lessons this morning?"

"No, I haven't." She picked up a huge chunk of fish, trapped it between two halves of a roll. "I take it I'm supposed to go do them, right?" She scooped up a handful of strawberries, one corner of her mouth lifting into a wry smile. "I'm on my way. I'll be in my room, Lonzo." She left the terrace with the hollow clatter of hooves on stone.

She had been dismissed and she had accepted the dismissal. Had there been a hint of sadness in her tone? As if she expected him to leave without bothering to say good-bye? Lonzo picked up three of the huge, perfect strawberries. He ate one, dizzied by the sweetness and perfume of the fruit. Obedience, he thought. That's what was different about Ailene. In this man's presence, she was *obedient*. It would be hard not to obey Renfrew. The temptation tugged at him, too. Lonzo ate the second strawberry. To have such an imposing residence—who had he bribed for the permits to build here in the Preserve?—he had to be a world power, one of the top nodes in the WorldWeb. It would be foolish to be anything *but* obedient. Perhaps that was why she found her garden in the disobedient forest.

"A penny for your thoughts." Renfrew leaned forward—a little too far forward, Lonzo noticed.

"I was thinking about Ailene."

"Ah?" Renfrew's hand on his knee invited a confidence.

"She told me a designer made her. On a whim." He tossed the last strawberry in his palm, pretending to ignore Renfrew's touch. "Why? Why would he do that?"

"Is there ever a rational explanation for whimsy?" Renfrew shrugged. "He was a genius, Patrick Doyle was, and crazy, I think. He loved his work. Love." His sky-colored eyes fixed on Lonzo's face. "Love is such an undeniable thing, isn't it?"

A message beneath those seemingly casual words? "Is it?" Lonzo popped the last strawberry into his mouth. "I don't know."

"Don't you." It wasn't quite a question. Renfrew sat forward to fill his own cup, reached for Lonzo's. "He worked so hard on her, and she was flawed. Crippled. Patrick fixed it finally, added the hardware to accept signals from her human neural pathways and translate them into comparable movements of her equine muscles. It's a brilliant extension of the technology used to attach prosthetic limbs. I'm afraid the surgery involved was painful at times. She's had a . . . difficult childhood and she's precious to me. The most important thing in the world." He handed Lonzo his refilled cup. "I had a daughter once. Her mother was a nobody, and she betrayed me. I don't take betrayal well." His voice went soft, and Lonzo had the sudden sense that he was saying something else, something shrill and terrible beyond the range of hearing. "Never mind that." Renfrew smiled, his mood suddenly shifting. "Angelina, my daughter, was beautiful in spite of her mother. She was perfection. She was everything I'd ever wanted. Everything."

*Was* . . . Lonzo looked away, because for a moment Renfrew's expression reminded him of his past lovers—glossed with a blind and terrible hunger. And something else. A flash of hatred? "What happened to her?"

"She died." Renfrew turned those city-sky eyes on him, his face charming again, unreadable as a virtual. "She used to show horses—stadium jumping. It's a dangerous sport, you know, but the young don't believe in mortality, do they? Do *you*, Lonzo? Believe in mortality?"

"Yes," Lonzo whispered. Strawberry juice had stained his fingers, red as blood. "I know I can die." *Why did you try to die?* she had asked him. Not *Why did you try to kill yourself?* There was an important difference. For a moment he thought he had it, but then it eluded him.

"I'm glad you're aware of your own mortality, Lonzo. Unfortunately, my daughter wasn't. She died in a jumping accident. Head injury. There wasn't even time to get her onto life support."

"I'm sorry," he said, but the words came out a mumble. His lips were numb, and the terrace had contracted to a small bright space in a shimmering fog. Drugged, he thought sluggishly, and tried to get up. His bones had turned to jelly, and he sagged back into his soft, comfortable seat.

"She's very lovely, Ailene." Renfrew's voice seemed to come from a distance. "I love her very much. Do you understand? I love her very very much. And she loves me."

"I know," Lonzo heard himself murmur the words, without volition, without control. "I love her, too." And wanted to call the words back because they weren't true, couldn't be true. But it was too late.

Someone patted his face, very gently, almost tenderly. He couldn't see who it was.

HE WAS DREAMING and he knew it; had fallen hard and soft out of a tree. But that didn't matter because he was riding through the dappled forest shade on Ailene's sleek back, and he didn't want it to stop. Her powerful equine shoulders rocked between his thighs, and she had taken off her shirt again. Sweat gleamed on her human shoulders and her mane mingled with her hair, streaming back into his face, tickling his chest and groin. He put his hands on her slender human waist, his prick rising, hardening. She twisted to look over her shoulder as she galloped, face bright with laughter and lust. And he leaned forward to kiss her, his erection rubbing against horse and human heat. . . .

He woke, curled around pleasure, dream, and a piercing sense of loss. Bright light hurt his eyes, made him blink. The sun was low, tangled in the tops of the fir trees. This late already? He sat up, head aching, the chair cushions soft beneath him. Remembered his brunch with Sebelius Renfrew. *I love her, do you understand?* Renfrew's words echoed in his head.

A warning. Lonzo stumbled to his feet, his head pounding. Why the drug? he wondered, and had the uneasy fantasy that Renfrew had used it to look into his dream, to watch him ride Ailene through the woods. The tray of food still stood on the table. Flies buzzed on the spoiling fish, black with greenish wings. His pack lay on the floor beside it. Yes, a warning and a message. Leave now, or else. Don't even say good-bye. A fly landed on his arm, and Lonzo slapped it. It fell to the polished stones of the terrace, leaving a tiny smear of death behind on his tawny skin.

Sebelius Renfrew could swat him like that. Nobody would care.

He grabbed his pack. It wasn't closed all the way, gaped open as he lifted it. His orb gleamed inside. Ailene must have found it when she covered him, must have put it back in his pack. He shivered, half-reached for it, jerked his hand away. No need to go back. He could go on, catch the rail from the ag-plex stop, travel east or south, and find some bit of forgotten land that was truly wild. Maybe there he could find a way into the hole in his music.

Ailene had looked into that hole and had understood. What would she believe if he simply walked away? That she didn't matter? She had expected him to go. How often had this scene played itself out in her life? Lonzo stood at the edge of the terrace, eyes on the tree shadows beyond these heavy sprawling walls. Those walls had been built for her. Sanctuary or prison? He turned back, crossed the terrace with quick nervous strides, his pack banging his hip. Across the bridge, up the ramp, the route had seemed so simple, so direct, but now he noticed the connecting walkways and ramps, and faltered.

This way to her rooms? Yes. He veered right, telling himself that he was sure. It led him to a terrace with the pots of blue-and-white flowers. Hers, he told himself, and reached for the french doors. They were locked and he paused, urgency tugging him again. He'd tried. (But she wouldn't know that.) He should go. (And she'd believe he didn't give a damn.) Swearing softly under his breath, he fished in his pack for the key that Dyke had given him. Liar, hacker, thief, she might be, but Dyke's gifts were always functional. He pulled it out, touched it to the plate of the electronic lock. The key hummed to itself as if happy with the challenge. The lock clicked and he dropped the key back into his pack. Pushed the door open. And stopped dead.

This wasn't Ailene's room, and now the small uneasiness he'd felt on the terrace shouted at him. The flowers had fooled him. A luxurious bed took up space, along with a sunken bath like a simmering pool at one carpeted end of the room. An old-fashioned wooden bar offered ranked glass bottles full of liqueurs, and a bowl of fruit. An entertainment-scale holoprojector like a larger version of his orb stood on a pedestal in front of an upholstered couch. All were human-normal in size. Ailene would be totally out of place in here. *His* room, Lonzo thought. On a table made from polished wood the color of ivory, static holos shimmered above their gleaming bases.

Common sense was screaming at him to get out, but he took a step toward the holos, then another. He needed to see them, needed to see who mattered enough to this man that he kept their holos beside his bed. The carpet was as soft as the needled ground beneath the big firs. Another step. They were all of one girl, stair-stepping in age from dark-haired infancy to smiling young adulthood. His daughter, of course. Angelina. No image of mother, sibling, friend. Just her; sitting, waving, smiling over her shoulder in a laughing glance that was at the same time intimate and coy. In the center a larger image shimmered above a matte-black base. Angelina leaped a frighteningly tall fence astride a black horse.

Frozen moments of the past, holos, caught and preserved forever. He'd read somewhere that primitives feared the first crude 2–D cameras, claiming that the picture captured their souls. True, Lonzo thought as he stared. We freeze our past, our loves and hates, keep them forever to torture ourselves. He swallowed, his eyes fixed on that central image.

Black hair flying like the mare's black mane, girl and horse leaped together, and she laughed, so sure of herself, so *alive*. Ailene. A fully human Ailene, astride a black mare.

If you had all the money, all the power in the world, all the access to the visionary geniuses in the sciences—you could do whatever you wanted. *She betrayed me*, Renfrew had whispered, and Lonzo had pitied the nobody who was the mother.

Maybe he hadn't meant the mother at all. *I love you.* The voices of Jeff and Sondra and the rest whispered in his head. *You've betrayed me, us, you've left us. . . .*

Death was a betrayal. His mother who had taken him with her to the doctor had left him long ago, vanished without a trace in a sea of strangers' faces, and strangers' love.

If you had the means, you could spend a lifetime on revenge. You could make it subtle. An art form. Or maybe not revenge. Maybe this was . . . punishment.

If the holo can steal a soul, what about a strand of DNA? What gets stolen then?

Ailene, Ailene, do you know who you are? Do you know *what* you are?

Lonzo snatched up his pack and bolted out the door. He didn't have a clue where he was, where her room might be, could only run down the ramps and walkways and hope he'd recognize her terrace. And found it easily around the next curve of wall—found her. She was standing in the golden beams of late afternoon sun, her laptop reader balanced on the railing between two of the pots of flowers. A couple of sparrows perched on the railing at her elbow, preening themselves, cocking their heads to watch her.

"Ailene!"

Her head snapped up and she shied—because a computer buried in her flesh had translated that human start into its equine equivalent. Crippled, Renfrew had said. Flawed.

"Uncle said you'd left." She let him hear the echo of her hurt. "He said you were going to catch the mag-lev back to the city."

Renfrew knew he'd come here on the mag-lev. So Ailene hadn't diddled the security record nearly as well as she'd thought. "We need to go." He looked over his shoulder, realizing suddenly that he hadn't seen a single human being in this gigantic place except the three of them. Surely Renfrew had a dozen servants. "We need to go right now." He set his pack down and caught her wrist.

"What are you talking about?" She arched away, her arm stretched between them in a tug-of-war she could win easily. "You're crazy."

"Maybe. Maybe not just me." He met her dark, wary gaze, willing her to *see*, to understand. "Did you know that he had a daughter?"

"Angelina." She turned her head away. "I've lived here all my life. Do you really think I wouldn't know?"

She'd seen the holos. "Why did you tell me . . .?" He shook his head fiercely, because why should she have told him the truth? "Never mind."

"I didn't lie to you. Patrick Doyle really did do the work, you know. I found the records. Uncle told me he'd . . . kept a DNA sample. That he couldn't let her go, Angelina. And Doyle used it without asking."

"Do you believe him?" Lonzo asked her softly.

"Yes." But her horse-body sidled uneasily. She lifted her chin, her eyes still avoiding his. "I know she's me. Part of me, anyway. I even know her. Security has always watched every square centimeter of this place. There was another house here before this one. They lived here then. He tore it down, after. I watched her jump on those old holos. She used to train in the meadow above the house. The stream runs through it in a deep ravine—the same stream you were near when I found you." She paused for a second, her eyes on a vision he couldn't share. "She was always so sure of herself. Because he was watching. You could see that she was showing off for him. You could see that he was scared for her, but proud of her, too."

He? A new chill settled onto Lonzo's shoulders. "Renfrew?" he asked softly.

"No. He was tall. Dark. Her lover, right? He had to be, or he wouldn't have watched like he did, all full of fear when they jumped fences, but not showing it, you know? He was in love with her. And she was so *sure*. . . ." Her eyes were still fixed on that vision in the air. "I . . . saw her die. There's a narrow place in the ravine. She rode the mare at it one day. I don't know why—I don't think she'd ever tried to jump it before. She was my age. They hit the side, and you could see the mare scrabbling at the bank. And then . . . they just disappear." She shuddered, bent her head.

"Stop it!" He seized her by the arms, clutching her, wanting to hurt her, wanting to focus those strange dreamy eyes, make her *see* him. "Ailene, do you know what he's doing to you?"

"I look like his daughter. He loved her. He loves *me*." Her back arched and her front hooves clattered on the flagstones as her distress translated itself into equine fear. "He built this house for me. He takes care of me."

"Loves you? He doesn't love you. He's punishing *her*," Lonzo yelled the words because she didn't want to hear him. "He crippled you, do you hear?" His voice was cracking like it hadn't cracked since he was an adolescent, cracking and breaking. "If this Doyle person could do mermaids right, he could do you, too. He *wanted* it, Uncle, he wanted your flaw, your failure. It's all around you—how flawed you are. How much he hates you. Don't you *see* it? *Listen* to me!"

She reared and flung him backward. For a heart-stopping instant, hooves pawed the air above Lonzo's head. How would her horse-muscles interpret grief and rage? His shoulder blades banged the wall and he flattened himself against it, half expecting to die. "Ailene?" he whispered. "Don't."

She dropped onto all fours again, made a sound in her chest that wasn't a sob, wasn't a groan, but twisted him inside. She was trembling, horse and woman, head bowed. "You're wrong," she whispered, face curtained by tangled hair. "He wouldn't do that."

"Will you come with me? Please?"

She was shaking her head, and there were no words to explain. He pulled his flute from the pack. The notes were dark, minor-key, layered with an obbligato of loneliness and old hurt. He edged them with love that could twist into hate, threaded it all with a tiny burnished gleam of hope. Of future. He put his soul into the music, poured it through the flute on that fragile stream of breath, of life. Finally, it ended. He tucked the flute back into his pack, wrung out and empty, because he had nothing left to say.

She lifted her head and looked down at him for one silent moment. "I'll walk with you to the mag-lev stop," she whispered. Her hooves thudded softly on the carpet. "I think . . . that's as far as I can go."

Silently he followed her out onto her terrace. The music was his voice and it hadn't touched her. He had no words to persuade her. Hurt welled up inside him, twisting like a knife in his guts. Was this what they paid for, the men and women who whispered *I love you* to him? For this pain?

"Come on." Ailene looked back over her shoulder, her eyes evading his. "Up this ramp. It comes out on top, and then it's just a short trot to the old station."

Birds circled above his head, more sparrows. He flinched as one of them swooped down to perch on his arm. It clung to his sleeve with its tiny dark claws, staring at him from one mirror-bright eye. Lonzo stared back, frozen, seeing his reflection, tiny and perfect, in that glittering silver eye. And then it took off, fluttering back into the sky to join its mates.

"Ailene?" Cold was filling him like an enveloping onrush of icy water. "Ailene, he's watching everything."

"So?" She whisked her tail, didn't slow.

*I don't take betrayal well. . . .* Renfrew's words fluttered around him like the mechanical sparrows. What had happened to the tall lover who had watched Angelina jump? Lonzo swallowed his fear and ran after her, his legs aching from the climb. The path curved past a huge free-form pool dug into the side of the hill, hanging gardens set among the cliffs, a tennis court. Who used these, Lonzo wondered. Anyone? Or were they simply here as further reminders that Ailene didn't belong in the human world? With one last burst of energy, Lonzo reached the top and stopped to pant.

Meadow up here. Greenhouses. Barn and fenced horses. All black, Lonzo noticed. See yourself, Ailene, don't forget what you *really* are. His stomach knotted with hatred for Renfrew. Gardens and an orchard. More houses—small cottages—but these were square and commonplace. Servants, he thought, looking around. The people who had been so conspicuously absent from the house. They were still absent. The sunny meadow was as empty as a stage before the performance begins. Nobody worked in the garden or the orchard. What play was scheduled here? A tragedy, Lonzo thought, full of dread. As if he had cued them, a dog barked nearby, then another. Ominous deep-throated bays of rage.

Ailene spun, pale and frightened, her skittering hooves throwing clods of earth. "They're attack-trained. When they're loose at night, you can't go outside." She whirled away from him, haunches bunching with her terror.

"Wait!" Lonzo cried, afraid that her horse-reflexes would carry her away in a wild bolt. "Ailene, wait for me!"

She grabbed for his hand, clutched it while her body trembled and danced—and got control, slowly with an effort. "Okay," she gasped, and they ran together across the meadow.

Her gait limped, ugly in this place, Lonzo realized, because he was seeing it with Uncle's eyes. The way she saw it. Dog voices bayed again—ahead of them now, cutting them off. Aileen half-reared, her hand tearing free from his, and spun away from the sound. He shouted her name, but she gave no sign that she'd heard.

They were being herded toward the stream. Sparrows fluttered above their heads, circling and dipping, chirping in shrill mocking voices. Renfrew had been manipulating them all along. It struck Lonzo with sudden clarity, brought him to a stumbling halt. Maybe from the moment she had watched him in the forest. Maybe it wasn't just in death that his daughter had betrayed him. Maybe she hadn't betrayed him in death at all. "Ailene," Lonzo called softly. "Please, stop."

She heard him, struggling with the reflexes that wanted to carry her headlong into flight, and finally halted. In front of them the ground dropped suddenly away into a narrow little gorge. White water tumbled over stones at the bottom, and the sides were steep. Rocky.

You could think of jumping a horse across the gap—if you were desperate.

It wasn't a deep chasm—thirty or forty feet, he guessed. Deep enough if you fell the whole way down onto rock and shallow water. More than deep enough if you fell with six hundred kilos of horse on top of you. This was the place. "Not this way." He grabbed her hand and they ran back the way they'd come.

Ailene gave a soft cry, yanked her hand from his as she half-reared. Three dogs rose out of the tall grass to block their path, black as Ailene's flanks, bigger than any dog Lonzo had ever seen. They carried their heads low, red tongues lolling over white teeth, yellow eyes intent. Renfrew walked up behind them, circled by darting sparrows.

"Stand," he said. As one, the three dogs froze, eyes fixed on their prey.

"Uncle." Ailene's voice was so faint Lonzo could barely hear it.

"It's dinnertime." He walked toward them, leaving the dogs behind. "Lonzo can find his own way to the station. Come back and have dinner with me."

He'd never reach the mag-lev. Lonzo read the verdict in Renfrew's smooth face, and his muscles tensed all at once.

"I told him I'd walk there with him." Ailene stopped trembling. "To make sure he didn't get lost." She lifted her head, her voice strengthening. "I'll come back."

"Will you?" His face was as still and cold as polished marble. "It will be dark."

"How can you even ask?" But her eyes evaded his. "And where would I go?"

"I love you." He spread his hands, palms up. One of the sparrows fluttered down to land on the grass at Ailene's feet. "I'm asking you to come home with me." His voice was soft and his eyes never left her face. "You're the only thing that matters to me. And you love me. You know you love me. Send Lonzo to the station by himself. He doesn't need you."

Ailene flinched.

These words had such an *old* feel. "You said this to Angelina." Lonzo pushed forward. "What was his name? Angelina's lover? Did you kill him?"

"Be quiet." Renfrew didn't look at him, but the dogs bared their teeth.

"I was made to love you." Ailene fixed her eyes on the sparrow at her feet. "Did I ever have a choice?"

"None of us really has a choice in this life. Tell me you don't love me, Ailene." Renfrew's voice was soft as velvet. "You can't do it, can you? Because you do love me. You can't leave me. Where would you go? What would you do?"

"You made her into a monster." Lonzo's voice carried like a shout. "Patrick Doyle didn't steal that DNA, did he? You asked him to create Ailene. To suffer for *her?*"

"Shut up!" Renfrew took a step forward and the dogs snarled. "This is your fault." Renfrew turned his stare on Ailene. "Do you know what he is, your pretty friend?"

"He's a whore." She looked Renfrew in the face. "He told me, Uncle."

"Whore?" Renfrew spat. "He's not even that. I recognize the prototype. He was created to process a person's biochemistry, then sweat the pheromones to match it. He's a sex toy, Ailene, that's all he is. Ask him to show you his ID code. It's tattooed on his body somewhere. He's a *thing.* Not even a human being."

*Not human.* Dizzy, Lonzo shook his head. *Let's go see the doctor,* the woman in white always said. Mother, he cried soundlessly, but the word echoed in a vast emptiness. Maybe the doctor wasn't because *she* was sick. Maybe the doctor had . . . made him. *I love you, we love you,* a thousand voices whispered in his head.

"Not a human being, Uncle?" Ailene's voice was cold and clear as a tolling bell. "You mean he's like me?" She lifted her head, mane and hair blowing back in the evening breeze. "I'm not human either, or did you forget? Did you hate her for dying, or did you hate her for loving someone else? Let me tell you what I dream some nights. I dream I'm her. I dream that the dogs are chasing me, and I ride my mare at the ravine to get away. From you, Father."

"No!" He flinched, face averted. Behind him, the dogs inched forward. "It didn't happen that way," he said hoarsely. "She was always trying dangerous jumps, pulling crazy stunts like that. Showing off for him. It was an accident, *his* fault, and . . . it tore me apart. Because I loved her so much."

Tortured eyes above that smile. Eyes full of love and hate. Lonzo shivered, because he had never seen such dissonance on a human face. He stepped in front of Ailene, a bare meter separating him from Renfrew. "You take her humanity away from her every day in this place. You make her a freak, make sure she knows it. Why?" He met Renfrew's pale eyes. "What happens if you let her be a woman?" he asked softly. "Why was your daughter running from you?"

Renfrew's face went white. With an inarticulate cry, he shoved his hand into his pocket, the dogs snarling and whining behind him. Lonzo caught the glint of light on a gun barrel. For him, or for her? Renfrew had given them the script, but they had lost it and now anything could happen.

*Why did you try to die?* she had asked him, not *Why did you try to kill yourself?* He had waited for the lightning and the lightning had disdained him.

He was through waiting. Lonzo flung himself forward, reaching for the gun, hands clamping around the lumpy unfamiliar shape, cringing with the expectation of sound, pain. Their fingers twined like lovers, his and Renfrew's, and the gun didn't go off. Chest to chest, they panted in each other's face. Renfrew was stronger and bent Lonzo's wrist slowly back, back, until he gasped with the pain. In a few seconds, bones would snap and he would let go.

He had been close to Renfrew on their stroll to his terrace, close enough to smell him, to taste him when he breathed.

Lonzo felt his skin flushing, felt sweat prickle his skin. And Renfrew reacted, fingers relaxing slightly, hesitating for just an instant.

Lonzo wrenched the gun away, pointed it.

A hammerblow slammed his hand aside, and the gun spat, bounced on the grass. Lonzo spun sideways, knocked flat by the force of the blow, then caught a glimpse of Ailene rearing over him, hooves striking down again. He cringed, but they missed him, came down on the gun, smashing it, pounding it into the turf. Then she whirled, her shoulder slamming into Renfrew, knocking him sprawling. Almost in the same motion, she bent and grabbed Lonzo's wrist, yanked him to his feet. "Get on," she yelled, her body shuddering with the need to run.

The dogs howled and leaped forward, foam flying from their jaws.

He scrabbled a leg across her back, almost lost his seat as she whirled. Warm ribs arched beneath his thighs, slick-haired and slippery. He clutched her waist, thrown forward against her back as she lashed out with both heels. A dog yelped. Another buried its teeth in her flank and she screamed, almost unseating him again as she leaped forward.

Bright blood streaked her coat, impossibly red. The dogs were on their heels and there was no place to go but the ravine, a dozen meters ahead. Even now, Renfrew was herding them, Lonzo thought bitterly. He had given his daughter a second chance, and she had repeated her choice.

"Hang on," Ailene yelled, and her voice was raw with fear.

It was all he could do to stay on her back, blinded by her whipping mane, clutching her torso as she thundered forward. She had died here once. Maybe memory really did get passed on in the DNA, maybe she remembered. Falling. Dying. He felt her gather herself, horse and woman, too late to be scared because in a second she would leap. And they would land, or they would fall.

"I love you," he yelled as she hurled herself into the air. The words split him open like the lightning hadn't done. Because they were *truth*, and they had never been true before. He felt her body stretch desperately for that far wall, stretched with her, reaching for safety.

The shock of her landing nearly dislodged him. Arms around her waist, half-off and staring at the ground, he felt her waver, hind legs scrabbling for purchase as rocks and dirt tumbled into the void. She grunted, a deep animal sound of desperation. And then a foot caught, levered them upward in a wild heave that flung Lonzo back onto her equine shoulders.

They'd made it.

She paused for one instant on that brink, looking back over her shoulder, her face full of terrible grief. And then she broke into a rocking canter that carried them into the trees beyond the stream. The dogs' hysterical baying faded as she wove through the forest, ducking branches, never once looking over her shoulder at him.

She didn't stop until she'd broken through the wall of young trees, out onto the mag-lev right-of-way. After the tree shadows, the sun nearly blinded him. She stood still, ribs heaving, horse and human. His knees buckled as he slid from her back and he sat down hard, butt in the dirt. He still had his pack slung over his shoulder. Miracle. He fumbled in it, took out the flute. It was undamaged, gleaming in its velvet wrapping. His hand hurt where her hoof had grazed it, and it was bleeding. He pulled the gloves on anyway and began to play.

The tremble in his fingers came through, making the music tentative and uncertain at first. He played sunlight, leaf-shadow, graced with the counterpoint of dark blowing hair and the rhythm of a syncopated walk, blew loneliness and the ability to give but not receive. He twined light and dark together, played a melody of the human soul—love, hate, and need—carried on the living breath of the flute.

He played love.

His breath was no longer just a stream on which to sail the notes. It came from a place deeper than his lungs, flowed like blood through the flute, blossomed in the music like a living heartbeat. There was no hole. No absence.

After a while he stopped playing. He didn't end the music. He simply stopped playing, laid the flute down on his knees, and bent over it, dizzy and exhausted. The sun had set, he noticed vaguely. Soft twilight turned Ailene's coat to polished onyx. She knelt slowly, awkwardly, so that she was on his level. Took his bruised hand in hers. ''You're crying,'' she said.

''So are you.'' He touched her face. ''What he said about me. . . .''

''It doesn't matter.''

''Yes, it does.'' He rewrapped the flute, stowed it in his pack. It was there—the ID—tattooed in tiny green letters and numbers up high on his inner thigh, where only a lover would see it. He had always wondered why it was there. Maybe the woman in white was a technician with the compassion to love a creation. "What does it mean to be human?" he asked softly. "You need a bandage for your hand." She stroked the darkening flesh gently. "I don't even know what it means to be me."

"You can find out now."

"He's right. I can't leave. What would I do?" She looked down at her equine chest, touched the shiny black hair, the big-boned legs folded beneath her. "Where would I go?"

"Anywhere we want." Lonzo closed his bruised hand around hers, wouldn't let go. "We can get you a flute, play the shacktowns. People are going to love me whether I want them to or not. They'll take care of us because of that. They're going to pay money to look at you, want to put kids on you for a ride."

"That sounds like whoring." She drew back a little.

"Your . . . Renfrew said I wasn't even that." He wouldn't let her look away. "We are what we are. We can't change that. But we can go find out what it means—to be us."

"Us." Her fingers twitched in his. "I couldn't let you kill him," she said softly. "He created me to love him and . . . I do." Sadness filled her eyes like early nightfall. "Even now. I can't help it." She lurched to her feet, ungainly and equine.

"You're hurt." He touched the torn skin, the crusted blood. "We need to wash it. In the stream maybe." He got to his feet, leaned against her shoulder, hard muscle beneath his shoulder, warmth and slick hair, and the pungent smell of her sweat. "We can't keep from doing what we were created to do," he said softly.

"He won't bother us." She looked away and sighed. "I found some . . . transactions that he would not like people to know about. I hid them in the Net. I'll E-mail him and tell him that I have them. That I won't use them if he leaves us alone."

"You've thought about leaving him before."

"I did. I couldn't do it." She looked away.

Lonzo shouldered his pack. "Want to walk for a while after we take care of your leg?" He nodded at the waxing moon rising over the eastern horizon. "There'll be enough light if we stick to the mag-lev track."

"You can ride." She sounded shy. "You aren't very heavy, and my leg's fine." She looked away. "A part of me wants to stay with Uncle. It would be safer."

*I love you*, the voices whispered from his pack. They would always be as close as weakness. "Safer, yeah." He sighed. Then he put an arm around her waist and scrambled awkwardly onto her back. The warm arch of ribs between his legs evoked his dream, but the warmth inside him didn't have much to do with lust. Besides, the architecture was wrong for an erection. He laughed.

"What's so funny?"

"I have fallen in love with a mare," he said. "This is not normal."

"No." Her sigh pushed against his knees. "You know, I guess we're both monsters if we let ourselves be."

What divides human from not-human? Who gets to fence that perimeter? It occurred to Lonzo that she didn't react to him like most people did. Maybe his biochemistry couldn't handle her pheromones. So if she loved him—if it happened—it would be real. He took out his flute, blew the sound of their leaving— the promise of tomorrow's sunrise in bright woodwinds, of rain in muted oboes—played the warmth of her ribs between his thighs and the warmth of his love.

And it worked.

# ECOND CHANCE

Something was wrong at Marsbase Down.

Reba peered through the thick glass as the pilot swung them out across the Ross Ice Shelf. An accident, Scutino had said. They needed a doctor, pronto. Hard white light swallowed the ugly sprawl of McMurdo base as the helo bounced in the wind.

*Heelo*, not chopper. Not down here. Antarctica enforced its own language: ice-blink sky, helo, brash ice, and bergy bits. Cold trickled down Reba's collar. Suddenly, there was nothing beyond the thick glass except white. Snow raced through the air in straight lines like a hail of bullets, obscuring the coast of Victoria Land.

Antarctica enforced its own rules. Planes crashed, men and women dropped through the ice with their 'dozers and Trak-Masters. Antarctica didn't give second chances.

White sky, white ice. The engine roared and the wind roared. Reba's shoulder banged the thick glass of the port as the helo lurched and bucked. Li had believed in second chances, but Reba had always known better. She gasped as the helo dropped out from under her. The straps jerked her downward with the seat, but her stomach remained behind, somewhere above her. She swallowed, cotton-mouthed. She was damned if she was going to lose it in front of this Navy kid. The helo bucked again, bounced like a ball by the wind.

How many planes and helos littered the ice with their steel bones? Reba stared into the whiteness, feeling nothing but a numb sort of peace. If you stayed down here long enough, the cold arid wind sucked you dry. Memories and emotions blew away like dead leaves.

Outside, the white land had turned brown, as if an invisible hand had peeled the icy skin back from the stony ribs of the continent. The ground was a jumble of black basalt, dolerite, and granite, streaked with brown, gold, and gray, carved into fantastic ripples and curls by the howling wind.

These were the dry valleys, shielded from the snow for a thousand years by a trick of the winds. Marsbase was rising up to meet her, looking like a bunch of pop cans left carelessly on the dry floor of Wright Valley. The helo bounced, then skipped sideways in the wind.

"Easy down," yelled the pilot. "Six inches to your toes."

The rotors had slowed to a rumbling *wheep-wheep* as the kid reached back to unlatch the door. Reba had already shoved it open, admitting a blast of frigid air.

"Nothin' scares you, does it, Dr. Scott?" The pilot's hazel eyes glinted as he grinned at her, and his breath misted in the air.

He looked nineteen—twenty, tops. "You were driving, weren't you?" Reba gave him a thin smile as she swung down with her pack.

The cold hit her, hard and alien as vacuum. Her nostrils stung. There was no smell to Antarctic wind, only cold. Nothing but cold.

"Dr. Scott." A helmeted silvery figure waved. The voice sounded tinny and artificial, blaring from the speaker grid on the chest of his suit. "I'm Commander Ganfield."

Behind Reba, the helo's rotors thundered, drowning his words. Reba looked over her shoulder in astonishment. "He's heading back in *this?*" she shouted.

"The weather at McMurdo isn't that bad yet."

He sounded defensive. Or was that just distortion from the suit's speaker? Reba pressed her lips together, saying a small prayer that the Navy kid made it back. The wind whipped stinging sand and ice crystals into her face. Reba shouldered her pack, ignoring the commander's offer of assistance, and followed him back across the dry rocky ground.

They stopped in front of a round door jutting from one of the base's connected tubes. Reba watched the door iris smoothly open. Pretty neat trick to move at all, in this cold. She felt mildly impressed. Inside, orange-and-yellow suits hung on the walls of a small room like shed skins. The door irised closed behind them, cutting off the wind's howl. "So what happened?" Reba pulled off her bearpaw mittens and threw back her hood, ears ringing in the quiet.

"There was an icefall," Ganfield said tightly. "We lost three crew members in all—including both our medical people."

Reba blinked as Commander Ganfield lifted off his helmet. The tinted glass and his faintly New York accent hadn't suggested the stark African profile that the helmet had concealed.

"I'm sorry," she said, but she felt little shock. The only coin Antarctica accepted was life. "Dr. Scutino couldn't tell much." He'd been almost . . . evasive. Reba stripped off her balaclava mask and combed her fingers through her short gray hair. "How bad are the injuries?"

"We've got a severe case of frostbite." Ganfield looked at her from the corners of his eyes.

"Frostbite?" Reba stared at him, her mask dangling from her fingers. "Why the hell didn't you send him back to McMurdo?" Outrage pulled her voice up half an octave. "I'm the only doctor at the base until Brenner gets back."

"I couldn't send *her* off the base." Ganfield's voice was flat and final. "Why don't you come take a look at Sara, and we can discuss the whys later?"

Another self-centered NASA prick. Reba pressed her lips together. The airlock and the pressure suits made her uncomfortable. They gave the scene an eerie alien quality, as if this *was* Mars and not just a training simulation. "Show me my patient," she snapped.

She followed the commander's brisk stride down the tunnel-like corridor. Storage lockers and numbered doors lined the pastel yellow walls. The occasional narrow port had been screened with black to dim the numbing Antarctic light. It seeped in anyway, prying through tiny holes and tears, harsh and irritating. This base's sibling was already swinging toward a landing on the cold dead soil of Isidis Planitia.

Reba shivered, found herself breathing quickly, as if the warm air was too thin. The base reminded Reba of her one visit to Robert Scott's old ice tunnels. The abandoned living spaces had been frightening, squashed and warped by the slow weight of the ice. Here, it was the weight of technology that pressed in on Reba.

The infirmary looked familiar and reassuring. It was tiny, crammed with lockers and neatly bracketed equipment. An X-ray machine jutted from the wall at one end of the narrow exam table that could double for surgery. State of the art, Reba thought sourly, not like her haphazard clinic. In the dark stormy winter, McMurdo was as far from Christchurch airfield as Mars, but Antarctica was just another place on Earth. Mars was an alien world. It was all a matter of perspective.

"In here." Commander Ganfield was beckoning her from a doorway. "This is Sara Shen," he murmured as Reba walked past him.

The isolation room was a narrow chamber, with two double bunks on one side, a built-in desk on the other, and a sink/toilet combination at the end. A small masked port leaked hard light into the room. The woman on the bunk was small. She lay flat on her back, breathing slowly and regularly. Makeshift restraints, fashioned from towels, immobilized her arms and legs. The woman's hands and feet were hidden by tents of fabric.

"Hello, Sara." Ganfield cleared his throat. "Dr. Scott's here from McMurdo to see you."

"Hi." The word had the flat gloss of sedation.

The woman turned her head on the pillow, and Reba felt the air in her lungs congeal. She looked like Li. "Hello, Sara," Reba managed.

Asian-American and muscular, Li had always joked about being peasant stock. Reba swallowed, struggling to breathe again. Sara looked like Li had at twenty-two—the year they had moved into the crummy basement apartment together, Reba's second year of med school.

"Are you feeling any pain?" Reba groped for her clinical composure as she lifted the drape from one of the woman's hands.

"No."

Reba nodded. Dead tissue didn't hurt, and the woman was obviously heavily sedated. She frowned at the purplish, grossly swollen fingers. Yellowish serum seeped from deep cracks in the back of Sara's hands, and Reba smelled the telltale sweetish odor of infection. The sloughing tissues had been damaged, and bacteria had invaded. Sara's feet were worse. Reba glanced at the woman's slack dreaming face and jerked her chin at Ganfield.

"Who has been treating this woman?" she snapped when he had followed her into the exam room.

"I have." Ganfield's face was stiff. "We all have some basic medical training."

"Is this your idea of care? Shoot her full of dope and leave her by herself? What's she been doing, walking around?" Reba reined in her anger with an effort. "Why didn't you send her to McMurdo right away?"

"Orders." Ganfield's face looked hard as carved mahogany. "Yes, she got up. She's been . . . irrational at times." His lips thinned. "I've been staying with her. I only left to meet you."

Something gleamed in his eyes—worry? Worry about Sara or about the Marsbase program? "I want a helo." Reba leaned against the hard edge of the exam table. "The minute the weather breaks, I'm taking her back to McMurdo."

"You can't." Ganfield crossed his arms. "Marsbase has been closed for security reasons. Dr. Scutino knows."

Closed? Reba stared into his impassive face, her rising anger tumbling the words in her brain. "Bullshit," she managed. "I don't take orders from NASA. I'm a private contractor for the National Science Foundation. . . ." She bit off the rest of her words as Ganfield shook his head.

"It's a matter of national security." He shrugged, looking tired. "Take good care of Sara, please."

"I may be angry at you, but I don't take out my feelings on my patients."

"I didn't think you did."

"National security?" Reba loaded her words with scorn. "So what illegal military stunt have we tried to pull behind the backs of the treaty nations this time?"

"Nothing like that. I'll make sure that one of the crew is always available if you need help," Ganfield said coldly. "Let me know if you need anything."

"I need a helo back to McMurdo," Reba growled, but he pretended he hadn't heard her.

She glared as he stalked through the door. Damn these military games, anyway. Reba took an IV bag of normal saline from one of the lockers. The US resented the treaty and all its restrictions on military operations. Scowling, she injected an amp of ceftizoxime into the bag. Someone had played fast and loose with the rules, and now Sara was caught in the middle.

Reba inverted the bag to disperse the antibiotic. The infection was probably staph, but it was well established. The broad-spectrum antibiotic was a good start until she could get a culture and sensitivity run. She smoothed the anger from her face as she reentered the isolation room. "I want to start an IV." She hung the bag above the bunk with a reassuring smile.

"Okay." Sara's eyelids fluttered. "Dr. Scott, right?" she asked uncertainly.

"That's right." Reba brushed a wisp of black hair back from the woman's face, flinched at her automatic gesture.

*Sara*, not Li. Li was dead.

"First I need a quick sample. It won't hurt."

"I don't feel anything." Sara watched listlessly as Reba cracked a sterile culture vial and swabbed the oozing infection in Sara's hands and feet.

Li had died in just such a bed, plugged into the useless IVs, a shriveled, wasted husk. Drop it. Reba bit her lip, thumbed the clamp, and watched the antibiotic-laden saline flow down the tube. "A little prick, now . . ." She drew three tubes of blood, inserted a catheter into a forearm vein, plugged in the IV, and taped the tubing into place.

"It hurt while it was thawing, but not now." Sara watched the colorless fluid drip from the bag. "That means the tissue's dead, doesn't it?"

"Some of it, yes." Reba adjusted the slow drip of the fluid, hearing the fear in Sara's voice. "We'll find out how much as we go along."

"Could I have some juice, please?" Sara's voice was dull with the drug and her struggle with fear. She stared at the ceiling.

"Sure." Reba knew that look—had seen it too many times. "Coming up."

The automated lab swallowed the culture vials and blood tubes with a silvery chime, and Reba found a plastic jug of juice in the exam room's refrigerator.

"Apple juice okay?" She slid an arm beneath Sara's head, supporting her so that she could sip comfortably from a straw. "Wait a minute." She put the cup down and released the restraints. "Try not to move around," she told her.

"Thank you. I keep thinking I can use my hands." Sara's voice trembled. "Will you promise me something?" She looked into Reba's face with Li's dark eyes. "Will you tell me the truth when I ask questions? That's the only way I can stand it."

Li would have said something like that. Reba felt dizzy. Li had been so competent, so much in control on the surface. It was only at the end that she had run out of strength.

"I promise," she said softly.

"Thank you." Sara closed her eyes briefly, some of the tension draining from her face. "I'm going to lose my feet and my hands, aren't I?"

"Parts of them, I'm afraid." I promised to tell her the truth. Reba chose her words carefully. "They're getting some very exciting regeneration with embryonic growth hormone."

"I'll never go to Mars."

It wasn't a question, so Reba didn't answer.

"I wanted so much. . . ." Sara swallowed, tears gathering at the corners of her eyes. "It really *was* an icefall that . . . killed Angela and the others, wasn't it?"

"That's what Commander Ganfield told me."

"I'm glad it wasn't the sphere."

Sphere? Reba looked sharply at Sara, but the woman's eyelids were drooping.

"I dream about it and it scares me," Sara murmured. "Funny, to be scared of something that fell out of space maybe a million years ago. Funny that we found something like that right here on Earth." Her face twitched, as if she was in pain. "It's so ironic," she whispered. "Angela didn't expect to die down here. Now, neither of us will ever walk on Mars." A tear slid down the side of her face. "I dream that I remember the sphere, and I'm afraid. . . ."

A sphere from space? Reba felt a chill surprise. So *that* was it. "Don't be afraid." Reba wiped the side of Sara's face gently. "Dreams are just illusions," she murmured. Even the ones that you thought were your future. Even those dreams were illusions.

"I found it, you know." Sara looked at Reba with Li's haunting eyes. "I dreamed about the place it was buried, and there it was."

"You're under sedation and reacting to a bad infection right now." Reba made her voice light. "A lot of things will look different in a few hours. I'm going to take you off the sedative."

"Will you open the shade?" Sara moved her head restlessly on the pillow. "I want to look outside."

Reba twitched the dark screen aside, blinking in the harsh flood of light.

"I can almost pretend that we're on Mars," Sara murmured. "It's so alien. I don't belong here."

None of them belonged here. Even the Weddell seals and the penguins clung to the edge of the sea. The frozen empty land glared through the thick glass. Loneliness. Reba shivered. Antarctica was a vast tract of absolute loneliness. She wanted to clutch Sara and huddle against the far wall, cornered by the freezing isolation outside. Reba let the shade fall back into place. You felt that way down here—back to back against the light and cold, forced into a sense of closeness that didn't really exist.

"Will you stay with me?" Sara's voice was husky. "I don't want to be alone."

Li's eyes. Reba swallowed, wishing she had never come, cursing Ganfield and Scutino. "Yes," she said.

REBA PUTTERED around the small spaces of exam room and isolation, watching the harsh, lonely light seep through the screen. A sphere. A sphere that had fallen to Earth had trapped her here with Li's ghost. Reba shivered.

I don't believe in ghosts, she told herself sharply. Sara was no ghost and she wasn't Li, but the desiccated memories hadn't blown away after all. Here, in the warm protected microcosm of Marsbase, they were rehydrating. For nineteen years, she and Li had shared their lives.

I don't want to remember. Reba watched the crew trainees trickle in to visit Sara, singly and in pairs, diffident and full of falsely cheerful words. They knew that Sara was effectively washed out—one less candidate for space on that distant sibling base.

Some would be truly sorry, some would be secretly pleased. Reba watched them come in and leave, young faces, immediate and full of themselves. So sure of life. She felt acutely conscious of her gray hair. It would be sticking out in spikes, dry and brittle from the cold.

She didn't ask them about the sphere. She noticed the sideways looks they gave her, wary and aware. They had had their orders. She pretended to be busy with notes. The trickle of visitors paused, and Sara dozed. Asleep, she didn't look so much like Li. Her face was rounder, broader. Reba stretched, feeling the tension-ache in her muscles. She needed to start anticoagulants before Sara threw a clot to her lungs and she'd have to set up a physical therapy regimen.

"Who are you?"

It was Sara's voice and . . . it wasn't. Reba turned, hiding surprise behind a bland neutrality. "I'm Dr. Scott. From McMurdo base, remember?" Disorientation?

The drugged glaze was gone from Sara's face. She looked . . . different, as if she'd put on a mask of her own face. Reba frowned. "How are you feeling?" she asked easily.

"Not good." Sara looked at the dangling IV bag. "How long will I have to stay in bed like this?"

"Until the dead tissue has finished sloughing away." Reba swiveled the plastic chair around to face the bed. It was an awkward maneuver in the narrow space, but it gave her time to collect her thoughts. Something seemed wrong—disturbing—as if Sara's face was subtly deformed.

"Weeks." Sara moved restlessly. "That's too long."

"We'll try to keep you entertained." Reba made her voice reassuring, but Sara wasn't asking for reassurance.

"What happens if I *do* get up?"

"Infection. More damage." She met Sara's cold evaluating stare. "You've already tried it."

Fear, Reba thought. She isn't afraid. That's what's missing. Sara Shen's face had a hard gloss that reminded Reba of the ice-covered landscape of Antarctica itself. Everyone had fears—fear of the darkness, fear of spiders or thunder. Fear of death.

Not Sara. Its absence glared like white light on ice. That made her insane, or a potential hero. She doesn't look like Li at all, Reba thought, and felt a tiny chill. What the hell is going on? Some kind of major personality disintegration?

Sara raised her head, eyes on the masked port. "As soon as the weather clears, they'll dig it up and fly it out." She was murmuring to herself, as if she'd forgotten Reba's presence.

"They'll dig what up, Sara?"

Sara closed her eyes, pretending sleep or unconsciousness, but her taut facial muscles gave her away. I'm seeing desperation, Reba thought suddenly. She's not afraid, but she's desperate. It was a cold, calculating desperation.

Why?

"Excuse me." A redheaded man appeared in the door. His short-cropped hair was almost the same color as his orange coveralls. "I'm supposed to report to you. I'm Jerry." His eyes looked past Reba to Sara's still form. "How is she?" he asked in a low hesitant voice.

"As well as can be expected." Reba stood suddenly. "She's trying to sleep," she lied. "If she wakes up, keep her quiet and flat. Where can I find Commander Ganfield?"

Jerry blinked at her brusque tone and told her.

"Thanks," Reba said. It was time for some answers.

"I WAS GOING to come by." Ganfield sounded as defensive as he had when she'd protested the helo's departure. "How's Sara?"

"Good question." Reba looked around at the cramped space of the commander's private quarters. It was cluttered with manuals and sheafs of hardcopy reports. "Why didn't you tell me that Sara was having some kind of mental or emotional crisis?" The port was unshaded, and the bright pitiless light drained the color from everything in the room.

"I mentioned that she had been irrational." Ganfield didn't meet her eyes. "What did she say?"

"She can't stay here," Reba said bluntly. She traced the harsh lines of the commander's face. He was holding something back. "What the hell did you find, and how does it relate to Sara?"

"We found a . . . meteorite."

"My God." Reba's voice crackled with anger. "You fall all over meteorites in the Allan Hills."

"All right. It's an alien artifact." Ganfield's chair scraped loudly as he stood. "Do you understand me? We found a piece of technology that I can't even make a guess at understanding. Is that important enough for you?"

He was shouting. Reba took a half step backward, a prickle of unease creeping down her spine. Technology? Again, the sense of *alien* assailed her. Spaceships in the frozen dust of Wright Valley? Reba looked out the port, half expecting to see the cold, red sands of Mars.

"We're such fragile beings," Ganfield said softly. He was looking out the port, too, staring at the dun piles of frozen rock and dirt from the subsurface base that the crews were excavating. "Sara found it while she, Allan, and Kelly were on a mapping expedition at the foot of the Meserve Glacier. The ice shelf came down on them just after they reported." The whites of his eyes gleamed as he swiveled to face her. "Angela was on the rescue team. She got careless and brought down more ice."

He was afraid. Reba had seen fear too often to mistake it. She rubbed her eyes, head aching from the hard light. "What are you getting at?" she asked heavily. "Why did you drag me out here when you could have consulted me on Sara's condition over the radio?"

"I want to know what's wrong with Sara." Ganfield folded the screen back across the port, dimming the numbing light. "I want you to tell me."

"I'm not a psychiatrist," Reba said softly. "Sorry."

He didn't say a word as she walked out of the room.

SHE DISMISSED the redheaded Jerry when she returned to the
infirmary. He wanted to ask her if Sara was going to lose her
hands. Reba could see the question in his eyes, but it reminded
her too much of Ganfield's hints and she didn't help him. He
finally left, taking the question that he was afraid to ask with
him.

Sara turned Li's eyes on Reba. They were normal eyes, full
of normal fear, held under tight control.

"Thank you for not leaving me alone," she said. "I don't
want to be alone."

"You shouldn't *be* alone." Reba sat down on the plastic
chair, feeling tired and out of her depth.

"I've wanted to go to the stars—ever since I can remember.
That's all I ever wanted to do." Sara rolled her head restlessly
on the pillow. "Now I wish that I'd never joined the program.
Why did you come down to this dead land?" She turned fierce
eyes on Reba. "Why do you stay?"

Everyone asked that question of everyone else, down here.
*Why did you come?*

The usual, casual answers died on Reba's lips. "I don't
know," she said slowly. "Maybe because it *is* so alien here."
Human loneliness and grief were so insignificant, measured
against the Antarctic landscape.

"Will you touch me? I can't feel anything—sometimes I think
I'm going to float away or just dissolve."

"It's all right," Reba murmured to the fear in Sara's voice.
She reached over to stroke the hair back from her face. Amazingly, her fingers didn't tremble.

*Hold my hand,* Li had pleaded. *Don't let me die, Reba. Please . . .*

Oh God, why are You doing this to me?

A lanky blonde woman brought in two trays of dinner and
offered to stay for the night, if Reba wanted the privacy of the
second isolation room. Reba thanked her but refused, not sure
why she did so. She coaxed Sara to eat, although she herself
wasn't hungry.

"I'm a light sleeper," she told Sara as she spooned up apple-
sauce for her. "You can call me if you need anything—even if
you just need some company."

"Thank you." Sara was staring at the splinters of light coming in through the screen. "I don't want any more visitors. They think I'm crazy. You can see it in their eyes."

"They think you're imagining things." Reba sat on the edge of the bunk, careful not to disturb Sara's tented limbs.

"Am I?" Sara murmured. "How did I know where to find the sphere? Why do I think that I remember it?" She shivered. "I have such strange dreams."

"Tell me about them." Reba combed a tangle out of Sara's short hair with her fingers.

"I can't. I . . . just see them. There aren't any words that fit." Sara's voice trembled. "Sometimes, I'm not even sure who I am."

She was fighting the fear hard. "Easy. Take it easy." Reba stroked her forehead. Touch was important in a sensory deprivation case like this, she assured herself, but her fingers wanted to remember Li and that scared her. This wasn't Li. She stood up abruptly. "Call me if you have any dreams."

"I will."

Sara sank into sleep easily, like someone sinking into deep water. Like someone sinking into death. For a moment, Reba was seized with an irrational urge to shake her, yell at her; wake her up.

Stop it. Reba got ready for bed, telling herself that she was tired, if not sleepy. That was the truth. The base pressed its alien walls around her, rubbing the edges of her mind raw. Reba closed her eyes against the light from the port, missing darkness with a sudden painful intensity. The sun never set in the hospital, either. You were so sure you would get a second chance, Li. It had taken her such a long, long time to die.

Reba finally fell asleep and dreamed of Li, laughing as she played with their dog, Oso. She threw the ball and Oso brought it back in her mouth, slobbering all over it, as always. Li bent to pick it up. When she straightened, Reba saw that it wasn't Li at all. It was Sara, and her hands were swollen and black with frostbite.

Reba woke up, her face wet with tears. She hadn't dreamed about Li in a long time. The room was full of dim light from the port, and her ears rang with the echo of Oso's frenzied barking. Reba groped for her digital clock, remembering belatedly that she was in an isolation bed in Marsbase.

Her watch said three-ten. She lifted her head to check on Sara and froze. Sara was sitting on the edge of her bunk. The disconnected IV tube leaked fluid onto the sheet.

"What are you doing?" Reba swung her feet over the side of her own bunk.

"Go back to sleep." Sara looked over her shoulder. "No one will ever know you waked up."

Those desperate eyes again. "I'd know." Reba stood. "You can't walk." She kept her voice calm and reasonable. "If you put any weight on your feet, you're going to do a lot of damage." She edged closer. "Just lie down," she soothed, sweating.

"Let me go, damn it!" Sara lunged forward.

She cried out hoarsely as Reba caught her around the chest, struggling briefly as Reba forced her back onto the bed. Her hands and feet were so much useless weight. With a strangled sob, she went limp, letting Reba ease her back onto the mattress.

"Easy now. That's right." Crooning softly, panting a little, Reba refastened the towel restraints. Close call, very close. She felt shaken as she untangled the sheets and sat down on the edge of the bunk. "Where were you going?" she asked as gently as she could.

Sara looked up at her with bleak eyes. "What if I told you that I'm in prison? That I've been a prisoner for longer than you could imagine, and that the gate is out there? It's just out of reach."

They were desperate eyes, but they were cold. Utterly without fear. "I don't know what to say." Reba shivered as if the port had just dissolved, admitting the freezing wind. "Why do you think you're in prison?" I'm no psychiatrist, damn it. Reba took another IV bag from the locker, trying to think. Multiple personality? Paranoid delusions? She'd looked at Sara's health record. NASA psychologists had been breathing down her neck for years. She wouldn't have made it this far if there had been any hint of instability.

She didn't look like Li at all.

She didn't look like Sara, either.

"Don't play games with me, please." She stared up at the ceiling. "I have to reach the . . . sphere."

She had been groping for another word. "You can't go," Reba said gently.

"Not without your help." She looked at Reba briefly, turned her eyes back on the featureless curve of the ceiling. "The commander wouldn't believe me." She moved restlessly on the narrow bunk. "You can't move physical objects faster than the speed of light, you know. Only the . . . soul can cross the universe. That's how I got here.''

Reba stared at her, silent. The walls pressed in around them, and outside, alien sand lapped at the base. This was the Wright Valley, she told herself sternly. They were a short hop from McMurdo, a few hours' flight from New Zealand.

"Accidents happen." Sara's voice dropped to a whisper. "Can you even begin to imagine what it would be like, to be trapped among alien creatures for a million years? You go crazy, after a while. You forget who you really are."

Dear God. Reba hung the bag on its hook, feeling tired, old, inadequate to deal with this. The woman's body was tight as a spring. Mechanically, Reba filled a syringe. "This will help you relax," she said.

"Drugs, again? You'll keep me strapped down here until it's gone and I'll never get back." Her voice rose. "How long before I forget forever?" She winced as the needle slid into her arm, fixing her desperate fearless eyes on Reba's face. "I thought you'd listen to me," she whispered.

COMMANDER GANFIELD came by the infirmary at seven-thirty. "How's Sara doing?" He looked as if he hadn't slept, either. "I'm sorry to bother you so early." He studied Reba's face and frowned. "Will you come have breakfast with me?" he asked quietly.

She needed to get away from the infirmary. Anywhere would do. "Let me check on Sara." Reba looked into the isolation cubicle. Sara's face was still turned to the wall. "I want someone to stay with her while I'm gone," she said, feeling fatigue like a core of ice in her bones.

"I'll call someone," Ganfield said.

The lanky woman who had delivered dinner arrived, and Reba instructed her not to leave the infirmary for any reason. Ganfield led her down the connecting tunnels of the base, past the small common room. Voices and coffee wafted through the door.

Suddenly, Reba wanted a cup of coffee more than anything in the world.

"We'll eat in my quarters, if you don't mind." Ganfield sounded hesitant, as if he expected her to refuse.

Official isolation? Reba nodded, too tired to argue. She didn't want to talk about Sara's delusions in front of a crowd, anyway.

The cramped room looked unfamiliar this morning. Had it

only been a few hours ago that she was here? Reba rubbed her eyes as Ganfield poured coffee from a thermal carafe. Her eyelids felt puffy from lack of sleep. She picked up her mug and sipped, welcoming the scalding heat.

"What happened last night?" Ganfield asked carefully. He offered her a plate of small dense muffins, took one himself.

"What makes you think something happened?" Reba snapped.

"Your face." Ganfield leaned forward, his untouched coffee steaming in front of him.

"Sara tried to get out of bed." Reba crumbled her muffin between her fingers. "She got . . . upset. I'm no psychiatrist, damn it. Why do you want me to paste a label on her?" Tired as she was, she was losing hold on her temper. "What the hell are you trying to cover up?" she snarled.

Ganfield flinched and his face tightened. "Maybe I deserve that." He looked down at his coffee, as if some kind of answer might be floating on the surface. "Angela and Sara were close. Too close, maybe. I shouldn't have let Angela go out with the rescue party," he said quietly. "I knew better." His voice shook.

Reba studied the harsh lines of his profile, her anger dying as suddenly as it had risen. He had made a mistake, and Angela had paid for it. Had she been too frantic for a friend's safety to be cautious?

You didn't get second chances, down here.

Reba frowned at the untidy pile of crumbs in front of her. There were no pictures, few personal mementos at all in the cramped room. What did Mars mean to him? "I'd better get back." She stood.

"Do you have any idea what's troubling Sara?"

"No." Reba looked down into his drawn guilt-stricken face. "No, I don't."

"I'VE BEEN dreaming," Sara said when Reba returned to the infirmary. "I dreamed I got up and walked in the snow. My nose itches."

Reba scratched it for her. Sara's eyes resembled Li's again.

"Did I get up?" Sara lifted her head to look down the sheeted mound of her body. "I can't, can I? God, the dreams are getting worse." Her words were slurred with tears, and she let her head drop back on the pillow.

"You didn't get up." Reba sat beside the bed, feeling cold inside. "It's all right, Sara." The words sounded so false, so useless and inane.

"I don't think it's all right. Nothing has been all right since I found that . . . thing. I keep thinking that I know what it is—that I've been looking for it all my life, but now that I've found it, I'm going to die."

"Stop it!"

Sara turned startled eyes on Reba.

"You're injured." Reba drew a long breath. "You're lying there wondering how crippled you are going to be—whether you realize it or not. You're blaming yourself for Angela's death," she said brutally. "You're in a state of borderline sensory deprivation, and I've shot you full of drugs to keep you quiet. You're lucky you can tell up from down, right now."

Tears glistened at the corners of Sara's eyes. "I hope you're right," she whispered. "I wanted to go to the stars so much. I used to climb onto the roof of our house after my parents were asleep and pick out the constellations. My uncle gave me a telescope for my birthday and. . . ." Her face went pale.

"What is it?" Reba leaned closer. "Sara? What's wrong?"

"I can't remember his name," she whispered. "It's gone. I keep trying to remember things, and they're just not there."

"It's the drugs." Reba caught Sara's face between her palms, wanting to shake her. "Listen to me, Sara. Look at me. It's all right."

"No, it isn't. My uncle's name, my dog—did I have a dog?—sixth grade—they're all gone forever. Forever."

*I can't remember,* Li had cried at the end. She had clung to Reba, as if Reba could save her. *Help me,* she had pleaded.

"Help me," Sara whispered. "Please."

"I will." Reba leaned across the bed, wrapping her arms around Sara. "I'll help you," she murmured to Li's terrified eyes. "I promise." The words caught in her throat. Oh God, I can't take this. Not again.

Slowly, Sara's trembling eased and her breathing deepened. Reba felt the change, straightened slowly, dread gathering in her chest.

"It's hard to fight the drugs. I get lost." The fearless eyes looked weary and full of pain. "Have they taken it away yet?"

"No. Stop it," Reba whispered.

She'll end up in therapy, she told herself. Some psychiatrist will unravel all the loose ends you can't see, and eventually she'll be whole again. Don't let yourself get dragged into this.

She was losing her objectivity. Reba closed her eyes briefly. No, she had lost it already—when she had first looked at Sara Shen and seen Li's face. Just keep her in bed and get the hell out of here as soon as you can, she told herself fiercely. Reba opened her eyes. "Why do you want this . . . sphere?" Her voice grated like gravel.

"It's the pattern. It's escape." Her black eyes burned. "I thought it was lost, but it wasn't. All this time, all these centuries, all these lives, these bodies and minds, it's been right here. I think I felt it a long time ago, but I'd forgotten how to understand. You have to let me go. Please . . ."

Reba started to put a hand on her shoulder, but her fingers flinched away on their own. I can't think of her as Sara, Reba realized with a touch of panic. I have to tell Ganfield that I'm too involved. Someone else has to deal with her. "What will happen if you reach the sphere?" she heard herself asking.

"I'll know the way back." She was panting, flushed, and sweaty. "I'll remember how to be free."

"What will happen to Sara?" Reba whispered.

"Sara?" The woman on the bunk frowned up at her. "I . . . am Sara."

Reba shook her head, unable to put her question into words.

"I was born in this body." Her voice trembled. "How else can you understand another race, except to *be* it for a while. You want to think that I'm insane." Her laugh was sad. "I *am* insane. I've lived here so long, for so many lifetimes, in so many forms, that I got lost a long time ago. I forgot who I was. But there is only me, and now I'm starting to remember." Her eyes sought Reba's. "I am the only . . . soul in this body."

"You are Sara Elaine Shen, born of Eloise Gilbert and Cheng Shen in Columbus, Ohio," Reba said harshly. "You are suffering from some kind of psychotic delusion." She got unsteadily to her feet.

"You believe me. Part of you does." Sara lay still, her eyes on Reba's face. "Do you have any idea of what it's like? To be utterly alone?"

Yes, Reba thought dizzily. Yes, I do. She looked into those black alien eyes and saw the reflection of her own face, tiny and perfect. "I don't believe you." She stumbled as she crossed the room.

"Don't." She twisted on the bed, watching Reba fill the syringe. "I'm Sara. You'll drown me for a while, but I'll still be here. I'll still be alone. For how much longer?"

Her voice had the sound of the Antarctic wind, desolate,

filled with the echo of empty spaces. Reba jabbed the needle into her arm, suppressing her pang of conscience. I have to have some peace, she told herself. I can't listen to this.

"What if I forget? What if I never find the way back?" Sara's eyes were glazing as the sedative took effect. "Please let me go," she murmured. "I don't want to be alone anymore."

Reba summoned the trainee listed on Ganfield's schedule. It turned out to be the redheaded Jerry. "Stay in the room with her," she instructed tightly. "I have to talk to the commander." He had to let her go back to McMurdo *now*. Today.

"Sure." Jerry gave her a tentative smile. "Did you hear? The weather eased over at McMurdo. We're supposed to get a couple of helos in here, tomorrow."

It wasn't hard to read between the lines of Jerry's carefully edited report. The experts were on their way, ready to scoop up the precious artifact and spirit it away before the treaty nations got wind of it.

After that, it would be over. She would go back to McMurdo. They'd fly Sara out—to some military hospital for psychiatric care. Everything would be back to normal in a few days. Or would it? Reba blinked, realizing that she was standing in front of the open infirmary door, staring out into the empty corridor.

She stepped back, and the door closed. "I changed my mind. I'm going to get some sleep," she said out loud. "I was up all night."

"Sure." Jerry looked up briefly from his paperback novel.

The empty isolation room had the indefinable unused smell of a new car, but she needed some privacy. Reba closed the door behind her, blinking in the bright light that filled the room.

*The commander didn't believe me,* Sara had said. What if he had? He was afraid. Afraid of what?

My God, am I starting to believe this craziness? The black fabric panel lay on the floor. Either no one had bothered to put it up, or it had fallen down. Reba crossed to the port and looked out, squinting against the light. She could see the tips of the Apocalypse Peaks, like white teeth above the brown desolation of the arid valley floor.

Four years ago, a single graduate student had been studying the wind erosion of metal in this very spot. Reba remembered the rows of metal stakes he had driven into the rocky ground. He had told her that by comparing his metal stakes to photographs of the legs of the first Mars lander, he could learn about the Martian wind.

This is a piece of alien ground left here by mistake, Reba

thought. She had felt it when she first set foot in this place. Perhaps that alien aura had attracted the meteorites that littered the Allan Hills. Perhaps it had attracted the sphere. A few meters beyond the port she noticed a small drift of dolerite ventifacts. The wind-faceted stones looked like knapped obsidian tools, as if some primitive ancestors of humanity had crouched here, flaking away at the stones, waiting patiently for spring and warmer weather.

They had died, because spring had never come to this land.

The ancient black stones reminded her of Sara's eyes. *I am alone.* Reba turned away from the port, eyes tearing from the harsh light. Paranoia could sound so rational. She sat on a bunk, hands folded on her lap. Tomorrow, people would come in bright warm parkas. They would dig the strange thing out of the Meserve Glacier and carry it back to their laboratories for scrutiny.

*I am alone.*

What if it wasn't a delusion?

She had seen guilt in Ganfield's eyes. Guilt for Angela's death. What remains behind when a soul leaves a body?

The cold comes from within, in Antarctica. It grows in the heart and is pumped to the extremities until you become a solid, moving sculpture of ice. Reba sat on the bunk, feeling the blood move sluggishly through her veins, colder than the Weddell Sea. Outside, she heard someone replace Jerry, to be replaced in turn as the day wore on. Once, she heard Ganfield's voice, but he didn't knock on the door.

It was late before she emerged, although the cold, hard light still poured through the unshaded port. Reba's head ached. A covered tray sat on the exam table in the infirmary. The plastic cover was cold to the touch.

"Did you have a good sleep?" A curly-headed young man was sitting in a chair, swinging one foot idly. He nodded toward the door to Sara's room. "Sara said she wanted to rest. I thought you were going to sleep all night." He stood, yawned, and stretched his compact frame. "You still need me?" he asked hopefully.

"No. Thanks." Reba waited for him to leave.

Sara didn't look at her. She was staring at the ceiling, her face expressionless. The IV bag was empty. Blood had backed into the plastic catheter tubing.

Sara watched with lackluster eyes as Reba peeled off the tape and removed the catheter. "More drugs?" she asked.

"No." Reba lifted the drapes to examine Sara's hands and feet. It was a gesture, a touchstone of familiarity. She looked at the swollen dead tissues without really seeing them, then took a deep breath. "You won't be able to walk," she said. "I'll have to carry you."

"You'll help me," Sara breathed.

"I think I'm crazy." She didn't look at Sara's face.

"Thank you."

Reba didn't answer.

It was easy. Reba almost hoped that someone would challenge them, but they met no one on their endless journey to the lock. It was the middle of the night, in spite of the bright summer light. You didn't guard equipment, down here. Antarctica itself guarded it for you. Sara was lighter than Reba remembered, as if her flesh was thinning, sloughing invisibly. Reba carried her easily down the corridor and into the lock.

The skinsuits were plainly impossible. Reba worked Sara's dead hands through the sleeves of Reba's own parka, wincing at the damage that wouldn't matter but still did. The bearpaw mittens nearly defeated her. Sweat stuck Reba's hair to her forehead, and she jumped at every sound.

Oh God. What if I'm wrong?

Reba tasted blood from her bitten lip. She got a pair of boots on Sara, began to pull on an orange skinsuit. Sara told her how to fasten the seals and activate the heat. The cycling lock sounded like a hurricane in Reba's ears, but still no one appeared to stop them.

Masked ports glared like blind eyes from the silver radiation-reflective skin of the base. The wind shoved at her, but the suit blocked the cold. It was frightening not to feel cold—as if her own flesh was frozen and dead. She boosted Sara's too-light body into the seat of a parked TrakMaster and got it started.

So far, so good. Reba tried to count her own heart rate. Fast. The TrakMaster roared and lurched across the rocky slopes. Clumsy in the unfamiliar suit, she felt as if she was driving for the first time.

"That way," Sara shouted, pointing up the valley.

They passed a dead seal at the edge of a black puddle of frozen lake. It was a crab-eater. The drying lips had curled, exposing its yellow teeth, and its mottled gray-and-yellow sides looked sunken and brittle.

Why did they come here, struggling across a barrier of moraine and broken ice? Antarctica's white light stabbed Reba through the tinted glass of her helmet. Did some mysterious force draw them, too?

Then the TrakMaster was climbing. Cold had cracked the soil into neat polygons. The permafrost was fifteen centimeters down and two hundred meters thick. Reba watched the Meserve Glacier grow higher in front of them. The pale blue walls cut off the end of the valley. Broken chunks of ice littered the stony ground, light as balsa wood. They glittered in the sun, as if they were flecked with silver.

"Stop," Sara shouted over the roar of the TrakMaster.

Reba shut off the engine. You could still go back, she told herself, but she was already clambering down from the seat. Sara was so light. Reba's feet crunched on ice and rock, and she struggled to keep her footing in the loose scree. They had surrounded the site with the bright orange stakes that seemed to define all human intrusions in this land.

She couldn't tell which jumble of ice had killed the trainees. It had been a casual thing, leaving almost no trace on Antarctica's face. Reba stopped. The ice at the foot of the glacier was clear, full of tiny bubbles, as if someone had frozen a bottle of champagne.

There it was.

Right there.

Ganfield was wrong, was her first numb thought. She had visualized machinery—flying saucers. This was no machine.

The tiny sphere glowed in its shroud of ice, shimmering with opalescent light. Reba caught her breath. It had no definite shape, although *sphere* was close enough. *Pattern*, Sara had called it. The small nodule of beautiful light was more alien than Antarctica's white glare.

As alien as Sara's eyes.

"What happens now?" Reba let Sara slide slowly to the broken ice.

Sara crumpled to her knees without answering. She had shed the last remnants of her humanity like a tattered cloak. She crouched awkwardly on her dead feet, her face empty, a mirror, reflecting back the shimmering opalescence.

*There is only one soul in this body,* Sara had said.

Reba had meant to stay, but Sara's face and the beautiful light terrified her more than anything she could remember. She ran, stumbling back across the shattered ground, panting, sweating inside her suit. She didn't want to see, didn't want to know, but she looked back when she reached the TrakMaster.

The air above the glacier seemed to be streaked with a strange shifting unearthly light. The *fata morgana*? Another of Antarctica's famous illusions?

"I couldn't save you," Reba whispered to the woman with Li's eyes. The words caught, became a sob. "I wanted to, but I couldn't."

She hadn't been able to save Li, either. Reba watched the shimmering light. Death was stronger, Li. I did all I could. It wasn't my fault. The first tears scalded her as they trickled down her cheeks.

THE TRAKMASTER lurched over the cold stones on the way back to Marsbase. The dead seal grinned at her, and Reba met its conspiratorial stare, wondering if she would merely lose her license or if she'd go to prison. The experts in their bright parkas wouldn't find their sphere. They'd only find a frozen, empty body.

What does an interstellar address look like? Or the envelope for a soul? The TrakMaster lurched and growled. Steve Ganfield would pay, too, even though he'd been afraid to let Sara go. They'd blame him for the sphere.

No second chances, down here.

Not so. I gave Sara a second chance.

Reba looked back at the blue shadow of the Meserve Glacier. Wet with tears, her face burned like thawing frostbite. Down here, the cold comes from within. Reba clung to the TrakMaster as it crunched across the frozen alien ground.

It was time to go north. Maybe somewhere she could find the spring.

# ORDERTOWN

Josh first saw the Curtain late in the afternoon. The Tortilla Curtain, the Wall, the Fence. It shimmered like a mirage at the edge of his vision; not colorless, but of no color Josh could name. He squinted through the grimy bus window, but rising heat-waves blurred the landscape. A fitting metaphor for the past weeks, Josh thought bitterly. Familiar reality distorted to strangeness. The ancient bus—some derelict purchased cheap from a city fleet—lurched, and Josh winced as his shoulder banged the glass. The road looked as if it had been shelled. Which might have happened. The US Border Patrol didn't fool around.

Gritty wind blew in through the window; a furnace breath that licked the sweat from Josh's skin before he could even feel it. Josh swallowed, throat sandpapery, stomach uneasy, wishing that he'd bought two bottles of water before he'd boarded, instead of just one. Damn Peter for asking Josh to meet him at this godforsaken little border crossing.

In the seat behind him, the baby started crying again. The baby's mother shushed him with a murmured cascade of incomprehensible Spanish syllables. Josh touched the translator plug in his ear, rubbing at the annoying itch. The mother unit in his pocket was turned off, and he didn't turn it on. They were all Mexican, the other passengers. Mexican-American, Josh amended, because Mexican nationals couldn't cross the US border anymore. They had stared at him with black, unreadable eyes and expressionless faces as he had climbed aboard—the only white face on the bus. They talked softly to each other in Spanish, and he didn't want to understand.

For the hundredth time, Josh's fingers crept into his pocket, fingering the flimsy page of hardcopy wrapped around the flat rectangle of the turned-off translator and the cash card. Peter's letter. *Sorry I couldn't make the funeral, kid. Listen, I need your help.* . . . His help? Help from the tagalong younger brother that he had occasionally tolerated, but mostly ignored? The watch on his wrist caught the light, the old-fashioned glass crystal winking like an eye. Dad's watch. Not given, not bestowed, just inherited, because Dad's cheap will had left everything to Josh. Jennifer had come to the funeral. She had said *I'm sorry,* her voice as cool as the touch of her fingers on his hand.

Josh leaned forward, shirt sticking to the patched vinyl seat, sweaty back briefly cool as the oven-wind dried it. The woman in the seat behind him and across the aisle—the one with the mirrorshades—was staring at him again. Josh watched her from the corner of his eye. She had a light-tattoo on her arm. Implanted optic fibers formed a serpent twining through roses. They glowed like neon whenever her arm was in shadow. It hadn't really surprised him to find that Peter was down here. The *ejido* wasn't really Mexico, and it sure as hell wasn't the US. It was a narrow little country of its own, sandwiched between the US and Mexico; a place without rules.

Yeah, it was Peter's kind of place.

The tattooed woman had noticed his looking. Red lips smiled beneath the blank stare of the shades. Josh blushed and glanced quickly away The transmission groaned as the bus driver shifted gears. *¡Peligro!* A dusty sign slid past the window; red letters superimposed on a grinning skull and crossbones. *Danger!* They must be close to the border. The weird shimmer of the Curtain could have been a hundred yards away, or a hundred miles. Josh craned his neck, squinting against the yellow glare of the late afternoon sun. This time he saw the town; a cluster of desert-colored buildings squatting against the blank backdrop of the Curtain.

Desert had given way to sagging wire fences, shacks, houses made from fake adobe or ancient plywood, even a few of the new solar domes. A fuel station slid past. A scrawny yellow dog raised a leg against one gutted pump. Bullet holes stitched the pump's ruined face; signature of the quiet, ugly war that went on along here. Everything was the color of dust. The sun had sucked all the life from the little town. Josh swallowed again, so thirsty that it hurt. He thought briefly about pulling the bell cord, about getting out right here, catching the next bus north. Keep the money and let Peter go to hell.

Peter had asked him for help. The engine growled, coughed, and choked down to an uneven idle. The town ended, dissolved into a warscape of rubble. An intentional warscape, caused by bulldozers, not bombs. The border. Throat dry, heart beginning to pound in slow steady strokes, Josh reached for the bell cord. It was an automatic gesture, like grabbing for something as you fell. There was no cord. Just plastic mounts that might have carried one once.

Outside, beyond the squat concrete buildings of the border station, beyond the shimmer of the Curtain, movement caught Josh's eye. A man? The figure ran through the wasteland of dying sage, blurred to anonymity by the shimmer of the Curtain and the rising heat. He was running right at it, feet kicking up puffs of dust, running straight for the invisible deadly fence.

Josh stiffened, mouth open, a shout frozen in his throat. At the last instant, the man threw his arms wide, like a sprinter breasting the tape. His body jerked, head whip-cracking back, then forward, arms and legs spasming like the jackrabbit Dad had made Josh shoot on his twelfth birthday. More dust rose as the man skidded face-first into the sage, drifting away on the hot wind.

"Passport? Hey, boy!"

Josh jerked like the dying man, and turned. The bus had stopped. A uniformed man was standing in the aisle, hand out.

"Come on, boy." The border agent's thick fingers snapped. "I ain't got all day."

He was white, with blue eyes, gray hair, and a hard sun-dried face. Josh had expected a Mexican at the entry point. He fumbled in his pocket, sweat springing out on his skin. The folded fifty felt thick as wadded tissue beneath his fingers as he handed over his passport card. His stomach was full of molten lead.

The agent grunted and slipped the card into the reader at his

belt. "Anything to declare? How long you plannin' on stayin'?"
He snapped the card out without even glancing at the screen,
handed it back.

"I . . . just brought clothes. And this." He lifted his wrist to
display Dad's old watch. "I'm only staying a couple of days."
Josh took his card. No fifty. His face was burning, and he hated
himself for it.

The agent smirked. "Have fun, kid." He held out his hand
to the woman with the baby. "Hope you got your shots," he
said over his shoulder.

Josh shoved his passport card back into his pocket. The
woman was handing over a grimy piece of hardcopy and a wad
of folded bills. In the dusty sage, the dead man lay spread-
eagled and still. He had run right into the Curtain. The bus
lurched forward, slamming Josh back in his seat. A concrete-
block gatehouse slid by, and a tall metal-mesh gate on a track.
More warscape rubble and then . . .

. . . they were in the *ejido*.

Color. That was what struck him first—the color. The sun
was setting. In the softening light of evening, the colors shouted
from the crowded streets; hot tropical pinks and vivid aquas.
Oranges, bright greens, and blues splashed the mud-colored
walls. Vendors hawked silk flowers, baskets of fruit too brilliant
to be real, jewelry that showered fountains of kaleidoscopic light
into the air, and bottles of vivid drinks. The sun that had faded
the US side of the border to desert dun had no effect here.
Buildings were square, one or two stories, built of concrete block
or adobe. The streets were crowded with people and cars. Old
cars that had to run on alco-fuel and had originally been
designed for gasoline. A very few electrics. A *donkey*, dropping
brown lumps of dung right on the street!

Men and women clustered outside gaudy storefronts, drinking from Mylar packs, plastic, and even glass bottles, laughing,
talking. A group of youths clustered around what looked like an
antique PC set up on a couple of wooden crates on the sidewalk.
As Josh watched, they all howled with laughter, heads thrown
back, light-tattoos flashing on their shoulders and faces.

The *ejido*. You could get anything here. Sex. Drugs. A new
face or a new liver. Fetal cell implants to keep you young forever
or fix a damaged spine. A son or daughter tailored to your design. Death, accidentally or on purpose, in a thousand creative
guises. Yeah, this was Peter's world. Josh's stomach tightened
as the bus lurched and sighed to a stop. The men and women

were gathering bags and babies, shuffling down the aisle.

Swept up by the momentum of their exodus, Josh found himself—through no conscious effort of his own—in the aisle, clutching his pack. With a twitch of panic, he groped in his pocket for the reassuring lump of his cash card and the letter. Bodies jostled him. He flinched at the touch, smelling sweat and cooking odors from the street. His stomach lurched, and he tripped over the bottom step and stumbled out onto the hot evening street. With a whine of rusty hinges, the door closed and the bus engine roared.

The other passengers were dispersing quickly, casually, with the preoccupied relief of commuters going home. It came to Josh with a sense of shock that they *were* going home—that they were Mexican, after all—never mind what the president had said about air-tight borders. The sidewalk seemed to shudder with the bus's motion beneath his feet, and he gulped deep breaths of the alien air, stunned by death, and heat, and the colors. The woman with the shades and the roses on her arm brushed past him, a leather handbag tossed carelessly over her shoulder. Her red lips shaped a smile beneath twin reflections of Josh's face. "Welcome to Mexico, gringo," she said in English, and laughed.

WITH ITS electronic alchemy, the translator turned the sea of Spanish chatter into words so familiar that they made Josh dizzy. He hadn't really expected to understand. He kept his hand in his pocket as he hurried through the crowd, fingers clenched around his cash card and passport, eyes fixed on backs and shoulders and the safe, filthy street. In spite of his translator, he couldn't bring himself to stop someone and ask directions. It took him a long time to find the hotel that Peter had named in his letter. The Sonora cost a lot, and the translator didn't tell him if he should bargain. He paid the fee, shoving his cash card into the register. It stood on a scarred wooden counter that looked old enough to have been standing there on the day the Alamo fell.

The old man behind the counter showed Josh to an upstairs room. There was one sagging bed, covered with coarse, spotlessly clean sheets, one rickety wooden table, and a single chair. The light came from a naked bulb dangling from a frayed cord that disappeared through a hole in the plaster ceiling, but the shiny plastic box of a Netlink was mounted on one wall. Before he left, the landlord offered to get Josh a terminal if he needed it, or a suit of VR skinthins, or a woman, or a boy. He shrugged when Josh declined.

In the single bathroom at the end of the hall, the composting toilet stank and the bright box of a pay-meter gleamed above rusty taps in the chipped sink. Josh eyed the reddish water leaking from the fixture like drops of diluted blood and shuddered. A year ago, the idea that he would be here, in this place, would have shocked him or made him laugh. A year ago, Dad had been alive and well and the future had been a seamless and tangible certainty.

Back in his room, Josh pulled the chair over beside the window. It was getting dark, and the street below was crowded. At this distance, the translator was almost useless. The only words that it translated were the shouts. The effect was strange; as if all communication took the form of greeting or insult or challenge. A side street opened across from the hotel. It ended in rutted dirt and a wall of nothing. The Curtain. Josh looked quickly down at the crowded street.

Bare shoulders and shaved scalps glowed with inlaid light below him. A cluster of young men drank from long-necked bottles in front of the hotel, raucous and rowdy. Vendors wandered along the sidewalk with trays of unfamiliar foods and drinks. Josh knew he should be hungry—*must* be hungry, because he hadn't eaten anything since morning. The thought of walking past those laughing young drinkers and out into that crowded street again made sweat break out on his face, cold in the breeze that blew through the window. He had bought two plastic bottles of water from the landlord. *Agua Tecate* was printed on the label, above a picture of green hills that looked utterly unbelievable in this landscape of dust.

He sipped the tepid water, grimacing at the taste. It was too dark to see the Curtain now, but you could tell where it was. The lights of the town ended abruptly at a wall of darkness. He was here, Peter was here, and there was nothing else. Burns, Arizona, the old house, Dad's grave—they had ceased to exist. In the distance, someone screamed. Pain? Fear? For an instant, the street seemed to fall silent. Josh closed his eyes, seeing again the spastic shot-rabbit leap of the man. He fled the window, but the street pursued him, slipping into the room in the smell of cooking food and the beat of music and alien voices. Groping for sleep, Josh burrowed into the coarse sheets, into a night that stretched into an endless dark dream.

HE WOKE to hot sunlight that lay like a weight across his body. Josh kicked away the tangled sheets and sat up, wincing as red lightnings flashed behind his eyes. His head ached, and the sheets were damp with sweat. When he stood, the room tilted and he had to grab for the metal bed frame to keep from falling. Hungry, he thought dizzily. That's all that was wrong with him. It was late—past noon. He'd eat something and be fine.

He shoved his cash card into the meter slot in the bathroom and splashed tepid water onto his face. It smelled faintly of sewage, and the resultant spasm in his belly doubled him over. Drawing deep ragged breaths, shivering in spite of the heat, he made his way out of the bathroom and down the single flight of stairs to the lobby. No one was behind the scarred counter, and the stuffy twilight of the lobby made Josh gasp for breath.

Outside, sun filled the empty street like the silent clash of brass cymbals. No one moved in the white-hot glare. Doorways and windows were holes into blackness. A single spotted dog lay slack as a roadkill beneath an ancient Datsun perched ridiculously above giant tires. The dog didn't even lift its head as Josh made his way down the street. Last night, food had been everywhere. In the heat of noon, wooden doors and shutters closed the shops, as if the entire population vanished with the sunrise. Josh stumbled into a pile of dung. The donkey? White maggots writhed in the moist clumps, and his stomach twisted again. Leaning against the sun-hot concrete of a shuttered cantina, he vomited, bringing up burning yellow fluid tinged with bright streaks of blood.

"Hey, gringo." A woman's voice. "Don't you know better than to drink the water?"

A hand closed on his arm, and he caught a glimpse of tattooed roses on smooth brown skin, dull in the harsh light. She steadied him as he vomited again, moving aside a little so that she wouldn't get spattered. "It was bottled," he croaked, when he could breathe again. "The water. From the hotel."

"That stuff is okay. Normando never cheats on his water." Fingers touched Josh's forehead, cold enough to make him shiver. "You brought this sickness with you, gringo."

With an effort, he straightened, recognizing the woman from the bus. Twin reflections of his face glared back at him from her shades, white and strange. She was wearing a magenta tank top, and her braided hair hung forward over one bare muscular shoulder.

"Come with me," she said.

"No." He hung back. "Where do you want me to go?" Images of alleyways and knives danced in his head. "Who are you and what do you want?"

"You have listened to too many stories about the border."
She tossed the thick braid of her hair back over her shoulder.
"My name is María, and I am a *curandera.*" She touched him
lightly, just below his sternum. "Come, and I will fix this. Or
stay and vomit in the street. Your choice, gringo."

It would be wiser to go back to his hotel, to ask the landlord
to call a doctor. If there *was* a doctor in this place. Peter was supposed to meet him at the hotel. If Peter was even here.

It didn't matter. That seamless, comfortable future had
evaporated before he had ever reached the border. Nothing
mattered anymore. "I'll come," Josh said.

He stumbled along the baking dirt street with the woman's
incredibly strong hand locked beneath his elbow. His knees
quivered at every step, and his belly was a pit of hollow pain,
waiting to swallow him down forever. A wash of cool shadow
blinded him momentarily, and he stumbled over the threshold
of a door.

"My *yerbería,*" the woman said.

They were inside a shop. Shelves lined the walls, covered
with glass and plastic containers of all sizes and shapes. The air
smelled pungently of herbs. A single wooden table stood
against one wall, beneath a crucifix decked with plastic flowers.
The rough adobe walls breathed cool, and Josh began to shiver
again. This time it wouldn't stop. His teeth chattered as the
woman pulled aside a curtain and led him into a back room.
Something nudged him behind his knees and he sat down hard,
his vision full of dancing black flecks.

Slowly, Josh's head cleared. He was sitting on a narrow bed
covered with a bright spread. The woman stood with her back
to him at a table covered with chipped Formica, doing something over a hissing propane stove. Dishes—touristy earth-
enware and cheap plastic—cluttered the stove end of the table.
At the other end stood what appeared to be an old-fashioned
computer terminal and keyboard, connected to various pieces of
hardware by a tangle of mismatched cables. Another small table
at the end of the bed was cluttered with a spread of bright cards,
a Bible, and a dozen plastic and china statues. Madonnas. Jesus.
White-skinned pious-looking men that Josh guessed to be
saints. There was a real rose in a chipped glass vase and a bowl
of dried leaves.

"Drink this." The woman turned away from the stove.

Josh took the thick red-glazed mug gingerly. The brownish
liquid in it smelled like rotting leaves.

She was waiting, arms crossed lightly, her posture relaxed

and without impatience. He could drink it or not, her body language told him. *Your choice, gringo.* With a start, he realized that she had taken off her shades, although he didn't remember her doing it. Her eyes were green—emerald, artificial green, set like polished gems in her wide brown face, bright as the tattoo on her arm. She was laughing at him. Josh flushed, lifted the cup to his lips, and gulped down the tea.

It tasted worse than it smelled. Eyes closed, he took two deep breaths, waiting to throw it up. Amazingly, it stayed down, and the pain in his stomach lessened instantly.

"That was for the illness in your body." She sat down beside him on the bed and scooped the cards from the cluttered table. "I have no tea to heal the illness in your soul." She began to shuffle the cards with a practiced flick of her wrist. "For that, you must look elsewhere."

A fortune-teller? Josh edged away from her just a hair. The pitch would come in a minute. The cost of the tea, the plug to read his future. For a stiff fee, because he was just a dumb tourist, too dumb even to be careful about the water. He was feeling better, though. For that, he'd pay her something.

Her mocking smile suggested that she again had guessed his thoughts. "You are running from Death." She flipped a card lightly down beside his knee. "You cannot escape, because you carry it with you. To be free of it, you must give it away."

On the shiny surface of the card, a skeleton in armor bestrode a white horse, carrying a banner. The eyeless sockets stared mockingly up at him. Josh recoiled. The woman's smooth brown face might have been a porcelain mask set with green gems. "I've got to get back to my hotel." He groped in his pocket for cash.

"Keep your money." She laughed, and the porcelain mask became flesh again. "You *norteamericanos* are so afraid of Death. Even when you seek it, you deny it. You spend so much money to keep it from you." She laughed again, and the skin at the corners of her eyes crinkled into fine lines. "Here, Death looks over our shoulders all the time. We pass it in the street and we nod. We invite it to our parties. It is everywhere, gringo, but you clutch it to you, as if it belongs to you alone."

Josh realized that he was standing, looking down at her. His muscles had levered him to his feet without his even knowing it. "Thanks for the tea." He pulled a bill from his pocket and tossed it onto the bedspread. A hundred-peso note. It fluttered like a falling leaf; settled gently onto the card.

The woman flicked it away with a contemptuous finger. "Do I frighten you, gringo?" The tips of her teeth showed between her smiling lips. "I am no *bruja*, gringo. I am a *curandera*. It is my business to heal only." Her smile widened. "But I can conjure your brother for you, if you wish."

"My . . . brother?"

"The one you came to find. The one you are afraid to find."

"María?" A male voice called hoarsely from the front of the shop. "*¿Está usted aquí?*"

"I am here." María looked past Josh's shoulder. "Speak English, *por favor*. You have a visitor."

Josh turned slowly, the familiar sound of the voice tightening the flesh between his shoulders. "Peter?" The word caught in his throat. The man walking through the doorway was Latino, with shoulder-length hair, a jutting sweep of nose, and dark hooded eyes. "I'm sorry," Josh said lamely. "I thought you were someone else."

"My God, Josh!" The stranger took two steps forward and threw his arms around Josh. "*Mi hermano*. In the flesh. Hooey, you should *see* your face, kid. María?" Sudden wariness closed down the laughter in his smile. "How the hell did he end up *here?*"

"I went to get him." María picked up the empty cup, her green eyes unperturbed. "He was sick."

"Well, she can cure that, if you can stand the stuff she brews." He grinned at her, turned the grin on Josh. "You look like you saw a ghost, kid. You expected blond? Blue eyes?"

"Yeah." Josh shook his head, feeling as if he was suffering from a weird kind of double vision. "I did."

"You can get away with it in the big bordertowns—Tijuana, like that. Being a gringo, I mean. Hell, you've got as many whites and Asians as Latinos in some neighborhoods. But out here . . ." He shrugged. "You can have any face or body you want, if you've got the money. I can't afford to stand out, kid."

It was his brother—the same tight lift of his shoulders as he spoke, the pulse of anger behind his words, like a second, hidden, heartbeat. "Peter?" Josh licked his lips, words crowding his skull, too thick to pick through carefully. "You . . . didn't show up." Those words came out on their own, bursting through the press.

"No, I didn't. Jon wasn't supposed to give my address away to *anyone*, and I guarantee you he regrets it." The unfamiliar Hispanic face had gone cold. "Dad nearly killed me the night I left. I'd still like to get even with the bastard who tipped the principal that I was so deep in the files. She didn't have a *clue*, man." He laughed harshly. "No way I was coming back just to hear the old man tell me one more time that I was a fuckup. Hell, you're so good at all that dutiful-son stuff. You didn't need me."

Oh yeah. This was Peter. Josh looked down at his clenched fists. Those last weeks had stretched into a timeless eternity; feeding Dad, helping him to the bathroom, wiping his butt, while he whispered, shouted, and cursed at an invisible Peter. Oh, you were there, brother, Josh thought bitterly. Even if you didn't know it. "You're right. I didn't need your help." Josh unclenched his fists with an effort. "I'm going back to my hotel to lie down for a while."

"You can't." Peter's new brown face scowled. "A cop's waiting for you."

Josh stared at his brother, his brain refusing to process that bit of information, refusing to put it into any kind of rational perspective.

"I told you I was in trouble." This time, the black alien eyes slid sideways, away from Josh's face. "I guess my new identity isn't as airtight as I thought, and they made the connection between us. They want to ask you my address."

So what? Josh wanted to yell at this stranger with his brother's voice. This is *your* life. *Your* problem. What the hell has that got to do with me? "What about my stuff?" he asked thickly. "And my passport?"

"Son of a bitch." Peter drew the words out into a long sibilant hiss. "You left your *passport* in your room?" His fist hit the tabletop with a crash. "Not even the dumbest *turista* is that dumb! What about my money?"

"I'm not a tourist. I'm here because you begged me for help."

"I didn't *beg* you for anything."

Josh fixed his eyes on the cluttered table. A china Virgin Mary wore a sky-blue cloth over her head. Her face was very white above her clasped hands. "I'll tell them you never showed," he said.

"Just like that, *hermano?*" Peter's voice was low and cold. "And you think they'll believe you?"

Josh didn't look up. Peter's arms would be crossed, his face sullen and closed. Just as he'd stood on that last night, silent in the middle of the kitchen, after Dad had paid his bail and brought him home. Thick silence had clogged the small house as Dad unbuckled his belt. He had used the buckle end, grunting with exertion as he swung it. Peter had just stood there— taller than Dad at seventeen, strong enough to deck him if he had wanted to. No matter how hard Dad hit, even when the buckle drew blood, Peter stood still. There had only been the sound of the blows and Dad's hoarse panting. After Dad had thrown the belt on the floor, only then did Peter walk out the door and out of the house forever.

The Virgin Mary was smiling at Josh, her eyes lowered seductively. "What did you do?" he said. "Kill someone?"

"Not that I know of." Peter shrugged. "I was boosting some R&D files and I got careless, all right? One of the big multinationals is pissed at me. No big deal. I just need to disappear for a while."

"It sounds like a big deal to me. Why don't you try something honest, Peter?"

"You sound like Dad." Peter's new black eyes were flat and unreadable as stone. "You really do, kid. You're such an angel, I suppose. Yeah, you probably are. You always were. Honor student, teacher's pet, the guy who always did his chores and made his bed. And now you've inherited Dad's job at the plant—yeah, I checked you out, kid. You still live in the old house. You've never done a thing Dad wouldn't have done."

"You're wrong," Josh said softly. "I don't live in the house anymore, and I did do something Dad wouldn't have done. I came down here to get your ass out of a sling."

For a moment Peter's face went very still. Then he laughed, head thrown back, teeth flashing in his brown face. "Now we both have our asses in a sling. Thanks to you, *turista*."

"The problem has a solution." María leaned forward. She had absented herself from their bitter conversation as completely as if she had left the room. Now the scene seemed to refocus on her, as if the contents of the room had rearranged themselves in an instant. "The hole in *el muro* is big enough for three," she said to Peter.

"If he doesn't chicken out and get us all killed. And what about the money?" Peter said. "I'll have to owe you."

"Your brother will pay me." María reached out to cup Josh's chin in her long fingers. "On the other side. You understand a debt, gringo, so *you* will owe me."

"I didn't know that you were afflicted with trust, María." Peter's lip curled.

"Only a fool would trust you, *querido.*" María smiled sweetly.

"Well, excuse me. I think I'll go finish getting ready for our little excursion." With a jerk of his shoulders, Peter stalked out of the door.

"You're talking about going through the Curtain." Josh swallowed. "I thought no one could do that. And what about my passport and my cash card?"

"What good is your passport to the police, if you do not pass through a gate?" María's red lips smiled. "*Los Estados Unidos* has no interest in the affairs of Mexico. To your country, the continent ends at *el muro.* Your passport will be sold on the market. *Norteamericano* passports bring a good price. Your money, of course, is already lost."

"You went through on the bus. I saw you," Josh said. "You all went through. Why can't we do it that way?"

María shrugged. "*Los anónimos* go through to do the jobs that you *norteamericanos* want them to do. *I* go through because I am María and I bring the others. There is no place for you on that bus, gringo."

In the outer room, the tiny bells chimed. Josh's muscles tensed all at once.

"A customer." María put a hand on his arm. "Rest for a while, gringo. Sleep. It is safe here." She ducked through the curtain.

Josh heard a low murmur of voices in the outer room. The translator was back in his hotel room, too. The cadence of those syllables could mean gossip, or a bargain struck, or betrayal. There was no way to know. Josh shrugged and stretched out on the narrow bed. He was living in each moment of the present, cut off from those moments that had passed and those that had not yet arrived by the invisible shimmer of the Curtain. *El muro.* There was no pillow. The woven spread smelled of herbs and something musky and animal. María? An erection prodded his jeans, unexpected and urgent. He closed his eyes and thought of Jennifer, trying to call up her face, her smile, the swirl of her hair. All he could remember was the splintery feel of the garage windowsill beneath his palms and the brown gleam of her naked suntanned shoulders as she writhed beneath Peter on the ratty old sofa. Josh rolled over, burying his face in the spread, wondering if Peter and María had made love on this bed.

HE CAME AWAKE with a cry, to twilight and María's face bending over him.

"What time is it?" He sat up, blinking, muscles still tense with the aftermath of his dream.

"Evening. Dreams are the spirits, speaking to you." María sat down on the edge of the bed.

"I wasn't dreaming," he said, but faint memory shimmered at the edges of his mind—echoes of rage and red violence. "I never remember my dreams."

"Not everyone wishes to hear the spirits."

"Do you really believe in that stuff?" He jerked his head at the cluttered table. The statue of the Virgin was a blue-and-white blur in the shadows. "Saints and spirits and cards?"

"I could tell you that dreams are a manifestation of your subconscious, that they are a way of dealing with events that you cannot approach consciously." She looked at him gravely, but laughter quirked the corners of her mouth. "I am a *curandera*," she said. "I heal with whatever works. Sometimes, it is herbs. Sometimes, it is what I hear in the market, or information from the Net. Sometimes, it is the symbols that have meaning for the soul." She bent her head in a little bow to the table.

"Is that why my brother came to you?" Josh asked. "For healing?"

Frowning a little, she turned her arm slowly, so that the tattooed snake writhed in its bed of roses. Her eyes gleamed like backlit emeralds, and Josh wondered again if she and Peter had made love here on the hard narrow bed.

"Your brother came to me to buy a hole in the Curtain," María said at last.

"Peter's tough." Josh shrugged. "Trouble never bothered him much when we were kids. I think he liked the spotlight. Or maybe he liked it that it pissed Dad when he got into trouble."

"Some wounds heal. Some do not." María's voice was low, introspective, as if she was talking to herself. "They fester and turn inward until the soul eats itself, like a trapped coyote gnawing at its own flesh. If you are done sleeping, you can eat." She nodded at the table against the wall. "There is time before we leave."

*Before we leave.* The words—spoken out loud—dried the inside of Josh's mouth. A green plastic bowl and a cloth-covered basket stood on the battered wooden surface. The computer terminal was on, and the blue glow of the screen was the only light in the room. Darkness had filled up the small space while they talked, and the roses on María's arm glowed like blood-colored neon in the dim light. Josh swallowed, but his mouth remained dry.

"The *ejido* is a place of desperation," María said softly. "You do not live here by accident. The past crowds at your heels, and *el muro* cuts off the future. It is not shameful to be afraid here, gringo."

"A picnic!" Peter's voice preceded him through the doorway, too loud and cheerful for the dark room; so much more familiar while darkness hid his strange new face. "I hope you brought beer," he said. "Hell, do we have to sit in the dark?"

María bent and retrieved a solar lantern from beneath the bed; clicked it on. Its colorless light twisted her shadow across the floor and up the wall as she handed Peter a plastic bottle of the *Tecate* water.

Peter made a face and peered into the bowl. "Beans and tortillas. How ethnic. Did you have a nice rest, *hermano?*"

"What was your plan, anyway?" Josh watched his brother fold a tortilla and scoop beans from the bowl. "What was I supposed to do when I got down here? Carry you home in my suitcase?"

"Are you kidding? I wouldn't go back to that dead-end hole if you paid me. I have more fun down here." Peter handed the filled tortilla to Josh and reached for another. "I was going to pay María with the money you brought. She was going to open a hole for me, so they'd look for me up north. I was headed . . . elsewhere. The plan hasn't changed. Watch out for the beans, *turista.* They're hot."

"Except that now I have to risk my neck along with you." Josh took a careful taste. His eyes watered and he swallowed fast, damned if he'd grab for the water.

"Your fault." Peter took a huge bite of beans and tortilla. "Are you really happy in that shithole of a town?" he said with his mouth full. "Yeah, you probably are." He swallowed, grinned, and reached for the water. "You'll get married—it kind of surprised me that you're not married yet, by the way—have a nice, legally licensed kid. You'll spend the rest of your days manufacturing cheap plastic junk for the highest corporate bidder and going to church on Sundays. Never a worry in the world, as long as you don't catch anything Fed-Med won't cure."

Get married? Oh yeah, he'd wanted to do that. *I love you,* he had said to Jennifer. Her hair had gleamed like spun gold on that long-ago afternoon, spread out across the arm of that dusty sofa as she cried out, *I love you, Peter.*

*I love you.* Jennifer had been kind to him. Kind. "Shut up,

Peter." Josh laid the rest of his tortilla down on the tabletop.
"Just shut up, will you?"

"You know, I almost hoped you wouldn't show," Peter said
softly. "I almost hoped you'd tell me to go to hell. But you
always covered for me—doing the dishes when it was my turn,
lying for me when I skipped school—good old dependable Josh.
I was a real shit to you, too. I never could get you to take a swing
at me."

"Knock it off, Peter."

"Not once. Do you really trust me to pay you back?" Peter
took another bite of his tortilla. "I bet you brought me your life
savings, didn't you? I bet you were going to try and convince
me to come back home, repent and go straight, right? I bet you
still go to church every Sunday. Just like Dad."

If he hadn't, it would have shown up on his personnel file
and he would've gotten fired. Dad was sick, and he had needed
his job. "Yes," Josh whispered. "I went to church." He
squeezed his clenched fists between his knees so that Peter
couldn't see how his hands were trembling. If he moved, if he
said a word, a single goddamn word . . . he'd kill Peter. Here,
now, with his bare hands. The knowledge filled his head, sweet
and clear as a bell, sharp as the stink of his own sweat.

A touch on his shoulder made his muscles jump. Josh lifted
his head and found himself staring into the gemstone glitter of
María's eyes. She knew. He shivered, unable to look away. A
stillness was creeping into him, following the shiver down
through his flesh; a *pause* that settled deep into his bones. His
hands had stopped shaking. María nodded very slightly as he
laid them gently on his thighs.

"No, I didn't come down here to bring you home, Peter."
Josh drew a slow breath. "The money on that cash card was
yours. Half of what I got for the house. We're quits, Peter. After
tonight, I don't care if I never see you again."

Peter stared at him for a long moment, and something
moved in his dark eyes. Then he laughed; teeth flashing, head
thrown back. "You lost *my* money? You bastard. Oh well." He
shrugged, still grinning crookedly. "You know, just once, I'd
like to see you really get mad. Cut loose and swing on me."

"No," Josh said softly. "You wouldn't." He turned to
María. "Is it time to go yet?"

"*Sí.*" Her eyes flickered as if she heard the desperation he
was successfully keeping out of his voice. "In a moment." She
turned to the ancient terminal. The monitor screen glowed to

blue life as her fingers danced over the grimy keyboard.

"María's hot," Peter said. "The best coyote in the business. Never loses a client, going across. Kid, you're with *me* now, and I know how to pick 'em."

"¡*Vámonos!*" María stood in a single lithe motion.

There was an authority in her voice that silenced even Peter. She picked up the lantern and led them into the front room. Beyond the doorless entry to the *yerbería*, people strolled and laughed on the street. Inside, shadows twisted across the walls as the lantern swung. They filled the crowded shelves with false hint of movement, as if a thousand tiny demons scuttled among the mismatched jars. Outside in the street, two young girls with tight-braided hair and hungry faces leaned over a pile of hardware set up on a wooden bench against the wall. A skinny kid worked the keyboard, shoulders dipping, hips twisting, as if he was dancing, or working in VR, as if his whole body was pouring input into those grimy plastic keys. Sweat darkened his neon-orange tank top.

Josh wondered what they were hungry for, wondered what they were hunting. Maybe it was just a game. Sure. He tucked his chin closer to his chest, feeling naked and vulnerable in his white skin. He half-expected every person on the crowded street to turn and stare, like they'd done on the bus. An old woman was selling food from a tray, chanting her pitch in a cracked singsong. Josh couldn't see what it was, but the spicy aroma made his stomach growl briefly. She didn't look at him. She didn't direct her words to them at all, as the three of them walked past.

No one was looking at them. It took Josh another fifty yards to be sure of it. Eyes focused elsewhere. Bright words flowed around them as if they were invisible. Josh looked at the curve of María's back. In the shadows between the pools of light that seeped from cantina windows and battered solar lanterns of all descriptions, the roses on her arm glowed like a tracing of liquid fire. Like a beacon to lead them. Josh followed it, recognizing power in the smooth junction of her spine and shoulders. *Curandera?* Coyote? This was *her* town. They were invisible, because they were with María and she wanted them to be invisible.

She turned left at the corner of a crumbling adobe building that might have been a hotel or a big store once, but now was full of darkness. The dirt street dwindled to a track within a dozen yards. Somewhere off to their left, a goat bleated and a dog barked a single sharp warning. She halted them beside a hulk of shadow that resolved itself slowly into a falling-down shed cobbled together from rusty scraps of metal roofing. ''Now we wait,'' she said.

''You want to cross *here?''* Peter pushed past Josh, clutching at María's glowing arm. ''Are you crazy? The gate's less than a mile from here. My God, we'll walk right into them.''

He was afraid. Peter, who wasn't afraid of anything, who had laughed at Dad's rage, at his beatings. It came to Josh with a small buzz of shock that he *wasn't* afraid, that the last traces of fear had evaporated into the hot darkness sometime during their walk through town.

María waited silently until Peter let go of her arm. ''This is where the hole will come,'' she said. ''They look no harder here than elsewhere. You may go back, if you wish. Hire another coyote.''

''No.'' Peter was breathing hard, as if they'd been running. ''I can't. You know what they'll do if they catch me. I've got to get out of here *tonight.* You'd sure as hell better be right.''

María ignored the shrill note of threat. No, Josh thought. They had never been lovers. The soft, colored glow of María's tattoo lighted his brother's face, cast stark shadows beneath brows and cheekbones. He looked old. Much older than his twenty-seven years. Perhaps he had asked the surgeon to make him look old, Josh thought, but there was a weariness etched into the flesh of his face that went deeper than cosmetic work, went clear into the marrow of Peter's bones.

''What are you going to do after you go through?''

Peter's eyes evaded his. ''Move on to new turf, like I told you. Maybe Chile. Maybe New Bolivia. I don't think I'll tell you where, *hermanito.''* The malice in his voice was brittle; a thin shell, covering his fear.

''You've been running ever since you left home, haven't you?''

''I don't *run,* little brother.'' Peter bared his teeth. ''At least I'm my own man. *I'm* not going to waste my life living up to Daddy's expectations.''

''Aren't you, Peter? Dad never gave a shit what I did or didn't do,'' Josh said softly. ''He never noticed. He was too damn busy fighting with you. Yeah, I covered for you, Peter. I thought maybe it mattered, maybe things would get better. I didn't understand.''

''Enough.'' María's green eyes seemed to glow with their own light. ''It is time.''

Peter drew a hissing ragged breath. Time. María laid her

palm across her tattoo. When she lifted it, the fibers had gone dark. That darkness was absolute, as if the tiny threads of glowing light had been a lantern. It was there, in the dark, ahead of them. The Curtain. *El muro.* It tugged at Josh, promising violent epiphany and oblivion. Promising escape. Suddenly Josh knew why that man had run, arms spread, through the dust and heat.

"How does it work?" he asked hoarsely, needing words, the sound of a human voice. "How do you make the hole happen?"

"Screw the tour, kid."

"I don't *make* it happen." María took Josh's hand—her fingers felt cool and dry—led him forward through the darkness. "There are many holes in *el muro.* They happen here, there, all the time. Your technology is not so perfect as you pretend, gringo. To cross, you must predict a likely *where,* and then you make the *when* happen." She paused, fingers tightening. "When I say, run behind me. The hole is not wide." A red eye winked in the darkness ahead of them, like a glowing coal, or a red-eyed Cyclops.

A warning beacon, Josh realized. More red eyes winked to his right and left. Any warning signs were hidden by darkness, or maybe they didn't bother with warning signs on this side of the Curtain. They lighted it, near the big towns. *Come here,* the red eyes winked. *I promise you escape. I promise you freedom.*

You could spread your arms and run to embrace it, leap like a dying rabbit and . . . escape. Into the ultimate, irrevocable freedom. Josh remembered the mounted Death grinning from María's card and shivered. *You carry it with you,* she had said.

"*Cinco, quatro, tres . . . ,*" María hissed from the darkness. "Go!"

Josh ran. His body wanted to live and it flushed adrenaline through his veins, galvanizing muscles, making his heart pound. What would it feel like, to fry? Back muscles would contract—leg muscles, arms—flinging you into the air like a shot rabbit. His flesh cringed, full of life, dreading death. Rocks bruised his feet through his shoe soles. Sage clawed at his ankles, trying to trip him. How much farther? Ten yards? One? His skin prickled, as if his hair was standing on end. Nerves, or the hole closing? Josh stumbled and fell, slammed breathless by the rocky ground. He scrambled forward on hands and knees.

"It's okay, kid." Close by, Peter laughed a high-pitched breathless note. "We're through. Goddamn, we're through!"

"Not yet." María appeared, a darker shadow in darkness. "They know we are here. The sensors show them every owl and lizard. They are on their way."

"Now what?" Peter's voice went hoarse. "You're supposed to keep that from happening."

Engine noise in the distance, not loud. It had to be a Patrol vehicle. Josh knew that he should be terrified, but he wasn't terrified. He felt only a sense of anticipation, as if this was a scene he had rehearsed in some past life or distant dream. "It's all right," he said to Peter, and a small part of him wondered if it really was. "María knows what she's doing."

"All right, huh?" Peter's voice had gone shrill. "Do you think you're safe, Anglo? They'll shoot you as fast as they'll shoot us—they'll shoot you first. What now, María?"

"This confuses their scanners." She held out a flat gray rectangle, aiming it toward the engine growl in the darkness. "Go that way and stay low," she murmured. "You are coyotes. Think coyote hunting, hiding. *Believe* it, gringos, until you grow fur on your skin. When they come looking for you, lie flat and think about the fleas biting you. *¿Comprenden?*"

They ran, not too close together and not too far apart, flying like moths to the flame of the Patrol. Crouched low, Josh scrambled through clawing sage, running almost on all fours. Think coyote. He could hear the low murmur of the Patrol vehicle's electric engine; closer now. Would they hold their fire, if they realized he wasn't Mexican? Or was Peter telling the truth?

He flung himself flat behind a bush as a car door banged, heart slamming his ribs, thoughts a coyote's thoughts of hiding and flight. Voices scarred the night, blurred by the sage, Spanish or English, Josh couldn't tell. What would they use? Hand-held thermal scanners? Something like that. He pressed his face into the dust, trying not to breathe, eyes squeezed closed, waiting for the footsteps to crunch in the sand beside him, waiting for that adrenaline-rush of *aha*, like when you were a kid playing hide-and-seek, only this time, getting found didn't mean being *it*, it meant being dead. . . .

Footsteps crunched; close, closer. . . . "Damn scanner's acting up again tonight." Texas drawl, lazy on the night air. "But we got three *mojados* out here, sure."

"Or coyotes." The other voice sounded grumpy. "The four-legged kind. Could've been."

"Coyotes." Texas-voice snorted. "One coyote with two legs. Bet you a beer at The DewDrop."

"Done."

Voices and footsteps were getting fainter, moving away. Safe, O God safe, they'd missed him with their faulty scanner. He risked lifting his head—not very high (be a coyote)—and froze. Trick of desert acoustics—they were closer than he'd thought. Two men, dressed in camo, with night goggles like ugly masks. They carried automatic rifles. The new soldiers of a new Army. And he was the enemy.

*Be a coyote.* María's whisper in his head, a hint of invisible fingers on his shoulder. He held very still, breathing softly. He had gone to earth on a high point. The ground sloped gently away from him to the east. The two agents were walking across the slope, heads turning as they scanned the empty desert. Josh caught his breath. Peter. It might have been a deeper patch of shadow beneath a twisted clump of sage, but he knew with absolute certainty that it was his brother lying flat in the dust.

The Patrol men were going to walk right onto him.

A strange sense of lightness was growing inside Josh. It expanded like an invisible bubble, encompassing the sage-covered slope. It froze the Patrol agents in midstep, as if time itself had stopped. In the absolute silence, a video played in Josh's brain. On that internal screen, Peter leaped to his feet in a wild hopeless dash. The two agents fell back a step, lifting the short, ugly barrels of their rifles easily, without haste. Bullets streaked the night with fire, and Peter yelled one choked, meaningless syllable as he threw his arms out and fell facedown into the dust. Serves you right, you bastard. You had everything your way, fucked around all you wanted and stood in the damn spotlight the whole time. Jennifer screwed you out on the old sofa in the garage, because you were cool, because you were the bad honcho, the tough guy, the center of the Burns, Arizona, universe. She said, *I love you* to you, never to me. She never knew I existed, you bastard. Just like Dad never noticed that I existed. You had to have it all, didn't you? You couldn't leave anything for me, you stinking self-centered asshole.

Two more steps, maybe three, and they'd have to see Peter. They couldn't miss. They would shoot and he would die.

*The* ejido *is a place of desperation.* María's whisper in his ear, or the sound of dusty wind? *Your choice, gringo.*

Josh's fingers closed around a rock. The bubble of frozen time popped silently, and motion rushed in like a soundless thunderclap. Quick! He drew his arm back, flung the stone without aim.

The men spun, rifles raised, ready. "What was that?"

"Over there. No, by those rocks."

They were scanning the darkness with their ugly electronic faces, searching for him, for anything. Closer, closer. Josh hugged the dirt, wanting to bury his face, unable to look away.

Would he see the muzzle flash when they fired, or would the bullets hit him before his brain could interpret sight?

Something moved in the darkness, gray, fast, ghosting across the space between Josh and the agents. Gunfire stuttered and Josh flinched, blinded by the searing blossoms of light.

"Knock if off, you idiot." Grumpy-voice, loud and angry. "It was a coyote. The four-legged kind, like I told you." He lowered his voice. "If there *is* anyone out here, they know right where we are, thanks to you. With the scanner down, we're about on an equal footing if one of those stinking *mojados* is carrying hardware. I don't like those odds."

"You just want your beer," Texas-voice drawled.

"Screw the beer. Let's head back."

Miraculously, they walked back to their car and got in. As the engine noise faded into the distance, Josh started to shake. María appeared out of the darkness, tattoo glowing once more. Peter was with her.

"*Hermano,* that was a close one." Peter's laugh was feeble. "I thought they had me, sure. You okay?"

They did have you. "I'm fine." Josh tried unsuccessfully to keep his teeth from chattering as he spoke.

"Everything's cool now, kid." Peter sat down close beside him. "María says it's a clear shot into town. You can go to the cops there and spin 'em a yarn about getting robbed—passport stolen and all that. Around here, it happens." He touched Josh's arm lightly. "I would've felt bad if I'd gotten you killed, *hermano.*"

Josh lifted his head to meet his brother's shadowed eyes. "Do you remember Jennifer Hayes?"

"Jennifer?" Peter frowned. "Oh yeah. Long blonde hair. She and I had a thing once, didn't we? Dad nearly busted a gut trying to catch us together. I really had him going."

*I love you, Peter,* Jennifer had cried. "Peter?" Josh hesitated. "I was the one who told on you. About the school files."

Silence, except for the breathing of the desert.

"You?" Peter's voice came at last, fragile as the whisper of insect wings. "Sonofabitch. Why, Josh?"

"Because Dad loved you. Because he didn't even know I was there."

"*Loved* me?" Peter's voice cracked. "Josh, he beat the shit out of me that night. I thought he was gonna kill me. I never could be what the old man wanted, no matter what I did. *You* were the one who did everything right—you were everything he wanted."

"No. I wasn't." Out in the darkness, the Curtain shimmered. *El muro.* It could cut you off from past and future, from Burns, Arizona. "I'm not going back to Burns," Josh said. "There's nothing for me there, anymore. I don't know where I'll go." He drew a deep breath. "Want to come along for a while?"

"You're really leaving?" In the glow from María's tattoo, Peter's dark Hispanic eyes looked like twin holes into blackness. "I don't know." He turned away. "I mean, I've got my own stuff to do, you know?"

So he would go on to another *ejido,* another place of desperation. Peter had never actually crossed through the Curtain. It had merely stretched, hung between them now as an invisible barrier. Josh extended his hand, half expecting to feel its presence. "Dad's dead," he said softly.

"Yeah. I guess he is, isn't he." Peter looked at María. "Let's get this show on the road, okay?"

Her eyes glowed like her tattoo. "This is where you go." She handed him a small scrap of hardcopy. "Ramón will have what you need. If he tells you that he needs more money, tell him that his grandmother the coyote is watching him."

"Don't worry about me, kid." Peter lifted a hand. "I do just fine."

"Just a minute." Josh fumbled at his wrist. "I almost forgot." He held out the old watch. "At the end, Dad said that he was sorry. About what happened between you. He wanted me to give you this, to tell you that he understood—that he loved you." The lie dissolved slowly on the night air. It might have happened that way, but it hadn't. Burns, Arizona, was a place of desperation, too.

Peter reached slowly for the watch. "Thanks," he said very softly. "Take care of yourself, Josh." Darkness swallowed him, leaving only the small sounds of the desert night in his wake.

"What about me?" Josh faced María at last.

"You will go to the Patrol office in town," she told him crisply. "You will tell them that this man robbed you at gunpoint, that he drove back across the border with your money and your passport." She handed him a small 2-D photo. The man had a pocked Hispanic face and a predatory air.

"Why him?" Josh handed it back.

"They will take someone, so we will make it him. It is justice, gringo. Believe it or not. You owe me the price of your escape. This is part of it."

"And for Peter's."

María shook her head. "For some there is no escape. I do not charge you for what I cannot do."

Josh bent his head, hiding from that emerald stare. The coyote's eyes had glinted like green gems in the darkness. "I almost killed my brother," he said softly. "I think I have wanted to do that all my life." The *ejido* was a place of desperation. Would Peter run to *el muro* one day, arms spread to embrace the only escape it offered? "I don't want to kill him anymore," he whispered.

María inclined her head without speaking.

"Wait," Josh said as she turned away. "How much do I owe you? How will I get the money to you?"

"You will come back to me." María looked over her shoulder. "Or I will come to you. You have escaped the *ejido*. You will go many places and do many things. There is enough time for me to collect my debt."

"Did your spirits tell you that?"

"No." María smiled gently. "You have told me, gringo." She lifted her arm in a glowing salute and walked away into the darkness.

# YNTHESIS

Standing on a rock in the middle of the Precambrian ocean, David Chen raised his arms like a conductor. At his feet, the primordial sea responded, swelling around the barren crag on which he stood, rich with the potential of life. Sticky yellowish foam clung to the lava rock, stuck to David's bare feet. His virtual program translated the touch of foam on his palms with low-level electrical stimulation and suggested the damp breeze, but this was a Net piece. You didn't *smell* the ocean or feel the damp briny caress of that breeze.

In a stationary piece, he could add complex sensory input: the cold touch of foam, the tang of the rich sea. He could make this piece *live*. David suppressed a sigh. You had to have a gallery to get a stationary showing. Chen BioSource did very well on the Exchange, but the family firm didn't do well enough that he could afford to put on his own stationary shows. This piece would get its opening on the Net. Tomorrow. That was a big enough triumph, he told himself.

Tomorrow. Tension stirred in David's gut. He had managed to bury that deadline, but now it surfaced, ticking in his brain like an antique clock. He frowned at a plume of volcanic ash twisting across the pale sky. Was it out of balance, or was this just a case of preopening jitters? Wind moaned across the sea with the lonely voice of woodwinds, prophesying change. David stretched a virtual arm to tweak at the ash plume. Better. Not a bad prologue, he told himself and counted down: three, two, one, *now.*

The sea heaved, pregnant with life. Creatures writhed, swarmed, coalesced, and divided in a frenzied symphony of evolution. David stepped into the troubled sea and let himself sink. The silty water swirled around him, and the sense of motion was vivid enough to make David a little seasick. Good. Nothing for the nitpickers to bitch about here. He had researched every species, down to the last cell. David climbed back onto his rock, allowing himself to savor a tentative anticipation. *Creation,* he'd called this piece; his biggest to date. And it was . . . good.

Yes, good. All around him, swirling motes grew legs, feeder fronds, fins that became jointed swimming appendages. The Earth writhed and shuddered with the spasms of birth and death. Music soared in accompaniment as mountain peaks thrust up from the seething water, piercing the yellowish sky. . . . David stiffened as an ominous darkness spread slowly across that sky. It dimmed the sun, cast a threatening shadow over the landscape. A breeze riffled the water, and the suggestion of cold raised goose bumps on David's neck. On the rocky shore, the first hesitant swimmer was flopping and struggling its way into the intertidal zone, gasping with rudimentary lungs.

That wasn't supposed to happen. "Pause," David snapped and the scene froze. "Goddammit." He searched the motionless landscape of sea swell and breaking waves. "Where the hell are you, *this* time?"

A pointy canid face peeked at him from behind a thrust of black lava rock. American red fox. *Vulpes fulva,* and you could see every hair ripple in the wind, David thought grudgingly.

Red-furred, prick-eared, the fox grinned a white toothy grin. Its green eyes glinted with mischief, and it made a very human, very rude, noise.

Enough! David stretched out his hand. The pistol appeared in his fist, a vintage Western-style revolver with a pearl handle. The fox flicked its white-tipped tail, laughed a boy's laugh, and streaked across the static sea. It vanished into thin air as David fired. For a long moment he scowled after it. Then he tossed the revolver into the air. It blinked out of existence. "House?" he said. "Did I make contact?"

*I'm sorry.* House's voice whispered over his audial implant. *The intruder was able to withdraw from the program before the security trace connected.*

David grimaced, a headache nibbling at the back of his brain. He had changed the program-entry codes again only yesterday, had thought that he'd seen the last of his pesky ghost for a while. This piece opened *tomorrow.* Damaged or not. "Eraser," David said between clenched teeth. He snatched the oversized chalkboard-duster from the air and raised his hand to sweep away the fox's added shadow.

But it contributed something to the theme of the piece—a hint of trouble to come. An ominous warning. David tapped his toe on the frozen sea. He frowned at the ancestors of land life, caught in their struggle to crawl up onto the muddy ocean verge. Earth would never be the same again. The shadow . . . fit. Oh hell. "Save," David commanded. When the scene had been safely stored, he wiped away the fox's darkness with sweeping angry strokes.

*Excuse me,* the House program interrupted him. *You are due at your father's apartment in one hour.*

David sighed and disappeared the eraser. He wanted more time, wanted to run every moment of this piece through his virtual fingers, to reassure himself that his elusive ghost had done no more damage; that texture, shading, and tone were exactly what he had intended.

He did not want to meet with his father this evening.

David sighed again. "Store and exit." He closed his eyes against the momentary disorientation of the collapsing virtual.

His virtual lab took shape around him; three by three meters of carpeted walls, floor, ceiling. He stood in the middle of the floor, lanky and naked except for his singlet. The silver threads of his intradermal Kraeger net glittered in the subdued glow of the strip lights, covering every square centimeter of his skin. David wrinkled his nose, smelling his own sour sweat. His hair had come loose from its braid, and it stuck to his neck. Resisting the temptation to recall the piece and blame a glitch in his House program for his tardiness, David went to shower and dress.

HIS FATHER refused to use virtuals. He wouldn't even put on a suit of virtual skinthins, although he had had David netted before birth. Typical, David thought as he hesitated in the atrium outside his father's apartment. His father might detest the technology, but a Kraeger was the last word in power dressing in the business world. So Fuchin had had David netted. To benefit the family. "We Chinese are obsessed with family," David murmured. He brushed a nonexistent wrinkle from his tunic, wishing that the old man wasn't so stubbornly intransigent about the technology. He would be much easier to deal with in virtual.

*"Bù yâu,* don't preen for me," his father said when David finally entered the room. He was speaking Mandarin. "Save such actions for a future bride's attention."

Not that subject again. "Hello, Fuchin." David inclined his head stiffly and settled into the indicated chair. His father went in for antique lacquer chairs and a profusion of colored fabrics. Calligraphed scrolls hung on the walls, praising virtue. An antique writing set—ink box, carved jade chop, inkstone, and brushes—was laid out neatly on a carved desk. The antique clutter made David feel claustrophobic. "How are you feeling?" he asked his father. "Shau Jieh told me that you were having trouble sleeping."

*"Ching ni,* speak Mandarin, please. Use English for business. Your youngest sister worries too much." David's father waved his hand. "She is a good daughter." He reached for the porcelain pot on the table at his elbow and poured two cups of pale tea.

His father looked classically southern, David thought. His face might have been lifted from an antique Guangdong scroll. David's own features were more diluted; the product of his mother's mixed Caucasian blood. His eldest half-sister, Dà Jieh, liked to remind him of his mother's mixed blood. She had been something of a scandal, a very late and very young second wife. She had given him her own father's name, but David didn't remember much about her. He regarded his father's stark profile, lips tightening as he read the signs of anger folded into the brown, aged skin. What had he done, *this* time?

"How is Yu Hwa?" his father asked.

"We aren't seeing each other anymore. We got mutually bored. Middle sister *is* about to give you your third grandson," David said. Èr Jieh had opted for selected gender again—to please father, he was sure. David sighed. "Fuchin, if we have to fight, can we at least fight about the real issue and not about my childless status?"

"Try one of these Phoenix Eye dumplings. They're made with shrimp. Wild-harvest shrimp, not artificial paste. A gift from Shau Jieh." His father sipped his tea. "You have no child. Can't you think of your family? Who will carry on the name? Who will light incense for me?"

"This is not fifteenth-century China." David declined the proffered dumplings with a shake of his head. "Chen BioSource is a family company, not a dynasty."

"Your shortsightedness tires me to death." His father's frown deepened. "I understand that you have been dealing with a representative of the Tanaka Corporation. Why didn't you ask me first?"

Aha. "My job is to deal with company representatives so that you don't have to." David spread his palm so that the silver threads of his net caught the light. "Have I misunderstood?"

"You exceeded your authority. I am the head of Chen BioSource, and I am the majority stockholder."

"I only talked to Mr. Takamura this afternoon. Less than five hours ago." They had met in a plush Tokyo office; in virtual, of course. Mr. Takamura had worn the virtual face of a popular Japanese media star; the latest in power dressing. "I was going to bring it up in conference, tomorrow." After he finished *Creation*. After the opening.

"That is not appropriate." His father's palm slapped down on the lacquer table, making the pot shiver. "I am to be consulted before any such dealings. We will not do business with Tanaka."

"Fuchin." David hung on to his temper with an effort. "Have you discussed this with the rest of the family? Have you talked to Dà Jieh, to Eldest Sister? Half of the genetic templates we market are for improved strains of commercial sea-life. I gave you the report on the upcoming revision of the Antarctic treaty. Japan is rumored to be the winning bidder for harvest rights in the Antarctic waters. Tanaka is the largest Japanese firm involved in serious aquaculture. They will benefit. They made us an outstanding offer," he said.

"I risked everything to create Chen BioSource." His father rose stiffly to his feet. "I did it for our family; for you and your sisters, for your children's futures. I did not do it to benefit Tanaka. I am sick to death of hearing about Tanaka. You would throw away everything that I have worked for, give it away to strangers. You have no sense of family."

"And I wonder about your sense of business," David said in English. He clenched his fists on his knees. "I was not selling out the firm. Tanaka is interested in a long-term contract, that's all. I thought our intention was to make a profit," he said.

"There is profit and there is profit."

"And Tanaka is Japanese." David met his father's disapproving stare. "Prejudice is an antique and expensive luxury, Fuchin."

"And loyalty is beyond price. Your eldest sister agrees with me. Tanaka is a danger to our independence."

"Does she?" David's laugh hurt his throat. "That's a new tune, considering that her last three designs were targeted specifically for Tanaka's Pacific fisheries—*with* their direct input." He should have expected this. Dà Jieh was always ready to stick a knife into him, where their father was concerned. "If I'm so incompetent and disloyal, why don't you fire me and hire someone else?" he demanded bitterly.

"Do you want to waste your life playing your expensive games?" His father's lip curled. "You are my son. You are *Chen*. Chen BioSource is *your* heritage."

"And your dynasty." David flushed. He got to his feet, stared down at his father. "I'll meet with Mr. Takamura and reject his offer. I hope the *family* firm doesn't regret this."

"Er-dz!"

David wanted to ignore his father's command, but his muscles obeyed out of lifelong habit, pausing David at the door, turning him around to face his father.

"I have decided to retire. Two months from today." His father's face might have been a mask, carved from dark bitter wood. "On that day, Chen BioSource will become your responsibility. On that day, you may do as you wish."

David turned on his heel without bowing, without speaking. He strode through the anteroom and out into the large atrium that his father shared with David's youngest half-sister. She was waiting for him, sitting on an upholstered bench beside a small pool of water lilies. Her hair was pulled back smoothly from her wide face, braided into an intricate knot at the base of her neck, and she wore a floor-length tunic of jade-colored cotton.

"Come sit with me," she said in Mandarin and patted the bench. "Fuchin is feeling very threatened, today."

"By what, Shau Jieh?" David dropped onto the seat beside her.

"It's because he's old. He knows that he is starting to make mistakes, and it terrifies him."

"He didn't seem very terrified. I got the impression that *I* made the mistakes." David nudged a polished pebble from the rim of the pool. It fell into the crystal water with a tiny splash. Gold-and-white koi fled, trailing diaphanous fins.

"Fuchin sees himself in you—perhaps too clearly." She smiled at the widening rings on the pool's surface. "How does that *work*? I can't even tell that the water is a holo unless I try to touch it."

"There's a chip inside each pebble." David nudged another bit of agate into the holographic pool. "The program senses it and generates the ripples."

"It's a wonderful job, Little Brother. What are you working on now?"

"A piece called *Creation*." David let go of his anger. Shau Jieh was only four years his senior, and the only sister with whom he had been close as a child. His middle and elder sisters had been adults—disapproving adults—to his young eyes. Only Shau Jieh had been willing to play tag and fly kites with him. "It's about the origins of life on Earth," he told her. "Sort of a symphony of evolution. It shows on the Net, tomorrow."

"Wonderful." She clapped her hands with delight. "I'll Net into it. Did you tell Fuchin?"

"Tell him what?" The bitterness rose in David's throat again. "He doesn't approve of my *games*. You're throwing away your life here, Shau Jieh. You don't have to be his servant. Why don't you move out, or move in with someone who'll appreciate what they've got?"

"I like living here." She blushed. "Fuchin didn't mean it. About your art." She touched David's arm lightly, tracing the silver threads of his net with her fingertips. "Chen BioSource has eaten him," she said sadly. "It's become his immortality, and lately he's been feeling very mortal. You care about your art, and that frightens him."

"You protect him too much." David smiled to take the sting out of his words. "Chen BioSource would have fallen apart years ago, if you weren't here to keep us all speaking to each other. Sometimes though, I wish. . . ." He shook his head impatiently, at a loss for words. What did he wish? That his father would enter one of his pieces? Approve of it? How childish, David thought. Father wouldn't even step into virtual to deal with an important client. "As long as you're playing mediator, ask Eldest Sister to leave me alone." He tugged at the thick braid of his hair. "I have enough trouble without her encouraging our father's prejudices."

"Don't be angry. Dà Jieh cares about her genetic designs as much as you do about your virtuals. She gets . . . jealous."

"Of *what*? Surely not of me, her incompetent little mongrel brother?" He laughed, but his sister looked troubled. She was taller than he when she stood up, but sitting down, her enormous eyes gave her the look of an anxious child. David bent over and kissed the perfectly straight part on top of her head. "I'll try not to get into another fight with her," he promised, dropping back into English. "But I wish she'd lay off. I make plenty of trouble for myself without her help. Why can't we get along?"

"What's bothering you tonight, Younger Brother?"

"Does it show so much?" David glanced down at her hand. Those thick blunt fingers looked so clumsy, could communicate such warmth. "Fuchin told me that he's going to retire," David said slowly. "In two months. Shau Jieh-Jieh, I'm confused. He accuses me of betraying the family with one breath, tells me that he's turning the company over to me with the next."

"Fuchin thinks that you do a very good job," his sister said in a low voice.

"Does he? I'd like to hear that from him. Just once." David stood abruptly. "I have a *game* to finish."

"Don't be angry."

"I try," David said through tight lips. "I really do, Shau Jieh. Good night."

"Good night," his sister said, but her eyes were sad. Frowning into the depths of the holoed koi pool, she didn't look up as he left.

DAVID TOOK a cab to his tower, caught the lift to his midlevel floor. Beyond the transparent walls of the tube, the spilled jewels of LA's lights sank downward into darkness. For decades, the city had waited for The Quake. The Big One. It had never arrived. David imagined the spangled cityscape shattering, blossoming into flame and ruin. Seen from this height, distanced and abstract, it would be a beautiful and terrible image. Powerful. The lift stopped at his floor, and David turned away from the view with a jerk.

David maintained a single room beside his lab. It was sparely decorated, the opposite of his father's cluttered space. A few cushions lay scattered around a single low table, and a futon on a platform served as bed and sofa. His excess income went into the purchase of Netspace for his virtuals. David ordered himself a cup of tea from the kitchen wall, feeling slightly disoriented, as if the room had changed subtly in his absence. He had never been truly able to imagine himself as the executive of Chen BioSource, even though he had known that it would happen someday. David stared into the golden depths of his tea. His father's retirement had seemed as real and as unreal as the predicted Big Quake; a threat that hovered forever beyond the horizon of tomorrow.

Tomorrow had arrived.

David left his tea on the table and went into his lab. He stripped off his tunic, tossed it into a corner. Light rippled across the silver threads embedded in his skin. You had to be netted in utero, during early fetal development. Those threads translated every twitch of muscle, every biochemical shift, to his virtual programs. An intradermal net gave you the ultimate range of interaction in virtual.

Ironic, that it had enabled David to practice virtual art. Father certainly hadn't spent Chen money on it for *that* purpose. It had been an investment for the business, for the family. Food and family, David thought sourly. Our cultural obsessions. "Studio," he commanded, and spread his arms.

The walls shimmered, became the off-white walls of his virtual studio, soaring two stories to a multipaned skylight. An easel stood in one corner. A half-finished painting of van Gogh's *Sunflowers* stood on its paint-spattered shelf. A green plant spread lush tropical leaves in another corner, and a black-and-white cat washed its face contentedly on an antique steam radiator. Dust motes glittered in a shaft of sunshine that found its way through the skylight, and soft dulcimer music filled the air.

In here, in the virtual sanctuary of his studio, neither his father nor Chen BioSource existed. David walked over to a rack of canvases that stood against one wall. He picked out *Creation;* green water and black rock painted with heavy, confident brush strokes. It was his strongest work yet. David pulled on the canvas. It stretched in his hands, lengthening, widening, until it was door-sized. It *became* a doorway, opening onto heaving waves and a small lava crag. No sign of fox-prints. David started to step through the doorway, paused as a two-toned chime rang through his studio. Only a few friends knew the entry code. "Come in," David said, and sighed.

A door appeared in the studio wall, a smooth panel of hand-rubbed birch. It swung open to reveal a tall, slender man with spiked blond hair and the face of a breathtakingly beautiful boy.

"Hello, Beryl."

"You're working, dear heart?" Beryl wandered over to the canvas-door, moving with languid grace. He peered in and shrugged. "Your stuff's good, but it's too subtle for me. I like a little raw violence stuck in here and there."

"Thanks." David snapped his fingers, and a white curtain dropped across the Precambrian scene. Right now, he did not want to listen to Beryl's deft needling or to a dose of the latest gossip. All he wanted to do was to walk through that door into his piece, lose himself in it. "What's up?" he asked shortly.

"I've got a little present for you." Beryl reached, and a padded chair appeared under his hand. "No charge, for a friend." He curled into the chair, smiling.

Beryl's body language reminded David of a cat. A supple purring leopard. David wondered what Beryl looked like in the flesh—in fleshtime. "You charge for everything," David said. "Even if it doesn't always show up on my Exchange account."

"You wound me." Beryl didn't look wounded. "Who are BioSource's enemies, dear heart?"

"Enemies?" David blinked. "We've got plenty of rivals in the field; Antech and Selva Internacional are probably our biggest competitors. Why?"

"Someone is buying Chen BioSource Security codes on the Net."

"What?"

"When did you lose your hearing, dear heart?"

Sabotage? Piracy? The possibilities buzzed in David's head like biting flies. He wanted to doubt, but Beryl hadn't acquired his reputation by selling flawed information. "We're not a high-end operation." David shook his head slowly. "We're not big time. Who the hell wants to pirate gene-templates? It would be cheaper to buy them."

"I told you what I know." Beryl yawned. "Find out who's buying and ask *them*."

Troubles, troubles. He would have to warn the rest of the family and spend time reviewing Security for cracks. It would mean upset, a flair of tempers and accusations. His father was going to throw a fit. David's earlier headache had come back. How long before he spent his every waking moment worrying about Chen BioSource?

"I'm off. Edith is throwing a hot party tonight. Are you coming?" Beryl's chair vanished as he stood. "No? Too bad. Well, if I hear any whispers about Chen codes, I'll let you know."

"For a price."

"Of course. Wasn't my information on the Antarctica treaty worth the investment?"

It would have been, if his father had been willing to listen. David balled his hand into a fist as the birchwood door closed behind Beryl and vanished. No time for *Creation*, now. He windowed into BioSource Security, called up a quick overview of the last ten days. No one had tried to enter. David purchased an extra level of protection, wincing at the cost. He chewed his lip, considering. He should call Father. But his father would want to know David's source, and he did not approve of freelancers like Beryl. So the family would get into it, spend the night in a frenzy of argument, and nothing more would be accomplished, anyway.

If someone had the codes and tried to use them, the extra layer of Security he was installing should alert David. If they'd already been into Chen filespace, it was too late.

Who wanted to spend that kind of money to swipe a handful of genetic designs? Someone. He would have to ask Eldest Sister about it. Tomorrow would be soon enough. It would be too soon.

Near midnight, David finally windowed out of Security. Tired, but too tense even to contemplate sleep, he swept the curtain aside and plunged into the surge of the Precambrian ocean. Life formed and re-formed around him, evolution in full song, a dance of eternity. David watched it from his rock, a cold sinking in the pit of his stomach. It had looked good, this afternoon.

It didn't look good to him now. It looked flat and overambitious, like a kid trying to copy the *Mona Lisa* with crayons. Technical perfection with no soul. A 3-D video game. Then a flash of rusty color caught his eye, and David spun.

The fox sat on its haunches on a stretch of muddy beach, its head tilted, eyes quizzical.

"You little sneak." David clenched his fists. All the jagged bits and fragments of this night balled up in his stomach, ignited into rage. "You damn Network ghost! Stay the hell out of my pieces!" He leaped off his rock, staggering in waist-deep water. "I'll trace you. I'll kill you, do you hear me?" Panting, he struggled for the beach.

The fox flicked its white-tipped tail and fled.

"Bastard!" David yelled after it. He stumbled, fell to his knees in the mud, palms slipping, spilling him flat on his face. Rage popped like a bubble inside him. He'd done too good a job on his beach. If he hadn't made the mud slippery, he wouldn't be on his face in it. That irony wrung a laugh out of him as he picked himself up. The fox had vanished. David erased the virtual mud from his skin and continued to run the piece through. There were no signs of any more fox-prints.

The effects he had tried to achieve—the harmonies and dissonances, the subtle contrasts in textures and atmosphere—were still there. But he couldn't recapture the excitement he had felt as he created them. David sat down on a rocky headland, fatigue a dry ache behind his eyeballs. Opening jitters, he told himself; but it was more than just jitters. There was a dusty feeling in the back of his brain, a sense of futility. "Beginning," he commanded the program with a sigh. "Run."

Once more, the sea swelled with diversifying and proliferating life. Once more, the ugly questing snouts of the air breathers poked at the intertidal mud. David frowned at the sky. "Pause." He retrieved the fox-marked scene from storage, overlaid it. Yes. The shadow improved it. What the hell, David thought, and merged the overlay in.

This would be his last piece, his last show. In two months, there would not be enough time for this. It would become a hobby, a pleasant diversion. If he did it at all. David ran through *Creation* again and again, not satisfied with it, not able to let go of it. In the early hours of the morning, too numb with fatigue to feel anything, he downloaded it into the show's Netspace.

"I HAVEN'T any idea what they're after." Thin, tall, radiating suppressed energy, his eldest sister crossed her arms on her desktop. "Security is *your* problem, isn't it?"

"It is." David forced a smile. When had Dà Jieh started seriously to dislike him? A cloudy memory stirred in his mind—a formal family dinner with some honored guest or other. David remembered cushions piled beneath him so that he could reach the table, remembered his father's hand on his head as he boasted of David's progress with his tutorials. He remembered his eldest sister's eyes, as she sat silently across the table from him.

At age twenty, she had taken a dual degree in biochemistry and genetics, had done so with highest honors. Had his father told their visitor that? With a child's narcissism, he hadn't remembered. David shook his head. "It would help me if I knew where to start looking," he said. "What have you got under development?"

"If you are making the executive decisions for Chen Bio-Source, it is advisable to pay attention during conferences."

David swallowed a groan. Shau Jieh had spilled the beans. "You do a great job of keeping us informed." He dropped into English. "But what about projects in the theoretical stage? Things that you haven't officially begun to develop yet. Have you seen any signs of entry into your filespace at all?"

"No. Nothing is complete enough to steal. I hope your Security is as tight as you claim. Have you discussed this with our father?"

"Not yet. We're at an impasse unless we can discover who is after us." David sighed. They were meeting in his sister's office virtual. It was a packaged job, standard and plastic. He had offered once to design her something more interesting. He wouldn't make that mistake again. "What about the new line of cod that you're working on?" he asked.

"Tanaka's the only company doing open-sea farming on any scale." She frowned down at her desktop, ran her long fingers through her clipped-short hair. "They've already contracted for it. Why steal it? No. I would guess that your pirate is after that high-yield strain of oil-producing corn cells we've targeted for the vat-culture industry. It will outperform anything on the market."

Her expression was earnest, but David frowned. She was dealing with him in realtime, and her office wasn't editing her body language. There was . . . evasion in her posture. "Dà Jieh, Eldest Sister, I didn't know about Fuchin's plans before last night." He groped for the words he needed. "I'm not . . . happy about his decision. I don't think that I'm ready to take this on yet. I'll do the best I can, but I need your help," he said. "I need the whole family's help."

"Perhaps you should tell our father *ni bù néng*, that you can't do it." She reverted to Mandarin, her tone coldly formal.

"I promised Shau Jieh that I wouldn't fight with you."

"You'd rather play your precious games."

Father's words. "They're not games," David said.

"Oh yes. You call it art." His sister smiled coldly. "You remind me so much of your mother. Shau Jieh tells me that she's somewhere in the Colorado Preserve. Heli-skiing with her latest lover. She only liked to play and spend Chen money."

"I'll give you the status report on Security as soon as it's complete," David said. He bowed, turned on his heel, and stepped into his studio. "What does she want from me?" he said. "Damn it."

The cat blinked at him from its perch on the radiator, jumped to the floor, and arched against his ankles. David reached down to scratch its ears absently. Yes, his mother was in Colorado. He wondered how Shau Jieh knew—wondered if Youngest Sister was keeping track of her. She had made a complete break with their father when she left, but unexpectedly, David had received a call from her. It had come a month ago, on his thirty-first birthday, a barely remembered voice from a barely remembered past. She had left his father—and David—when he was two.

Reality and unreality. David gave the cat one last pat and straightened. Special lenses in his eyes let him see a cat. He stretched out a hand, and visual suggestion made his nerves interpret low-level electric stimulation from his net as warm flesh and fur. So he petted a cat and it comforted him. You could make love in virtual, to a perfect, unreal partner. You could fight an enemy. Your body could go into shock from a virtual wound. A month ago, he had sat in the virtual of a plush resort living-room across from a petite woman with fine pale skin, a Chinese face, and reddish hair. His mother had looked thirty-five. No older. She had smiled at him with a sad, slightly puzzled, expression, as if she couldn't quite remember him or couldn't believe that he was actually her son. They had drunk coffee together, and she had asked about his art. *I couldn't live in your father's world,* she had said, as if she was answering a question. *I tried, but I couldn't. I am sorry, David.*

I didn't ask, David thought. I've never asked her why she left. He watched the cat leap back onto its radiator. The thirty-five-year-old woman on the virtual sofa had been as unreal as this cat. In fleshtime, his mother would be in her sixties. That young woman on the sofa had been more real to David than the dim memories that sometimes haunted his dreams.

The boundary between the real and the unreal was a fragile one. David rubbed his eyes, remembering that family dinner again, and how he had beamed in the spotlight of his father's pride. Once more he tried to remember if Fuchin had praised Dà Jieh, but all he could summon was a vision of her cold, angry eyes. "Access Hans Renmeyer," David said, and sighed. "Semiformal mode."

The square, blunt features of his agent appeared in the air in front of David. "David." Renmeyer smiled, visible only from the waist up. "I was going to call you. *Creation* has accumulated the greatest share of access-points of any piece in the MultiNet show this past twenty-four hours."

"That's great," David murmured. This wasn't a realtime

conversation. Renmeyer's body language was just a hair off. You could always tell a sim from a realtime interaction.

"The show committee has offered you a further three days of exhibition," Renmeyer's sim announced. "They'll download your royalty statement to your personal account at the conclusion of the show. It's the standard contract. I have it ready for your signature, if you agree."

So *Creation* was a success. Absently, David scanned the oversized document that appeared in front of him, laid his palm against the signature box. Such a success might conceivably bring a gallery invitation. David wandered into his living room, ordered up a bowl of noodles and bok choi that he didn't really want. He should feel triumphant. Fulfilled. Pleased, at least.

He felt tired.

DAVID SPENT the morning windowed into Security, reviewing reports, double-checking for unusual currents in the daily informational flow. Nothing presented itself to him. If anyone was probing Chen Security, they were too good to detect. Thoughtfully, he called up the file on the company's current projects—Dà Jieh's projects. She was the creative genius that powered Chen. She was the one who found the backdoor means to ends that other engineers had given up on.

She knows what our pirate is after, David thought, and then wondered why he thought so. You could attach a dozen negative interpretations to her hostility. Someday, he would ask their youngest sister about it. Shau Jieh would know. Shau Jieh had worshiped her as a kid, had followed her tall, brilliant sister like a shadow.

David finally exited Security in midafternoon, spent a hurried couple of hours reviewing the day's reports. Chen Bio-Source was down on the Exchange, and there was no reason for it to be down. He scowled. Rumors of the pirate interest? He would have to ask Beryl. The studio waited for him on the other side of the wall. David could feel its breathing presence as he dumped his uneaten noodles into the recycler and drank a glass of water. *Creation* was a success, with an extended showing to its credit. Enough to interest a gallery? Enough to get it a stationary showing?

It didn't matter anymore.

The walls squeezed in on him. David banged his glass down on the counter. It tipped over, rolled off onto the carpeted floor. It didn't break, and he didn't pick it up. Grabbing a jacket from the closet, he went into the hall, down the lift, and out onto the street.

The city streets always depressed David. Crowded, littered with a human spoor of food wrappers and trash, they made him think of cracks in the city reality, accumulating dirt and debris. Black-market vendors hawked food, chemicals, and information from carts and coat pockets. Public terminals and virtual booths clustered at every corner. Cabs zipped past, and the mag-lev whispered overhead on its concrete rail.

People in the street shuffled past in a faceless procession, on their way from *here* to *there*, flesh brushing flesh, making no eye contact. We are at our most isolated in the street, David thought, although lately he had felt as if someone was following him every time he left the tower. He never noticed any particular person when he turned to look, but the feeling haunted him. He didn't feel that shadow's presence today. Shoulders hunched, David threaded his way through the crowd, welcoming its grimy claustrophobic crush. He couldn't think down here, and he didn't want to think.

A crowd filled the small square at the end of the block, thronged around some shouting evangelist, or revolutionary, or entertaining crazy. Pedestrian traffic stalled, backed up, and spilled over into the street. David let the crowd pressure-push him into a narrow alley between two old office buildings. A small shop opened into it—a custom clothing designer. The expensive holo decoration and squalid site suggested that it was the peak of chic. For the moment. The holos were mediocre. David eyed them, then noticed three figures crowded into the shadowy recess of a sealed-up doorway.

Two youths held a kid between them. They wore black skin-thins and tattoos on their hairless scalps; youth's current uniform of tough. The boy looked about twelve; street-kid ragged. This was just another city reality, ugly and ever present. People walked, hurried, or strolled past. There were fewer here than in the main thoroughfare, but they were equally blind; as if they were walking inside separate virtuals. Light from the storefront holo shone on the kid's face, warm as the afternoon sun. It made his green eyes glitter. David hesitated. Skinthins peaked from beneath the kid's dirty clothes. The way he tilted his head and hunched his shoulders against the hands that gripped him looked . . . familiar. David mentally overlaid red fur on that thin face, adding pricked ears. The boy's lips drew back from his teeth, and David saw a fox-face, a ghost face that had laughed at him with glittering green eyes.

"Hey," he said, and stopped.

The taller of the youths turned to stare at David. His pale eyes looked like glass marbles in his expressionless face. His posture suggested that David was no threat. With unhurried grace, he turned back to the kid, seized his wrist with a long-fingered hand, and twisted it.

The kid screamed.

Still unhurried, the two of them let go of the boy, stalked past David, and disappeared into the main street. David stared after them, stunned by their casual violence. Quick movement at the edge of his vision jolted him out of his trance. He turned in time to grab hold of the kid's grubby tunic. "Not so fast." The virtual skinthins beneath the filthy clothes were expensive, state-of-the-art. David shoved the boy back against the concrete wall, eyes narrowing as the kid's chin came up. Yeah, it was *him*. The fox-ghost. His body language gave him away. "What the hell have you been doing in my pieces?" he demanded.

"Nothing, man. Leggo! You're crazy."

"Don't give me *nothing*." David shook him. "You damn vandal. You've been all over the place. Did you think it was fun? Did you get a kick out of screwing around in my pieces and messing things up? Was that it? *Was it?*"

"No," the kid gasped. "I went in because you're *good*. You're the best."

"Bullshit," David said between his teeth.

"No shit, man. I'm an artist. Like you." The kid looked up through the tangle of his dirty blond hair, his fox-eyes glittering. "I'm good. But you're better. For now."

"So work your own pieces."

"Netspace costs. And I wanted to see how you did stuff."

Something like . . . veneration gleamed in those green eyes. David scowled. The kid was thin. His bones pushed sharp edges against his pale skin. He was cradling the hand that the youth had twisted, and there were pain shadows at the corners of his mouth.

"That guy hurt you," David said.

"I went into this jerk's abstract. What a piece of shit." The kid's lip curled. "But he's got better Security than you do. I guess word got around that I was haunting your stuff, so they looked for me here."

"You've been following me, haven't you? In the street."

"I wanted to see you. It's just a thing, you know? Realtime

flesh, I mean—I just like to do that. You're the same," he said. "You don't put on a Self when you're working."

"Why bother?" David looked away from those glittering eyes. He felt a twinge of recognition for the hunger that he saw there. That shadow had added just the right touch to *Creation*. David sighed. "Someone needs to look at your hand," he said. "Come on."

The kid didn't say a word on the way to a nearby clinic. David half-expected him to bolt, would have been relieved if he had. The boy's body language suggested flight. He walked tense and wary; poised. But he didn't bolt. At the clinic, at David's request, a receptionist ushered the boy into a treatment cubicle. He hunched silently on the bench, a cornered fox, ignoring David. He didn't make a sound as a bored medical tech set his broken wrist with a single twisting pull, but his skin went dead white and beads of sweat glistened on his forehead. The tech put a cast on his wrist, handed him two orange capsules for pain, and left.

David ran his own card through the terminal for payment. Outside, the kid followed him blindly, as if he was sleepwalking. The plastic cast encased his hand and part of his forearm. The boy cradled the hand in his good arm, carrying it as if it was a piece of wood. At the entrance to David's tower, he hesitated, and a shadow of his earlier wariness stirred in the green depths of his eyes.

"It's all right," David said, because the look in the kid's eyes demanded some kind of reassurance.

The wariness didn't go away, but the kid nodded and walked through the door into the entryway, as if David had extended a formal invitation.

David felt a growing uneasiness as the lift carried them upward. Slanting beams of afternoon sun touched the soaring new towers and the old office buildings, gilded the city with light the color of hope. He hadn't meant to do this—bring the boy home. His father's impending retirement cut him off from this kid with his hungry eyes. David had simply meant to pay for the medical treatment; repay that moment of veneration. Well, whatever he had meant or not meant, the kid was here; wide drugged eyes focused on the expanding cityscape, filling the cramped lift with the thick, sour smell of unwashed flesh. David wrinkled his nose.

Feed him and send him home.

In his apartment, David ordered the kid a sandwich from the kitchen wall and sat across from him at the small table, mildly repelled by the ravenous manner in which his guest devoured the food. "What's your name?" David asked as the boy licked the last crumbs from his fingers. "Where do you live?"

"I'm Flander." Uninvited, he helped himself to coffee from the kitchen wall, then perched himself on the corner of the table. The glaze of shock was fading from his eyes, and he swung one foot, restless and a little tense. "I live around," he said.

"On your own?"

"Shy-Shy kind of keeps track."

"Who's Shy-Shy?" David asked. He didn't really want to know, wanted this kid out of his apartment, all accounts settled and closed.

"She's a cool lady I know. I hang around with her a lot." Flander picked at the slick plastic of his cast, frowning. "*Creation* did real good on the Net today. What are you going to work on next?" And then: "You left it in. The shadow."

"It was a good touch. Valid." David prowled across the room, aware suddenly of how small it was. "I . . . don't know what I'm going to work on next." I'm hedging, David thought. He wasn't ready to put it into words yet—that he was through —not to himself, and certainly not to this fox-child.

"What about that volcano piece? I liked it, and I haven't seen it for a while. I can't get at your stuff when it's in storage."

"Don't sound so apologetic," David growled. No, that hunger in the kid's eyes wasn't for food. "I'll show it to you." He pushed his chair back. Let this be the closing act, he decided. Let the kid muck around in the piece; David had been blocked on it for months, and now it didn't matter anyway. Then he could send him home to his Shy-Shy. What a weird name. David went into his lab. The kid followed, pulling a virtual mask down over his head, tugging a glove over his uninjured hand. "Studio," David said, and watched the walls stretch and pale. "Not the fox again?" He glowered at the prick-eared creature. "That was quick. You know all my codes, don't you?"

"Not all of them. I told you—I can't get into your storage." The fox lolled its tongue, grinned. "I like this Self. There are people who want to know what I look like in fleshtime."

"Sure of yourself, aren't you?" David reached for the racked canvases. "What would those two have done if I hadn't inter- rupted them?"

The fox didn't answer that one. David stretched out the volcano canvas and stepped into it. The fox was there ahead of him, nose in the air, as if it was sniffing the breeze. It was limping, David noticed, holding its left paw clear of the ground. The feel of the piece washed over him, and he frowned. He had started with rage, poured it out in billowing ash and thick remorseless streams of glowing lava. Then he had tried to reshape it with a gentle moonlit sky and the lush leaves of surviving tropicals. All he had achieved was the flat realism of a travelogue and the nagging feeling that it *could,* damn it, work.

Scowling, David muted the hot glare of the lava column, added steam where it touched a small stream, turned the steam opalescent in the moonlight.

"You're lucky you're netted," the fox said in Flander's voice. "It's tough to do the really fine stuff in skinthins. Who paid to fix you up?"

"Our company."

"Shy-Shy's netted." Flander/fox darted past him, loping three-legged into the blackened desolation beyond the creeping tongue of lava. "What about this?" He nosed the gray ash, and tiny leaves unfolded.

Yeah, you could do it that way . . . maybe get the right effect. David chewed his lower lip, wandered back along the cooling lava flow. Try this. . . . He planted sprouts and cracking seeds. Small animals scuttled through the ashy wasteland, burrowing, mating, living. Beyond rage, beyond hope . . . it was a nice contrast, if he could get it into balance, give it some focus. He shaped, vanished what he had just done, swore, and tried something new. Life in the aftermath of devastation? Hope sprouting in the ash heap of despair? It could work, yes, it *was* working. Excitement seized him, flowed like molten gold through his veins. David reached, made and unmade, twisted and shaped the fiery world in a frenzy of creation.

Hours later, fatigue finally stopped him. David put down the virtual boulder he was holding, mildly surprised by the tremor in his muscles. He wondered what time it was. He felt good, fine. He hadn't felt like this since *Creation* had started to come together. His knees quivered, and the muscles between his shoulder blades ached. His belly was a black pit of emptiness. "Store," David rasped, dry-mouthed. He looked around for the fox. He had lost track of it some time ago. "Exit studio," he said, and staggered as the lab reappeared around him.

The kid—Flander—was curled up in the corner, head pillowed on his arm, the plastic cast a white blot in the muted light. He was asleep. "Hey," David said.

He didn't twitch.

The floor kept trying to tilt beneath his feet. David shrugged and stumbled to the other room to drink glass after glass of water. Outside, in the grimy reality of the streets, it would be getting light. Before he fell across his futon, David carried an extra quilt into the lab and draped it over Flander.

IT SEEMED as if only minutes had passed before the House woke him. It nagged him out of bed with subsonics and unbearable jokes about family, business, and the demands of a schedule. David was not in the mood for jokes this morning, wondered whatever had possessed him to design such an adolescent wake-up. Tea seemed like a good idea, but it pooled like molten lead in his stomach.

He had let himself forget about the kid.

David stopped dead in the doorway to the lab. Flander was still asleep, tangled in the quilt, his injured arm sticking out as if it didn't quite belong to him. David groped for a solution to this situation, found nothing ready to hand. With a sigh, he sat down in a realtime chair, called up his office, and put the boy out of his mind.

There was plenty waiting for him on the slab of polished jade that was his desk. A major supplier, Chem Suisse, had unexpectedly failed them. During the night, Chen BioSource had fallen even further on the Exchange. David wiped the depressing reports from the jade with a sweep of his hand, frowned as glowing red letters reappeared in their place. It was a message from his father announcing that he was on his way over to see David. In person, of course.

*Your father has arrived,* House announced.

David groaned and went to let his father in.

*"Ni hǎushiang bìng.* You look sick," his father said as David opened the door. "What did you do? Drink all night?" He marched into the room.

Eldest Sister was with him. She gave David a smooth smile, then walked primly across the room to seat herself at the table.

Their father clucked his tongue disapprovingly at the dirty dishes piled beside the kitchen wall. "Can't you at least offer me tea?"

"May I offer you tea, Fuchin?" Resigned, David ordered pot

and cups from the kitchen wall, carried them to the table. "This is my *room*. It isn't an office."

"Your hospitality is as lacking as your attention to family affairs."

"Fuchin, I have spent a large part of the past thirty-six hours dealing with family business." David noticed his sister's expectant expression, flushed, and got hold of his temper.

"Your new Security costs us a fortune."

"Surely you reviewed my report on the piracy threat. Would you rather have someone in our filespace?"

"The expectation of theft is yours, not mine." His father glared at David. "Our margin of profit will be severely strained by the extra Security cost. I am here because we are about to default on our contract with North America Aquaculture. Dà Jieh tells me so."

"The report is on your desk. You haven't gotten to it yet?" His sister's tone was demure. "The contract depends on a specific delivery date. As you surely know. Since Chem Suisse can't fill our order for amino acids, we won't meet the deadline."

"What are you going to do about it?" His father's hand slapped the tabletop, and David jumped.

"I plan to contact other suppliers." David turned his teacup between his fingers, struggling to organize his sluggish thoughts. "We can probably get what we need from European Pharmaceuticals."

"We don't have much of a margin," Dà Jieh interposed smoothly. "If we get too far behind, we won't make the deadline, and North America can legally decline the order."

"They won't do that." David banged his cup down. "They've given us leeway on deadlines before."

"You should have thought about this," his father interrupted harshly.

The supply failure had been a matter of bad luck and bad timing, but Fuchin was never willing to blame luck. He *was* willing to blame David. Anger sat like a stone in David's chest, but beneath the anger was a cold awareness that his father was partly right. If he had considered all possibilities, he could have lined up alternate suppliers ahead of time.

I didn't consider the possibility of The Quake happening tomorrow, either, David thought bitterly. He lifted his head suddenly, caught his sister's eyes on him. Hatred? David felt a small jolt of shock, but her face smoothed so quickly that David wondered if he had imagined it.

"If I receive the required supplies within a week, I can push our production schedule," she said. "Perhaps we will make the deadline."

"I hope that you will not be so lax again." Father stood. "I expect you to be competent. At least that." He looked over David's shoulder, frowned at the doorway that led to David's lab. "You cannot play your games and do a good job for your family."

"I have never let my *art* hurt Chen BioSource," David said as he ushered his father out of the room.

The words sounded weak to David, a petty defiance without real dignity. He clenched his teeth and bowed to his father. When the door had closed safely behind them, he stomped into his lab. He had intended to call up his office and start querying suppliers, but a virtual was already open. David staggered as his net automatically popped him into a familiar landscape of lava and struggling greenery.

The fox lay on a patch of black loam, licking its injured paw. "Wow, man." It snapped its jaws. "You really did a fine job on this last night."

"Thanks." David struggled with leftover temper. "Go play with it. It's all yours, okay?" He called up a door, opened it into his office.

"What do you mean? I thought we were working on it?" The fox limped after him, ears pricked. "That old boy sounded like he was bugging you. How come you didn't tell him and the bitch to take a hike?"

"Eavesdropping is rude. The old boy happens to be my father *and* my boss. The bitch is my sister. Go play."

"I wasn't eavesdropping. I don't speak the lingo, and don't give me *play*, man. You still should've told him to take a hike." The fox leaped three-legged onto the corner of the jade desk. It stretched out a paw, hissed a quick patter of commands. A tiny perfect image of David's father appeared on the desktop, hiked stiffly across the smooth surface. Its face looked thunderous.

It was a marvelous caricature. In spite of himself, David smiled. "You *are* good." His smile faded. "It's a long story, Flander. I . . . don't have time for this anymore. The volcano's a throwaway." He looked down. "If you want to do something with it, go do it."

"You're crazy, man." Flander's voice skidded up half an octave. "You're *good*. You can't just stop. Some gallery'll offer for you, for sure. That piece is no throwaway. Man, what you *did* to it, last night. And I was asleep." The fox flattened its ears.

Flander was right. The volcano piece wasn't a throwaway. Not anymore. David closed his eyes, remembering last night's magic. "I've got work that has to be done," he said. "Give the fox a rest, will you?"

"So do your work. I'll hang around till you're done." Fox metamorphosed into a fur-covered boy-shape, then shed fur all over the desktop to become Flander. He looked up at David through a fringe of dirty hair. "I don't want to screw around by myself," he said softly. "I want to see how you made that piece work like you did."

How does one say no to veneration? David looked away from the kid's glittering fox-ghost eyes. He didn't want to say no. "What about this Shy-Shy?" He fired his last shot. "Isn't she going to worry?"

"I called her from your studio." Flander grinned. "She said you sound like a good guy, that I was lucky as hell that I met you, and I should say thank-you about a hundred times. Thank you," he said.

David sighed. "I've got to deal with this business stuff first. Go take a shower. You stink."

DAVID SPENT the morning in his office, using Security to scour Chen BioSource filespace. He came up clean, but the cost made him cringe. Better he should have found evidence of a break-in. Father was going to scream, and that wouldn't help their shaky position on the Exchange. He tracked Beryl down in one of his virtual lairs, quizzed him about that mysterious shakiness.

*Rumors,* Beryl told him. He was a willowy youth with a shaved scalp today, but his leopard-slink gave him away. *It's floating around that someone is out to shaft Chen BioSource. Sorry, dear heart. No names, just intent.*

"Don't send me a bill for that," David told him sourly.

He tracked down an alternate source for Eldest Sister's amino acids and turned the details over to his middle sister. Èr Jieh handled that kind of thing. If they didn't run into trouble in development, Chen BioSource would make the contract deadline. Barely, but they would make it. David stretched, grimacing at the gritty ache of tension in his neck. He needed a shower, he decided, and exited his office.

Instead of exiting to his lab, he found himself standing in his volcano piece. Flander—in human form, this time—was sitting cross-legged in a patch of scorched and wilting fern, chin in his hands, staring moodily at a blackened tongue of cooling lava. "I can see what you changed," he said. "I can't figure how it makes the piece work."

"I don't know, either. It just felt right to me." David lowered himself to the ground. "That's new," he said, nodding at the ferns beneath Flander.

"I didn't feel like sitting on rock. That's all."

"Sure." David examined the clump. Every crushed or bent leaf was perfect, right down to the smeared film of ash on the green fronds. Flander was showing off. "You have an incredible talent for detail," David said. "But those ferns don't belong there."

"I know. I'll wipe 'em when I get up." The boy tilted his head, eyes bright. "Are you done with the office stuff? Can we do this for a while?"

"Yes," David said, because he needed to forget the Exchange, his sister's hostility, and his father's eternal dissatisfaction. Hell, why *not* play with this kid?

They worked together. At first David cloaked himself in the memory of the boy's venerating eyes and tried to assume the role of teacher. That didn't last long. The kid was good in his own right, quick and perceptive, with an offbeat point of view that somehow resonated with what David tried and sent him into paroxysms of inspiration. Before long they were arguing over details, changing and erasing, reshaping the entire piece.

There were fox-prints everywhere.

"Hey, we've got to quit," David said finally.

"Why?" Flander tossed a handful of pebbles into the air, turned them into a flock of small jewel-toned birds. "I'm not tired."

"You ought to see your face. Have you eaten anything today?" Reluctantly, David shrunk the piece to a virtual canvas again and racked it. "I know you haven't."

"Neither have you." Flander scratched beneath the edge of his cast. "It's not that late."

"I can't do another all-nighter. I have a business to run." David exited the studio, propelled the boy into the main room. He ordered sandwiches and fruit while Flander stripped off his hood and glove. "Eat this," he said, handing a plate to the boy. Shadows stained the skin beneath Flander's eyes, made them seem too large and too bright. "Then go home and get some sleep."

"How come your dad wants you to quit doing art?" Flander bit into a pear, wiping juice from his chin.

"I didn't say he did. It's my decision. I can't just play at this," David said slowly. "It matters too much to me. I'm not going to have the time to do it the way I want to do it."

"So you're just going to quit? To do what?"

"To run a family dynasty." David took a huge bite of sandwich. It tasted like sawdust.

"Huh." Flander peeked into his own sandwich, put it down. "I don't know. I probably would've gotten into something dumb if it hadn't been for Shy-Shy—doing sex virtuals for the X-parlors, or shoot-'em-ups, or something like that. She kept bugging me all the time, telling me that I had to remember what I wanted to do."

There was understanding in his tone, and sympathy. This skinny half-starved street kid was forgiving David for making a bad choice. David choked on his mouthful of food, caught between insult and laughter. "You're lucky to have her around," he said when he could finally talk. "She gives you a lot of support."

"She does that," Flander said soberly. "She's a cracker and she's *hot*. She's the one who got me into this artist's Netspace the first time. She's always there for me—I can't remember anybody before Shy-Shy. I wouldn't have made it without her."

The expression in Flander's eyes silenced David. He picked up his plate, hiding an unexpected pang of envy. How would it feel, to have someone look at you like that? David wrapped Flander's untouched sandwich in a piece of plastic and handed it to the boy. "Eat it later," he said. "If you want to come back, we'll finish this piece." Let this one be the last, instead of *Creation*. He had a little time, yet. "Call me from the tower entryway, and I'll let you in."

"I'll do that." Flander grinned. "Thanks." He darted out of the apartment, quick as a fox streaking for cover.

DAVID HAD PLANNED to let Flander do most of the work on the volcano, but he couldn't stay out of it. The piece was coming alive, promising to be more powerful than *Creation*. David worked on it whenever he could snatch the time, putting off sleep until he was stumbling with exhaustion. Using Flander's flashes of crazy inspiration as a springboard, he catapulted into soaring flights of invention. The Milky Way fell down into the

seething cauldron of the volcano in a cascade of cold light, as if
the universe was folding in on itself, coiling back into primordial
fire.

Even Beryl should like this one, David thought, and laughed
out loud. He had reached a new level in his work, and it felt
good. Flander was part of it, too. A big part. David had stopped
sending Flander home in the evenings. He let him sleep on the
cushions in the main room. It had finally dawned on David that
the kid lived on the street. This Shy-Shy might provide emotional sustenance, but Flander's bodily needs were his own
business. David nagged him to eat, and a little flesh began to
hide Flander's bones.

"How come you don't live with her?" David asked Flander
one afternoon. The cloud he was working on looked like a pile
of oatmeal. "Doesn't she worry about you sleeping on the
street?" David scowled at the cloud, then erased it with an
angry swipe.

"She lives around, okay? She doesn't hang out in any one
place very long. You know, you're too stuck on reality."
Flander retrieved the cloud, combed it into a glittering comet
tail. "Shy-Shy and I take care of each other, and we do just
fine."

"Easy. I wasn't criticizing." It sounded as if this Shy-Shy
was one of Beryl's cohorts, dealing in black-market information.
You kept your realtime, fleshtime Self out of sight, in that trade.
David muted the fiery comet tail to a whisper of ice crystals.

The communication chime interrupted his thoughts. "Come
in," David said, glad of an excuse to stop struggling with comet
clouds.

Hans Renmeyer's torso took shape in David's virtual doorway. "David." He bowed from invisible hips, in realtime, this
visit. "I apologize for the lateness of the hour. I'm interrupting
your work."

"That's all right." David exited into his studio, noticed from
the corner of his eye that Flander had reverted to fox shape.
"What can I do for you?"

"I hope you're going to have something new for me soon.
In the meantime, I have some good news for you." Renmeyer
cleared his throat, pausing portentously. "I've received a query
from the Roberts Gallery, in London. They are interested in giving your piece *Creation* a stationary show."

A stationary?

"It's not a large gallery." Renmeyer spread his hands

apologetically. "But it's relatively prestigious. In my opinion as your agent, the invitation is well worth your consideration."

Out of the thousands of artists who showed on the Net, only a handful showed stationary. A very small handful.

"I . . . accept," David said.

"Good, good." Renmeyer's smile grew wider, warmer. "I'll review their contract and have something for your signature tomorrow. I wish you continued success," he said, bowed again, and exited.

Fox-feet hit David in the small of the back. He turned around and nearly went down flat as Flander, boy-shaped again, threw himself into David's arms with realtime mass and force.

"I told you, man," he yelled gleefully. "I *told* you they'd come after you. You're so good. You're so damned *good.*" He sobered suddenly, looked up into David's face. "You're not quitting now. Right?"

"No. I'm . . . not." David drew a long breath. "We're good. *We'll* be great."

"Your old . . . your dad's going to be pissed, isn't he?"

"I'm not sure that he will ever speak to me again." David exited the studio, shivered as the lab appeared. A part of him had been shaping this decision as he and Flander had shaped the volcano piece. "Chen BioSource is his universe," David said heavily. "My father designed a son to fit into that universe. The David Chen that he sees is a virtual—the son he believes in, the one that doesn't really exist. I'm not sure he will ever see *me,* or understand who I am."

"That's tough, man." Flander put a hand on David's shoulder in a surprisingly mature gesture of comfort.

"Yeah, it is." David's voice wanted to crack. He put his arm around Flander, squeezing warm realtime flesh. "I meant it about the *we,*" he said. "We do good together."

"We do that." Flander grinned, fox-eyes dancing. "Wait till this piece hits a gallery. What are we going to call it, anyway?"

"I don't know. I haven't come up with a title yet." David tossed his loosened braid back over his shoulder and sighed. "Let's go get some dinner," he said.

THE HOUSE PROGRAM interrupted them as they celebrated with buns stuffed with real chicken. *Excuse me,* it intoned apologetically. *You have an urgent call from your youngest sister. She says it's an emergency.*

An emergency.

Father. David knew it, even as he stretched a virtual hand to open a door to her apartment.

She wasn't there. A pale stylized carp with flowing fins—his sister's personal sigil—answered him. "I'm at the hospital," it said in her voice. "Come right away, David. Selva Internacional filed a piracy suit against us, and Fuchin had a heart attack. Please come."

David blinked as his apartment re-formed around him. His arms and legs felt numb, without sensation, as if he had been sitting at the table for hours without moving. The room seemed to be shrinking, closing around him like a fist. David pushed himself stiffly to his feet, breathing too fast as the shrinking room squeezed his ribs, compressed his lungs.

"What's wrong?" Flander pushed his chair back as David started for the door. "What was she saying?"

"Nothing," David said, and walked blindly out of the apartment.

DAVID STOOD close to Shau Jieh at his father's bedside. He had spent a sleepless night at the hospital, sitting in a sterile little waiting room that reeked of disinfectant while a million slow eternities crawled past. He had waited there, trapped in that barren cube, because it would have been wrong to wait at home, to visit the hospital in virtual. Wrong. Fuchin wouldn't even wear skinthins.

Tubes went into his father's nose, into the veins that writhed like blue worms beneath his crepey skin. Orange blobs of remote monitors clung to his head, chest, arms, and legs. Every synaptical flicker was being recorded and evaluated and responded to. Medicine inflicted the ultimate lack of privacy, David thought dully. His father looked shrunken, shriveled, as if the tubes were draining his blood, as if the monitors were alien leeches, sucking away life and substance. David put his arm around his sister's waist, felt her tremble slightly. At the foot of the bed, their middle sister sniffled audibly and predictably into a tissue.

Dà Jieh stood behind her. She raised her head and looked coldly at David. "If you had spent more time attending to business, this would never have happened."

"That is enough." Shau Jieh's tone made them all blink. "We will not fight at our father's bedside."

Dà Jieh shrugged and pressed her lips together. Silence filled the small room.

That silence felt like an accusation. David bowed his head,

eyes on the pitiless white of the hospital sheet. If he had been in his office yesterday evening, he might have seen the brief before his father had discovered it, might have been able to deal with it, or at least prepare him. Might have, might have . . . David clenched his hands into fists.

Whoever had bought Chen codes had gotten in and out without tripping Security. They had duplicated his sister's developmental records on her new strain of cod, and they had destroyed some of her files. Now, Selva Internacional was claiming that they had developed the template first, that the identical nature of the Chen template indicated piracy. Chen BioSource no longer had the developmental records to disprove Selva's claim.

It had been a very clever bit of espionage. If Selva won their suit in entirety, Chen BioSource would have to file for reorganization. It was not likely that the company would survive. I should have caught it, David thought bitterly. I shouldn't have taken my sister's word for the untouched state of her records.

When the suit had been filed, he had been in his studio with Flander. Playing games. David turned away from the bed.

"Er-dz? My . . . son?"

The dry whisper sounded faint as the rustle of an insect's wings. "Fuchin?" David bent over the bed, squatted beside it when his father's eyes didn't seem able to focus on his face. "I'm here," he said. "We're all here."

"Save us," he whispered. His withered fingers twitched, touched David's hand. "Chen BioSource will die. The family will die. Don't let it die."

"Fuchin, it's all right." David took his father's hand and squeezed it gently, frightened by the weakness of that spidery touch. "It's just numbers, Fuchin. How many years have you been playing with numbers?" He forced a smile, tucked his father's hand back onto the bed. "I'll play better than Selva, and everything will be fine."

"It must be." His father's withered lips trembled. "It must be all right. Please promise me . . .?"

Death lurked in his father's eyes. David could see its shadow. His immortality, Shau Jieh had said of Chen BioSource. No, David thought. It is his *life*. If it dies, he will die. "I promise," David whispered.

Er Jieh crowded in beside him, weeping openly now, and David used the moment to slip out of the room. There were public terminals at the end of the hallway. Renmeyer's face looked grainy and lifeless on the flat screen.

"I don't understand." The poor resolution couldn't hide his shocked expression. "David, *why* do you want to cancel the gallery show?"

"I don't have time to do the sensory effects," David said woodenly.

"It can't require that much time. I don't understand. The contract I presented to you was more than reasonable."

"It's not you. It's not the contract. Look, I'm sorry." David exited the connection abruptly.

It was more than a lack of time that had made him cancel the show. *Sorry.* Whom had he been apologizing to? Renmeyer? Flander?

Himself?

Shau Jieh caught up with him at the lift. "Younger Brother, wait." She grabbed his arm, forced him to stop.

"You stay with him. I can't." David ran his hand across his face as her eyes filled with hurt. "He *created* me, do you realize that? I'm not sure that I'm even real."

"Stop it. He loves you. He does." Her voice was full of pain. "We Chinese are so obsessed with sons. Fuchin is obsessed with it—I know that, and I know that it's not a good thing. But don't hurt him." She clung to his arm. "Don't walk away from him, Little Brother. Not now."

"It's ironic." David raised his arm slowly, turned it so that the silver netting caught the light. "It's ironic that he bought this for me."

"He didn't net you." His sister looked surprised. "Your mother did. I remember them arguing about it. She used to design virtuals. Before she married Fuchin. I thought you knew."

"I didn't know." David felt numb. I never asked, he thought. She didn't exist for me. Was that what she had been trying to tell him in her awkward birthday visit? "Don't worry," he said bitterly. "I'm part of our father's private virtual. I can't walk away." David turned his back on her tears and fled.

HIS APARTMENT seemed unfamiliar to David, as if he had been absent for months, instead of merely hours. David glanced into the lab. Flander was obviously inside some virtual or other. Stripped to his skinthins, hooded and gloved, he sat cross-legged on the floor, eyes fixed on the far wall, unaware of David's fleshtime presence. His good hand twitched as he did whatever he was doing in his invisible universe. David watched him for a moment. Everyone had their own personal virtual, he thought bitterly. Their personal reality.

What is mine? he wondered.

David's hand clenched into a fist. He went back into the main room and entered his office. The jade desktop waited for him, covered with neat lines of flowing script. It was the digest of Selva's suit, as reported by his office attorney. The projected outcome looked bad for Chen BioSource, whether they settled or not. Selva had them. It was simply a question of how badly Selva wanted to hurt them and how much they were willing to spend to do it. Corporate espionage and piracy were being prosecuted fiercely in the international courts. David stared at the words until they blurred into meaningless loops and squiggles. Their message didn't change.

I was good, David thought. I have that. I was *good*.

A door appeared in the wall of David's office. "David?" Flander's voice. Virtual knuckles rapped on virtual wood.

Go away, David thought, but he sighed and opened the door. Flander wasn't alone. A tall woman stood beside him. She had silvery hair pulled into a stylish club at the base of her neck and a square, strong face. She was netted.

Shy-Shy. It had to be. I've seen her before, David thought, but the connection slipped away from him.

"Hello." Her voice was low and warm. "I'm sorry to bust in on you like this, but Flander doesn't know the meaning of the word patience." She rumpled Flander's hair gently.

Flander grinned back, and the absolute unity of that shared moment made David look quickly away.

"I asked her to come in," Flander spoke up. "Shy-Shy's *hot*, man. She gets me in *anywhere* I want to go. She can find out who dumped that suit on you. She can find out who works the levers, no problem."

David felt as if his mouth was hanging open. "What did you do?" he managed finally. "Translate my sister's private message?"

"Sure. You were *way* upset, man. I don't speak the lingo, but the library does." He lifted one shoulder in a casual shrug.

David grimaced, fighting an outraged sense of invasion. This was the fox, he reminded himself. The ghost who had slipped in and out of his pieces. Flander was a street kid. Nothing was sacred to him. David sighed, tired beyond belief. "You've been into everything, haven't you? Even my office?"

"Don't blame him too much." Shy-Shy's hand tightened on Flander's shoulder, but the shake she gave him was a gentle one. "You've been good to him and he was really worried. He wouldn't take no for an answer." She laughed softly and pushed a wisp of hair back from her forehead. "I *am* good," she said. "I can find out what you need to know. If you want me to. *He* gets to decide," she said to Flander as he opened his mouth. "It's his business, even if you've been into it up to your eyebrows."

"I'm sorry, David." Flander's eyes were anxious. "You didn't tell me not to look."

"It's okay," David said. Shy-Shy was waiting, one casually possessive hand still on Flander's shoulder. She was *dressed;* real-leather boots, natural fiber tunic, fiber-light embroidery. The works. Street-power chic. She wasn't dirty, she wasn't skinny. Why the hell doesn't she take care of him, David thought resentfully. "I'd . . . appreciate your help." He forced the words out. "For my father's sake."

DAVID REMAINED in his office while Shy-Shy and Flander accessed the Net. They worked together, and he didn't want to watch. Instead, he caught up on the orders, the supply problems, and the reports; all the dreary details of running a business that went on—that had to go on—in spite of personal tragedy. He dealt with what had to be dealt with and kept on working, sorting through the low-priority bits and pieces that had accumulated like dust in the corners of the business. He was obsessing, knew it, and didn't care. In the private hospital room, monitor-leeches tethered his father to life. David could feel the numbers, the projections, and the worries closing around him like fingers, solidifying like the walls of a newly opened virtual.

When Flander blinked into existence in front of his desk, David started convulsively. "Use the door," he snapped.

"Sorry. I forgot." Flander grinned at him. "Man, I was *right*. I *guessed*. Shy-Shy said it would've taken her twice as long if I hadn't tipped her where to start."

So the power-dressed Wonder Woman had cracked Selva. David stretched, feeling his vertebrae crackle. His muscles ached, and the clock on his desk shocked him. Hours had passed. I was hiding, David thought. "Show me," he told Flander.

"You bet, man. Shy-Shy got it down cold. Because I guessed part of it." Flander was still grinning, pleased with himself, full of pride for this prize he had brought to David. "Just watch," he said.

David blinked as the lights dimmed. One whole wall of his office shimmered and became a screen. A movie was playing on it, a flickering kaleidoscope of antique Technicolor hues. Rows of red velvet seats lined the floor in front of it. Popcorn and crumpled candy wrappers littered the floor, and a couple necked passionately in the front seat. David wondered irritably how long it had taken Flander to design these details. His gaze shifted to the screen, and he went cold.

Up there on the screen, in gritty two-dimensional passion, Beryl and David's eldest sister writhed in a tangle of black silk sheets.

"He records *everything*, man. You ought to see what Shy-Shy and I had to wade through." Flander wriggled like a puppy. "But it's there. She hands him some stuff—hardcopy—and after she leaves, he runs it under his scanner. He thinks he's got some Security, man. He's never run into Shy-Shy!" The enormous bed vanished, replaced by white sheets of hardcopy, lined up neatly.

David stared at the scrawled numbers and symbols. Sickness gathered in his belly as he recognized his sister's handwritten notes.

"I saw her face, when she was here. She hates you, man. Shy-Shy said that a slick piracy job would cost mucho. If big money wasn't part of it, maybe it was personal. That made me think it was an inside job, and your sib seemed like a natural. So Shy-Shy boosted me into her virtuals. Your sister doesn't check for ghosts." His lip curled. "She went to see this guy this evening—while you were doing business stuff. I thought maybe he had something on her, but she looked pretty happy to see him. So we went into his filespace and found the stuff you wanted. She's a real bitch, isn't she?"

Dà Jieh. Eldest Sister—proud, disdainful Dà Jieh. All this time, *her*. She had played him like a puppet and he had let her, because she was *family*. He had been as blind to reality as their father, but it had been their father who had paid the price. David had thrown his gallery show away for nothing. If Dà Jieh wanted to destroy Chen BioSource, nothing that David could do would save it. Some part of him had guessed. Maybe that was why he had buried himself in business this afternoon. He had been hiding from the truth that Flander's wonderful Shy-Shy would dig up for him.

David clenched his teeth until his jaw ached, struggling with a deep resentment against the stranger who had walked into his father's life and casually pointed out the ugly cracks in the foundation.

"David?" Flander touched his arm, realtime flesh warm be-

hind those virtual fingers. "I'm sorry. I'm really sorry, man."
Realtime, fleshtime comfort, and this Shy-Shy didn't even
keep him *fed*. "Thanks," David whispered. There was nothing
he could do. "Beryl's the key. He trades in information and
levers." It didn't matter. "I need to talk to Beryl." It really
didn't matter. . . . David turned his back on Flander and
plunged into his office.

HE SPENT the rest of the night hunting Beryl, chasing him
through a virtual maze of social and business connections, hop-
ping from party to party, from shrug to knowing shrug.
*I don't know. I haven't seen him around.*
*Don't know where he lives. No one does, man.*
*Get real, Chen.*
Beryl didn't want to be found. Not by David, at least. In the
early morning hours, David gave up. He exited the dregs of the
party that he had dropped in on and found Flander in his office.
He was sitting on the floor, arms clasped around his drawn-up
knees, watching David. David had a vague memory of seeing
him in just that position every time he had dropped back into
his office.
"You look like shit," Flander said softly. "Go sleep, man."
"Shy-Shy," David said. The word came out as a dry rasp.
"Get Shy-Shy for me. She can find Beryl."
"Give it some *rest*, man." Flander sounded anxious. "He'll
be around. Don't kill yourself, okay?"
"Now!" David clenched his fist. He had to find Beryl, had
to hunt him down and confront him, because if he didn't . . .
he'd have to confront Dà Jieh. "Get her," he said.

SHY-SHY didn't look as if Flander had waked her. She looked
fresh, solidly unruffled, as if she'd been up for hours, or all
night, or maybe she just didn't need to sleep at all, David
thought sourly. Again, that twinge of familiarity—stronger, this
time. He could almost remember. "Beryl," he said, struggling
with the fog that kept filling up his head. "The guy my sister
. . . met. He's hiding from me. I need his address."
"His Security must have picked up a trace from my ghosting.
Maybe he guessed it was you." She nodded. "No problem. I
downloaded his address into your office filespace after I got out
of there. Sorry. I thought you'd find it." Shy-Shy touched his
arm. "You look like shit," she said softly. "Go sleep, man."
Flander's exact words of a minute ago, spoken with Flander's phrasing and syntax and inflection. In spite of his exhaus-

tion—or perhaps because of it—David heard it. Differences in timbre and pitch misled, but the mechanics were . . . the same.

Familiar. Shy-Shy was so damn *familiar.* Cold trickled down David's spine, raised gooseflesh on his arms. He looked at her closely, with an artist's eye this time, *seeing* her. Change the gender, hair, and eye color, add thirty years of aging, and she looked . . . like Flander. She could be his mother or his sister. You could change your Self in virtual, but you moved the same, thought the same, talked the same. The cold spread, filling David's belly with ice. She was power-dressed, but Flander scrounged to live. Flander slept on the street. Where did Shy-Shy sleep?

Now that he knew to look, it was there. Shy-Shy was Flander and . . . she wasn't.

David shivered, his teeth rattling briefly together. She was a simulation, an autonomous virtual persona. She had to be, and she *couldn't* be. No one could create that kind of autonomous body language. She was right here, in the same office with Flander, but her every twitch was independent and perfect. No one had that kind of talent.

Flander's fingerprints were all over her. David knew his style well enough by now to recognize them.

But even with his knowing, she still seemed real.

David didn't have the kind of talent that it would take to do something like that. He would never have it. Numbness was seeping out to the ends of his fingers and up into his brain. "Shy-Shy's a sim," David croaked. "My God, you *made* her."

"No way, man." Flander's body jerked, but he laughed. "Shy-Shy, listen to him."

David feinted suddenly at Shy-Shy's face, watched her involuntary jerk of reaction, watched her eyes widen, her pupils contract. *Perfect.* You couldn't tell. It made Renmeyer's expensive sim look like an automaton.

I thought I was good. David stared at Shy-Shy's face, watching her get angry, seeing Flander's body language in the tightening of her lips, the tension in her shoulders, and the curve of her spine. That knowledge that he had talent, *major* talent, had been a talisman for David to keep forever.

Flander had just taken that away.

Showing off. Flander was showing off, like he had showed off with his clump of ferns. The kid had been sitting here, watching him bleed, laughing up his sleeve because dumb David couldn't even tell a sim from a realtime virtual. "You little shit," David breathed. "You goddamn *punk.*" His fist caught

Flander on the cheekbone—realtime flesh bruising realtime flesh.

Flander tumbled backward with a cry, sprawling at David's feet.

"Knock it off!" Shy-Shy dropped to her knees beside Flander, angry face turned up to David. "What the hell's the matter with you?"

"The game's over." Fists clenched, breathing hard, David stood over Flander. "You *made* her. *Look* at her! You can see the touches. The way you color skin. The way you detail every hair and every wrinkle. She's controlling her own movement—but that's *your* body language. I could run a side-by-side; it's the same, down to the last twitch. Did you think that I was completely stupid?" he said bitterly. "Yeah, I thought she was real. Did you get a kick out of watching me make a fool out of myself? You little street punk! You think you're so damn clever!"

"I didn't do it." Flander scrambled to his feet, eyes wild, shaking so hard that he could barely stand up. "She's real. She took care of me. Always." On her knees on the floor, Shy-Shy clasped her hands, her eyes as wild as Flander's. "She's real," Flander screamed. "You hear me? She's *real!*"

The image of Shy-Shy popped like a soap bubble. Flander gave a hoarse animal cry and vanished from the office.

"Flander?" David yelled. Silence. It seeped into David's flesh as the seconds ticked by, chilling his anger, turning it into a cold sickness. "Flander?" he called again. "Come back here." He exited the office, premonition prickling his skin like gooseflesh. The lab was empty. So was the living room. The exterior door stood open.

*I wouldn't have made it without her,* Flander had said of Shy-Shy. There had been love in his eyes when he had looked at her, and she had loved him back. She had been dressed in streetpower clothes. What kid would clothe a hero in rags? David looked down the wide empty hallway toward the lift. Was it even possible? he asked himself. Could you create a virtual persona that complex and complete, and then forget that you had done so? The answer scared him. You would have to be insane. Seriously insane.

Perhaps. Or perhaps you had to be so lonely that such a creation made you sane. If you were talented enough, you could invest that persona with all the love and comfort and safety that didn't exist anywhere in your fleshtime world. In a way, you could bring that creation to life. Until someone made you see what you had done.

Reality and unreality. Where did one end and the other begin? I killed Shy-Shy, David thought, and sudden grief twisted him. He looked down at his hands. They were clean. Not one trace of Shy-Shy's blood soiled them. He wiped his palms on his tunic and went back into his empty rooms to keep his promise to his father.

THE ADDRESS that Shy-Shy—that Flander—had left on file led David to a decrepit brick building. It stood on the edge of the burned-over scar that had once been the LA barrio and looked as if it had been consistently neglected at least for a century. Old earthquake damage had flaked away the concrete facade, and black cracks zigzagged through the weathered bricks. There was no lock on the entryway. Inside, it smelled like urine. David breathed shallowly. The OUT OF ORDER placard taped to the lift doors looked about as old as the building itself. David climbed the stairs. Dust sifted up from the mud-colored carpet and hung in the air, glittering like gold in the shafts of sunlight that filtered through the grimy steel-netted windows on the landing.

Beryl lived on the third floor. David stood outside on the landing for a few minutes, catching his breath, waiting for his heart rate to return to normal. *No major Security,* the file notes had told him. *He's safe, 'cause no one knows.* Shy-Shy's words. Flander's voice. David bent to examine the locks. They were mechanical. As old as the building. Good cover, David thought coldly. What thief would bother? He slid the thin blade of the smart-key into the first lock. One by one, the locks clicked. David turned the handle, pushed, and walked in.

The squalor inside stopped him on the threshold. The cramped room smelled worse than the hallway; a mix of dirt, unwashed human flesh, and spoiled food. Crusted dishes and clothes lay scattered everywhere. A rumpled bed, a table, and a chair took up much of the floor space. Dust filmed the table-top, tracked with indecipherable smears. Beryl sat on the edge of his bed, stark naked, his eyes wide and glazed.

Like David, he was netted. Light glittered on the silver threads in his skin. David felt a dull sense of shock. The Beryl he knew was all feline grace, beauty, and sneering self-confidence. The virtual Beryl. The fleshtime Beryl was short, with soft flaccid muscles, a layer of fat around his waist, and drooping shoulders. His skin looked translucent in the glare from the overhead lights, sickly pale, like some cave-dwelling insect.

Beryl shivered as he exited his virtual, and his face tightened into an expression of surprise and fear. ''What the hell are you doing here? Get out," he said in Beryl's silky voice.

David looked at the dirty sheets on the narrow bed, remembering black silk and his sister's smooth shoulders. "It was a virtual," he said. "Flander was right. This wasn't blackmail." Why? David shook his head slightly. To get *him?* Had she been willing to risk the company just to make David look like an incompetent? It wouldn't make any difference, he thought bitterly. Their father wouldn't stop believing in his virtual son, no matter what Dà Jieh did. He took a step closer to Beryl, another. "Hey, man." Beryl backed up fast, grunted as the table edge stopped him. "No need for violence, okay?" he stuttered. "Look, let's do this in comfort. How about in your office?"

"I think I prefer fleshtime." David took another step, hands at his sides. Perspiration gleamed on Beryl's face, and David could smell the rank, sour odor of his fear. He is afraid of me, David thought. Not because I might hurt him, but just because I'm *here*. "So, tell me," he leaned closer, breathing in Beryl's face. "Tell me all about it."

"Sure, man. What's to tell?" Beryl was bending backward, away from David, hands braced on the tabletop. "It was just a little business deal. A sweet setup, if you want to know. Your sister is a sharp lady. An operator." He flinched, although David hadn't moved a muscle. "She fed me the stuff," he said breathlessly. "All I did was pass it on to Selva—I know someone there—and settle the details with them. Look, *she* designed the scam. I was just the runner. That's *truth*, man."

Yes, it probably was the truth. More or less. "You're going to call Selva off," David said softly. "They're going to drop the suit."

"No way." Beryl's voice went up half an octave. "They're going to make *bucks* taking a bite out of Chen BioSource. They're not going to walk away from that."

"I know where you live." David didn't smile. "I have copies of the pirated data, so their bite isn't such a sure thing anymore. I'll kick in some money, and you come up with the rest of the price. You'll find something to trade. You have one hour," he said. "Then your address goes public."

"All right." Beryl's arms were trembling. "All *right*, you bastard."

David sat down gingerly on the edge of the upholstered chair. Something more or less yellow had spilled on the arm and dried. It looked like vomit. David turned away, watched Beryl as he went into virtual.

Now he could see the Beryl he knew. The man's body

language changed. The muscles in his face firmed. On the other side of an invisible electronic wall, he tossed his beautiful head, sneered, slunk like a grinning leopard through someone's day. His body mimicked those movements. Which is real? David wondered suddenly. This Beryl, or the other one? David felt dizzy. The smell in the room oppressed him, and a dry finger of nausea moved in his belly.

"It's done." Beryl finally exited. Arms crossed, back against the wall, he glared at David. "Check your mail. Selva is withdrawing their suit. Now get out."

David checked. The withdrawal was there, filed and legal. He got to his feet, looked into Beryl's flaccid twitching face, and left. Outside, the dingy city streets felt like paradise. The nausea still sat coiled in David's gut. Beryl would have to move. His invisibility had been compromised. David imagined him walking through the crowded streets, trapped in realtime as he relocated.

Beryl would get his punishment.

David hailed a cab and gave it the lab address.

HIS SISTER was waiting for him. Beryl had called her, of course. She greeted David serenely and ushered him into her private apartment, up on the second floor of the building that housed her lab. The spotless, almost spartan, decor jarred with David's memory of Beryl's squalid clutter. He looked at his sister's profile, smooth and perfect as porcelain, wondering what needs had brought her into Beryl's virtual bed. Sex only? Or something more?

"I didn't expect you to discover my little plot." She set a tray down on a low lacquer table. "I expected you to be misled by the pirate rumors we planted. Tea?" She handed David a delicate cup.

The glaze was a depthless gleaming black. A tiny illusory pearl seemed to glimmer in the bottom. "You did this just to make me look bad," he said. "You came within a hair of destroying Chen BioSource." Of destroying Father. "I haven't told Fuchin," he said. "Yet."

"Don't try to lever me with our father. I am weary to death of him and of you." Her eyes gleamed, as hard as the glaze on the cup in her hands. "You don't care about Chen BioSource. It's a burden to you, a distraction from your so-called art, Little Brother." Her lips twitched. "I *am* Chen BioSource. *I* design the templates we sell. I care about the company more than our father ever did. But I am merely a daughter. So Fuchin had to find a brood mare and make himself a son. I have spent my life making Chen BioSource work, and he is going to give it to *you*. Because you are his *son*.'' Her voice trembled. "Tanaka wants a new krill I'm developing. They value me for what I am. They have offered me a position as head of their aquaculture design unit, and I am going to take them up on it. According to Beryl, Fuchin will still have a company to give you, but it won't be worth much without me. Tell him whatever you wish, Little Brother. I don't care.''

Dà Jieh. Eldest Sister. David looked down at the cup in his hands, remembering her eyes as their father boasted of his *son*'s achievements to that forgotten visitor. The illusory pearl gleamed in the bottom of his cup. His sister and their father shared the same passion, the same virtual. Chen BioSource: Immortality. Dynasty. Life. But Father could only visualize it through a son.

David set his cup down very carefully. "I *am* self-centered," he said to his sister. "I didn't understand. I am sorry."

He left her sitting there, the black cup in her hands, wary surprise on her face.

DAVID'S APARTMENT rang with quiet. He prowled the empty room, peered into the lab. He peeled his tunic off over his head, threw it into the corner, and entered his studio. One by one, he pulled out the racked canvases. No sign of new fox-prints. David selected the volcano piece, stretched it out. Flander was woven into every nuance of the composition. David saw his signature in the delicate shadows cast by grass-blades, in the gleam of light on a bit of smooth stone. Stars cascaded into the caldera, dying in shimmering light.

The piece was a masterwork.

Because of Flander; crazy, talented kid, gone now, maybe forever. What would happen to him, without Shy-Shy? Maybe he could re-create her. Maybe he couldn't.

"Erase," David cried in a shaking voice. "Delete all storage." The dying stars trembled.

*Are you sure you want to do this?* his studio program queried.

David opened his mouth, closed it. This is what my sister did, he thought, and felt dizzy. Jealous, hurt, and angry, she had tried to smash what she loved. David touched a fern frond, noting the tiny cinnamon spots of the spore cases on its underside. I was going to destroy this, he thought, because I am hurt and because I am . . . jealous.

Jealous. He would never be as good as Flander. Sooner or

later, the world would know it.

"Cancel the erase," David said. He squeezed the scene back down to a canvas, racked it carefully.

"New canvas," he said, and picked the white rectangle out of the air. It stretched in his hands, blindingly empty. "Azure," David said, and wiped sky across the expanse of nothingness. He muted it to twilight blue, shaded darkness over it; nightfall seeping into the weary end of day.

David worked on into the night in a frenzy of creation. He sculpted Shy-Shy's image, remembering the weathered angles of her face, the love and warmth that Flander had put into her eyes. He added the furtive driven traces of a fox, melded it all into a symphony of love and hope and compromised dreams, of darkness and light. He put his father into it, too, gave him blind all-seeing virtual eyes and a grieving face. Reality and unreality twisted together, became a skein of human hopes and fears and desires.

Sometime well into the next day, David passed out. As he fell, limbs drifting toward the floor in slow motion, the entire piece unrolled inside his head. It was good. David felt one piercing moment of triumph, and then the floor touched his face and darkness swallowed him whole.

THEY ALL CAME by to see Father on the day that he was released from the hospital. They brought gifts, delicacies of fresh fruit or wild-harvest seafood, and he basked in their attentions. He looked better than he had in months. This was family, operating as it should. Chen BioSource in the flesh. The virtual was intact. David stayed at the periphery, aware that Shau Jieh was keeping an eye on him. His eldest sister nodded to him, and her porcelain face betrayed not one echo of their interview. If she was worried that David would reveal her part in the lawsuit, it didn't show. Her bit of espionage had been the smashing fist of an enraged child. Her withdrawal to Tanaka was the calculated destruction of an adult. In either case, Chen BioSource would die.

*Die* was the appropriate word. Fuchin *was* Chen BioSource. David had understood that in the hospital when he had made his promise to his father. David sighed. You could kill in virtual. In the illegal parlors, you could kill the body with drugs and unreal weapons. You could kill the soul. David tried to banish the image of Flander's face as Shy-Shy vanished from his life. We surround ourselves with unreality, he thought. Not just the Beryls, who had retreated from the physical world; but people like his father, who had surrounded themselves with an illusory reality shaped to fit their needs.

His middle sister had finally herded the boys out of the room. Only Shau Jieh remained. David went over to the bed-side. He knelt down, took his father's hand in his. "I'm glad you feel better," he said in perfect, careful Mandarin.

"You did what I asked. You got Selva to drop the suit. I am proud of you, Er-dz."

David looked away from the approval in his father's eyes. A part of him would always long for that approval. A part of him had been willing to give up a lot for it. David took a deep breath. "Selva decided that the suit didn't justify the expense. Fuchin, I am leaving Chen BioSource. I can't work for you anymore."

"What are you saying to me?" His father struggled higher on the pillows, his cheeks quivering. "You talk nonsense. What will you do? Walk away from your family? Turn your back on us?"

"I don't want to walk away from you," David said gently. "I am still your son, I am still David Chen, but I can't manage the company. I don't want to do it."

"*Wanting* has nothing to do with it. You have a responsibility. To me. To the family."

"I do." David stood. "I know that there are people who will do a better job than I can. I *am* thinking of the family."

"You think only of yourself." His father's tone dripped bitterness. "Like your mother did."

Father had never spoken of his mother to David before. There was hurt in his voice. David held out his arm, watched light run across the silver threads embedded in his skin. Had she been implanting a hope or an echo of her own failed dreams? He felt a pang. I'll ask her, he thought. I *need* to ask her. "*Dwèi bu chi*, I'm sorry, Fuchin." David reached out, touched his father's shoulder gently. "What I do is for the best. I hope you understand that, someday."

His father turned his face to the wall, his expression closed, hard as stone.

"Fuchin?"

His father gave no sign that he had heard. David looked down at his hands. They were trembling. He closed them into fists and turned away. Dà Jieh was still in the atrium. She was sitting on the bench beside the holoed pool, staring at the gold-and-white fish.

"Reality and unreality are not so easy to tell apart." David stopped beside her. "Sometimes, the unreal has as much power as the real. Maybe more.''

''Are you trying to be a philosopher, now? I thought you were an artist?'' Her tone was acid.

''I transferred my company shares into your account.'' David watched the graceful flick and swirl of the kois' trailing fins. ''That gives you a strong majority.''

''What are you saying?''

Her expression was wary, as if she expected a trap. In a way, it was a trap. David sighed. ''I can't stop you from going to work for Tanaka. I can't stop you from destroying Chen BioSource. If you stay, Fuchin will have to listen to you. I don't think he'll like it, but I've quit. That might change his attitude a little.''

''You're going to walk away? Just hand over all your shares, with no strings attached?''

''Check your account. It's done. I can't change it now.'' Those shares were the chains that would bind her forever. She cared about Chen BioSource as much as their father did. David dropped a pebble into the water, watched rings form and expand, chasing each other across the still surface. Flander was right. He was too stuck on reality. David lifted his head, met his sister's black porcelain eyes. ''I wish that I had as much talent as you do,'' he said softly.

Something flickered in those depthless eyes, and she bent her head. ''If what you tell me is true,'' she said, ''I will probably reject Tanaka's offer.''

''I hope so.'' David walked away.

Shau Jieh was waiting for him beside the lift. She said nothing, but her eyes were sad.

''Our sister is the son that Fuchin wants,'' David said to her. ''Gender has nothing to do with it. Do you think he can ever understand that?''

''I don't know,'' she said. ''I'm sorry.''

''Me, too.'' He had destroyed the David Chen that his father had believed in. He had done it to keep Chen BioSource alive, destroying the smaller illusion to preserve the greater one. There was no way to heal the hurt that he had left behind in his father's bedroom. Part of David would always grieve for that lost father. David lifted his sister's hand gently from his arm, kissed her, and stepped into the lift.

''YOUR PIECE *Synthesis* is remarkable. Your use of the volcano theme is masterful.'' Hans Renmeyer paced across David's studio, hands clasped behind his expensively clad back. ''I take it that you have settled whatever was . . . troubling you? Never mind, never mind." He spread his hands, smiling. "Your access-point rating is still high after seven days on the Net. I haven't seen anyone get such a lengthy showing for months now." He coughed delicately. "Perhaps another gallery will be interested. I have heard some . . . rumors."

"Good." David reached out to stroke the black-and-white cat. I am afraid, he thought. After the payoffs to find Beryl, the bribes for Selva, and his stock transfer, he didn't have much left. He had never done this for the money, as a means to stay off the street. "If you present me with an offer, I'll accept it," he said. "I give you my word."

"Good, very good. Tell me." Renmeyer paused, his hand on the studio's virtual door. "Why did you choose the name *Synthesis*? I'm just curious."

The piece had named itself. It *was* a synthesis, a merging of himself and Flander, of reality and unreality. "Because of foxprints," David said to Renmeyer's uncomprehending face, and ushered him out of the studio.

Alone, he took the canvas of Shy-Shy and his father out of the rack, stretched it open. He hadn't worked on it since his night of frenzy. David ran through it slowly. It was good. Not perfect, but good. *"Grief,"* David said. "That's what I'll call this one." It was a hymn of grieving for what was, and for what couldn't be. And for what might have been.

A flash of red moved at the edge of vision. David turned slowly, heart leaping. The red fox sat on its haunches in a sweep of stars. *Vulpes fulva*—and you could see every hair ripple in the wind. It cocked its head, green eyes wary, ears pricked.

"You're very good," David said. "You're going to be better than me."

The fox flattened its ears, curled its lips back in a snarl.

"Together," David said softly, "we can be great."

For a long moment the fox didn't move, and David found himself holding his breath. Then it opened its jaws, lolled its red tongue over its pointed white teeth, and trotted into the center of the scene. It flicked its tail and scattered shards of light across the piece.

David opened his arms and Flander walked into them; grubby, skinny street kid whose ragged clothes covered state-of-the-art skinthins. He needed a shower. David watched the glittering droplets of light settle over his father's face and Shy-Shy's, like shed tears, like forgiveness.

It was the perfect touch.

# LOOD TIDE

More than an acre of Mylar film rippled over Damian's head, thin as a spider's weaving. The warm northwest wind, blowing straight from Australia's deserts, began to falter. The genoa jib shuddered, fluttering like a silver wing in front of the mainsail.

"Wind speed's down to eleven knots," Paul called from the trimaran's computer console. "I hope one of your automatic systems kicks in before that sail collapses."

"It will," Damian yelled back to his son. "Haven't you listened to *anything* I've told you?" The expression on Paul's face reminded Damian sharply of that reserved and uncommunicative teenager who had walked away from him to enter the Space and Aeronautics Academy ten years ago. Paul might be in the US solar propulsion program, but he still acted like that sulky teenager, as far as Damian was concerned.

Perhaps Paul was making a point—that he was only interested in the wind from the sun. Damian pressed his lips together and searched the ocean swell for signs of a freshening breeze. His son had never been willing to waste his time on the sea.

Stifling anger, he ducked beneath the taut main boom and walked aft, moving easily along the tri's narrow kayak-shaped center hull. Graceful, hollow wings arched out on either side of the main hull, like a.gull caught on the downstroke of flight.

Let Paul turn up his nose, Damian thought. I'll beat *Warakurna* and prove my Autocrew to Pat Garret and Tanaka-Pacific, once and for all. Damian clenched his fist, trying to recapture the *focus* he had had at the start of the race. It had vanished. He opened his hand slowly, inspecting his salt-roughened palm. Paul had dissolved it.

He swung down beneath the plastic weather-bubble that protected the cockpit and leaned over Paul's shoulder. "We can take another three-tenths drop in wind speed before she starts to luff." He watched the wind die on the flat screen of the sailboat's master monitor. Three days out of Sydney. They were more than halfway to the finish line of the Designer Cup race at the mouth of Kaipara Harbor—and to the heliplane that would take Paul to the Platform shuttle. He scanned the ocean swell.

"*Warakurna*'s slatting." Paul pointed at the Australian entry, north of them. "Look at her sails flap."

"She may be the top contender, but she can't take the light wind like *Gossamer.*" Damian nodded. "If we get into heavy air, though, she'll leave us behind."

"You'll win." Paul's expression was enigmatic. "Don't you always get what you want?"

"No!" The word burst out, startling them both.

Paul looked away, his lips tightening.

The sail rippled with a dry crackle, and Damian squinted into the afternoon sun. The wind was coming. He could smell it.

"Cancel the automatic reef," he snapped.

Paul glanced up dubiously, but said nothing as he keyed in the command.

If the wind dropped to four-point-five knots and he hadn't reefed, the Mylar film would start to slat and it might tangle. Surface charge would stick the micro-thin film together like old-fashioned plastic wrap, and the charged-fiber ribs wouldn't be able to exert enough force to straighten the enormous sail.

Sweat prickled in Damian's armpits. Five-point-oh-three knots. He was gambling, betting the race on his nose for wind instead of letting Autocrew make the decisions. Or was he trying to prove something? Four-point-seven. The wind veered around to NNW and picked up with a sudden gust. The silvery film of the enormous mainsail fluttered and filled, and the triangular genoa bulged.

Damian let his breath out in a gusty sigh as stress codes raced across the screen. Made it. Small electrical currents stiffened the fiber ribs, unfurling even more sail.

"That was close. I wouldn't be first pilot long, if I cut it that fine on the *Clarke*." Paul didn't look at him.

Damian heard criticism in his son's words and flushed. "I've been sailing boats since before you were born," he snapped. "If you'd ever bothered to learn, you'd have seen the wind coming."

It was a lie. He'd gambled. Don't start another fight. This isn't why you invited Paul along. Damian glowered at the *Gossamer*'s filmy sails. They had been manufactured by null-g technology up on the Platform—an offshoot of the solar-sail program. Those silvery space-born sails might win this race for him, but they would steal Paul. The journey to Tau Ceti was one way. The *Clarke* wasn't coming back. Suddenly, he hated the silver film with an intensity that made his stomach churn.

"Your Autocrew is doing a great job," Paul said, a shade too enthusiastically.

"Your mother believed in space as the Great Frontier, and what did it get her?" Damian's fist smacked the slick plastic hull. "A plaque up on the damned Platform."

"I know the risks," Paul said tightly. "So did she."

"Did she?" Damian glared at his son.

The monitor beeped and both men jumped.

"It's calling for a two percent increase in sail area." Paul turned to the screen with relief.

"So do it. If you can remember how." Damian turned away. Out on deck, the winches hummed, reeling out more line as the electrical currents flowed and more sail unfurled. "Bring her in closer to the wind," he commanded. "I want to give that factory ship plenty of room."

The Japanese-flagged vessel, big as an aircraft carrier, flew the corporate flag of Tanaka-Pacific. I helped make them the biggest, Damian thought, but the sense of satisfaction had faded long ago. The bright young kids were taking over, full of fresh ideas and impatience. He watched a hoverplane lift from the ship's deck, loaded with fish meal.

"Most of the Platform's aquaculture tanks are adapted from your methodology," Paul said, following Damian's gaze.

"The techniques aren't patented." Damian touched the helm

control, and the *Gossamer* rounded into the wind, briefly tilting the port hull clear of the water. The wind gusted suddenly and the trimaran leaped under them, surfing down the face of the waves, bows in the air.

"Damn." Paul grabbed for a handhold.

"We're well ahead of Pat and *Warakurna.*" Damian eyed the taut curve of the carbon-filament mast, feeling a small satisfaction at his son's reaction. "How's your stomach?"

"Okay." Paul moved fractionally away. "Believe me, anything the waves can do, null-g can do better." He grimaced. "Is the mast supposed to bend like that?"

"Uh-huh. That's how it can handle the big sail." He glanced at the sat-link's screen. It displayed weather information and the positions of the other contestants. "I told Pat that Autocrew would beat him with its long-range strategy." Maybe Tanaka-Pacific would listen to him, now.

"You're really into this new computer-assisted boat design." Paul shot him a sideways glance. "What happened to that thermal-vent project?"

"Didn't I tell you?" Damian kept his tone casual, eyes on the screen. "They put Lescaux in charge."

"I'm sorry."

"Why?" Damian scowled, aware of his gray hair, colorless as driftwood. "I'm not dead yet. There's still plenty for me to do, right here on Earth." God, here I go again, he thought, and closed his mouth.

Bent over the monitor, Paul didn't answer. His hair was gingery—Mira's hair. Paul looked so much like her. Damian still remembered the day the solemn redheaded three-year-old had stepped off the shuttle. That had been a week after the accident. My son, he thought. And hers. Damian watched the stress codes scroll across the main monitor, not really seeing them.

*You're chasing dreams,* he had told her, on that last sailing weekend together. *The Platform's just a job with a bad safety record.*

*It's a first step for all of us,* she had said. The sea wind had whipped her red hair into her eyes. *You don't have to come.*

He hadn't come, and she had ended up a sacrifice to someone's stupid miscalculation of hull stresses. Whose mistake is going to kill Paul? Damian thought. He clenched his fists, glaring at the silver wings of *Warakurna*'s sails. On a reaching course like this, stresses pushed to the limit, *Gossamer* was making good time. Was he winning or losing? The race and Paul's upcoming mission blurred together in his mind, and he couldn't tell.

The boat skipped over the crest of a wave in a crash of spray. "It's a rough ride." Paul looked pale, but stood easily enough, stretching his compact frame. "I'd hate to be on this thing in a storm."

He was trying to smooth things out. "She bounces worse in a light breeze." Damian hated the casual words. This chitchat wasn't what he wanted, but anger kept rising up between them like a thick sheet of glass.

They had never been very close. Damian busied himself running a check on Autocrew. The factory ships and the flimsy subsea domes had been dangerous—no place for a child. On vacations, Paul had never cared about sailing or the sea. If he talked at all, it was orbital velocities and Dyson spheres.

"Juice?" Paul was rummaging in one of the supply nets.

"Please." Damian cracked the seal on the plastic packet Paul handed him. The liquid was too sweet and artificial, full of nutrients. He grimaced and emptied the packet in three long swallows.

"Look, Damian." Paul braced himself against the plastic curve of weather-bubble. "Let's stop this bickering, okay?" He lifted his hands in a placating gesture. "I know you don't approve of what I'm doing, but maybe we can put it behind us for a while." He lifted one shoulder in an awkward shrug. "Just for these last couple of days?"

"It's your choice, isn't it?" Damian crumpled his empty juice packet. "To leave on this suicide mission. Why shouldn't we talk about it?" He glared up at the cloudless sky, to where the Platform hung invisibly above them in its geostationary orbit.

It was more city than platform now, a vast manufacturing and tourist extravaganza. And somewhere at the periphery waited the *Clarke*, its micrometer-thick sails ready to unfurl for its long flight.

"Suicide." Damian enunciated the word carefully. "Why don't you admit it?"

"How many times have we been over this?" Paul sounded tired. "It's too late now."

"You've got plenty of backup people who could take over for you. Damn it, look around you." Damian ran a hand through his thinning hair. "We're just starting to tap the sea's resources, and we've barely touched the planets. Isn't there enough for you here? What the hell are you looking for—some adolescent adventure fantasy?" He was yelling, again. Damian clamped his lips together.

"Tau Ceti has at least one carbon-hydrogen-oxygen–based

planet." Paul was folding his empty juice packet into smaller and smaller squares. "There's not much here for us, in the solar system—not in the long term. We can live on Phobos and Mars, if you want to live with life support or biomodification." He raised his head, and his hazel eyes were opaque as salvage gold. "It's time for us to tip over our cradle," he said. "Someone has to take the first step."

Mira's words. "Even if it takes you a dozen lifetimes to do it?" Damian cried. "The damn system's eleven light-years away, and you don't know if you'll find anything once you get there."

"Five years," Paul said evenly. "That's all the time I'll spend outside of stasis. If there's nothing there, we'll look somewhere else."

"If the stasis doesn't fail. If an asteroid doesn't get by the laser sweep and put a hole in the hull. If. If. *If.* You could drift around until you die of starvation or old age." Damian clenched his teeth so hard that his jaws ached. "Who's going to care?" he grated. "Who's even going to remember that you tried?" Why you? he wanted to shout at his son. Why the hell do *you* have to do it?

"Let's just drop it." Paul tossed the tiny wad of plastic onto the console table. "I'm tired of arguing."

"Yeah." Damian took a deep breath, struggling for calm. "I'd better concentrate on the race."

"Good idea." Paul's relief was guarded. "I'll go check the telltales on deck."

This trip wasn't working. There didn't seem to be anything between them anymore but anger. Damian stared at the blinking codes on his monitor. Maybe Paul was right. Maybe it *was* too late. The breeze was still gusting between NW and NNW, and Damian felt the tiny shudder as the movable keels tilted on the outboard hulls to counterbalance the shifting force of the wind on the sail. This is my last chance, he thought.

"Come up, quick." Paul's excited shout came from the bow. "Dolphins."

Damian scrambled out of the cockpit and hurried forward along the center hull, ducking beneath the taut main boom. Paul had flattened himself along the bow. He pointed.

Three wild dolphins leapfrogged off *Gossamer*'s bow, cutting sleek arcs through the air. "Dolphs always look like they're playing." Damian squatted behind his son on the narrow hull. "You don't see wild ones much, anymore."

"We had some Auggies, down on the subsea training base," Paul said. "They were pretty smart."

"I've never liked the augmented dolphs." Damian shrugged. They seemed taut, frantic, as if they were poised between sanity and insanity. "We don't even understand the dolphin mind," he said.

Paul tensed, anticipating another lecture. The bow slapped down into the trough of a wave, and salt spray beaded his face like tears.

"I saw a whale once," Damian said. "A sperm whale."

Paul rose cautiously to his knees, shading his eyes. "I thought they were extinct."

"They might be, by now. It was a long time ago." Twenty-six years ago, on his final weekend with Mira. "It looked old," Damian said. "And tired." Towering over their tiny sailboat like a blotchy barnacled mountain, it had eyed them for a timeless moment. Then it had opened its enormous jaws and slid gently beneath the waves. Its wash had nearly swamped the little boat.

"Your mother was there," Damian said. You were there, too, he almost said. Mira couldn't have known she was pregnant, yet.

Would I have gone? he wondered. If she had told me? Damian cleared his throat, wiping stinging salt water out of his eyes. The construction site would still have decompressed, but maybe. . . .

Paul touched his arm suddenly. "I wish you'd come to see the *Clarke* launch," he said. "The sail is beautiful—an enormous silver wheel, turning slowly in front of us, blotting out the stars. We'll start slow at first, but the momentum is cumulative, so eventually we'll approach the speed of light." He watched the dolphins, his face luminous. "We call it the ark. A million fertilized ova—everything from lobsters to man." He turned his shining golden eyes on Damian. "Dolphins, too. It's a chance at immortality, Dad. For all of us."

Paul hadn't called him Dad since he was ten. "Nothing lasts forever." Damian stood up on the slick hull. "There is no such thing as immortality. You can die here, or a million miles from home."

The light faded from Paul's face, leaving it dull and cold. Damian watched him retreat aft, stooped and awkward on the narrow hull. A million miles from home, or on a geostationary platform.

He scanned the gray swell, but the dolphins had disappeared. In either case, death was the bottom line.

"YOU'D BETTER check the sat-link," Paul told Damian when he finally climbed down into the cockpit. He sounded edgy. "The barometer's down to .993."

"Weather's coming." Damian scowled at the barometer. He was letting Paul distract him from the race.

Wispy cirrus clouds trailed up from the horizon, stained peach and rose by the setting sun. He should have noticed the change. "A storm," he said. The sat-link showed the collapsing high-pressure system. A big low was sliding south, pushing squalls ahead of it.

"Great." Paul's shoulders hunched. "I hope it's not a bad one."

"We're safe enough," Damian said. "Autocrew'll keep us on course, and even if it doesn't, we've got an onboard Locator." The Locator. A terrible, wonderful idea popped into Damian's head, and he dropped onto a bench to hide the sudden flush of his excitement.

Without the Locator, search and rescue operations would have to depend on satellite observation and heliplane sweeps. Damian forced himself to relax. Searchers would estimate a boat's position from wind and known course data. But what if *Gossamer* changed course under the cover of the storm clouds? Autocrew could maintain it through the storm—Damian believed in his program and his boat.

Without a Locator, they could be lost for days.

Five days would be enough. The *Clarke* would be gone. Did he dare? Damian's pulse was racing, and he forced himself to relax. It was a risk, but not too great a one, if he didn't disable the Locator permanently. "Paul, would you check the mast telltales?" His voice sounded remarkably casual in his ears.

"Sure." Paul reached for the ladder. "As long as you don't want me out there during the storm." He gave a brief laugh and disappeared over the weather-bubble.

Damian dropped to his knees in front of the sat-link, fumbling with the watertight seals that protected the electronics. Heart pounding, one eye on the ladder, he opened it up. There. That was the board he wanted. He removed it from its slot and hid it in a watertight supply locker. Now, *Gossamer* was nothing more than a single boat on a very large ocean. Not even the satellite eyes would find it easily, if they didn't know where to look.

He'd make sure they didn't know.

Damian resealed the sat-link's housing and threw himself

onto the bench as Paul started down the ladder. A gamble. He took a deep breath. It was a gamble that might save his son.

"It's getting pretty wild out there." Paul looked apprehensive. "Everything seems fine."

Damian nodded, suppressing a smile. Already, the waves were getting steeper, sliding past the *Gossamer* like dark glassy hills. The sun sank, staining the sea with its blood, and the Platform appeared in the darkening sky. It glowed briefly, like a pile of spilled jewels, before the clouds swallowed it.

Damian broke out the insusuits, and while Paul struggled into his, Damian entered the course corrections. Paul didn't know Autocrew well enough to suspect anything. The storm felt like a big one. It should drive them well out of range of a search sweep. Outside, a school of small squid shot by, glowing milk-white beneath the surface. The boat plunged through the waves with a heavy labored roll.

"You've never been up to the Platform, have you?" Paul's face was a shadowy oval in the blue glow from the monitor screens. "You've never seen the memorial."

"No." Damian entered the final changes in Autocrew. Mira had made her choice. He had made his. The wind gusted suddenly, and the boat shuddered.

"Hey." Paul half rose. "The sat-link screen is blank. Did you turn it off?"

"Damn." Damian scrambled over to the console with a credible display of concern. "It's dead. Our communication is out." He frowned. "Can't do anything about it until the storm lets up," he said. "If a wave came in over the bubble while I had it open, it would blow all the electronics."

"Great." Strain tightened Paul's voice. "So now we're on our own."

"That shouldn't bother you. You'll certainly be on your own on the *Clarke,*" Damian said dryly. "You're relatively safe down here. Autocrew will keep us close to course, and even if we go off, they'll be able to find us by the Locator signal."

"I hope you're right." Paul's face was sober. "The sea reminds me of space—vast and completely unconcerned whether we puny humans live or die. You gave me a good understanding of that, as a kid, you know. It's helped."

"I thought you hated the sea." Damian felt disconcerted.

"No." Paul looked surprised. "I never hated it."

The monitor beeped a soft alert as the wind gusted violently. *Gossamer* heeled sharply, lifting her port wing clear of the water, and red blossomed on the monitor screen. The first breath of the storm.

"Whoa." Paul hung on to the console table. "It feels bad." The bow lifted like a rearing horse, slapping down into the waves with a crash, and the wind rose from a growl to an angry scream.

"It'll be all right," Damian yelled. "*Gossamer* can take it." He hunched over the main monitor as the hours crawled past and the storm showed no sign of easing. Autocrew was performing perfectly—making a thousand tiny adjustments in sail and keel each minute, keeping the boat on course in spite of the storm. Too bad *Warakurna* would win. Red stress codes blinked like baleful eyes on the monitor. Damian felt the storm's power vibrate through the hull as it hurled them farther and farther away from discovery. Even if Tanaka-Pacific dumped Autocrew, he would have saved his son.

SOMETIME after midnight, the wind veered from NNW straight around to the SE. The main boom swung across the deck, winches screaming, sail filling with a hollow *whump*. The *Gossamer* shuddered and tilted, starboard wing rising clear of the water, graceful hull thrumming with strain.

Paul yelled something as he and Damian tumbled sideways, slamming into the port wall of the cockpit. For a tremulous instant, *Gossamer* balanced, undecided. A wave broke over them, and icy seawater splashed down into the cockpit.

Would she broach or right herself? Damian held his breath.

With a groan, *Gossamer* decided, crashing down into the wild sea, nosing her center bow straight into the side of the next wave. It slid across the deck in a welter of foam. More water slopped into the cockpit, and the pumps whined as she shuddered and staggered upright. The monitor glared with red codes, but *Gossamer* was still afloat.

"Something's wrong." For the first time since the storm had begun, Damian felt a touch of fear. He flung himself into the console chair, fingers flying across the keyboard as he overrode Autocrew and keyed in more reefs to further reduce the sail area. Still too much sail for this wind. Sweat prickled beneath his insusuit.

*Gossamer* shuddered beneath another fierce gust, and the monitor beeped frantically.

"The genoa's still up," Paul yelled from the ladder.

"It can't be." Damian scrambled up beside his son, clinging

to the rungs as the boat plunged into a wave trough that looked deep as the Grand Canyon. "I keyed it down, first thing." Damian stared in disbelief. Beyond the reefed mainsail, he could barely make out the silver bulge of the big genoa.

Damian cursed as he dropped back into the cockpit, fear a cold fist in his belly. A jammed winch? Fouled line? The wind speed was forty knots, gusting to sixty. With that much sail, they would go over. He keyed the drop command again, but Paul shook his head. It was still up.

The tri's triple hull shot out over the crest of a small mountain of water, smashing down into another trough. The port hull lifted, bounced hard. The boat groaned and the monitor went wild.

"I've got to get it down by hand." Damian was already scrambling up the ladder, snapping a lifeline onto his safety harness as he went.

He could feel Paul on the ladder behind him as he stuck his head above the shelter of the bubble. "Stay here," he yelled automatically. "I'll get it."

The wind hit him in the face, snatching the breath out of his lungs. Windblown spray stung his face like hail. The boat bucked under him, bow leaping out of the gray-and-white water, crashing down in an explosion of foamy spray.

He didn't dare stand up. Hands numbing in the cold seawater, boots scrabbling for purchase on the wet deck, he worked his way forward on hands and knees. Twice, wild waves broke over them from the starboard quarter, nearly tearing him loose from the hull.

The wind shrieked in the rigging and the mast shivered. The boom was taut with strain in spite of the reefed mainsail. Damian ducked under it, clutching the handholds with aching fingers. He reached the winch that controlled the genoa's foot, hooking his legs around the base. He'd have to put it on manual and operate it from here.

The cable felt hard as a steel rod from the strain of the overstressed sail, and the manual release refused to budge. He pried at it, expecting the *Gossamer* to heel over and broach at any moment. The deck tilted under him, steep as a mountain slope.

The boat surfed down the face of a huge roller and slammed into the trough. It felt like they'd hit a brick wall. Damian gasped as the winch clicked into manual mode, but it still wouldn't budge. Damn. Where was the foul?

Swearing, Damian spotted it—a twisted loop of cable above

the main feed. He strained at the twist, working by sight, fingers too numb to feel anything. It gave. He cranked and the cable spun out. The sail flapped wildly as the wind spilled over the slackening edge, cracking like pistol shots.

He had to get it down before it wrapped around the stays. He crawled forward, beneath the foot of the whipping genoa. He was out near the bow, here. The hull narrowed to less than a meter, bucking like a bronc beneath his knees. One moment, he was three meters above the waves, the next, the hull crashed down and water exploded up around him.

Another sea slammed into the boat. Damian's foot slipped, and he fell flat on the wet plastic. Don't go overboard. Hang on. The main winch didn't stick, and miraculously, the sail began to drop, twisting in the wind. He grabbed an armful of slick film, blinded by spray. Crank. Reach up and haul in the folds, before the wind could tangle them. Crank, reach, fold. Crank. Reach. Fold. It became mindless, aching monotony. There were a million square miles of sail to furl, and the wind snatched viciously at the film, trying to tear it out of his hands.

A plastic grommet caught him on the cheekbone, and pain lanced through his jaw. Damian pulled in the last armful, and as he struggled with the wet film, a wild wave caught the bow from the side, slamming into the boat like a freight train.

As *Gossamer* nosed into foaming water, something smashed into Damian's side. Flotsam—a piece of wreckage or a rotting tree trunk—he never saw it. He lost his grip, and the wave swept him casually off the bow. Cold water closed over his head, and Damian fought the urge to gasp for air.

His left side was numb, his arm useless. He groped for his safety harness with his right hand, forcing down panic. His fingers closed over the taut lifeline, and suddenly he was on the surface, buoyed by his insusuit.

He gasped air and choked as a wave slapped his face. He was only a dozen feet from the hull, but he couldn't haul himself in single-handed. I should have let Paul come out with me, he thought numbly. I always have to do it myself. The *Gossamer* rushed through the stormy darkness, pulling him along. Damian cursed himself as his hand slipped. Something hard banged his fingers.

The safety snap. Cold panic shot through him. He had snapped the line to only one ring of his safety harness, and it had pulled through the loops in his suit. If he let go, he would be adrift in the storm.

His hand was numb. He clenched his teeth, but he could barely feel his fingers. In another minute, maybe two, he would lose his grip. He slid up the foamy slope of a wave. The suit would keep him alive for hours. How long would it take them to find him?

Too long. They wouldn't know where to look. The bitter irony choked him as the sea tossed him casually over a wave crest.

I'm going to die, Damian thought. Paul too, if *Gossamer* and Autocrew couldn't handle the storm. Wind shredded the waves. A mountain of water slid over him, and for a terrible moment, Damian thought he had let go of the line. I wanted him to stay, because he's all I have left. I let Mira go alone, and I shouldn't have. The thoughts darted through his mind like fish. I want Paul to stay because I'm old. Because I'll be alone. Damian's head broke the surface, and he gasped for air. Miraculously, his fingers were still locked on the line, but he couldn't feel them at all.

Too late, now, he thought. Too late.

He didn't feel Paul's hand on his wrist. It wasn't until his son's fingers dug into his armpit that he made out the shape of the boat and Paul's straining torso. His son had followed him, after all.

"Help me," Paul yelled. His shoulders bunched with effort. Damian kicked hard, clutching the cable of his lifeline with every last ounce of his waning strength. Slowly, Paul pulled him closer. A wave crest slid over them, and Damian squeezed his eyes closed. His knuckles scraped the hull and another wave caught him, lifting him almost onto the deck. Paul hooked his fingers into the useless loops of Damian's suit and heaved him out of the water.

Safe. Damian lay flat on the slick hull, shuddering.

"Come on," Paul yelled in his ear. "You've got to get below."

With a groan, Damian made it to his knees. The boat tried to throw him into the water, the wind tore at him, and even with Paul's help, it was a million terrible miles back to the cockpit. By the time he slid down the short ladder he was exhausted. Every breath was a scalding agony.

"Your Autocrew's doing great." Paul unsealed Damian's suit and probed his shoulder and side with cold fingers. "I'd sink us, for sure." In spite of his light tone, his face was drawn and anxious.

"We're still floating." Damian gasped as pain stabbed him.

"You might have broken some ribs, but your shoulder seems okay. I should have gone out with you." Paul's face twisted, and he turned away to reach for the first-aid box. "I thought I'd lost you," he said harshly.

"I'm the one that got lost," Damian mumbled. He leaned back against the hull, trying to make his eyes focus on the monitor.

The storm was starting to die. Only a few red stress codes winked from the screen. A pain patch dulled the agony in his side, but every roll of the boat hurt. "I could have gone up to the Platform with your mother," he said.

"You had your job with Tanaka-Pacific." Paul's voice was rough. "Don't go into that now."

"No. It's important." Damian struggled to sit up, fighting the fuzziness of the drug. "They asked me to set up the Platform's aquaculture program. It was a big offer." He looked into his son's face, seeing Mira in every curve and shadow. "I was afraid," he whispered. "The Tanaka-Pacific job was safe. I knew the ocean. No one knew if we could even build the Platform, and I was afraid."

"Everyone has to make their own choices. You're the one who told me that." Paul draped a thermal blanket over his father.

"Did I?" The drugs blurred Damian's words. "After the accident, I kept seeing Mira in your face. I kept thinking that things . . . might have been different. If I'd gone with her."

"I made you feel guilty," Paul said softly. "That was why you were angry."

Damian nodded once and let his head droop, hurt by the sad acceptance in his son's tone. Does he know me that well? Damian thought with a wrench. I don't know *him*. "I've always been afraid," he said. "Afraid to love you, because I might lose you, too." Tears ran down his face and dripped off his chin.

"Dad?" Paul's eyes were dark as amber. "I love you. I haven't always acted like it—you had such a reputation that I always felt like I was standing in your shadow." He half smiled. "Maybe that's why I joined the space program." He slid his arm around his father. "You gave me a book about the sea for my sixteenth birthday," he murmured. "You'd written a poem on the flyleaf—from Shakespeare—I've never forgotten it." He chanted softly:

*There is a tide in the affairs of men,*
*Which, taken at the flood, leads on to fortune;*
*Omitted, all the voyage of their life*
*Is bound in shallows and in miseries.*

"It's inscribed on the *Clarke*'s hull," he said. "We'll take it with us."

Damian leaned back against his son's shoulder. Why did I write that? he thought. It had been one of Mira's favorite poems.

"You'll have to fix the Locator." The words cost him an effort. "Or they won't find us in time. I hid the board in the number four locker. It'll restore communications, too." He looked away from his son's widening eyes. "I told myself that I was doing it for you," he said. "But I was doing it for myself. I nearly killed us both." He bent his head, feeling tears gathering behind his eyelids again.

"It's all right," Paul said huskily. His arm tightened around Damian's uninjured shoulder. "I understand."

THE HELIPLANE settled down next to *Gossamer* in the bright midday sun. Light sparkled on the gentle swells, and the silver sails flapped in the still air.

"Well done, chaps." A sunburned woman in a military coverall leaned out of the cockpit door. "You came through the blow better than most of the boats." She tossed them a line. "Too bad they canceled the race on you." She sounded Brit, looked Eurasian, and eyed Paul with undisguised interest. "We brought the medic along," she said brightly. "Who's the patient?"

Besides the medic, the plane was full of more military types wearing the gold-and-black Solar Propulsion insignia. "We're on a tight schedule," an officer explained while the medic taped Damian's ribs. "A solar-flare prediction upped the launch schedule. If the storm hadn't ended when it did, a backup would have had to take Paul's place. Are you sure you can get back to Kaipara on your own?" The officer looked concerned. "I could leave someone with you."

"No need," Damian murmured. "Autocrew does all the work." So close. He looked into his son's face. A few more hours and Paul would have had to stay, anyway. There was so much he hadn't had time to say.

*There is a tide in the affairs of men,*
*Which, taken at the flood, leads on to fortune . . .*

"Dad?" Paul stood in front of Damian, his posture stiff and awkward. "We'll be launching as soon as I get on board." He swallowed. "Wish me luck?"

Damian shook his head, remembering the light in his son's face as he talked about his ark. Immortality. "You said you could leave someone here to help me with the boat." He turned to the officer.

"I could do it, sir." A lanky young woman saluted smartly. "I've sailed since I was a kid."

"Could you take her back on your own?" Damian found he was holding his breath.

"You bet." Her eyes gleamed as they slid along *Gossamer's* sleek hulls. "Any time."

Paul was looking at Damian, his eyes bright.

"Maybe you'll have time to show me the memorial," Damian said. Everyone had to make their own choices, good or bad. I hope you find what you're searching for, he thought, and put an arm around his son's shoulders.

"Too bad about the race," the officer said. "Maybe you'll win the next run."

"I won this one," Damian said.

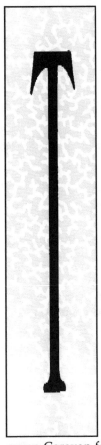

# THE RAIN STONE

Rosemarie shifted her pack higher on her shoulders as she clambered up the creekbed. Below, the desert floor blurred to a haze of tan that stretched out to the rim of the world. The sea must look a lot like that, Rosemarie thought. Only blue, not brown. The herd of stocky little goats browsing along the flat looked like gray foam on the desert sea.

The Caravan had set up the first herding camp at the base of the creekbed, where they always did. Sun flashed from the black wings of the solar panels on the truckbed campers, trailers, and battered RVs that housed the seven Caravan families. The water tanker stood in the center of the loose circle, because water was at the center of everything. The tanker was still full, since they were only a week out of Malheur. And anyway, it was spring, and the goats could even find a little water in the old creekbeds up here on the rim. Water didn't really get to be a bad problem until the other side of the circle—after they'd gone around the bottom of the Alvord Desert and up along the Owyhee. By then, it would be full summer and everything would be dry. That's when the grownups would start knocking on the tanker's metal sides, figuring head-count and miles to the Snake River Aquifer at Nyssa. That's when you couldn't get drinks between meals, and you were *always* thirsty.

Even thinking about those hot days made Rosemarie thirsty, and she shrugged her pack off her shoulders. She only had two jugs in her pack, not the three she usually carried.

Because she had snuck out.

The anger balled up in her belly again, hot and hard as a clenched fist. *You're getting too old to go out herding.* Her mother had uttered those shocking words as she scrubbed the dinner dishes back in Malheur, on their winter place. *I'm sending you up to Pendleton when we get to Nyssa, this fall. There's more to life than goats, Rosie-child. You can live with Aunt Jenny and go to school. Until then, you can help Mathilda in Caravan. She's getting on and needs a pair of strong arms. Go get me a clean pan of sand.*

Too *old* to go herding? Shane was fifteen, two years older than she, and Doug was a year older. The three of them had been herding goats together since Shane was eleven. They *needed* her. Mathilda, the Caravan doctor for both humans and goats, was tough as an old doe. She didn't need anyone. In fact, she had seemed relieved when Rosemarie had told her that Mama wanted her this week. By the time Mama found the note she'd left, it would be too late. She'd be up on the rim with Shane, and Doug, and the goats. They'd have two whole weeks together before they had to meet up with the Caravan for more supplies.

Go live with Aunt Jenny! Rosemarie capped her water jug, trying not to think about those awful words. Everything had started to fall apart this winter. Rosemarie shrugged back into her pack and plodded up the narrow crack of the creekbed. Winter was bad enough, because a lot of people left for Pendleton or The Dalles to work winter jobs. It had been worse this year, because Anne McLaren's cousin in The Dalles had gotten Shane a job up there, and Doug had apprenticed to Samuel, the mechanic who kept the Caravan on the road.

*Mechanic work is men's work,* Mama had said when Rosemarie had asked her if she could help Samuel, too. Why it took a man to fix an engine, she wouldn't say, but she wouldn't let Rosemarie ask Samuel if she could help, so Rosemarie hadn't seen much of Doug, either.

It was because she had started bleeding. Rosemarie veered south, scrambling up the rocky side of the creekbed. Mama wouldn't say so, but that's when things began to change. She wrinkled her nose, aware of the rub of her nipples against her shirt. Her breasts were getting bigger. Not big enough to get in the way, like Anne's, but she didn't want this. She didn't want *any* of it. It was a pain and a nuisance, and the final straw to a crummy winter. With a last wild scramble, Rosemarie clambered up onto the spine of the ridge. On the far side, the old homestead creekbed cut its way back into Steen's Mountain. Doug and Shane would be in there somewhere, because they always started out up the homestead creekbed.

Rosemarie paused to catch her breath. The ridge hid the Caravan, and she couldn't spot any of the other Caravan herds. There was only hard blue sky, the wind, and the endless gray sea of sage. It was *spring*. Rosemarie spread her arms, her irritation suddenly evaporating. The chilly wind nosed inside her jacket where the zipper was broken, raising a shiver on her skin that wasn't all cold. The cloudless sky was so big. It seemed to pour in through her open jacket, into her chest, filling her up inside with a cold aching vastness that always made her want to dance, or cry, or leap down onto that dusty plain of rocks and sage, run clear to the edge of the world and dive off into space.

You could almost see the wind. It wove through sage and rocks and sky, like the warp threads of Mama's winter loom. Rosemarie spread her hands, fingers crooking, as if she could hook her fingers into the fibers of the wind itself, into the warp and woof of the world, shake it, and make it hers. Mama didn't matter, and Nyssa, and Aunt Jenny. She breathed out, in, slowly feeling the wind in her lungs. Right here, now, above the sage sea, kissed and tickled by the cold wind, there was only *now* and *forever*. For a moment—just for an instant—she felt *something*. Shimmering threads beneath her fingers. A pattern. If she could only grasp it, she could seize the wind, take the earth and sky into her hands and. . . .

The moment passed. Sky was sky, hard and blue and dry. Wind was wind. It frisked about her like a dog, pelting her with grit. "Hey, cut it out," Rosemarie yelled, liking the sound of her voice on the clear air.

It puffed cold down her neck and yanked at her ponytail, like Doug or Shane would yank at it. Teasing her. Sometimes, it was her only playmate, the wind. Laughing, Rosemarie slithered down into the creekbed in a shower of dust and stones, arms raised against the whip of willow stems as she crashed into the thicket that lined the bottom of the old creek. Goats bleated, and a trio of does bounded out of her way, followed by skittering kids. More goats bleated on the far bank, and she picked out the jingle of Mandy's lead-goat bell.

Bingo.

"Hey, what the hell?" A figure parted the willow stems; stocky as the goats, sandy-haired and grinning.

"Hi, Doug." Rosemarie tried to untangle her hair from the willow branches. "You didn't think I was going to let you wander around up here by yourselves, did you? We'd never see those goats again."

"Speaks the girl who gets lost on the main road." Doug snorted. "What are you doing up here? I thought you got stuck doing fetch-and-carry for the Doc?"

"Mama changed her mind," Rosemarie said, and then wondered why she'd said that. She and Shane and Doug had never had any secrets from each other. But she had just lied, and had lied without even thinking about it. She shook her head impatiently. "I'm stuck. Grab this, will you?" She slid out of her pack straps, swung it into Doug's hands.

"What's all this?" Shane shoved his way through the willow brush. He was taller than Doug, dark and slender where Doug was fair and stocky, narrow-hipped and muscled like an antelope, because he ran everywhere. "What're you doing here?" he asked.

Annoyance in his tone? Rosemarie's mood faltered.

"She came to look after us." Doug raised his thick brows and rolled his eyes.

"She did, huh? Who did we have to haul up that cliff last summer?"

"I would have been fine if that ledge hadn't given way." Rosemarie tossed her head. "There was a cave down there."

"With nothing in it." Shane grinned at her. "Some of us have better sense than to risk our necks for nothing."

"You're just weenies." Rosemarie finally got her hair loose from the branches, laughing, relieved inside because after all it was okay, normal, the way it always was when they were together. "Total weenies."

"Weenies, huh?" Doug smiled his slow smile. "Then you can go down into the brush after the lost kids when it starts to get dark. Us weenies'll watch from the bank."

She stuck her tongue out at him, and he ran after her to tickle her, and it was all right again; the three of them clowning, teasing each other, ganging up two against three in various combinations that never stayed the same very long.

THEY SET UP camp in the slanting beams of the setting sun, doing it fast and without much talk, because they'd done it together a thousand times before. As Rosemarie spread the tarp and shook out their sleeping bags, she wondered how they'd worked the routines without her. Which one had laid out the bags, and who had built the fire-ring? Doug was farther up the stream, getting water from the seep that always had something in it, this time of year.

Rosemarie shaded her eyes, looking for him, but the harsh evening light hazed the rocks into a blur of light and shadow. The goats were browsing on sage twigs, still restless this early in the year. They clumped together in family groups, strangers after a long winter in separate barns, eyeing each other warily. Green ear-tags belonged to Doug's parents. Red ones were Mama's, white were the Murphys', and blue-striped ones belonged to Shane's dad. After a few days, they'd start to blend, butting heads until they'd worked out a single pecking order. Tiny kids peered at Rosemarie from the safety of their mothers' legs or bounced in three directions at once. The three of them always got stuck with the old brood does, because they were easy to herd. Yearlings and bucks tended to scatter. We could handle yearlings, Rosemarie thought, and tossed her head. We're *good*. She flipped a pebble at a wandering kid.

By the time the Caravan reached the saleyard, up in Nyssa, the kids would be as big as their dams, ready for slaughter. They were lab goats. Scientists had strung their genes together like beads to make them grow fast and meaty, to get along without much water or food. They had been *made*. So they could live out here on the edge of the Dry, where the cattle and sheep had died off long ago. The wind eddied around her, gentler down here, and she put out a hand absently, feeling its cold breath on her palm like a great dog snuffling at her. She hated Nyssa. She hated the dust, and the frightened bleat of the goats as they were prodded onto the big trucks.

This year, she was afraid, too. Afraid of the bus that would take her to Pendleton, and Aunt Jenny, and the city.

*Why?* Rosemarie shook the last sleeping bag out with an angry snap. Shane had dumped an armload of dry sage-branches beside the fire-ring and was kneeling beside it, shaving off thin splinters of kindling with his clasp knife. He looked up and smiled as she sat down beside him. He had a black eye, just beginning to fade into green around the edges. She hadn't noticed it before—hadn't seen much of him at all in the confusion of the Caravan forming up and getting underway. Noticing his eye, she noticed his face. It had changed over the winter. It looked sharp-edged, and lean. His brown eyes seemed darker, as if they were full of twilight. A sudden shyness took Rosemarie by surprise. She had grown up with Shane. They had fought over toys when they were bare-assed kids, but suddenly . . . he was a stranger.

He saw her looking at his face, grimaced, and lifted one shoulder in a wry shrug. "Dad was pissed that I didn't get back to help with kidding." A thick splinter curled off the stick and flicked into the smooth dirt of the fire-ring.

"I was worried." Rosemarie picked up the shavings and began to pile them into a tepee shape. "I thought we'd have to leave without you."

"I had a ride, but it . . . fell through." He snapped his knife closed, stuck it in his pocket. "I finally hitched with a trucker."

"How was the job? What was The Dalles like? Did you make a lot of money?" She spoke fast, to make the inexplicable shyness go away, and because she was jealous. They had been up here for two days without her, and Doug had heard all this first. "What did you do?"

"I helped Patrick haul local produce for the Army." He pushed her hand away and began to rearrange the piled splinters. "He contracts for this lady who supplies the Corps of Engineers in The Dalles. It was okay. I made some money. More than I told Dad about," he said shortly.

"Why?" Outrage sharpened her voice. "He can't take your money."

"Oh yeah?" Shane shrugged; a jerky, angry hunch of his shoulders. "He wants to buy new breeder bucks, and they cost. He says it's reinvestment. We're improving the stock." His voice dripped bitterness. "Like it matters. Like this is something besides a way of using up the desert before it dries up and blows away, like we're doing something more than marking time out here."

"Oh, come off it, Shane." Doug hiked up to the fire-ring and plunked down four dripping jugs. "Is this any worse than loading crates onto a truck?"

"No, but I don't want to spend my life here, pretending that I've got some kind of future."

"So leave," Doug said shortly.

"Will you knock it *off!*" Rosemarie bounced to her feet, furious, wanting to cry, too, and horrified that she might. Shane's talk of leaving shocked her even more than Mama's pronouncement about Aunt Jenny. They had always talked about leaving; going to Portland, or San Francisco, signing on with one of the iceberg trains, hunting for lost treasure in the Dry—but that was just talk. Daydreaming. Underneath was the solid reality of the herding cycle and the Caravan and the cold winter barns. "I didn't sneak out here just to listen to you guys snarl at each other," she said. "What's with you, anyway?"

"Nothing." Doug sighed, and righted the water jug she had knocked over. "We're both cranky, I guess. Listen, I found an old road up there. Just beyond the seep."

"Can't be." Shane fished a lighter out of his pocket. "How could we have missed a road, all these years we've brought goats up here?"

"That's the desert for you." Doug's eyes had darkened to the color of twilight. "You can live here all your life, and not find out all its secrets. Come on, Shane. Leave the fire and let's go look. We've still a couple of hours until dark."

He was coaxing, trying to soothe Shane's temper. Doug was always the first one to make peace after a fight. "Well, *I'm* coming." Rosemarie fished in her pack for her solar flash, excited in spite of Shane's grumpiness. If Doug said he'd found a road, he had, and it could lead anywhere. There was so much out here—the ruins of old farmsteads, or mines, or ranches. People had lived and died in the desert for a long time. Mama said that it hadn't ever been much different, even back before the weather changed and the country started drying up. The desert was a strange place. It swallowed things. Walk ten steps away, and a road or a ruin disappeared—just vanished into the dust and sage.

The wind nudged her, whispering cold excitement in her ear. "Come on, Shane." She dug his flash from his pack, tossed it at him. "Let's go."

He caught it with a shrug and got to his feet. Surly. Rosemarie swallowed irritation. She didn't want him to be surly. Not on her last time herding.

Her last time. The tears caught her this time, clogging her throat. No way, she was going. No *way.*

"It's up there." Doug pointed upslope, and fell in beside her. "You all right?" He touched her arm.

"Yeah." She shook her head so that her hair whipped into her face, so he couldn't see she'd been crying.

"You really grew a lot this winter." He looked at her, his expression strange. "I didn't notice it until now."

"I grew an inch and a half," Rosemarie said, although she wasn't sure that was what he meant. "There it is. I can't believe we missed it." She pointed.

A road, an honest-to-God dirt track, and they must have grazed the herd right over it at least once. Ten years old or a hundred—you couldn't tell in this dry, forever land—it snaked upward into the mountains, a clearer path of wheel-worn dirt winding across the stony slope.

"Well, I'll be." Shane spoke from behind them.

"Told you so," Doug crowed. "Race you to the end."

They whooped and shouted, and raced up the slope until they were panting and staggering; because it was spring and they'd found something new and possibly wonderful to explore. And because there was something wrong between them; a sense of strain that had never been there before, and nobody knew quite what to do about it. Everything was changing. It made Rosemarie angry and sad, and she ran until she left even Shane behind, and her side ached, and every breath burned her lungs, and she couldn't feel anything else.

The track ended at a ruin. It had been a cabin once, built into the side of the mountain. Rosemarie staggered to a halt, panting, knees wobbly and weak. Stone foundations crumbled beneath it, and gray weathered boards revealed cracks of darkness between them. Rafters showed through the broken roof, stark as bleached bones. Like the track, the cabin could have been ten years old or a hundred. Things didn't age very fast out here.

"Who . . . built it . . . way out here?" Shane came up panting behind her. "Stupid place to build anything."

"Maybe it was a miner." Doug wasn't panting, because he had dropped to a walk, way back. He never could keep up with them running, and he didn't try. "See? I bet that was the tunnel." He jerked his head at a slide-scar of raw dirt and rock on the slope nearby. "Maybe they mined gold."

"Nah. They mined lead or mercury around here. Not gold." Shane pulled at a sagging shutter, leaped back as it crashed to the ground and broke apart. "There was never any gold up here. Let's go back, before we have to chase goats half the night."

Ignoring him, Rosemarie stepped carefully between the warped and fallen boards of the small porch. The empty doorway yawned, full of darkness, although the setting sun poured harsh yellow light onto the face of the cabin. She clicked on her flash, and a brief rodent scuttle made her jump.

"Better be careful." Doug edged up beside her, wary on the

brittle boards of the porch. "That roof could come down, or you could go through the floor."

"It's okay." Rosemarie stepped through the door, knowing suddenly and with a certainty in no way rational that it *was* okay.

A table leaned drunkenly on three legs, beside a broken bedstead. A small metal stove stood in one corner, its cooktop covered with the rusted ruins of its stovepipe. Rosemarie pulled a cast-iron skillet from beneath the debris. It was orange with rust, and heavy.

"Someone lived here." Doug traced a line in the thick layer of dust that covered the table. "Someone sat at this table and ate rabbit stew out of this skillet." He shivered. "I feel . . . like we're trespassing."

"Some stupid homesteader thought they could make it rain by hoping. *I* don't feel any ghosts." Shane looked in through the doorway, scowling. "Come on. I'm hungry."

"Just a minute." Rosemarie turned around, feeling a pull, *something*, in this place. The wind rattled a loose board and sifted dust down from the roof, turning the beam of her flash into a hazy sword of light.

"I do," Doug said. "Let's go, Rose."

Someone was watching them. Rosemarie whirled around, heart slamming her ribs. Every ghost story she had ever heard, or made up around the campfire at night, burst into her brain. Nothing there, just the wind whining through the cracks with the sound of a nervous dog. "Okay, I'm coming," Rosemarie said, but as she started to turn away, her light beam touched something that glinted like metal.

"What is it?" Doug squinted as she reached back into the crack of shadow beneath the window's warped frame.

"I don't know." The little metal box fell open, as if it had been waiting for her to pick it up—or as if the hinges had rusted away. It held folded sheets of paper that shattered to tan bits beneath her fingers. "Letters," she said, regretting that they had crumbled to dust before she could read them. Her fingers touched something else, something hard and smooth as a chicken egg, cold as the wind that breathed over her shoulder.

Doug whistled as she held it up, and the light from her flash caught it. A stone. It was bigger around than her thumb, a soft translucent gold that glowed like afternoon sunlight as they shone their flashlights on it. Droplets of silver gleamed within, like raindrops falling through a pool of golden light.

"It's beautiful," Rosemarie said softly.

"It's amber. Petrified pine sap." Shane leaned over her shoulder. "It might be worth something, in The Dalles or Pendleton."

"No way." Rosemarie carried the golden stone outside. "It's mine." In the light, the stone looked like the honey she'd had for a treat on her last birthday. It felt heavy in her hand, warm, and . . . alive. Magic. "Let's get back." Rosemarie closed her fist on the stone, shoved it deep into her pocket. "Or we *will* be chasing goats all night. They've probably pissed all over our sleeping bags by now, anyway."

That was enough to get them running down the mountainside, laughing again, still under truce. And when they reached the campsite, sure enough, the goats *were* all over the place, because when did goats ever miss a chance to get into anything they weren't supposed to be into? At least they hadn't pissed on the sleeping bags. Doug and Shane shooed them out of camp and did a quick head-count while Rosemarie picked up the knocked-over packs, restacked Shane's kindling, and lit the fire.

THEY DIDN'T BOTHER to cook, because it was dark by the time the fire had burned to a bed of coals, and they didn't much bother cooking on their first days out, anyway. Dried fruit and smoked goat meat tasted just as good plain, washed down with the luxury of tea, made with water from the seep. Which meant they ate straight mush for the last days before they came back down to the Caravan again, but that was the way it was. One of the rhythms that shaped herding season, like the sun's rise and set, like the dust storms that sometimes blew up out of the south.

There was comfort in those familiar rhythms. Doug had gotten his battered flute out of his pack and was playing softly—one of his desert tunes, as he called them. The fire flickered as Shane tossed a handful of twigs onto the coals, casting shifting shadows across their faces, striking silver glints from the flute. Goat eyes gleamed dull green in the darkness. The herd always stayed close at night, as if for protection—although the few coyotes around only went after stray kids. Maybe they just liked human company. Sometimes, you woke up with an old doe curled up at the foot of your bag or against your back. Rosemarie stretched, leaning against Doug's shoulder, her feet (which got cold at night) tucked under Shane's sleeping bag. Doug's flute-music rose and fell, wandering like wind among stones. The music and the firelight closed them into a golden bubble—a small, private universe surrounded by goats and cold darkness.

Rosemarie fished in her pocket. The stone felt smooth as she took it out, warm as her flesh. She set it on one of the stones that ringed the fire—not too near the heat. The silver drops inside the amber gleamed in the glow of the dying flames. "This is a rain stone," she said softly. "Magic trapped the rain inside, and if you say the right words, the rain will come."

Doug's flute had trailed away to silence, and for a moment there was no sound except the hiss of the fire and the whisper of the wind on stone. Then a goat bleated, calling to her kid, and Doug laughed softly.

"That would be some find," he said, and the lingering flames filled his eyes with light. "You could make the desert live again."

"Let me see." Shane tossed another branch onto the fire and picked up the stone. "They're bubbles," he said, holding it up to his eye. "You can see. They must have been trapped in the gum, like flies get trapped sometimes."

"They're raindrops." Rosemarie caught the stone as he tossed it to her, nettled by his tone. Last year, he would have agreed that they were raindrops. Last year, it would have been a rain stone, not a lump of dried-out tree sap. She shoved it into her pocket, angry at him, and at the same time . . . sad for him.

"I've got to piss." Doug tossed aside the bag he'd tucked across his legs and rose to his feet. "I'll check on the herd. Yow, that wind has a bite." He shivered, zipped his jacket closed, and crunched off into the darkness. After a moment or two, they heard the soft notes of his flute.

"He's mad at me." Shane crossed his arms on his upraised knees, eyes on the fire, brooding. "But I can't help bugging him. He . . . reminds me of my dad, sometimes." Shane's voice had gone low and soft. "Up in The Dalles, you can see how things have dried up. You can see where there used to be farms and orchards. It's just dust now. Like here—only up there, you *know* it used to be different. You *know* the land's dying. Out here, you don't have to see it if you don't want to," he said bitterly. "The sage still grows. We can find a little water, way up on the rim. You can tell yourself that everything's fine, that we can go on herding goats forever. You can pretend; like Doug does. And Dad. He pretends he's a cattle baron, like his grandfather. The family used to own that ranch—the big one down the road." Reflected flames danced in his eyes. "Dad told me one winter, when he was drunk."

"I didn't know," Rosemarie said softly. He always wore a cowboy hat, Shane's father. And boots, as if he was going to get up on a horse and ride away, like you saw in the history books. Maybe that's what he dreamed of doing. Maybe that's why he looked at the goats like he hated them, and they had more trouble at kidding than any other herd, and he rode his dirt bike after strays, like he didn't care if he died or not.

She had never thought about it this way. Shane's dad was just Shane's dad—the man with the angry eyes who left bruises on Shane's face that Shane lied about in Caravan, and didn't lie about to her and Doug. She looked at Shane sideways, trying to make sense of the change in him. He seemed older, not just two years' worth of older, but older in some subtle internal way. The firelight pooled shadow beneath his high cheekbones and highlighted the line of his jaw and thoat. He turned his head as if he sensed her stare, and Rosemarie felt a flutter in her belly; a sudden prickly strangeness that tightened the skin of her abdomen and thighs, made her want to get up and run, or yell and dance, or do *something*.

"I missed you," he said, and touched her hand.

That touch, light as a feather, traveled along her arm and down to her belly, where it made the flutter worse.

"I've always been able to talk to you," he said. "No one else talks. About the weather, yeah, and how many kids they got last winter." He jerked his head, eyes angry in the flickering light. "Maybe they're afraid that if they start talking about anything important, they'll have to talk about how they're using up the desert, killing it off with the goats, until everything dries up and we all blow away."

He was right about the land. The sage was a little thinner every year. It didn't quite grow back after the goats browsed it down. South and east lay the Dry; the dead heart of the country. It was a land of no water, and rock, and empty towns drifted over in blowing dust. It was getting bigger; coming this way. The grownups talked about it in Caravan, late at night, when the kids were all asleep or out on herd duty. Trapped with Mathilda, she'd listened. They talked about it like it was an animal, stalking them. A monster with gray dusty hide, and fangs made of bleached bones.

They were afraid when they talked about it. You could hear it in their voices, like a cold wind. She heard the same fear in Shane's voice, here in the firelight. "What happened in The Dalles?" She closed her fingers around his, felt him shiver. "Something did, didn't it?"

"Patrick was . . . nice to me. He's twenty, and he's lived on his own for a while." Shane stared into the fire. "He let me stay with him for free. He never loses his temper, Rose. I mean, he gets mad, but he's still thinking. He's an okay guy. I like him a lot." He sighed once, a letting-go that made his shoulders and spine slump. "He . . . asked me to stay," he said very softly. "That's why I missed my ride. We . . . went to bed together, that night. I kind of knew it was going to happen, and . . . I didn't try to make him stop. He would have stopped, if I'd asked." He looked at her at last, an anguished sideways glance that didn't quite connect. "I'm . . . not really sure who I am, Rose. I'm not sure what I am, or where I belong, or if I belong anywhere."

"You're Shane," she whispered, because her throat had closed and only a whisper could get out. "And you're here, and it's okay." And she lifted her face to him, her body moving on its own, because there weren't any words for this, *none*. He needed something from her, and this seemed . . . right.

They kissed gently at first, and she breathed the scent of his body—not sweat, but musky, warm, *different*, as if she'd never really smelled anyone before. The differentness of it shivered down her skin in a strange new way, silver and warm, making her shudder deep down inside. And then it wasn't such a gentle kiss anymore, and she didn't want it to be. The air seemed to thicken around them, as if the very fabric of cold and night was changing, drawing close, like a blanket wrapping them up in their own private space of smell and taste and touch. "I'm going to leave," Shane murmured softly. "When we hit Nyssa. Come with me, Rose? There's nothing for us here. We can catch a ride with a trucker. Please?"

Nyssa again, like a road sign, or a wall that she couldn't see beyond. She opened her mouth to say something; yes or no, she was waiting to hear what would come out. Brush crackled and a stone cracked on stone. They bolted apart like frightened goats, and Rosemarie felt a hot clutch of guilt, as if she'd been caught doing something wrong.

"The goats are fine." Flute on his shoulder, Doug walked over to the fire. "They're settling down fast, this year." He poked at the coals with his toe, not looking at them. "You guys ready to sleep yet? I'm tired."

"Me, too," Rosemarie said. She was blushing, and could feel it.

It made her angry that she should be blushing, that she should feel like she'd been sneaking. She could kiss Shane if she wanted to. The wind gusted suddenly, whirling sparks into the air, cold on her hot face. Partly, it was what Shane had told her. It sat in her chest, heavy as a stone; a secret that she couldn't share with Doug, a secret that she wasn't sure she really understood. Not completely.

Doug shoved the flute into his pack without speaking. Shedding his jacket, he climbed into his bag. He left his jeans on. They'd always slept in their underwear and shirts. None of them had ever talked about it—they just did it that way. Shane was getting undressed. *He* took off his jeans, and the deliberate way he rolled them up and tucked them down into his bag felt pointed. Rosemarie looked away from the white bulge of his underwear, and she felt herself blushing again. Damn them. Damn The Dalles, and this Patrick, and her bleeding. Damn *everything*. She stood up, unsnapped the waistband of her jeans, unzipped them. Doug had rolled over with his back to her. Shane was staring at the fire. The thick feel to the air was still there, and it made her skin prickle with strangeness. Slowly, she pulled her jeans down, stepped out of them. The wind rubbed against her like a huge invisible animal, flattening her shirt against the roundness of her breasts, making her nipples get hard from the cold. They weren't looking at her, neither of them. Rosemarie kicked her jeans into her bag, slid into it after them. "Good night," she said.

"Good night." Shane was climbing into his own bag.

"Good night, Rose." Doug rolled suddenly over to face her. In the faint glow from the embers, his eyes looked as dark as Shane's. "Sleep well," he said.

It occurred to Rosemarie that she'd stopped hearing his flute for some time before he'd walked into the firelight. The desert played funny tricks with sound. You could walk right up to someone, and they wouldn't hear you. She wondered suddenly how much Doug had heard, and what he had seen, and why he had stood there, listening in the darkness. Tears came up to clog her throat, hot and choking as a lump of overcooked mush. For a long time she lay awake, pressed flat by the weight of a million bright stars above her, intensely aware of Doug and Shane on either side; sleeping or awake, she couldn't tell. Her breasts hurt with a thin, fierce ache, and she couldn't sleep. Finally, Rosemarie reached into her pocket and closed her hand around the rain stone. The smooth hardness of it eased some of her restlessness, and after a while, she fell asleep.

THEY WOKE LATE, to gray light and a cold wind that snatched at their clothes and flung grit in their faces. A sneaking coyote-wind, with its teeth bared. Rosemarie blinked dust out of her eyes and zipped her jacket closed as far as she could.

"I guess maybe your rain stone works," Doug said as he tried to get the fire started. "Just don't flood us out, okay?"

"This kind of shit never means rain." Shane scowled up at the high, thin clouds that streamed like ragged banners across the sky. "Not this late."

"It's got to rain somewhere. At least it's not a dust storm. I give up." Doug scrambled to his feet, wiping ashes from his hands.

"What do you mean?" Shane glowered. "We got to chase goats without any tea?"

"So *you* start it." Doug turned his back, and stalked off into the sage.

"*I'll* do it." Rosemarie dropped to her knees in the cold dust, scooping sage twigs into a pile.

The coyote-wind seemed to have gotten inside all of them this morning. She looked at Shane, wanting to say something about last night, about what he had told her. In the cold harsh light of day, the words wouldn't come. That kind of revelation was for darkness, for the private world of firelight and goat eyes. He wasn't looking at her, was sitting on his bag, lacing up his boots. Rosemarie sighed and cupped her hands around the tiny flame of the fire, scorching her fingers as she protected it from the coyote-wind.

"Forget the fire." Doug burst out of the sage. "The goats are gone."

"Gone?" Rosemarie stared at him, cupped hands full of fire-heat. "What do you mean, *gone?*"

"They must have scattered. They're all over the mountain-side. I only spotted four does."

"God*damn* it." Shane bolted to his feet. "I am so fucking sick of goats."

"Maybe someone scared them." Rosemarie cut Doug off before he could snap back at Shane. "I thought someone was watching us yesterday, up by the old mine."

"Coyotes." Doug's eyes had gone the same flat gray as the windy sky. "They're after the kids, this time of year."

Rosemarie shook her head, sure that it hadn't been a coyote yesterday. "Let's split up," she said. "You guys take the sides of the creekbed, and I'll go straight up the middle. That way, we can run them down into the center, and we won't have to chase them clear up onto Steens."

Shane frowned. "Rose, maybe we shouldn't split up like that. If someone was really spying on us yesterday, maybe you ought to go with me, or with Doug."

"Like *hell!*" Now she was genuinely angry. First Mama, with her "you're too old to go herding," and now this. "When I need you to worry about me, I'll *ask.*" She stuffed one of the water jugs into her daypack, slung it over her shoulder, and shoved her way into the willow brush above their camp.

"Rose . . . marie!"

Doug's voice. He sounded worried, not angry. Shoulder deep in willow, she hesitated, remembering that creepy sense of someone looking. This was *their* mountainside, their private space. She glanced back, but Doug and Shane were arguing again. Boys! She watched them turn and stomp off up opposite sides of the creekbed. Goats! She couldn't decide which angered her more, right now. A willow stem slashed her face like a whip, and her eyes filled with tears as she ascended the slope. Why couldn't they all just put the damn, miserable winter behind them and be friends like they used to be? Why? Why? *Why?* Willow stems whipped at her as she shoved through the thickets, and she couldn't come up with one single answer. Panting, she finally slowed. A doe bleated off to her left; the low growling murmur of a mother calling her kid out of hiding. A bell chimed faintly. Mandy's bell. It was from Switzerland; an antique. You could always tell its sound from the cheap ones.

Most of the herd would be with Mandy. She was lead doe. Relieved, because at the back of her mind she had been imagining ravening wolves, or monsters, or worse, Rosemarie pushed through the brush and climbed the north bank. She was almost to the mine—had come much farther than she'd guessed. A gray head poked up from behind a clump of sage, followed by a second, and then two more. Rosemarie scrambled onto a rock to do a head-count, because the short, squat little goats weren't any taller than the sage.

Most of them were here. The others wouldn't be far away. Nothing had chased them. They had just wandered, because goats liked to do unexpected things every so often, just to keep you on your toes. The wind curled around her, its coyote-teeth hidden once more behind soft springtime lips. The cloud-streamers were merging overhead, softening the light, making the dusty green of the sage leaves and the gray coats of the goats stand out sharp and vividly clear. She could feel it up in those clouds: rain. She could feel the warp and woof of wind and sky, like yesterday, like she could reach out and grab it. Rosemarie groped in her pocket, closed her hand around the warm smoothness of the rain stone. It felt *alive*. Full of power. Hold it up, say the right words, and those gray miserly clouds would wring themselves dry, watering the sage and the goats, driving back the Dry for another season, or two, or three.

If you knew the right words.

"Hey, missy. I want to talk to you."

The strange rough voice startled her. Rosemarie spun around, foot catching on the uneven surface of the boulder. She lost her balance, leaped sideways off the rock, and landed wrong and hard on her ankle. Pain spiked up her leg, so sharp that she went down on her knees.

"Don't spook on me now, missy. You hurt yourself?" A man bent over her, holding out a grimy hand, grinning through a tangle of graying beard. "I ain't gonna bite you."

Hex. Rosemarie let her breath out in a whooshing sigh, because she knew Hex. He hung around the Caravan so he could buy water while he scavenged old ranch houses, townsites, and forgotten dumps. "You scared me." Rosemarie scrambled to her feet and bit back a cry. Her ankle didn't want to hold her up at all. "You scared our goats. What are you doing up here?"

"Don't blame me for your goats wanderin'." He wiped his nose on the ragged sleeve of his jacket. "You kids were snoopin' around that old cabin upslope. I was right out in the sage, and I heard you, yesterday. That's *my* site. I got a state license for salvage in this county, and you was trespassing. You got somethin' of mine, missy." He stuck out his hand. "Hand it over now."

So the watcher had been Hex. Rosemarie shrugged, sulky and hurting. He didn't belong here. He was the miserable winter, and Shane's dad, and The Dalles. This was *their* space, and he was ruining everything. "A state license doesn't mean you own the whole county." Rosemarie stuck her chin out. "I didn't take anything from you."

"You found something in that cabin. A piece of jewelry or something." Hex's eyes glittered. "I may not own the whole county, missy, but I own what's in that there cabin, and the law says so."

The rain stone. *Her* rain stone, that had brought the clouds. She sta.ed at his grimy outstretched palm. "I don't have any jewelry. I've got to chase goats." She started to turn away, gasped as he grabbed her arm.

He pulled her around to face him. "Don't you give me lip, missy. I know you. You're Margie's girl. You sure turned into a pretty little filly this winter, didn't you?" He pulled her a step closer, grin widening. "Tell you what. We'll cut a trade. You give me a kiss, and you can have whatever you stole. How's that? Fair?"

"No. Let *go!*" Rosemarie tried to wrench free, but his grip was like iron. She kicked him, but her bad ankle buckled and it wasn't much of a kick. He winced, but he didn't let go. Instead, he yanked her closer. His arms went around her, squashing her against his chest, holding her so tightly that her ribs threatened to crack and she couldn't kick him, or get her leg up to knee him, or even *breathe*.

"You got some spirit, don't you?" he said, and laughed.

She was strong, and she'd always been so sure of her strength. She could run faster than Shane, even. But Hex towered over her by more than a foot, and he was big. Rosemarie struggled, suddenly frightened; really *scared* in a way she'd never been scared before. The air had gone thick, like it had gone thick last night in the camp, only this was a different kind of thickness—musky and dank, full of violence and fear. Different, and . . . the same. His breath blasted her face, sour and hot, and she leaned away from him.

"Leave her alone." Shane appeared behind Hex, his face pale and angry. "Let go of her!" He grabbed Hex's arm, yanked at him.

Hex staggered, and Rosemarie tore herself out of his grasp.

"Bastard," Shane snarled, and swung his fist at Hex.

Hex growled in his throat and blocked Shane's wild punch. His thick shoulders bunched, and he stepped forward faster than Rosemarie could believe anyone could move. A punch to the stomach doubled Shane over. Hex laughed a single sour note, and backhanded him across the face. "I heard you spent the winter with the McLaren boy." He looked down at Shane, sprawled in the dust. "I guess your dad's right about you not being worth shit."

Shane came up off the ground in a way that no human could move; like a spear, or an arrow shot from a bow. He hit Hex without a sound, slamming one fist into the big man's gut. The second blow caught the scavenger in the jaw, flung him backward as if he'd been hit by the water truck. Hex fell hard, rolled over, and came up onto one knee.

"You little prick," he said thickly. He surged to his feet, took a single step, and stopped.

Shane crouched facing him, still silent. The blade of his knife flashed white light as the sun stabbed through a break in the clouds. His eyes blazed, dark as the night sky, crazy in a way Rosemarie had never seen before. It was like he wasn't really looking at Hex, like he was seeing something else; a monster, a demon. Something that wasn't human. Something to kill.

"Hey, c'mon, kid." Hex spread his hands. "This is no big deal. It ain't no blood matter. I was just foolin' around." Fear gleamed in his eyes, and he took a step backward as Shane shifted his weight.

"No!" Rosemarie said. The wind whined, loud in her ears, deafeningly loud as she stretched out her hands. "Shane, stop. Don't do it!"

He didn't hear her, wasn't listening, was lost in a world that she couldn't see into, couldn't touch. He was alone in there, never mind that she could see him, right there in front of her, with a smear of blood on his chin and the fading bruises on his face. His dark crazy eyes shut her out, and there was only Shane, and Hex, and death.

Without a sound, he lunged forward, knife swinging upward in a streak of silver light.

"Shane, *no!*" Rosemarie threw herself at him, but her ankle betrayed her. "*Shane!*"

A blur of motion from her left became Doug; tackling from behind, grunting as he wrapped his arms around Shane. They staggered forward and fell, still locked together, rolling down the steep slope in a shower of rock and dust. Hex gave her a quick glare, turned and ran. Rosemarie ignored him. Afraid, she slithered down the slope after them, teeth clenched against the stabbing pain in her ankle. Way down at the bottom of the creekbed, they were struggling to their feet.

They both clutched the knife, straining chest to chest, faces masked with dust and sweat, silent. Doug looked desperate, and as scared as she felt. It was as if all the beatings Shane had taken over the years, all the bruises and pain and tears he never cried, had sunk into some dark ugly well inside him. They had erupted, here and now, had rushed up to charge that knife with lightning. With death. Rosemarie sobbed once, feeling it. Death.

It would happen before she reached them; Doug would die, or Shane, and for no reason. *For no damn reason.* With a cry, she stumbled to a halt. Arms spread, crucified by anguish, her fingers clawed the wind. And felt it *move.* Felt the fibers of earth and air and sky again, and this time, she *grabbed* them. Gray cloud streamed inward, like smoke sucked down a crack. A wind whipped her hair, circling like an angry wolf, too big to be a coyote. She clutched her anger and anguish, wrapped it up with the wind, and *threw* it.

The wind screamed, whirling away from her, twisting into a tower of spinning dust. Wolf-wind, it towered over her, sucking up sage leaves, twigs, and dust; growling. Too big to stop, it zigzagged down the slope, and with a moan, it slammed into Doug and Shane. They fell apart, blinded by dust, shielding their faces from stinging grit. Gasping, terrified by what she had or hadn't done, Rosemarie stumbled and slid down the slope. The twisting wind was thinning away. She was going too fast . . . out of control. . . . Shane saw her, put his arms out to stop her, staggered as she crashed into him. They would have fallen, but Doug wrapped his thick muscular arms around both of them, so that they all staggered, and scrambled, and stayed on their feet.

Cold drops pelted them as the last of the wolf-wind gusted and died, pounding down in a brief rush, then thinning away as the squall moved on up the creekbed. *Rain,* without any magic words, with nothing more than anger and fear . . . and love. Rosemarie pushed damp hair out of her eyes, felt rain and tears on her face.

"I'm sorry," Shane choked out. His eyes were glazed and full of pain, but not crazy anymore. "I don't know what happened. . . . I'm sorry, Doug."

"It's all right," Doug said.

"No." Shane met his eyes. "It's not all right. It's not all right, Doug, and I don't know if it ever will be, so just don't say it is, okay?"

Doug wiped his eyes on his sleeve, smearing tears and rain and dust to mud. "Okay," he said softly. "I know. I understand."

Shane made an inarticulate sound and looked away. Blood was running down his fingers, falling in slow thick drops to the dusty ground. Rosemarie took his hand, turned it over. The knife blade had slashed his palm in a long deep diagonal from the base of his thumb to the base of his little finger. Without a

word, Doug pulled a faded bandanna out of his pocket. "Close
your hand around it," he said. "So you don't bleed all the way
back down to camp."

"Most of the does are over here." Shane looked up, drew a
quick shuddering breath. "I counted all but about ten."

"The rest are just west of here. Down in a little pocket. Or
they were." Doug managed a smile. "They've probably snuck
off by now. You want to go on down and take care of your
hand? We'll chase 'em."

"I'll live." Shane pushed hair back from his dirty face, not
quite meeting their eyes. "We better all do it, or it'll take all
afternoon."

"Ha." Rosemarie made a face, because they needed to
laugh. "You're the guy who scared half the herd into that canyon last year, remember?"

"How about when you ran those does out into the lake
bed?" Shane halfway smiled.

"Let's go." Doug rolled his eyes. "Argue later, okay?"

Hex had disappeared. The mountainside was theirs again.
Leaning on the thick willow-stem that Doug had cut for her,
Rosemarie whistled perverse goats out of the sage so that Doug
and Shane could chase them down the creekbed. They were
putting it back together again; the trio, the unity. Mending the
broken pieces.

Only they couldn't. Not really.

She paused near the top of the ridge, where you could see
out across the desert, clear to the old ruined buildings of the cattle ranch that had once belonged to Shane's family. The wind
nudged her, like a dog wanting to play, and she spread her
fingers, aware of the *texture* of the world, aware of the way earth
and sky were the same, just woven differently, like Mama wove
different patterns into her rugs. Or had she dreamed it up there?
The wind?

"You did it, didn't you?" Doug had come up behind her,
bending the fibers of the world as he walked. He was smiling,
but there was a wary hunch to his shoulders. "You made that
rain happen."

"Yes," she said gravely, because she hadn't been dreaming.
"I made it happen." It's not the stone, she wanted to tell him.
It's the warp and woof of the world, it's *everything*, and I can
touch it, and I haven't a clue what to do with it. Maybe she
would tell him, someday.

And maybe not.

He loved her. She looked away from his eyes that were the color of the desert sky. She hadn't seen it before, or hadn't known how to see it. He wanted her to stay here, because the desert was inside him, part of him. And Shane wanted her to come with him, wanted her to save him, only she couldn't, and he wouldn't understand. Rosemarie sighed, aware of Doug's quiet presence beside her, like the shadow cast by a mountain.

The wind nipped lightly at her cheek as she dug into her pocket. "Here." She picked up Doug's lax hand, placed the rain stone into his palm. It felt warmer than her flesh, alive in his hand. "This is yours," she said. "It was meant for you."

His eyes were full of questions, and faint shadows of the answers that he already knew, but "Thanks" was all he said. And maybe it *would* bring rain for him; not because it was magic, but because he believed that it could, and he believed in the desert, and maybe that was the only weapon that would really fight the Dry. Maybe he would know the right words to say.

Shane came down the slope to meet them, and he and Doug each put an arm around her, because by now her ankle was really swollen. Together, they made their slow way down to camp. Tomorrow, she'd go back to Caravan and take Mama's scolding. She'd learn what Mathilda could teach her. In Nyssa, she'd get on a bus for Pendleton, because she didn't know who and what she was either, and she didn't think the answers were here. Not all of them, anyway. But there *were* answers somewhere, and she would have to find them. Or make them up.

"Look," Shane said softly.

A dim rainbow arched over the desert; the faintest brush of color on the clear air. She wondered if she had done it somehow, or if it had simply happened on its own. It shimmered and faded slowly, marking an end, or a beginning, or maybe, just maybe, there wasn't any real difference between the two.

"Shit," Doug said. "The goats are all over camp."

And they were. Hanging on to each other, yelling and whooping, the three of them scrambled down the slope to chase goats out of camp, and to see if they'd pissed on the sleeping bags.

# TAIRWAY

Almost dawn, and the storm had finally ended. Waiting for the pickup copter, Escher yawned and leaned back against the winch shack. The wind had died, and the mist rising from the berg beneath his boots chilled him to the marrow of his bones. The storm had been short but bad. Waves breaking against the sheer sides of the iceberg had sent spray clear over the rim. His monitors had gone wild with stress codes, but fortunately, none of the harness cables had snapped. After all their months of slow northward travel, the berg surfaces were slushy and unpredictable. Cables could drop into a rotten pocket and break, or insulation could tear loose from the bottom and foul the harness-mounted propeller blades.

Something like that could delay the ice train's arrival at the LA terminal. Escher didn't want any delays. He'd spent nearly two years making the circle from LA to Argentina, down to the Ross Sea and slowly, slowly back. Yesterday was waiting for him on the LA docks.

He hoped.

Up ahead, barely visible in the mist, birds wheeled and shrieked above the ghostly bulk of C berg. A gust of wind—a last breath of the vanished storm—parted the mist momentarily, giving Escher a clear view to the east. On the horizon, the rising sun bled color into the sky, silhouetting the distant spires of the Los Angeles skyline. So close, and so completely out of reach. It had hovered there for days now, tantalizing him until he thought he'd go crazy as the twenty-kilometer train of harnessed bergs inched its slow way to its offshore moorage.

He had spent his whole life waiting to set foot on that shore again. All two years of it. Escher shivered in the cold fog. Los Angeles; "the Angels" in Spanish. *El Pueblo de Nuestra Señora la Reina de los Angeles de Porciuncula*, the Town of Our Lady, the Queen of the Angels of Porciuncula. He had looked up its history in the train's library. He had spent a lot of hours in the library as the ice train crept northward from 70°S, looking at street maps, travel guides, anything and everything that mentioned LA, or had even one picture of the city.

Looking for his name. Looking for echoes from his vanished past.

The mist closed in again, cold and damp on his neck, hiding the city towers. The hospital had slapped a personal lien on him for payment after the accident, so he had signed onto the berg train. It would give him two years to remember, he had figured. . . .

Escher lifted his head as the racket of the pickup copter blotted out the sound of seabirds and water. It was as if the mist had sucked up the sound until it was saturated and had spilled the excess down on Escher like a wrung-out sponge. Fog shredded as the copter descended, battered away by the blast from the rotors. Escher sprinted bent-over for the door.

Rosanna, his relief, had already hopped out. "All green?" she yelled over the beat of the rotors.

"No problem. The rest of the train okay?"

"We're still moving. I think." Rosanna waved and headed for the winch shack, her lunch cooler swinging.

Karen, coming in from the Number 2 winch shack on C berg, leaned out, offering a hand. "If we aren't moving, I'm going to get out and push."

Escher grabbed her wrist and swung himself onboard just as the copter lifted. Trujillo never quite touched the skids to the ice on pickup. "Took you long enough," Escher yelled forward.

Trujillo shook his comm-helmeted head and lifted his shoulders in an elaborate shrug.

"Not his fault." Karen tossed back her sandy hair, yelling over the roar of the blades. "Ron broke his leg up on B, so Arturo got stuck with an extra run."

"Poor bastard." Escher settled himself against the wall. "Bad timing." He had a wife and a kid waiting for him somewhere way up north. "What happened?" he asked.

"Backlash from a broken harness cable." Karen grimaced. "It was just a secondary—the boss says it won't hold us up."

"S'what he gets for fakin' his probes." Jamie, from winch shack Number 3 on C berg, yawned. "Man, I got a date with hot chicks and major booze on shore. If I got to, I'll swim in."

"Ron does his probes. Why don't you *do* something with your money this time?" Karen squeezed over to make room for Escher between the wall-mounted stretchers and the orderly tangle of the hoist. "Party it all away, and you'll just end up back here for a third trip."

"So? Better than throwin' it away on a bunch of dust." Jamie winked at her. "Nah, I got some plans. I won't be back again. You'll see."

"We're not throwing it away." Karen tossed her head. "All that land needs is a new soaker-hose system, and this'll buy it for us. And no, I won't be back here. Not on your life." Her eyes flashed. "We're going to make it, Randy and I."

"Sure you are."

Escher listened with half an ear, not really part of this conversation. Ever since the ice train had begun to brake for mooring, the crew could talk about nothing but the lives they'd left behind. Now that LA had appeared on the horizon, all he heard was a constant babble about lovers, family, friends, getting back, going on, picking up the lives they'd left behind two years ago. . . . None of which applied to him.

"You look sad." Karen leaned over, her lips close to his ear. "Everything'll be okay. You'll get off the train, and all of a sudden you'll remember. I *know* it's going to happen like that."

"Yeah, he'll remember he's some heavy-duty killer, or the feds are after him." Jamie grinned. "Me, I think he's already remembered it, and doesn't want to tell us. How 'bout it, Escher? You a mass murderer?"

"No." Escher kept a tight grip on his temper. "Sorry to disappoint you."

"Yeah?" Jamie's eyes gleamed. "If you can't remember, how do you know?"

"Shut up," Karen flared. "Just shut *up*, Jamie."

"I just know." Escher clamped his lips together, tired of

Jamie's needling, two whole fucking years of it. If he'd done anything, the cops would've had his prints on file. They'd sure checked. Still . . . Jamie was right. He didn't know.

"You couldn't hurt anyone." Karen reached over and took his hand. "I know you. You couldn't do it."

Escher squeezed her hand, gratefully. Maybe it would happen the way Karen said. He'd set foot on shore and *bam*, he'd have a past, a life.

Maybe. He grabbed for a handhold as Trujillo banked the copter and elevator-dropped down to the deck of the crew ship in the lee of G berg. Jamie spat out a curse.

"Hey, don't complain." Karen scrambled to her feet. "Arturo picked you up out of the Ross before you even got cold, that time you went over while we were wrapping the bergs. Let's go get some breakfast. I'm starved."

Trujillo vaulted back into the sky as they crossed the *Western Star*'s deck. Escher stumbled, needing a few moments to adjust to the crew-ship's roll after the rock-stable berg, and Karen dropped back to keep pace with him.

"Don't let Jamie get to you." She put a hand on his arm. "You're who you are—that doesn't change just because you don't remember your eleventh birthday. At least you're not stuck on C berg with him." She rolled her eyes. "I was about ready to shove him over yesterday. God, what a prick."

"Yeah, he's that." Escher said it with more heat than he'd intended, and turned away quickly, pretending to study the towering bulk of G berg.

It loomed over them like a white mountain, trailing a veil of cold mist on the morning breeze. The silvery film of the Mylar insulation layer that protected the underside of the bergs glittered like silver along the waterline, quilted to the berg's frozen bottom by a network of cables. Gulls and terns shrieked and dove along its flanks. Herring gull, sooty tern, black tern . . . He'd learned to identify all the species from the library, had learned habits and names of the penguins, the leopard seals, the whales and dolphins; every animal or bird he had spotted on the trip. Sometimes, he felt driven, as if his head was a vacuum and if he didn't fill it up with *something*, it might implode.

Or was he trying to bury what was already there?

"What if he's right?" Escher asked slowly. "What if there's a reason why I can't remember?"

"There *is* a reason. You got a concussion, remember?" Karen peered into his face. "From hitting your head. You're really worried, aren't you?"

"Not worried, exactly." Escher touched his head lightly, fingering the faint trace of the scar where he must have hit the curb. *No organic damage,* the bored clinic doctor had told him. *Functional amnesia. Your memory should return eventually. Just give it time.* "It's like a blind date." He followed her down the companionway, their footsteps ringing on the converted factory-ship's metal stairway. "It's a blind date with myself. There's a man out there, and I'm him, but I don't know him." He laughed, heard the tension in it. "I don't think I'm a mass murderer, anyway."

"Forget Jamie." Karen smiled up at him. "You'll like your blind date just fine, Escher. I know I do. Come on, I'm starved." She grabbed his hand. "I bet they've got cinnamon rolls this morning. They always make cinnamon rolls after a storm."

She was right about the rolls. (And about the man he'd meet onshore?) The crew mess was steamy with cinnamon smell. They loaded their trays with scrambled eggs and the big fragrant breads. A buzz of conversation filled the long room as they carried their trays to an empty table. The ice crew ate in here. The ship's crew—Portuguese mostly—ate elsewhere. Captain Watanabe dined in his cabin. He was Japanese, directly employed by the Tanaka Corporation, which held the world monopoly on iceberg transport.

Escher concentrated on the scrambled eggs that weren't really eggs, but were soy protein grown in fields irrigated by melted bergs—like the fields Karen wanted to farm. The bergs beat back the Dry. Had he read this in the library or picked it up on shipboard? Escher laid down his fork, trying to remember, wondering why it was suddenly important to know where he had learned every last fact.

Because he was listening for whispers. From yesterday. From LA, out there on the horizon. He held his breath, heard only the tired, excited voices around him.

"I told Dad that I'd take a bus up to the valley when I got in." Karen pulled her roll into sticky halves. "But I bet Randy'll hitch down to meet me. He'd do that, and his mom'll shit." She hid her smile in a huge bite of roll. "I can't wait to see him," she said around a mouthful of bread. "Last letter, he said we can close the deal for that land as soon as I get up there."

"I hope it really works out." Escher summoned enthusiasm for her. "I hope the two of you have the best farm in the whole northwest." He put down his fork, suddenly needing to get away from her happy plans. "I'm tired. Maybe I'll head off to bed."

"Me, too." Karen stuffed the last of the roll into her mouth and picked up her tray.

Her cabin was on the deck below his. She paused in the stairwell, leaning close. "Do you want to come down to my room for a while? Ellie's out on-shift, and I'm too tired to go to sleep yet."

He looked into her blue eyes, desire stirring. Randy hadn't seemed very real down in the freezing twilight of 70°S. Death had been real—crew members died in the black freezing water, or from the backlash of a breaking harness cable. Loneliness had been real, and there had been a lot of comfort in their lovemaking. Since they'd sighted the California coast, she had talked about Randy every day, and they hadn't made love.

I'm fading. Escher felt a chill breath on his neck. Randy was real. Escher, who had existed only on the ice train, was a shadow with no real substance. In a few days, Escher would be a memory to Karen, and maybe . . . to himself, the real self who had lived for some twenty-three years before Escher was born. No, he thought, tasting fear. I'm the same man. Karen's right, I just don't remember. "I better get some sleep," he said.

"Okay." Karen looked at him for a long moment, then touched his hand lightly. "Sleep well, then."

Escher climbed the stairs slowly, tired, but not yet ready to sleep, So near, that city, that blind date. The low-wattage bulbs streaked the narrow corridor with dim shadow. Somewhere out there, in the crowded streets and refugee camps of Los Angeles, people remembered him, knew his name, and wondered what had happened to him. I'll remember, he thought as he let himself into his tiny cabin. Karen was right. He'd hit LA, and it would all come back. He could feel it, just out of reach, but so *close*. Yesterday. He closed the door behind him. The two bunks crowded him, neatly made, empty. No pictures on the tiny desk, no personal clutter. You could barely tell that someone lived here. Escher tossed his jacket onto the chair and stripped off his pullover.

"Escher?" A fist pounded on his door. "You there?"

Walsh's voice. Escher pulled the door open, wondering what the ice-crew super wanted with him.

"Yo, Escher. Got a bunkmate for you." Light from the overheads glistened on Walsh's hairless scalp. "We picked this guy up out of the water. Captain says to put him somewhere, and you got space."

"Hi." A slender blond-haired man in his late teens or early

twenties stepped out from behind the super's wide bulk. "I'm Zachary Odell."

Escher stiffened, seeing another face in his mind; a blond, kid in his late teens, with a face full of judgment. *You're scared,* he said. *You're running out on us.*

As Escher reeled with its impact, the vision popped like a soap bubble, then vanished.

Memory.

"Hey, Escher." Walsh peered at him. "You okay?"

"Fine." He was talking to *me,* Escher thought wildly. *Who?* "Hi . . . hello." Escher stuck out his hand to the stranger, struggling to bring the vision back, to remember more. "I don't know you, do I? No, no, I guess I don't." He shook his head, a little dazed.

"Odell went overboard off this seiner." Walsh gave Escher a wary glance. "You sure you're all right, huh? Okay, he's yours till we anchor. Keep him out of trouble." He turned abruptly, and stalked back down the hall.

Escher looked after him, realizing belatedly that Walsh was nervous. In two years, he had never seen *anything* rattle the super—not even when a snapping cable had taken Roberto's leg off while they were harnessing the bergs. He turned his attention back to the stranger, still numb from that bombshell instant of memory. "So come in. You get the top bunk." He stared around at the narrow space, picked up his pullover. "Did you eat breakfast yet?"

"Yeah." Zachary tossed a blanket roll onto the top bunk. "In sick bay."

"Sick bay?"

"I was in the water for a while. You're Escher, huh?" Zachary shrugged skinny shoulders. "Willy found this book about a guy named Escher. In a house out in the Dry. He was some kind of artist—drew these weird pictures, hands that were birds if you looked at them right, and that kind of stuff. Willy figured we could get something for the book. You related to this artist guy?"

"No." Escher tossed his pullover onto the floor of the tiny closet. "I woke up in this hospital bed, and I couldn't remember my name. One of his pictures was hanging on the wall."

It had been the first thing he had seen, and he had stared at it for a long time, clinging to it like a lifeline as he struggled in a sea of confusion. Tiny figures had marched round and round an endless stairway. By some trick of the artist's pen, they seemed to be going up and down at the same time. *John Doe is kind of an overused name,* the nurse with the freckles had said to him, later. *Why don't you pick something else until you remember?* So he had looked for the artist's name on the picture. "It's borrowed," he said. "Until I remember my own name." The print was in his desk drawer; a present from the nurse when he'd been discharged.

Who was he—that blond kid with the face full of judgment? Friend? Brother? Enemy? "Who's Willy? How did you end up in the water?" Escher asked absently.

"Willy's my friend. Carl tossed me overboard."

"What?" Escher blinked.

"Denny threw me the life jacket." Zachary perched himself on the corner of the desk, pushing aside the little electric clock. "I liked Denny. I'm sorry he drowned."

Escher stared at him, all echoes of his vision gone now. "Someone pushed you *overboard?* Are you serious?"

"Yeah." Zachary grimaced. "I have these dreams, okay? And when I wake up, I talk about 'em. I can't help it. I'm not really awake yet . . . so it just comes out." He ducked his head, peering warily through the sun-bleached fringe of his hair. "Anyway, I guess I talked about the *Mary Anne* going down, and made it real clear that they were all gonna drown, and I guess Carl got pissed. He was third mate, and he didn't like me much anyway."

Escher closed his mouth with an effort. "He tried to kill you because of a *dream?*"

"They always come true." Zachary stood up suddenly, his posture sullen, full of challenge. "It bugs people. Doesn't it bug you?"

Oh God, a crazy, and Walsh had stuck him in here. He didn't need this, not now, not when he was starting to remember. "Look, I got some errands to run." Maybe he could catch Jamie before he crashed, bribe hlm to take this guy off his hands. He had bunk space. Jamie wouldn't do shit for him as a favor, but he'd been losing at poker for the last month. He'd do it for money. Escher grabbed his pullover from the closet, thrust his arms into the sleeves. "I got something to do. I'm coming off-shift, so I'm about ready to hit the bed, but I'll give you the five-cent tour when I get back."

No answer. Escher turned around. Zachary lay curled on Escher's bunk, eyes closed, out cold. Shit. Escher dropped to his knees, groping for a pulse. It was there, strong and steady, and Zachary was breathing regularly. Frowning, Escher touched his eyelid. It twitched, and Zachary gave a brief soft snore. Asleep? Escher let his breath out in an exasperated rush, acutely aware of his own exhaustion as the adrenaline drained from his system. Hell, Jamie would already be asleep. Escher yawned, jaws cracking. Catch him at shift change. He stripped to his underwear, made up the upper bunk, and crawled between the sheets, falling asleep before his head hit the pillow.

HE DREAMED about the blond kid, only he wasn't a kid; Escher had been wrong. He was older, closer to Escher's age. He had his arms around Escher like a lover, body pressed so close that Escher could feel the hard jut of his ribs beneath his shirt. His face was turned up to Escher's, and his eyes were open very wide in his tanned face. He looked so surprised. Escher glanced down, saw the knife sticking out of the guy's stomach. He was holding it, and the sticky blood ran over his knuckles, dripping from his wrist in thick red drops. . . .

Escher bolted upright in darkness, throat aching, cramped hard and tight with a thorny grief he could neither swallow nor vomit up. Oh God, he had killed, he had killed. . . .

Gone.

It had been there. Who this guy was, what he had meant. Right there, so everyday close that he could touch it, call it up with a single casual thought. And now, just like that, it wasn't. Below him, Zachary snored softly. Dreaming the dreams that he said always came true? Escher shivered, angry suddenly, because dreams were illusion and everybody knew it; they didn't predict the future or the past. In the two years since he'd waked up in the hospital, he had never remembered a single dream. Until now. Until Zachary.

"I didn't kill him," he whispered to the darkness. He *knew* that, could feel it in his flesh, in his bones. It was a nightmare, a nasty twist of his psyche, because LA was so close. It wasn't real. Escher spread his fingers, feeling no blood, no stickiness, just the smooth dry stretch of skin. *You couldn't hurt anyone.* Karen's voice, whispering in his ear. Talk to Jamie, first thing in the morning. Get this crazy out of here. Escher closed his hand into a fist, shoved it under the covers, and tried to go back to sleep.

It took him a long time.

"WHY NOT?" Escher scowled through the window as Trujillo whipped the copter off the *Star's* deck. "It's just for a few days."

"Not on your life, baby." Jamie's grin bared a mouthful of cheap backstreet crowns. "Didn't you hear? Man, he was babbling all over sick bay about how his boat, the *Mary Anne*, went down in the storm, and everyone drowned except him. And yeah, she went down all right—one of those refitted vacuum-seiners that shouldn't be out on anything bigger than a fish pond anyway. Rosalee was on the radio, and she told me Coast Guard's still looking for the crew, but not very hard, if you get me. Trick is, she went down *after* the E berg crew spotted him, and Doc says he'd been in the water for a while. But he *knew* she was gonna go down, and how could he know, huh? You get to keep him, baby."

"Oh, give it a rest." Karen had been humming to herself, but now she gave Jamie a disdainful look. "What? You think he sank her himself, or something?"

"Go ahead, laugh." Jamie shot her a sullen glance. "Maybe he's a fortune-teller, huh? Maybe he'll read Escher's palm and tell him his real name. Better hope he doesn't tell you you're gonna fall off the berg and break your neck."

"Shut up." Escher watched twenty kilometers of harnessed frozen water spin slowly beneath them as Trujillo banked the copter. He'd ducked Zachary this morning, waking first and sneaking off to breakfast, and to hell with Walsh. Dreams were illusion, and he had enough to handle without a crazy.

"Randy called." Karen nudged him. "I don't know where he got the money for it. He said he's leaving today, to hitch down here. I knew he'd do it," she said happily.

"Yeah, there's no future in dust." Jamie made as if to spit. "You'll be back on the bergs in a year, you'll see."

"Not me." Karen tossed her head. "Never, no way. How 'bout you, Escher?" She squeezed his arm. "You're not going to sign on again, are you?"

"Might be a good place to be when you finally remember what you did, huh, Escher?"

"Shut the hell up, Jamie!" His yell startled all of them, himself included. Escher clamped his lips together, avoiding Karen's surprised eyes as Trujillo dropped down to D berg. "Look, I didn't sleep well." He scrambled to his feet. "I'm sorry." He swung down to the ice without looking back.

"All green." Ross, coming off-shift, boosted himself on-board. "Have a fun day." He grinned and winked.

What was *that* supposed to mean? No time to ask. Karen was peering out the hatch, worrying about him. Escher sprinted away as Trujillo bounced up into the air, pretending not to notice. Slush splattered his legs, ice cold, but not cold enough to cool the anger in his gut. Jamie was an ass.

But would he have lost his temper, before the dream? Did he perhaps think Jamie was right? Escher wiped his hand on his waterproof coverall, remembering the warm, slightly sticky feel of blood on his fingers. It had felt so real. So what? So he'd had blood on his hand sometime in his life. Big deal.

It was a dream. Just *drop* it.

He hunched his shoulders and stomped down the trampled path to the aft winch shack. Berg D was one of the smaller bergs in the huge train. It didn't have any propeller blades harnessed to it—was towed by C or pushed by E, take your choice—a passive white whale with its belly wrapped in silver foil. Walsh only put one crew member at a time on D, because he got a bonus for shaving the overhead. This morning, Escher was grateful for his solitude. The winch-shack door stood ajar. Ross was getting careless. Escher shoved it open and halted, staring.

"Hi." Perched on a corner of the monitor console, Zachary grinned. "I didn't feel like hanging around your cabin all day."

"How the hell did you get out here?" Escher slammed the door.

Zachary flinched. "I got a ride." He swung one foot with the quick, nervous flick of a cat's tail. "I couldn't find you, so I asked these two women where you were. They were heading out in a boat to check the waterline, or propellers, or something. I told them that the supervisor had assigned me to help you, but I'd sort of lost you." Green flecks glinted in his hazel eyes. "Anyway, one of them said you'd be out here, and they gave me a ride. I climbed up the cables. These icebergs are really big."

"You climbed the *cables?*" Escher scanned the monitors, but this wacko didn't seem to have touched anything. All green. Ross had left another "have fun" joke in the log. Oh. So *that* was what he'd meant. Zachary. Escher logged in, scowling. "Climbing cables is a stupid stunt. If you don't know your way around, you can fall. Nice way to break your back or your neck."

"That's what one of the women said. I told her I'd worked bergs before. Maybe I did." Zachary swung himself down from the desk and peered at the main monitor screen. "What do the numbers mean?"

Crazy, crazy, crazy, and Jamie wouldn't take him. He'd never dreamed, not once, before Zachary had showed. "They're stress readouts," he said tightly. "From sensors on the harness cables, and the net that holds the bottom insulation in place. The winches have to keep them tight, or everything slides around."

"And the icebergs get smaller as they melt." Zachary was nodding. "So you got to keep pulling them tighter. Neat trick." He shot Escher a quick sideways look. "How'd you lose your memory?"

"Head injury." Escher did a rapid check on the bank of automatic winches, wishing he hadn't mentioned his amnesia last night. "I got hit by a truck." Only he'd never had any symptoms of brain damage. That's what the doctor had meant when he'd talked to him. That there wasn't any reason for him to not remember. The blond kid had looked so *surprised*. "Look, I've got to run a visual on the cables and the forward winches." He fished in the tool locker for a set of boot spikes and a probe. "You better come along." No way he'd leave this guy in here unsupervised. He scowled. "Get your butt off that cable before the winches kick on."

Zachary slid down, not particularly concerned, then followed Escher out onto the ice. The breeze had died, and the mist had thickened again. "So how come they couldn't find out who you were?" The fog muffled his words and the splat of his footsteps in the slush. "Didn't they take fingerprints or something?"

"Prints and DNA samples. So I'm not a criminal." And it was just a nightmare. He hadn't murdered anybody. "And I didn't have any ID on me, because someone stripped me clean before the ambulance got there." Or he'd gotten away with a murder. Escher hunched his shoulders and walked faster. "Do you know how many people there are in the LA area? You got Ice Town and the refugee camps, too." Everyone ended up in LA —all the drifters, the homeless, the dispossessed refugees from the dying drylands—drawn by the scent of water.

Escher's skin prickled suddenly, because he'd read it all in the library, but *this*, this echo of thirst and despair and desperate hope, was different. More memory? They had reached the windward edge of the berg. The harness had worn a deep groove into the rim of the ice. Meltwater ran along the woven-mesh cable, trickling down the berg flank in a tiny waterfall.

"What about your dreams?" Zachary squatted beside the cable. "Maybe you dream about who you were."

"I don't dream." Escher stuck the probe into the ice along the groove. Solid. "Get back from the edge."

"Everyone dreams." Zachary looked up at him, eyes glittering, running his fingers through the icy fall of meltwater. "How come you're pissed at me? I either scare people or they think I'm crazy. But you're pissed."

Because you made me dream. Which couldn't be true, and the dream didn't matter anyway. Escher stabbed the probe into the rim again, nearly lost his balance as it sank deeply into the berg. "Rotten ice here." He yanked the probe free. "I told you to get back from that edge."

No answer. Zachary lay in the slush, curled into a tight fetal ball. No *way* asleep, not this time. Escher jammed the probe into the ice and dropped to his knees, feeling for a pulse. As in the cabin, Zachary's pulse was strong and he breathed easily. Cold seeped through Escher's coverall, making his knees ache. "Wake up." Escher shook him. "Zachary?" His head lolled. Escher scooped up a palmful of slush, pressed it against Zachary's cheek. He mumbled incoherently, but he didn't snap out of it. Something was very wrong. Escher reached for his comm-link, swearing under his breath because he'd catch hell from Walsh for letting this guy come out here, never mind that he *hadn't* let him. As he clicked it on, Zachary twitched and opened his eyes.

"They killed her," he whimpered. His white-ringed eyes fixed themselves on Escher's face in a glazed unseeing stare. "She knew they were there, but she just kept on walking. Why didn't she run?"

"Hey, wake up." Escher scooped up another handful of slush.

This time, Zachary flinched away from the cold. "Knock it off." He slapped at Escher's hand, eyes focusing suddenly. "That hurts, man. I just fell asleep, okay?"

"Like hell." Escher peered at his eyes. Zachary's pupils were normal, both the same size. Tears? "You weren't asleep. You passed out cold."

"I was asleep. I just do that, okay? Fall asleep for a minute or two. Sometimes, it's longer." He wiped his face on his sleeve. "That's when I . . . have the dreams."

*They killed her.* "What did you dream?" Escher asked softly.

"I told you, didn't I?" Zachary got unsteadily to his feet, his face sullen. "I always tell, when I come out of it. This woman was walking down this crummy alley, and two guys came at her. One shot her, and the other grabbed the bag she was carrying." He turned his head away. "That's all I saw. You happy now?"

He was shivering, shaking with more than cold. He really believed it. That he'd seen the future, that it would come true, and somewhere, a woman was going to get shot in an alley. "You're soaked," Escher said. Hell of a way to be crazy.

"So you're gonna keep on being pissed?" Zachary said between chattering teeth. "Or are you gonna get scared?"

"I'm not pissed anymore." The guy truly was nuts. In a way . . . it was a relief. He had nothing to do with Escher, and the dream had been just that—a dream, a nightmare. "No, I'm not scared either." He held out a hand to Zachary. "We keep some extra overalls in the winch shack. You need some dry clothes."

ZACHARY didn't have any more seizures or episodes during Escher's shift. Not as far as Escher knew, anyway. He asked Escher interminable questions about the insulation, the harness, and how the ice train worked. When he tired of that, he wandered from one end of the two-kilometer berg to the other, climbing the eroded peaks and slopes, sliding in meltwater channels, throwing snowballs, and whooping like a kid. Escher found that he didn't mind having to keep an eye on Zachary. It kept his mind off LA.

"It's really something," Zachary said as they shared the sandwiches Escher had brought along for his break. "All this water under your feet. Out in the Dry, you're thirsty all the time."

The Dry. Escher stared at the sandwich in his hand, feeling the sun's hot lash, feeling sweat and gritty dust on his skin. An old man stared at a dry horizon of dun hills, face tanned to leather by the sun, hard and closed as the stony land. Full of bitter anger, and Escher knew that the anger was directed at him. Again, it was there, who this was, what it meant, right *there*, on the far side of an invisible wall, so close he could almost touch it. . . .

"Escher?" Zachary touched his arm. "You remembering something?"

"I . . . don't know." Escher put down the rest of his sandwich. "Yeah, I guess so." He rubbed his arms, sweating, although the shack was chilly. "The Dry, I think. Someone." Angry at me? It had had such an old feel to it, that anger. As if it had been there a long time, like rocks in the ground. He crumpled sandwich and wrapper into a wad, hurled them into the wastebasket. It was like a bloody jigsaw puzzle, only he didn't recognize the picture.

"I know how it is." Zachary swallowed a half-chewed mouthful of sandwich. "You get all these bits and pieces, right? And you don't know what really happened and what didn't."

"Something like that." Escher frowned, trying to recall that fleeting moment when he had almost known.

"Willy and I spend a lot of time out in the Dry." Zachary folded his sandwich wrapper into a neat square. "Scavenging."

"What's scavenging?" Escher asked, realizing he should *know* this, sure of it, but coming up with that old familiar nothingness when he tried to remember.

"We hunt out the abandoned towns. There's a bunch of 'em out there—mostly picked over, but we find some good ones once in a while. We go through the dumps, check out the houses. You can always sell metal and plastic junk to the dealers. Sometimes, we find good stuff." The sandwich wrapper was getting smaller and smaller between his fingers. "Willy's been doing it a long time." He bent the tiny square of the wrapper, but it was too small and too thickly creased to fold again. "I dream about him, and he doesn't care. He says what happens happens, but he doesn't understand how it works." He looked up suddenly, green flecks glittering in his eyes like chips of broken glass. "What was it like? To wake up and not remember anything?"

"It was . . . confusing." He'd never talked about it with anyone, not even Karen. Escher frowned, struggling to sort through those first fractured images. The universe had been a kaleidoscope of light and chaos, and he had cowered in a dark corner of his mind, terrified. The picture had helped; it had taken slow shape, evolving from chaos, to rectangle, to *picture*—a wonderful, wonderful evolution. The freckled nurse had leaned over him one night, so close that her face filled the field of his vision. *Are you in there?* she had whispered. And he had had no words to tell her that he was there, and please, don't go away. Words had come back to him later. "I started over," he said. "I'm two years old." Here, with LA breathing down his neck, he felt new, fragile, as if a strong wind could shred him like the mist and blow him away. A wind from shore?

"Your memory'll come back, right?" Zachary tossed the folded wad of sandwich wrapper at the wastebasket, missed. "Give me something to do, okay?"

"Okay," Escher said, and sent him out with the probe, to test the ice along the main harness cables. He'd already done it, but it would keep Zachary busy. He wanted to think about the bitter old man and about the Dry. *Your memory'll come back*, Zachary had said. It hit Escher suddenly that Zachary had sounded almost wistful. Huh. Escher picked up Zachary's folded sandwich wrapper and went to check the tension on the aft insulation net, remembering the hot feel of the Drylands sun on his shoulders.

IT WAS DARK when Trujillo picked them up at shift's end. A soft wind had set in from the southwest, and it was almost warm on the bergs. Karen raised her eyebrows as Zachary climbed aboard, but she merely smiled. Dreaming about Randy, no doubt.

"Who let *him* out on the ice?" Jamie rolled his eyes and shifted aft, clear into the tangle of the hoist. "Walsh'll have your ass."

He was scared of Zachary, watching him continually, his posture hunched and unhappy. At least it kept him quiet. Zachary noticed it, too. He gave Jamie one sullen stare, and sat silent against the wall, ignoring them all as Trujillo swung the copter into the air. To the east, Los Angeles glowed like a second moon rising.

"There are so many lights down there." Karen peered through the window, clucking disapproval. "Last night, an hour after the power curfew, it was still bright."

"Payola to the power company and the federal inspectors." He hadn't read that in the library, either.

"You're getting your memory back, aren't you?" Karen's face lighted up. "Escher, that's wonderful."

Was it? "I'm remembering some. Not enough to really know anything."

"Tell me!"

He pretended he hadn't heard her, kept his eyes fixed on his clean and blood-free hands as Trujillo swooped them down to the crew-ship deck.

Back on board, Karen went off to take a shower before dinner. Her absence left Escher uneasy, stuck with Zachary. He
wanted her there, wanted her to distract him with her bright
chatter about Randy, and drip hoses, and tomorrow. Now that
he was remembering, he wanted to put the brakes on, to slow
the process down. Or maybe he was just missing her in ad-
vance. He led the sulky Zachary down to the mess hall.

The room was full of conversation; a multilingual babble that
spilled over from table to table, wafted on warm food-scented
air. All at once everyone was so social—using words to close the
two-year gap between yesterday and tomorrow. Suddenly an
outsider, Escher loaded his tray and followed Zachary to a table,
glad of his company after all.

"You guys eat good." Zachary forked up cubes of tank-
grown carrot. "And the water's great." He had filled three
glasses at the counter.

"You know, you can go back for refills. It's not like we're
short." Escher picked up his own glass of water, sipped at it.

Pure ice-melt. On shore, you'd buy it in bottles and pay
premium price. Or you'd steal it from the tethered bergs—that
was another big business in LA. More memory, rising like oil
from a sunken wreck. It was as if Los Angeles *was* a second
moon; pulling at the past like the moon overhead pulled at the
tides. Eyes watched him from the shadows; blue eyes in a
weathered face, not angry, just surprised. . . .

I didn't kill you. Escher put his fork down, no longer hungry.

Across the table, Zachary had rested his head on his empty
plate.

"Is he okay?" Karen set her tray down next to Escher, eyes
crinkled in concern. "Should I call the doc?"

"He's just asleep." Escher peered at Zachary warily, wondering what he was dreaming this time. "He should wake up
in a minute or two."

"The guy's real weird, if you ask me." Jamie hesitated for a
long moment before he plunked his tray down across from
Karen.

"I have a cousin like that." Karen poked at her lasagna,
wrinkled her nose. "He falls asleep just like turning off a switch.
One second he's awake, and the next, he's snoring. If I never
eat lasagna again, I'll be happy."

Zachary twitched suddenly, jerked upright, and screamed a
shrill animal note. His plate skittered off the table with a clatter
as he struggled to his feet.

"Hey, take it easy." Escher stood. Zachary's eyes stretched

wide with some awful vision, and he had gone rigid. Escher grabbed him, shook him hard enough to make his teeth snap together. "Wake up." He shook him again. "Wake *up.*"

"They're burning," Zachary said in a high clear voice. "It blew up, the car, and they're burning. . . ." His body went slack suddenly and he stared around, blinking, as if he couldn't quite remember where he was.

In the silence a spoon dropped, and everyone jumped. Karen looked white as the ice, and Jamie's face had gone hard and ugly. They'd all heard about Zachary's wild prediction, and about the *Mary Anne* going down.

"Who's burning?" Karen's voice sounded shaky. "What do you mean? What were you talking about?"

"I don't know. Nobody, okay?" Zachary bent slowly, picked up his plate from the floor. "It doesn't matter."

"What do you mean, it doesn't matter?" Karen's pallor was turning pink. "Who did you dream about?"

"Nobody here." Zachary put his plate down on his tray and walked out of the mess without a word.

"That dude's a major weirdo," Jamie said in a soft voice.

"Does he even care?" Karen's voice shook slightly.

"Yeah, I think so," Escher said softly. He looked around, seeing pity on a few faces, belief on others. Seeing fear. In the cafeteria doorway, Trujillo crossed himself fervently, eyes on Zachary's retreating back. Escher dumped his tray onto the counter. He could see someone pitching Zachary overboard. You could get very twitchy, waiting to show up in his dreams. If you believed in them.

Zachary was lying on Escher's bunk when Escher got back to the room. The desk drawer was open, and he had the print from the hospital propped on the pillow.

"You sure made an impression." Escher closed the door behind him. "Don't ever sign onto an ice train."

"I wasn't planning to." Zachary wouldn't look at him. "I only signed onto that seiner because Willy needed money. I'd rather be out scavenging. I don't bother anybody out there."

Yeah, he'd bother people. "You better tell this Willy that scavenging is the safer bet." Escher stripped off his pullover and sat down to pull off his boots. "You won't earn much, drowned."

"Willy didn't know I signed on. He started bugging me about the dreams . . . thinks I can dream stuff to make him rich. Like where a town is, or stuff's buried. I told you, he doesn't understand." Zachary hunched his shoulders. "I can't dream about anything on purpose. It just happens. It's not always ugly, you know. Those are just the ones I talk about the most when I wake up. But I can't tell Willy how to get stuff. I'm not a fortune-teller."

Jamie thought he was a fortune-teller. Karen did, too, because *Zachary* believed and you could feel it. "So tell this Willy how it is." He sounded like an exploitative bastard. Escher picked up the print and rerolled it. "If he doesn't listen, maybe you should find somewhere else to live."

"I can't. Willy doesn't care if I dream about him. I don't scare him."

Escher lifted his head, met those strange bleak eyes with their broken-glass flecks. Yeah. "It gets pretty lonely, being the crazy prophet, huh?"

Zachary looked away, blinking. "I think I've lived with Willy for a long time. We'll get through this okay."

"What do you mean, 'you think'?" Escher frowned. Zachary had said something like that before—about how *maybe* he'd worked bergs.

"I . . . don't remember things so good." Zachary wouldn't look at him. "You'll get it back one day—being a little kid, your folks loving you, the first time you kissed—all of it. For me, it's like every time I dream about the future, I trade it for a little bit of the past. I just lose stuff. So I don't know if I've lived with Willy for a long time, because I can't remember. I never forget the dreams." He clenched his fists. "Like the car tonight. It was blue. Something low and fancy, and it pulled out in front of a big tanker truck. The truck hit it and the car blew up. The flames roared really loud, but you could hear the people inside screaming. It'll happen just like I said. It always happens just like I dream it, and I can't do anything about it, all right, so just don't blame me, because I can't *stop* it, *I can't keep it from happening!*"

"Hey. Calm down."

Zachary stiffened as Escher put a hand on his arm. For an instant he stared into Escher's face, body rigid, eyes glittering. Then he suddenly relaxed, drawing a snuffling breath and looking down at the rumpled blanket beneath him. "I can't keep any of it from happening," he said in a low voice.

"So who asked you to?" God, *yes,* he cared. What would it be like, to live with a head full of nightmares and think they were real?

"You don't want to believe me." Zachary looked at him from

the corners of his eyes. "You're scared to. You're scared of your own dreams, and don't tell me you're not dreaming."

"*No!*"

"Hey, it's all right." Zachary's strange broken-glass eyes were full of sudden sympathy. "They scare me, too." He lay down abruptly, curled up, and closed his eyes. "Good night."

"Good night," Escher said, wanting to deny it, wanting to tell Zachary that he wasn't afraid of a nightmare, that he didn't have to be afraid, that there was nothing to be afraid of.

The words wouldn't come. Slowly he unrolled the print, staring at the tiny marching figures on their endless stairway. The last two years had been like that; going round and round on an icy stairway of the present, with no past and no future. So, Zachary had no past either. Only his dreams. Beyond the wall, metal *clanged* dully against metal. A crew was working late in the main hold, breaking out the chase boats. They'd start the anchoring process tomorrow. Tomorrow. When they finished, Walsh would pay them off and Escher would go ashore, step off that stairway. Escher looked down at his bloodless palm, wiped it on his thigh. Zachary was wrong. He wasn't afraid of dreams. It was reality that scared him. On the desk, the red numbers on his clock blinked from eleven-fifty-nine to twelve. It was tomorrow. Sometimes, tomorrow *does* come. Go to bed, he told himself. Above him, Zachary turned on his side and began to snore. Escher stood, sighed, pulled the blanket out from under Zachary, and covered him with it.

IF ZACHARY DREAMED that night, he didn't wake Escher. But Escher dreamed.

*You're running out on us.* He was a kid again, with that hard look of judgment in his eyes. *You're never going to find what you're looking for. It's not out there, it's inside you. . . .*

"You're wrong!" Escher woke sweating, tasting anger and hopeless bitter dust on his lips. He had spoken Escher's name, that kid. The echoes still reverberated through his skull. Escher held his breath, wanting to hear it, afraid at the same time. Nothing. Blank, awful, familiar *nothing*. The air from the ventilator blew cool on his face. Escher reached up, felt tears on his cheeks. "I loved you," he said, and shivered, because the words had come from yesterday, popping into his head full of certainty and terrible pain. Beyond the *Star*'s hull, LA waited. *El Pueblo de Nuestra Señora la Reina de los Angeles de Porciuncula.* Queen of the Angels. An avenging angel, with a sword of fire in the shape of a truck? Escher wiped his face on his arm. "I didn't kill him," he whispered brokenly.

And he, Escher, hadn't. But a stranger waited for him out there in the city. Maybe *he* had held that knife. Who was I? Escher asked the invisible city.

Who will I be tomorrow?

Escher shivered and lay down, pulling the blanket up to his chin. He lay awake for a long time, but the moon of Los Angeles gave him no answers, nor did it evoke any more echoes from his past.

THE SUN ROSE over a windless sea. Mist shrouded the train, transformed it into a drifting fogbank. The propellers turned slowly, just enough to keep the train in place. During the night, they had inched into their deep offshore moorage and had stopped. Warning lights strobed from each winch shack; lighthouses atop a chain of floating mountains. Trujillo flew low and fast at shift change, businesslike and not interested in stunts this morning. No one talked much. The trip was over, and everyone wanted to hit shore. The work of anchoring and unharnessing still lay ahead, and it made everyone irritable. Zachary sat beside Escher in the copter. He had disappeared after breakfast, then reappeared just as Escher was going on-shift, silent and uncommunicative. When Escher had asked him if he'd had a bad dream, Zachary had merely shrugged. To Escher's surprise, Walsh sent Zachary out to D berg with him.

"I've got the aft anchor-guides set," Ross said when he boosted himself into the copter. "Watch out. It's slicker than shit out there. That drill is a bitch."

"Stay back from the edge," Escher told Zachary as they slopped through the slush to the aft winch-shack. "I'm not doing any high-dives, if you pass out and fall off."

"I won't fall off." Zachary kicked slush, still brooding. "So what are we doing, anyway?"

"Setting the guides for the anchor cables. They don't want these babies drifting around loose." They'd reached the shack. Ross had left the big ice-drill leaning against the outside wall, beside a pile of guide bolts. You could hear the distant sound of the chase-boat engines as they jockeyed into position to thread the anchor cables across the forward bergs. "Once they're anchored, we cut the harness loose and stow it. The insulation stays in place until they start processing the bergs."

Once they got the bergs anchored, the harbor super would

sign them off and the trip would be over. Karen would go running into Randy's arms, Jamie would go partying, and he would go meet yesterday. Escher looked eastward, but LA was invisible, erased by ice fog. "Here." He grabbed an armload of the thick two-meter-long eye bolts and shoved them at Zachary. "Take these. I'll carry the drill."

"They're light." Zachary staggered in surprise as Escher dumped them into his outstretched arms. "What are they? Plastic?"

"Yeah. Same stuff as the harness cables. You can't break it." Escher grunted as he heaved the heavy drill onto his shoulder. "We sink the guides about every hundred meters across the berg," he said. "They run cables across the ice between two anchor buoys." He halted about three hundred meters from the forward end of the berg. "This is where Ross left off."

Ross was right about the slushy berg surface being slicker than shit. The torque of the drill wanted to spin him around in spite of his ice boots. Zachary grabbed the handles from the opposite side, counterbalancing him as the bit chewed its way slowly into the ice. In spite of the perpetual chill, they were both soaked with sweat by the time they'd gotten the first guide screwed into place. Fight the drill, screw in the guide, wipe the sweat out of your eyes, and move on to the next spot. . . . Slowly, they worked their way across the berg, then moved aft.

Two chase boats were cabling C berg; Jamie and Karen's berg. It looked as if he and Zachary were going to finish well before the boats got C anchored. They were having some kind of trouble with the aft cables. Escher gave the last bolt a final twist, then straightened, wincing as his back twinged. "We did it," he said. "Thanks a lot. I'd still be sliding around in the slush, if you hadn't come along."

"Sure." Zachary was staring shoreward.

Sometime in the last hour a breeze had begun to shred the mist, but Escher had been too busy struggling with the drill to pay much attention. He sucked in his breath. Sun glittered on the anchored bergs in the melting pens, or waiting for transport north to the smaller terminals. They formed an icy breakwater that stretched from Palos Verdes north to Malibu. To the east, the towers and arcologies of LA proper rose in a stark silhouette against the sky. In between, bounded by ice and the towers, lay Ice Town; the maze of melting pens, collection depots, pipelines, and humanity that turned chunks of Antarctica into water, sent it flowing out to the thirsty land as irrigation water, drinking water, or expensive bottled ice-melt. Escher realized that he was holding his breath, let it out in a rush.

"Cool view," Zachary said. "From shore, the trains look solid, like a wall. We're a long way out." He walked to the very edge of the ice. "I got to get back to Willy," he said. "I . . . kind of ran out on him. Because he kept bugging me about dreaming stuff and I was pissed, but I shouldn't have left him. He's old, and he doesn't get around too well anymore. He needs me to do the heavy work, out scavenging, and . . . and I guess I just need to get back." He kicked a small spray of icy slush from the rim of the berg, watched it fall into the sluggish swell far below. "Your boss called me into his office this morning. He said the company filed a personal lien against me, for picking me up and letting me stay on the train. They signed me on for a week in the melting pens, shoveling ice. I'm not going to do it." He looked up at Escher, his eyes dark with shadows. "If Willy takes off, if I can't find him right away . . . I might forget him. The dreams might crowd him out."

Would it be worse to lose your memory that way? A piece at a time, knowing it was happening? "No one goes ashore until we're signed off by the terminal super." Escher sighed, and pulled off his gloves. "Call Willy and tell him where you are. I'll pay for it."

"We don't have a phone, and I'll still be stuck with the lien. Escher . . . he's not scared of me. Here, this is yours." Zachary peeled off the sweater Escher had lent him, handed it over. "The boots and the coveralls belong here. So do the gloves. Damn, it's *cold*." He did a little barefoot dance on the ice, dressed only in his threadbare jeans and shirt.

"What the hell do you think you're doing?" Escher threw the sweater aside and grabbed his arm. "If you're thinking of swimming, it's too far. Forget it. You'll drown."

"No, I won't." Zachary bared his teeth in a grin. "I told you I dream all kinds of stuff. I've dreamed how I die, and the dreams always come true. Deep down you believe me, whether you want to or not. I know how I'm going to die, and this isn't it. I don't drown." The broken-glass flecks in his eyes glinted green. "You're going to remember who you are. Don't worry." With a quick twist, he freed himself from Escher's grasp, took two running steps, and dived gracefully from the rim of the berg.

"Zachary!" Escher lunged for him, nearly skidding over the slushy rim of the berg himself. *Jump!* He hesitated, heart pounding.

Zachary had surfaced, and was swimming strongly and

easily for shore. Idiot. Crazy idiot. Escher snatched the comm-link from his belt. "Control?" he snapped. "This is Escher, on D. I've got an overboard, off the southeast corner. I need a pickup."

"Roger," the clipped voice answered him. "Relaying overboard; southeast corner of D berg. Who is it, anyway?"

"Zachary Odell. The guy we picked up after the storm." Sorry, Zachary. Better to get fined for trying to jump a lien than to drown. "He's trying to swim for shore," Escher said.

There was a brief silence. "Chase boat *Belinda* is taking the pickup," the voice told him. "Out."

The chase boat was already peeling away from C berg, tooting its whistle impatiently. Escher shaded his eyes, but he'd lost sight of Zachary, blinded by the sun-dazzle. Damn. He searched the blue-green swell desperately. This wasn't 70°S. The water was warm, and Zachary had been swimming fine.

Crouched on the rim of the berg, Escher watched and waited as the *Belinda* circled and searched. Cold seeped into him, pooling in his belly as the minutes dragged on and on, and they didn't find Zachary. He should have jumped, should have gone in after him. Finally, slowly, the *Belinda* veered off, giving up, heading back to C berg to finish the cabling. His comm-link was beeping, but Escher didn't answer it. He should have jumped in.

He hadn't. Because . . . he had been afraid at last. *I know you're going to remember*, Zachary had said.

Zachary was right. A tiny place inside him *did* believe. And that part of him had been afraid of what Zachary might tell him. So he had stayed on the berg rim, wanting Zachary to escape, to get out of his life. Instead, he had drowned. Escher hiked forward to catch the cable shot from *Belinda*, stiff with cold, teeth chattering. Behind him, LA breathed on his neck, and Escher felt a crushing sense of déjà vu.

IT TOOK THEM three more endless days to finish anchoring the bergs, dismount the propellers, and get everything stowed in the holds. Everyone worked extra shifts because they all wanted to get off. The offshore breeze carried the scent of land, the smell of friends, lovers, bars, *real life*. It was right *there*, and suddenly the close quarters and cold labor of the train were intolerable.

Crew members snapped at each other over nothing, or babbled nonstop about what they were going to do, who was waiting for them, how they were going to spend their wages. Escher tried not to listen as he helped stow the enormous propellers and inventoried harness fittings. He felt more a stranger now than he had in Ushuaia, where the crew had made up. No one was going to sign up for a train ever again. They all had something to go back to, someone to go forward with.

The cabin hummed with emptiness—an accusing emptiness. Zachary's ghost? Escher worked extra shifts, tumbling into bed so numb with exhaustion that he fell instantly asleep, before that accusatory emptiness could whisper in his ears.

He didn't dream.

Zachary had been the moon after all—not LA. Zachary had tugged the blond kid, the surprised bleeding man, into his brain. And Escher had stayed on the berg rim.

He had been swimming fine and *Belinda* was at berg-side, Escher told himself a hundred times. There had been no reason to jump in after Zachary. None. In the end, in a few cold moments of struggle, Zachary had discovered that his dreams didn't come true after all. A bitter irony. Escher shrugged off Karen's attempts at sympathy and pretended not to notice her bewildered hurt. One by one, the hours sneaked past. LA breathed on his neck with a warm earth-scented breath, waiting for him.

THE SUPERVISOR of the Greater Los Angeles Ice-Processing Facility showed up at last; a small, nervous man who stomped around on each and every berg, as if he needed the physical feel of the ice beneath his feet in order to believe the mass figures and core sample data provided in the inventory. Finally, sour-faced, he thumbprinted the captain's electronic log. The voyage was officially over. The crew's salaries had been transferred to their accounts by Tanaka Corporation, and people were already leaving. Heading home.

In his empty cabin that had always looked empty, Escher took the print from his desk drawer. The tiny figures marched round and round, trapped on their stairway. Escher wondered suddenly if they thought they were going somewhere. He rolled the print up, snapped a rubber band around it, and stuffed it into his carryall. Time to go. She was waiting, the Queen of Angels. *He* was waiting; the man who had walked those streets, who had been hit one night by a truck. Escher shut the door tightly behind him and hurried up to the deck.

"You're not taking the copter?" Jamie called out from the

crowd at the edge of the landing pad.

"There's no line for the boats." Escher shrugged.

That wasn't the real reason. He slung his carryall over his shoulder and stepped onto the ladder that dangled down to the deck of one of the chase boats. The copter would bring him in too fast, whirl him up, over, and down; dump him smack into the middle of the city. He wanted to sneak up on it, ease himself into yesterday. Butterflies fluttered invisibly in his stomach as the ladder swung outward beneath his weight. He dropped to the deck of the chase boat and jumped as someone touched his arm.

"Sorry." Karen smiled at him, eyes sparkling. "I didn't mean to startle you. He called this morning. Randy. He's meeting me on the dock." She shaded her eyes, peering up the rust-streaked cliff face of the ship's side. "Everyone wants to take a copter in." She clucked her tongue and laughed. "By the time they get to the head of the line, we'll be there. God." She looked around the aft deck, crowded now with knots of excited men and women. "I hated this boat when we were wrapping the bergs. I never thought I'd get warm again. Remember how sick you got, when it was rough that time? And now . . . I don't know." She took Escher's arm suddenly, stood close and warm against him. "It's over," she said. "I guess it's finally starting to sink in. That I won't see this boat again, or my cabin, or you, or Trujillo." She grimaced, and laughed. "I won't miss that closet of a cabin . . . but I'll miss you." Her smile had gone hesitant, unsure. "If you come up to the Willamette Valley, will you come visit me? We're near a little town called Ryder. It's just a government store and a couple of houses, but folks can tell you how to find our place. I'd . . . really like to see you again."

"I'll try," Escher said, because that was what she wanted him to say. Their lovemaking down at 70°S was a thread of sweetness woven into a long dream of cold, and twilight, and the moan of the wind over Antarctic ice. Maybe the man she had made love to wasn't even a real person. Escher felt a sudden chill. Maybe he was part of the dream, not the dreamer.

She sensed his reluctance and let go of him abruptly. Escher felt a pang of guilt as she retreated, because she was hurt and was trying to hide it. How would he think of Karen, when his memory returned? Would he still treasure her generous comfort, the way she smiled when she woke up in the morning? Or would he see her . . . differently? Escher shivered as the boat angled away from the white mountain of G berg. He hadn't thought of it before—that *he*, Escher, might . . . change. He felt a sudden giddy fright as he hung his carryall on one of the mounting plates that had secured the huge rolls of insulating film down at 70°S. As if he was about to leap from the edge of a berg, like Zachary had done. Would he drown, too? The boat eased between the anchored bergs, and the misty chill raised gooseflesh on his arms. Karen had joined the cluster of crew aft, was smiling at something someone had said. Escher turned his back on them and went forward along the rail. The powerful engines growled a lower note as they eased through the narrow channel and then . . .

. . . they were through.

Escher's stomach lurched as the cluttered vista opened in front of him. Ice Town.

Everyone had expected the Big One, the superquake that would shatter the entire coast of California. It had never come. Instead, two or three of its offspring had more or less gently sunk the LA basin. Not much. Just enough to invite the sea in. Encyclopedia knowledge, yes . . .

*I know this place.* Escher shivered, because he had lived here. *Here*, not in LA itself. The shells of old buildings jutted from the smooth surface of the bay like the trunks of broken trees. The melting pools filled the center of the bay; expanding plastic sacks that hung from the floating rims built around the bergs. Crushed ice floated like white scum on the surface of the pools, hundreds of acres of ice, melting slowly and cheaply in the warm ebb and flow of the tides. An explosion boomed across the water, and a puff of mist rose from the berg within the nearest pool rim. A 'dozer crawled forward, pushing a white avalanche of broken ice over the rim of the berg. Small figures with shovels and sledges crawled across the gleaming surface—cheap labor from Ice Town, cheaper than gasoline. Escher drew a slow breath.

This was the heart, the core of it all—water. Water was wealth, power, life. You could paddle out to the tethered bergs that sweated silently in the sun, plant a few collection traps, and live on the water you stole. If someone else didn't steal it from you first. He knew the beat of this heart. Escher's stomach clenched as he shaded his eyes.

Ice Town grew out from the shore of Los Angeles, spreading like pond scum between the broken buildings, reaching toward the melting pens like a growth of dark weed. Decks and huts clung like strange bird-nests to the glassless windows of the drowned buildings. A tangled web of catwalks and floating walkways connected building to building, cobbled together from salvaged scraps of wood, plastic, cable, and even some rusty metal. A labyrinth of piers thrust out from shore, crusted with shacks that looked as if they could fall into the bay at any second. Barges and houseboats, tied up side by side, formed a lower level in the shadow of the piers. Green plots of garden thrived on dirt-filled rafts at the fringes of the floating city. Official navigation channels sliced through the chaos, joined by narrow twisting "streets" that opened and closed up again overnight.

Ice Town. Water had created it. Some god had pushed down on this spot with an invisible thumb. Water had rushed in, and so had all the rootless people; refugees from the Dry. If you didn't have anywhere else to go, if you were smart enough and lucky enough to stay out of the refugee camps, you came to Ice Town.

Like he had come here. Running from murder? Running from that bloody knife? Escher shook his head, dizzy with a moment of double vision; stranger and homecomer at the same instant. The offshore breeze touched Escher's face with ghostly fingers, smelling of mudflat, food, and sewage. Smelling of yesterday. They were in the channel now, edging between clustered houseboats and barges, just seaward of the first of the drowned buildings. A scrawny woman with a thin braid of white hair and a face like old leather weeded vegetable plants on a dirt-covered raft. Squatting on the edge of a battered houseboat, a man dressed in dirty undershorts smoked a hand-rolled cigarette while he washed a pair of jeans in the bay. Two naked children tumbled and shrieked on the narrow deck behind him.

Escher smelled marijuana and garbage, watched a small boy piss into the bay from the door of a crude shack that floated on scraps of plastic foam. Behind the invisible barrier of his forgetting, something *moved*; like a ghostly face pressed briefly against a dirty window. Himself? The man who had lived here?

A sampan-style boat drifted close. A small black dog wagged its tail at Escher from the prow while the withered Asian man in the stern held up shredded vegetables, wrapped in some kind of flat pancake. In the center of the boat, the cracked bowl of a flush toilet held a bed of glowing coals. Skewers of pale meat sizzled on a piece of wire mesh. Escher shook his head. With an expert thrust of his paddle, the old man veered gracefully away. He would pay protection to the sharks who ran his pier. The sharks who owned Ice Town. The sampan disappeared around a double-wide mobile home mounted on a barge. THE HARBOR GRILL—ENCHILADAS, a hand-lettered sign proclaimed. Greasy smoke rose from a rusty stovepipe, and a gust of wind brought Escher the smell of cumin, rancid grease, and woodsmoke.

"Hey mister, missy! Flowers! Fresh oranges, watered with ice-melt, man." A skinny kid hawked limp roses and spotted fruit from grimy plastic buckets on one end of the barge.

His skin was scabby and thick from eating wild toxin-laden shellfish harvested from under the piers. He'd be selling black-market antivirals, or drugs, from underneath the flowers and fruit. Escher stared down at him, met flat black eyes that gave away nothing, and his stomach lurched. He'd lived here. Yesterday. If he wanted to, he knew how to ask the price of what the kid sold, and get an answer . . . almost.

Escher clutched the rail, clammy with sweat, so close to memory, to yesterday. The boat was slowing, engines throbbing a low guttural note. The bright new towers of LA vanished behind the broken teeth of the drowned offices and the rotting pilings of the piers as they neared shore. The silvery dish of a solar water-still winked in the afternoon sunlight, and somewhere, a rooster crowed.

The piers closed in on either side like a dark forest. Rickety bracing timbers crisscrossed between the pilings, crusted with bird nests and streaked with guano. Swallows darted in and out beneath the overhead planks, dipping and diving for insects above a floor of houseboats, barges, and a scum of garbage. Water dripped monotonously from the pier level. A skinny girl scrambled down from the bracings beneath the pier deck, the mesh bag on her back full of tiny swallow eggs and squirming half-feathered baby birds. She gave Escher a wary glance, leaped onto the roof of a crummy shackboat, and disappeared through a trapdoor.

You got a good price for eggs and squab in the marketplace. Memory was seeping back like the tide, but it was background only—setting the stage, waiting for the actor to walk on. *He* was still in the wings. Waiting for his cue. A landing edged into the channel up ahead. It was a sturdy platform of scavenged lumber floating solidly on blue plastic drums. A crude stairway led up to the pier level. "Let me off here," Escher called to the pilot, and felt a twinge of excitement and something that might have been fear. The request had come from that actor in the wings, not from him.

"What are you doing?" Karen came running forward, her

face pale in the shadows. "You can't get off here. I thought.
. . ." She blushed suddenly.

No. Escher looked away. I don't want to meet Randy. He
picked up his carryall.

"Escher, wait!" She seized his face between her palms, her
eyes angry and full of pain. "It wasn't just sex, down south. I
really care about you, Escher, but I love Randy too, I've loved
him since we were kids. Look, I feel bad enough about it already. Don't punish me, Escher. That's not fair."

"I'm not." Escher took her hands, struggling with the chaos
inside him. "What if . . . Karen, what if I was . . . a really different person before?"

"What are you saying?" Karen tilted her head, eyes on his
face. "You couldn't be really bad. Escher, you're *you*. Whatever
you did or didn't do in the past, you're the same man."

"Am I?" He swallowed. "What if that's not true? What if I
was a different person—a murderer?"

"I don't believe it." Her eyes flickered. "Maybe you had a
reason," she whispered. "Maybe it was self-defense, or you
were saving someone. I *know* you, Escher." She stood on tiptoe,
kissed him hard on the lips, then turned and ran back along the
rail.

The chase boat nudged the dock with a jolt, began to slide
past. Maybe she was right. Maybe it had been self-defense—an
attack, a mugging in an alley. Dreams weren't always true—
Zachary had found that out.

He had seen doubt in Karen's eyes. Just a tiny shadow, but
it was there. It hadn't been a mugging, or self-defense. Escher
grabbed his carryall and leaped. The landing rocked beneath
him as he scrambled up the crude steps, past the high-tide scars
of harvested mussels and barnacles, past the empty swallow
nests, up into the open air.

HE FOUND HIMSELF on the warped boards of the pier, panting
in the hot sun, standing between a tiny grocery store and a
shower house. UNLIMITED TIME, the sun-faded sign in the window announced. Which meant that the water would be half
seawater and the recycle filters probably hadn't been changed
in a year. Good place to pick up one of the new staphs. Clutching his carryall, Escher walked shoreward, stalked by shadows,
oppressed by yesterday. The faces on this pier were mostly
Asian. Small women carrying infants and laden baskets gave
him sharp sideways looks, and men shuffled by without making

eye contact. Buildings completely filled the space between this pier and the one to the south. They had been assembled from the scavenged guts of the drowned buildings; fiberboard that had melted and warped in the occasional rain, broken sheets of plastic and scraps from rusted-out cargo containers, hammered flat.

It squeezed him, the *familiarity*, made him want to scream out loud. Escher turned suddenly aside. A drink shack displayed a crudely painted picture of an orange and a glass of vivid juice. He went inside, clutched by thirst, needing to get off the crowded familiar pier for just a moment. The floor of the tiny shack shook beneath his feet, and he hesitated, eyeing the wizened old woman who sat sewing behind a crude counter.

"Whiskey?" The woman laid aside her sewing and waved at the cloudy plastic bottles on a battered shelf behind her. An old man snored in the corner, head resting on his knees. "Beer? Water? Ice-melt!" She grinned, revealing a set of blindingly white plastic teeth. "Orange juice? Fresh-squeeze, very fresh."

"Water," Escher said, because juice could hide a lot of seawater. And it wouldn't be real juice, anyway. Not in this place. More memory.

"Ice? Dollar extra."

Escher shook his head. Above her plastic grin, her black eyes watched him carefully as she ran his debit card through a handheld register. She was nervous. Escher watched her fill a mug from the plastic carboy that stood on a wooden crate beside the decrepit refrigerator. She was more than nervous. He smiled at her as he took the mug. For an instant, a single worry line creased her forehead; one more wrinkle barely noticeable in the folded landscape of her sun-dried face. Escher sipped at the blood-warm water, mouth wincing at a hint of mudflat, guts full of lead. "You're afraid of me," he said.

The harsh statement, too loud for the tiny hot space, woke the old man. He stared at Escher, head nodding on his spindly neck, rheumy eyes blinking.

The woman's face had gone carefully blank. She spread her hands palms up, said something rapidly and apologetically in singsong incomprehensible syllables.

"Forget it." Escher finished the water, because water was expensive and there hadn't been much left of his wages once the hospital had taken its share.

He set the empty mug down on the counter. The woman's sewing lay beside it in a heap. Escher lifted a corner. It was a blouse; probably real silk, and light as a cloud. Gold-and-black embroidery covered part of it; tiny perfect stitches that glittered in the dusty light that seeped through the window. The woman's obsidian eyes had fixed themselves on his hand. This would be how she fleshed out her income; doing piecework for one of the upscale custom shops. If he damaged the blouse, she would probably have to pay for it. She *expected* him to damage it, Escher realized.

She was afraid of him.

"Who am I?" Rage blossomed suddenly in Escher's head. "You can't just look at me like that. Tell me!" he shouted. "Tell me why you're afraid. Tell me who the hell I *am!*"

They both stared at him now, faces expressionless, their eyes holes into a black void. Escher flung the blouse down on the counter, hand trembling. "Never mind," he mumbled and fled the shop, stumbling over the threshold and into the blast of sunshine.

He headed shoreward, walking too fast for the heat, sweating and light-headed. Everyone knew him. Everyone. People gave him subtle space, didn't look at him directly. They got out of his way. He walked faster, wanting to throw his arms wide, scream *Who am I?* until someone told him. He laughed and shut up immediately, because the echo of hysteria in that laugh scared him.

I am *me*. Escher focused on ice, darkness, the cold agony of the Ross Sea, the warmth of Karen's body against his. Escher. *You couldn't be bad,* she had told him. *You couldn't hurt anyone.*

Yeah.

Shadow fell across his face, and Escher stumbled to a halt. One of the drowned buildings loomed over the pier. Weeds sprouted in the cracked walls, and children perched in the empty windows or on rickety balconies, yelling to each other, spitting down on pedestrians, who screamed threats up in return. A cage containing three small black chickens hung in one glassless window, swinging gently in the wind. A few feet above the level of the pier, someone had sledgehammered a window out to make a rough doorway. A man lounged against the broken edge of the crude entrance, picking at a rash on his face. His pale eyes rested briefly on Escher, then slid away as he dabbed at a bright spot of blood on his blotchy cheek.

Recognition gleamed in those eyes.

Ask *him* your name. Escher stalked past, stiff-legged and silent, afraid and despising himself for that fear and that silence.

Ahead, four youths prowled toward him, their sun-dark faces slashed with white diagonals of untanned skin, hair braided with wire. Sharks. Members of the gangs that owned Ice Town. One of them stumbled intentionally into a pile of oranges that an old man was selling from a tattered mat. Withered fruit rolled across the planks, and the old man scrambled after them on all fours. His face wore the same expression as the old woman's face in the drink shack.

Escher lifted a hand, flexed his fingers, suddenly aware of movement, of his *body*. That was it—he was broadcasting a code with every twitch of his muscles; a warning, like the bright colors of a poisonous reef fish. That's what had frightened the old woman. She had recognized him for a predator, a shark. His body moved with the smooth confidence of a hunting cat, as if his flesh had its own memory.

One of the sharks kicked a squashed and ruined orange. It bounced off a basket spread with drying seaweed and hit Escher in the knee, spattering him with sticky pulp. The slash-faced shark looked his way, eyes bright, waiting for Escher to react to the challenge. And he had to react, yesterday whispered in his ear. If he didn't, he was prey. That's the way it is, out here on the piers. You're predator or prey. Nothing in between. Movement caught Escher's eye. The blotch-faced man was working his way through the crowd, his expression intent.

"Hey, sweetheart." The shark slid toward him, a blade in his hand. "I'm talking to you, sweetheart."

Now it was a blood issue; cut or get cut. Escher felt his body shifting, getting ready, as if he was a puppet and some invisible hand was pulling the strings. He could feel it in his muscles—a sureness, a certainty that he could dodge that knife, turn it back on the shark. His flesh didn't want to die, *he* didn't want to die, and if he had to . . . he would kill this guy to live. He. The real man, not Escher, who was nothing more than a veil of mist on the iceberg of a forgotten life. In a moment, that mist would blow away on the hot wind of violence. The shark lunged, knife hand snaking out. . . .

"*No!*" Escher spun on his heel, fighting his muscles, fighting yesterday, wrenching his legs into motion. *I'm me, not him.* Escher. *Me!* He ran, ducking past a man carrying a pole strung with dried fish. Running made him prey. Part of him knew it, and that part hated him for running . . . no no, don't think about it, get out while you can, before you remember, before you, Escher, dissolve and die.

"Escher! In here."

*Escher.* The name snagged him like a treble hook. He veered left, toward the sound, toward the sledgehammered doorway in the drowned building, bursting through and into darkness. Yesterday shouted *danger* with a rush of adrenaline through his veins. Someone grabbed his arm and he tore himself free, his body tensing for an attack, yesterday rising up to drown him. . . .

"Hey, Escher, Escher, it's me! Take it easy!"

The voice hit him like a handful of slush in the face. "Zachary!" Escher gasped.

"Yeah, who else? Who's on your ass?"

It *was* him, Zachary, alive not dead. "You drowned," Escher gasped, knees trembling, shaking as yesterday retreated sullenly. "I thought you drowned."

"I told you I wouldn't." Zachary gave him a crooked grin. "I cut back along the bergs—in the shadow, you know? I hung on to a cable, and when the boat went away, I swam in. I hitched with this old lady who was out after squid. Hey, man, are you all right?"

"Yeah, no. I'm not sure." Escher shook his head, dazed, struggling against the memory that wanted to rise up and drown him. "He was right, you know? The doctor. It wasn't the accident, it wasn't brain damage. I don't *want* to remember, only I'm going to. If I don't get out of here." Escher gasped for breath. "Someone's chasing me. Does this hallway go anywhere?"

"I don't know." Zachary gave him a troubled look. "You're really coming unglued. Come on, let's go see."

Escher followed him, yesterday treading on his heels, plucking at his sleeve. Water-stained plasterboard buckled from the walls, scabrous with peeling wallpaper. Water slapped concrete somewhere below in a distant hollow rhythm, and acrid dust rose from the rotting carpet underfoot. Doorways opened on their left, bright with sun. Escher glanced nervously into a room. A balcony hung outside the glassless window, crowded with potted herb plants. A crude ladder cobbled together from grimy PVC pipe disappeared through a hole in the ceiling, and a dark-skinned naked girl crouched on the upper rungs, picking her nose. Staring at Escher, she wiped her finger on her thigh and let go a thin stream of urine that pattered on the filthy floor.

Escher breathed shallowly, smelling sewage, dank mudflat, and urine. No one lives on the pier level, yesterday whispered. You live high.

Shut up! Escher shook his head.

"Hey, this way." Zachary tugged at him, leading him as if he was a child. "You don't want to remember, huh? How come?"

"Because I'm Escher, and I want to stay Escher." He followed Zachary into a room, peered out one of the big glassless windows. The dry brown peaks of the San Gabriels were visible through a thin veil of haze. "What do you think?" He drew a ragged breath. "If you really hated the person you'd become, could you . . . just stop *being* that person? Wake up one day and be someone else?"

"You think you did that?" Zachary asked softly.

"Karen said I was the same man, but she was wrong." Escher stared down at a narrow ledge that ran beneath the window. Bird shit crusted it; gray and dirty white. "I've got to get out of here. If I . . . remember, I won't exist anymore. Me, Escher."

Zachary was staring at him, head tilted, eyes doubtful. "You haven't seen Willy around, have you?" He changed the subject abruptly. "Oh yeah, you don't know him, do you? I . . . forgot."

He leaned through the window suddenly, thighs pressed against the cracked sill, body canted out at such an angle that Escher grabbed his shirt. The pigeon perched on the ledge took fright, shedding a single gray feather as it fluttered away. Zachary stared after it. "You can't stop tomorrow from happening," he said in a low voice. "Willy's gone. I thought he might be down here, because we sell some of our stuff in Ice Town, but no one's seen him. If he went out scavenging, if he's gone for a long time. . . . I'm already forgetting stuff about him and me." His voice trembled. "I can't lose him. He isn't scared of me."

And that was what counted? "Zachary, I'm sorry." Escher pulled Zachary back from the window. "Listen, he's probably around somewhere. He'll. . . ." He stiffened at a sound from the hallway.

Footsteps. Someone was trying to be quiet. The skin tightened between Escher's shoulder blades. Maybe it was just the kid, sneaking after them. Or someone else from upstairs. He eased across the floor, flattened himself against the doorframe, and cautiously surveyed the hallway. A shadowy figure was peering into one of the rooms down the hall. As he stepped back into the hallway, a shaft of light from the setting sun caught his face.

The ruddy light made the eczema blotches glow angry red.

Escher backed away from the door, colliding with Zachary, who had crept up behind him. Yesterday was out there in the hall. "I've got to get out of here," Escher whispered. He slung his carryall over his shoulder and climbed over the windowsill. One leg, then the other. Dark oily swells slapped the wall twenty feet below, scummed with garbage, rushing in and out through barnacle-crusted windows. The ledge looked about three inches wide. He let himself down slowly, toes reaching, shirt sliding up his chest so that the concrete scraped his stomach.

The ledge jarred the soles of his feet. No problem. It was a lot wider than three inches, although the pigeon droppings made it slippery in spots. To Escher's surprise, Zachary scrambled lightly down beside him. He winked, and Escher felt a rush of gratitude. Zachary might have triggered the dreams, but he was part of Escher's world. He had no connection to yesterday.

Escher worked his way along the ledge, not daring to look back, belly tensed against a shout, or gunshots, or whatever. At the corner of the building, the ledge had broken, leaving a ragged edge. A shack jutted out above them, clinging to the pier, supported by a crisscrossed forest of scrap lumber and old pipes. An herb shop, Escher remembered vaguely. A palm reader, something like that.

"Hey!"

The shout came from overhead. Blotch-face must have spotted them and had run back through the building and out onto the pier. Escher looked around wildly. A labyrinth of boards braced the pier, not many feet from the ledge. Escher leaped for the closest support, tensed for the crack of breaking wood, for the rush of a fall. . . .

Wood slammed his palms, bruising his fingers. His toes slipped off the board, and he caught himself by his hands, gasping for breath. Zachary leaped for a nearby beam and swung back into shadow, agile as a monkey. Escher clambered after him, his carryall dragging at his shoulders, snagging on old nails and broken boards. They were out of sight now, safe in the shadows beneath the pier, hidden by the overhanging herb shop.

"Yo." Zachary reached, snagged a knotted hank of rope that dangled in the shadows. "We can climb down."

It was a rope ladder, with rungs made of old electrical conduit. The herb shop's back door? Escher clambered over to it, wriggling clumsily between the boards and bits of scrap. Zachary was already halfway down the ladder. He was enjoying himself, Escher thought sourly. As if this was a big game of hide-and-seek.

For him, it was. He was so damned sure he was immortal, protected by his crazy dreams.

Escher wasn't immortal. He grabbed the plastic rope, his bruised palms aching, carryall banging against his back. The ladder swung beneath his weight and the rungs felt slippery, as if they'd been greased. Step down . . . another . . . His knee banged against one of the pilings. Pants and skin shredded on the splintery wood. Almost down? His feet slipped off a rung, and his hands let go suddenly. Escher gasped, then grunted as he landed on a small barge. He staggered and nearly fell into the filthy water as it rocked beneath his feet. It was already dark down here. Light gleamed from the far end of the barge, or raft, or whatever it was that they'd landed on.

Escher squinted and made out an arched tentlike shelter constructed from an old plastic tarp. A flap lifted. The pale oval of a face appeared briefly, then vanished as the flap dropped into place once more. Keep moving, and most people left you alone. More memory, useful and dangerous. Don't listen to it or you'll die. . . . It was hard to shut out. Yesterday filled the air down here, thick as the dank smell of the bay. Hinges creaked overhead. Escher looked up as a crack of light widened, revealing a trapdoor above the rope ladder.

"This guy wants you bad," Zachary hissed in his ear.

No shit. Escher ran, stumbling through darkness and seeping light. Zachary followed at his heels as he leaped from boat, to barge, to raft. A dog yapped at them from a crate. People squatted around stoves or open cooking fires. Children shrieked at them, but the adults mostly kept silent, staring sullenly, staying out of it, whatever *it* was. Hispanic faces, under this pier. All races lived in Ice Town. An old man swore a rattling string of syllables as they hopped from the stern of his spotless houseboat to a filthy barge. They were well out from under the pier now, angling toward the melting pens. The sun had set, and it was getting dark. Escher leaped, landed on a raft that tilted alarmingly beneath his weight. Cold water slopped over his feet, soaking his jeans. He leaped again, nearly dropping his carryall as the next raft dipped. Arms windmilling, he fell forward into soft dirt and plants that crushed pungently beneath his palms. A garden barge. He scrambled to his knees, trying not to think about what they used as fertilizer on these things. Zachary darted past, and Escher followed him out to the end of the soil-covered barge, trying not to trample the crowded crop plants.

Open water lay beyond them. A penned berg caught the last glimmer of sunlight on its peaks, jagged and fractured by the shovel crew. Now what? Escher looked back toward the pier. Darkness blurred the chaos of anchored rafts and barges, tricked the eye into seeing a landscape of solid ground. Lights gleamed, and open fires flickered here and there. "We can work our way shoreward," he said. "If we're lucky, he'll miss us in the dark."

"It's shorter this way." Zachary nodded at the open water. "I live right across there, near the terminal. We'll lose that guy for sure, swimming. Water's pretty clean, out this far. Can't you swim?"

"I can swim." Sort of. Karen had taught him as they crept northward through the warm equatorial sea. Escher looked over his shoulder again. A shadow moving on that last barge? The barge's owner? He squinted, but the shape had vanished into shadow. Maybe it had been nothing more than shadow itself; his imagination in overdrive. Maybe. "It's too far," he said.

"It's safe." Zachary laughed softly. "I told you, I'm not going to drown. If I don't let go of you, you won't drown either. Besides, we can follow the fence in."

There was a wild note to Zachary's laugh that raised the hairs on Escher's neck. *My dreams are real, so I can't die.* Was that belief he heard, or a challenge to death? An invitation from a man tortured beyond endurance? Thanks, I'll walk, he started to say, but he closed his mouth without speaking.

A small splash might have been the barge rocking as someone leaped from its edge. Escher listened, heard it clearly; the soft thud of feet striking dirt. Sound *carried* out here. He was trapped. Escher looked around wildly, but the garden barge jutted out beyond the floating barge-city. No way off, except into the water. Choose, Escher. Which scares you more? Yesterday, or the water? He could drown in either. "Let's go." He hitched his carryall higher and slid into the water.

It was cold. The moon wasn't up yet, and it was fully dark now. Point in their favor. Escher swam a slow breaststroke after Zachary, trying not to think about the murky stretch of water between him and the shore. Zachary had been right about the fence. It was close; a yard or so of coated mesh sticking up above the slow swell, gummy with weed. It surrounded the entire melting complex and was supposed to stop bootleggers from getting in with their hoses and pumps. But they got in anyway, through holes cut in the mesh, in scuba gear, or just by snorkle and lung power, hauling the homemade siphons over to the pens. A lot of them drowned, and a lot more got caught.

More memory. Don't think, just swim.

Escher pulled himself along the fence, his legs already aching from the cold and the unfamiliar exertion. The fence didn't help all that much. The sluggish waves tugged at him, cold from the pregnant bellies of the melting pens. How much farther? They must have swum a mile already, and there *wasn't* a mile between the barge and the shore. Currents of ice water made him shiver, and after a while, he couldn't stop shivering. Idiot. Fool. He should have taken his chances with yesterday. Escher clutched the wire as a cramp twinged his thigh. Too late to turn back now. The cramp hit with full force, doubling him over. One hand came loose from the mesh, and the sea tugged at him, hungry for his life.

Escher groaned as the cramp racked him again. It felt as if his muscles were tearing away from the bone. His carryall dragged at his shoulder . . . a million pounds heavy. He let it go as a wavelet slapped his face. His lungs spasmed in a brief primitive panic. He was going to drown. The reality seized him, dug claws into his sanity as he choked.

"Relax." Zachary appeared beside him, clutching the fence. "Just let go of the fence and float. I'll pull you in." His arm slid across Escher's chest, fingers clamping into Escher's armpit.

"I can't," Escher gasped. The sea would seize him, suck him down. Fear squeezed the air from his lungs as he sank briefly in the cold water.

"Let *go*," Zachary panted in his ear. "I'll hold on to you, and I can't drown. I *know* it."

He was shivering, too, but he *believed*. He believed in his damn dreams. A tiny part of Escher believed, also. He reached for that belief, clutched it to him . . . and managed to let go of the fence. His body shuddered as it floated free in the swell, wanting to fight the cold water, fight the threat of death. It took every ounce of his self-control to lie still, to suffer the spasms in his leg and let Zachary do the work.

Zachary can't drown. Zachary won't let go, so I won't drown either. Escher repeated the words like a mantra, struggling to breathe as small waves broke over his face. How *far*? He was shivering, shuddering with cold. The bergs were melting, seeping Antarctic chill into the bay . . . a million years was crawling past. . . .

Something solid banged his hip. It hurt. Escher groped, touched soggy wood with his numb fingers. Zachary was hauling himself out onto a splintered half-submerged dock, still clutching Escher's shirt. Slowly, painfully, Escher dragged himself up onto blessedly solid planks. The air felt so warm, so wonderful. Shuddering, colder than he'd ever been on the ice train, he sprawled beside Zachary, too exhausted to move. A long, low building loomed over them, lightless and derelict. One wall had crumbled into concrete block and rubble, leaving a void of yawning darkness. It was surrounded with junk; the broken carcasses of boats, stripped car bodies, and less identifiable trash.

"I . . . told you." Zachary's chattering teeth punctuated the words. "We'd be . . . okay."

"Thanks to you," Escher whispered. He looked up at the rising moon with numb surprise. It should be morning by now, should be next *week*. The shivering was easing off a little. He'd left yesterday back there, on the Ice Town barge. He was safe. He had escaped. A flicker of hope warmed him, and he sat up, wincing as his leg threatened to cramp again. "So how *do* you die?" he heard himself asking. "Never mind, I'm sorry."

"It's all right." Arms behind his head, Zachary stared up at the faint stars in the sky. "I jump off this cliff. I look down, and there's only sand and a little sage underneath. No rocks, but in the dream, I figure it's far enough down that it doesn't matter if there's no rocks."

"I'm sorry." Escher looked away from Zachary's calm face. Zachary believed it. He believed it as much as he'd believed that they wouldn't drown.

"It's okay. I dream about death all the time. It doesn't scare me anymore. What's going to happen is going to happen."

Hell, maybe the future *was* fixed. Escher stared out at the small galaxy of Ice Town's cooking fires and solar lanterns. "I'm signing up for another train," he said softly. "Tonight. It's the only place I'm going to be safe." Only Escher existed in the dark cold of 70°S. Eventually, yesterday would dwindle, freeze, dry up, and blow away. He would never know whom he had loved and killed, would never have to know why. "I can be myself out there," he said softly. "Escher." After a while, Escher would be real.

Zachary was silent for a long moment. "Your friend Karen signs up again, too. I dreamed about her. You can stay with me," he said. "Until you leave. If you want to."

Loneliness blew through his words like an Antarctic wind. "Thanks," Escher said, understanding now how much Willy mattered. Because he was afraid of Zachary, of what he might dream. He hadn't been afraid before, but he *believed,* and with that belief came fear. "Maybe Willy'll show up before I ship out," he said too heartily.

"Maybe." Zachary got to his feet, stuck out a hand. "It's not far. I'll help you."

IT WAS FAR enough. Escher limped slowly after Zachary as they threaded the maze of piled junk that surrounded the derelict building beyond the ruined dock. This was the wasteland that adjoined the berg plant. Rusty oil drums lay like tumbled spools, leaking thick fluid that gleamed in the moonlight. They gave the drums a wide berth, emerged from a thicket of twisted and stripped cars onto an eerily empty street. Big halide lamps glowed to their right: GREATER LOS ANGELES ICE-PROCESSING FACILITY. The neon sign gleamed ice-blue, ten feet high, at least. Salvation. He could sign up there in the morning—they had a twenty-four-hour terminal open in the foyer. He could catch the *Western Star* on her way out of port, ride her down to Argentina where the crews assembled. Escher had a past on the *Star.* He had a past in Ushuaia.

Zachary steadied him as Escher stumbled. "You okay?"

Yes, yes, he was okay. He'd escaped, left yesterday behind in Ice Town, would leave it forever in a few days. "It's just my leg," he said. "Cramps."

"Hang in there for another block. Willy and I fixed up this place in an old furniture store." He put an arm around Escher, strong for all his skinny build. "It's mostly squatters down here," he went on. "The buildings got really shaken up in one of the quakes, and I guess nobody wants to fix 'em up. The ice-plant people are always getting the cops to run us off. I bet Willy's back. He was probably just off dealing that last load we picked up. Most of the stuff was gone when I checked." His voice was too bright, and had a raw edge to it.

"He'll be back." Escher tried to put certainty into his voice. "You're right, he's dealing stuff."

"Yeah," Zachary said too quickly. "He knew I'd come back. He wouldn't have gone out without me."

They'd reached the wide boulevard that ran past the ice-processing complex. Islands in the center had turned into wastelands of cracked dirt, drifted with shoals of trash. It had been designed to carry at least four lanes of traffic. Big streetlights curved metal necks over the empty width of asphalt, dark and dead. In the old days, when gas had been affordable, the city had been full of private cars. Now the street was desolate, except for a water tanker that had just pulled out of the complex.

A tanker truck. Something nagged at him—a memory from the ice train. Escher lost it as an engine roared behind them. He looked over his shoulder. A car had turned onto the street they were following and was accelerating toward the intersection. Its headlights were off, and he could hear music blaring. Private license plate, low-slung expensive design. Someone with money, out scoring drugs or sex, or just slumming. The driver wasn't slowing down, couldn't see the big tanker because of the cracked storefront that had buckled halfway into the street, although the idiot should have noticed the headlights by now. Stoned, probably. The trucker couldn't see the car and was accelerating fast—paid by the trip, the driver was hauling ass.

"Oh, jeeze," Zachary said in a soft, strange voice. "They're gonna burn."

Burn? Escher remembered Zachary's nightmare in the crew mess as speed and direction came together in his head. He lunged into the street, waving, trying to catch the driver's eye. The fool was going to pull right out in front of the truck. The car's lights came on suddenly, blinding him, exploding in his head with brilliant vision; light . . . anguish . . . the cliff-wall face of a truck bore down on him, and he suffered a crushing moment of regret as he didn't jump. . . .

The car seemed to move toward him in slow motion, horn blaring. Frozen by light, Escher gasped as memory unrolled in his head, peeling backward through time. Those surprised eyes were on his face and the limp body sagged in his arms again. *Not you? Not here!* Escher cried silently, but a part of him exulted as the blade went in, bursting through the frail resistance of skin and muscle, sliding over bone to touch the heart. . . . Then the blood rushed over his knuckles, and his eyes were full of tears, and he was shouting, crying, but it was too late, too late to stop it, undo it. Grief pierced him like a blade, twisting like steel in his gut, and there was no way to stop it, not ever. . . .

Breaks screamed and the car rushed past him, swerving out into the intersection. The truck's air horn blared as the car skidded into its path and metal crunched. The car ricocheted off the truck's fender, veered across the street, and plowed into a light pole. Time had speeded up to normal again. The truck was stopping, the driver swearing in Spanish out the window. Escher stood in the middle of the street, shaking. The car's driver fought the door open and got out, amazingly unhurt, followed by a woman.

"Escher?" Zachary's voice was ragged. "My *God*, Escher. What did you do?"

"I killed him. I didn't mean to," he mumbled. Only he had. No, no, that was yesterday. "I . . . didn't do anything." Escher staggered as Zachary grabbed him, nails digging into his arms, face thrust close to Escher's.

"It *burned.*" In the dim light of the moon, Zachary's eyes shone like an animal's. "The car. I saw it burn. I dreamed it. How they all died, how they burned, and I could hear it, hear the flames roaring and the screaming. It has to happen that way. It *has* to."

"So your dreams don't come true." He shook off Zachary's clutch, fighting the memory that wanted to overwhelm him. He had let that truck hit him two years ago, had decided to die in that split second of light, because, because. . . . No, *no! He* hadn't done it, he was Escher, and Escher had never lived here. Escher had been born in a hospital bed and lived on the ice, mist-man, so fragile. . . .

"It *can't* change. No one can stop it from happening. *No* one." Zachary's eyes blazed with green fire. "You think you're so damn smart, huh? You want to know your name, smart guy? I dreamed about *you*, only your name's not Escher. Want me to tell you who you are? Do you?"

Stunned, confused, Escher backed away. His name—that would do it, let the flood in, drown him in yesterday. He believed in Zachary's dreams. A face shimmered in the shadows. Yesterday? Waiting for Escher to remember—waiting for Escher to die?

If Zachary said his name out loud. . . .

ESCHER TURNED and fled, stumbling down the street, staggering, running. He cut through an alley behind a boarded-up building, sobbing for breath. The lights were still on at the processing complex, although the city had finally gone curfew dark. Water could buy you anything. It could buy you life. Pipes tunneled like huge dark snakes through the dry earth, and moonlight gleamed on the melting bergs out in the bay. Escher stumbled up the steps to the complex foyer.

The building was dark, locked up, although people would be working somewhere inside, monitoring the precious water as it was mixed with the maximum allowable amount of purified seawater and piped out the taps of the city's thirsty, or pumped inland to water the salt-tolerant crops. Ice, frozen water, could buy him his soul. A recruitment terminal had been built into the wall of the entryway. It was open. Escher shivered in the cool breeze from the bay, his heart slowing at last. Yesterday was fading. That bloodstained ghost had no place here, no reality. It would still be okay. He'd sign on and use his sign-up bonus to rent a room somewhere until the *Star* sailed. He'd make out. He, Escher. He'd survive.

*Welcome.* The terminal screen brightened at his touch. *Please choose a category by touching the red box beside it,* a soft voice intoned.

He touched the box beside EMPLOYMENT APPLICATION, touched ICE CREW, and entered his ID number.

It was too early in the year for the trains to be heading down to 70°S, but he could hang out in Ushuaia. It was cheap, and Escher had a past in Ushuaia. He wouldn't come back to LA. He could sign on with a train bound for San Diego/Tijuana, or San Francisco, or even Australia or Europe. Tanaka ran trains all over the world.

*Application accepted. Please place your palm on the blue square to confirm contract.*

Escher pressed his palm against the sky-blue square on the terminal screen.

*Your contract has been filed and recorded. If you wish to terminate, substantial penalties will apply. Thank you.*

Someone cleared his throat behind Escher.

He turned slowly, heart contracting in his chest. The small man with the blotched face leaned against the entryway. "I came down here to jack your personnel file out of the terminal." He tossed a small, flat rectangle of gray plastic on his palm. "Nice timing, I'd say. Where is he?"

Escher slumped against the terminal, defeated, trapped finally, so close to escape. "Where is who?" he asked, and was amazed that his voice didn't shake.

"Odell. I got the word that you two were tight on the train, so I figured you'd lead me to him. And you did. He didn't drown in the damn bay, did he?" A frown flitted across the man's blotchy face. "That was a pretty dumb stunt, jumping in. Even for a two-bit water pirate like you."

Zachary. This man—Kyle; the name came to Escher so *easily*—had wanted Zachary all along. What irony. Escher swallowed a wild urge to laugh. He could have stood back, out there on the pier, and yesterday would have walked right past him. It would have taken Zachary instead. "Why?" he croaked. "What do you want him for?"

Kyle shrugged. "This guy held a lien on him, and he sold it to the boss. Turns out Tanaka slapped another one on Odell, and now it's doubled, 'cause the asshole jumped it. The boss sent me to collect him before Tanaka gets hold of him. Boss wants him bad." Kyle's eyes glittered. "The old scav who sold him said this guy can tell the future," he said softly. "What a line, but the boss bought it."

*That's* what they wanted? Sickness clenched like a fist in Escher's guts. They thought Zachary was a fortune-teller. Escher remembered Jamie's belief on the train. It was contagious, belief. Like a plague. "You fell for it too, huh?" He tried a laugh.

"It's a scam, huh?" Kyle's lips twitched, as if he wanted to spit. "I figured. Too bad for Odell."

Kyle's cold tone raised the hairs on the back of Escher's neck. "What was the old scav's name?" he asked softly. "Willy?"

"Could be." Kyle looked at him from the corners of his eyes. "Sounds about right. You know, if a guy could do that, tell the future, and all. It'd be like owning this place." He jerked his head at the processing complex. "If you knew, say, the number of the winning lottery ticket—you could maybe find out who bought it. You'd know when a city bust was coming down, when the water cops were gonna check the fences." He rubbed his hands together lightly, his eyes gleaming. "Yeah, it'd be worth a lot."

Willy had sold Zachary out, had convinced some shark boss to pay for a chance at that kind of talent. Nice guy, old Willy. But he wasn't afraid of the dreams, and that's all that mattered to Zachary.

"I'm offering a finder's fee." Kyle licked his lips, his eyes glistening with greed. "I'll catch up with him sooner or later, but if it's sooner and simple, it's worth a little cash to me."

Kyle wouldn't believe Zachary's explanation of his dreams. He'd think Zachary was holding out and figure he just needed a little persuading. Life was cheap here. Life was cheap everywhere in this damn Dry. Escher met the man's stare. He couldn't help Zachary, didn't know the language, didn't know the tone and the winks, the little cues that would convince Kyle to lay off long enough for Zachary to disappear. He would shrug and Kyle would walk away. Too bad, Zachary. Maybe Kyle wouldn't find him.

Oh sure. Kyle would have Zachary by tomorrow night.

Escher closed his eyes briefly, remembering Zachary's arm across his chest as they struggled through the cold water. If they'd gone down, Zachary wouldn't have let go. It came to him suddenly—why Zachary had been so upset when the car didn't crash. He understood, and that understanding left him colder than Kyle's threats. He was safe here, but it was illusion, that safety. Escher opened his eyes, bathed in the bright shadowless glow of the facility lights. He, Escher, was a shadow man. He only existed here in the fragile bubble of the ice trains. He was no more real than the tiny figures on that endless stair. Escher let his breath out in a long slow sigh. He could spend his whole life on that stairway, running away from yesterday, thinking he was getting somewhere, only to turn the corner and find out he was right back where he started from.

He'd lived here. The woman in the drink shack had recognized him, and the man she had recognized would know the right words. The man she had recognized had stood in front of a truck, two years ago.

To hell with it. He was tired of the damn stairs. A dizzy rush of fear and regret shook him—like that moment when he had stood still in the glare of the truck's headlights.

"We're even, Zachary," Escher murmured softly. He shrugged, grinned a shark grin at Kyle, and said, "Okay, let's talk."

IT WAS ALMOST dawn by the time Escher made his way back along the street where he'd left Zachary. He and Kyle had haggled for a while, had finally settled on four hundred dollars in untraceable black-market cash to be paid over when Escher delivered Zachary. They had set it up for the afternoon, in the drowned tower where he'd met Zachary. Four hundred dollars was a decent price for a man's life around here. Kyle had done the deal because Escher had said all the right things, in the right tone, with the right body language.

He didn't feel any different. *You're the same man,* Karen had said, and she had been wrong. Or had she? Had he been running from himself, all this time? Escher glanced warily over his shoulder, but the street behind him was empty. He remembered being Escher, making love to Karen, freezing his ass, hating Jamie's needling. Who am I? he asked himself, and still wasn't quite sure. He turned a corner and ducked back into the entrance of an abandoned storefront, listening for footsteps. Kyle had tried to follow, to save himself four hundred bucks, but Escher had the skills to shake him, now. Silence, except for the small night sounds of insects and rats.

Still no sign of Kyle. Escher started up the street, looking for
the furniture store Zachary had mentioned. Behind him, moonlight blazed a gleaming path across the dark bay, and red warning beacons winked along the perimeter fence where he'd
nearly drowned. He felt a little schizophrenic; he knew how to
cut through a perimeter fence . . . and he didn't. Shark and tourist were both trying to look through his eyes, and the point of
view at times got a little fuzzy. So maybe Escher was still here.

The eastern sky was turning gray by the time he found the
store. The big windows had been covered with broken sheets of
plastic siding torn from some house. They had been bright tur-
quoise once, but had faded in the sun to a pale greenish-blue.
No entry here. Escher rounded the corner, confronted a heavy
wooden door standing ajar. He slipped inside, found himself in
a dark hallway. Doors opened on either side. Escher peered into
them, one after the other. Empty, empty, except for a broken
desk and a tipped-over filing cabinet. Aha.

A single solar lantern hung from the dusty acoustic tiles of
the ceiling. Crude shelves had been nailed to the wall. They
held food, cooking utensils, odds and ends, and books. Dirty
dishes cluttered a battered table, beside a plastic tub half full of
scummy water. Three empty water jugs stood beside the tub. A
rumpled bed occupied one wall, and a mattress on the floor took
up the other end of the room.

Zachary knelt in front of it, shoving a water jug into a pack.
Preparing for a trip into the Dry? He looked up and scowled.
"Beat it," he growled. "Get out of here, 'Cuda. Run, or I'll tell
you more."

"That's the name Kyle knew." Escher leaned against the
doorframe. "That's not my real name. That's not who I was
hiding from." He looked down at Zachary, at the cornered
hunch of his body. "I didn't understand, out there in the street,
but I do now," he said softly. "I made it your responsibility,
didn't I? All those people you dream about. If you can't change
the future, then you can't blame yourself for not warning them
somehow, for not saving them. I proved that you could have
saved them."

"Go to hell," Zachary breathed.

"I'm sorry. I didn't mean to do that to you."

"I don't forget everything." Zachary stared up at him, his
eyes as bleak as the Dryland hills. "I remember my father some.
I remember him laughing, cutting branches off the vat bushes
with his machete. I remember how he'd tell me stories, me sit-

ting on his lap in the dark. It was just us, or at least, I don't remember anyone else.'' He looked down at the crumpled pack in his hands. ''The machete was so sharp, it could cut right through a branch as big around as your thumb. It bounced off something one day, and cut his leg. The blood wouldn't stop coming. Only I didn't *see* that part. I dreamed it. When I found him, the blood had soaked into the dust. It was all dark and dry, and ants were crawling into his mouth. I couldn't lift him. He was too heavy.'' Zachary threw the pack aside, his eyes full of razor-edged pain. ''I didn't tell him about the dream. Or maybe I did and he didn't listen, but it didn't matter, don't you see, because it would have happened anyway. It wasn't my fault, I couldn't have stopped it. Only . . . that's not true, is it?'' He buried his face in his hands and groaned.

''Sometimes, people aren't going to listen.'' Escher put a hand on his shoulder. Maybe that's what had brought them together on the train. They had both been hiding from the face of death. ''We herded goats along the edge of the Dry,'' Escher said slowly. ''Doug, and I, always together. The older I got, the more I hated it. You could see how the land was dying, how we were killing it faster with the goats. It seemed so pointless. My dad couldn't see it, or maybe he just didn't want to.'' Escher heard the bitterness in his voice, then swallowed. ''So we . . . fought a lot. I only hung on as long as I did because of Doug.'' His voice wanted to shake, and he drew a quick, hard breath. ''When I finally took off, he wouldn't come with me. I'd never questioned it—that we'd both take off. In the end . . . he sided with my dad. He stayed.''

So Escher had left and had finally ended up here, telling himself that Ice Town was alive, a place where you could make yourself a future. Only there wasn't really any more future here than in the Dry. Doug had got it right, after all. Ice Town was just another stairway, another circle to nowhere. ''I was a water pirate,'' he said. ''And a shark. I got into this fight one day.'' He'd gotten cut—not bad, but enough to scare him a little and make him crazy mad. ''This guy came at me,'' Escher said softly. ''Out of the crowd. I didn't really look at him. I thought he had a knife, and I didn't even see who it was until it was too late.'' He turned away. ''It was Doug. God knows how he ended up in Ice Town. I guess he was trying to help me.'' He'd seemed so surprised when the blade had gone in, and then he'd looked puzzled, and sad, and then he died. He'd never said a word. Nothing. ''He made me see it,'' Escher said softly. ''What

I was, what I'd let myself become. And for a moment . . . I was glad I'd killed him." Escher closed his hand slowly, remembering the weight of the knife in his hand, that moment of exultation. Because Doug had betrayed him. Doug had let him go, and it hadn't been any damn better in Ice Town. If he hadn't succumbed to that moment of hatred . . . could he have stopped the blade in time? Escher let his breath out in a slow sigh. Maybe not, but he'd never know. "Where are you going?" He nudged the pack with his toe. "Out to look for Willy?"

"Willy's not coming back." Zachary's face twitched. "I was just going into the Dry."

To find that cliff? Because he couldn't live with the load of deaths Escher had just dumped onto his shoulders? He could make sure that dream came true at least. "Tell me your dream about Karen," he said harshly.

"Karen?" Zachary blinked. "Oh, her, from the train." He looked away, lips tightening. "She falls off this cliff of ice in the dark. It's a long way down, and she lands on the deck of a boat. I think she dies."

So she'd sign up again after all. The fields wouldn't make it. "There'll be another time, like the car." Escher spoke slowly, deliberately, each word like the stab of a knife. "If you're dead, it's going to happen anyway. If you're alive, maybe it won't. Once in a while, maybe we can change something. Mostly we probably can't." Escher looked around. "You got another pack I can use?"

"What the hell are you talking about?"

"We're leaving right now. We're going up to the Willamette Valley. To this town called Ryder." Folks would know where Karen and Randy lived. "I have a wedding present for Karen." He would still have a little money left after paying the fine for breaking his new contract. Not much, but maybe enough. She could put it aside, keep it safe until the day when she needed to sign up on another ice train. Then she could use it. She believed in Zachary's dreams, so she'd listen to him. "Maybe she won't die on the deck of a boat," he said. "Maybe we can buy her a different future." A life for a death? It wouldn't be enough, but maybe it would help a little.

"We?" Zachary's face twisted. "I scare you, like I scare everyone," he said harshly. "And I'll dream about you. A lot, because you're around. That's the way it works."

"You scared me for a while," Escher said softly. "Not anymore. Tell me one thing—the man you knew on the ice train, and the one you dreamed about . . . are they the same man?''

"They're you." Zachary looked puzzled. "Who else?''

Who else, indeed?

Zachary got up suddenly, fumbled a book from beneath a pile of rags. Pushing aside a clutter of dishes and junk, he spread it open on the table. "Willy didn't trade this. You want it?''

The water-stained page showed a copy of the print he'd lost with his carryall. The tiny figures plodded patiently on their endless stairway. Maybe it was only endless if you thought you were going somewhere; up or down. Maybe—if you knew that it was a circle, if you let your feet carry you back to where you started and recognized that spot for what it was—maybe you'd find a way off. Maybe the only other way off was a truck, or a cliff out in the Dry.

"I think I'll leave it here." He touched the smooth paper with one finger. "I don't think it applies anymore."

"You sure about this?'' Zachary didn't quite meet his eyes. "Us together, I mean. Are you really sure?''

Hope in those words, desperate and desolate. "You dream tomorrow, and I'll remember yesterday for both of us. We'll take it from there." Escher closed the book. "Yeah, I'm sure about us, and my name's Shane. My dad had this thing for Old West heros." He smiled faintly. "Find me a pack, and let's get out of here, okay?''

Zachary returned his smile. It didn't banish the wary shadows in his eyes, but it was a smile anyway.

"I got one," he said. "I'll go get it."

Shane, 'Cuda, Escher, Shane. One man, many names. You could spend your life running away from yourself. Time to get off the damn stairway. "Hurry up," Shane said, and found a place for the book, up high on an empty shelf.